FED UP

FED UP

Jessica Conant-Park
& Susan Conant

BERKLEY PRIME CRIME, NEW YORK

THE BERKLEY PUBLISHING GROUP
Published by the Penguin Group
Penguin Group (USA) Inc.
375 Hudson Street, New York, New York 10014, USA
Penguin Group (Canada), 90 Eglinton Avenue East, Suite 700, Toronto, Ontario M4P 2Y3, Canada
(a division of Pearson Penguin Canada Inc.)
Penguin Books Ltd., 80 Strand, London WC2R 0RL, England
Penguin Group Ireland, 25 St. Stephen's Green, Dublin 2, Ireland (a division of Penguin Books Ltd.)
Penguin Group (Australia), 250 Camberwell Road, Camberwell, Victoria 3124, Australia
(a division of Pearson Australia Group Pty. Ltd.)
Penguin Books India Pvt. Ltd., 11 Community Centre, Panchsheel Park, New Delhi—110 017, India
Penguin Group (NZ), 67 Apollo Drive, Rosedale, North Shore 0632, New Zealand
(a division of Pearson New Zealand Ltd.)
Penguin Books (South Africa) (Pty.) Ltd., 24 Sturdee Avenue, Rosebank, Johannesburg 2196,
South Africa

Penguin Books Ltd., Registered Offices: 80 Strand, London WC2R 0RL, England

This book is an original publication of The Berkley Publishing Group.

This is a work of fiction. Names, characters, places, and incidents either are the product of the author's imagination or are used fictitiously, and any resemblance to actual persons, living or dead, business establishments, events, or locales is entirely coincidental. The publisher does not have any control over and does not assume any responsibility for author or third-party websites or their content.

PUBLISHER'S NOTE: The recipes contained in this book are to be followed exactly as written. The publisher is not responsible for your specific health or allergy needs that may require medical supervision. The publisher is not responsible for any adverse reactions to the recipes contained in this book.

First edition: February 2009

Library of Congress Cataloging-in-Publication Data

Conant-Park, Jessic
    Fed up / Jessica Conant-Park & Susan Conant.—1st ed.
        p. cm.
    ISBN 978-0-425-22598-1
    1. Carter, Chloe (Fictitious character)—Fiction.   2. Cooks—Fiction.   3. Boston (Mass.)—
Fiction.   I. Conant, Susan, 1946–   II. Title.
    PS3603.O525F43 2009
    813'.6—dc22
                                                                                                2008045433

PRINTED IN THE UNITED STATES OF AMERICA

10   9   8   7   6   5   4   3   2   1

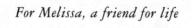

For Melissa, a friend for life

ACKNOWLEDGMENTS

For contributing mouthwatering recipes, we thank Angela McKeller, Ann and Michel Devrient, Meg Driscoll, Josh and Jen Ziskin, Nancy R. Landman, Barbara Seagle, Raymond Ost, Bill Park, and Dwayne Minier.

And for testing some of those recipes, we thank Mary Fairchild, Gina Micale, and Rita Schiavone

For detailing icky restaurant health code violations, we thank Deborah M. Rosati, R.S., food safety consultant.

Many thanks to Natalee Rosenstein and Michelle Vega from Berkley Prime Crime and to our agent, Deborah Schneider.

And for rescuing the real Inga, Jessica thanks her husband, Bill, who knew that the starving, neglected Persian would be the perfect addition to our home.

FED UP

ONE

I peeked in the rearview mirror of my car, touched up my lip gloss, and ran my hands through my hair. I was, after all, going to be on television, so I had every excuse in the world to double-check my appearance. Okay, well, it was actually my boyfriend, Josh, who was going to be on television. Still, I was going to be in the vicinity of the taping of a television show, and if the camera just so happened to find its way to me, I had to be prepared. My hair disagreed; far from behaving itself, it was doing everything it could to fight the anti-frizz and straightening products that I had slathered on this morning. I got out of the car, slammed the door, and cursed Boston's triple-*H* weather: hazy, hot, humid. I should've taken my friend Adrianna's advice about wearing my hair curly. I had taken her advice, however, about wearing a cute, if uncomfortable, outfit. I tugged at the hem of my lime green and sky blue retro-print dress and tried to smooth out the wrinkles that had developed during the drive. And these darn toeless pumps that matched the green in the dress were going to be hell; I could already feel my big toe whining about being squashed. *You have to suffer to be beautiful, you have to suffer to be beautiful,* I repeated to myself.

The parking lot of the upscale grocery store, Natural High, was moderately full for four o'clock on a Monday afternoon in late August. I was there—on location, as I liked to think of it—because Josh had been invited to participate in a local cable reality TV show called *Chefly Yours.* I was tagging along, but Josh was one of three local chefs competing to win the prize of starring in a new eight-part cooking show. The other two contestants were Josh's friend Digger and a woman named Marlee. *Chefly Yours* was scheduled to have nine episodes, three for each chef, with the contestants competing in rotation. Josh, Digger, and Marlee had each filmed one episode. Today was Josh's second turn. When all nine episodes had aired, viewers were going to call in to vote for the winner. Each episode followed the chef contestant into a grocery store, where the chef approached a shopper and persuaded the surprised stranger to participate in the show. The chef then selected and bought food and accompanied the shopper home to cook a gourmet meal. The hope was that the chosen shopper would have a spouse or partner at home, an unsuspecting person who'd provide moments of drama by expressing astonished delight—or filmworthy rage, maybe—when the TV crew burst in. *Crew:* considering that the cable station, Boston 17, provided one producer-director, Robin, and one cameraman, Nelson, the term struck me as a bit generous. Also, the premise of *Chefly Yours* hit me as disconcertingly similar to the premise of a big-time national program hosted by a hot Australian chef, but when I'd told Josh that Robin was copycatting, he'd brushed me off.

Still, my boyfriend's first episode had gone well in spite of an unexpected challenge. Because the "lucky shopper," as Robin called her, turned out to have numerous food allergies, Josh had been forced to cook an incredibly simple seared fish fillet with practically no seasoning. To his credit, instead of throwing up his hands in frustration, he had used the episode to showcase his technical culinary skills, and he'd taught his shopper and the audience how to break down a whole fish and cook it perfectly. Nonetheless, I was hoping that today he'd find a truly adventurous eater. I hadn't been present for the taping of Josh's first show. When Robin had given me permission to watch today's taping, she'd made me swear that I wouldn't make Josh nervous. I'd given her my promise.

The location, Natural High, was an elite market in the Boston suburb of Fairfield, which our local papers always described as the wealthiest community in Massachusetts. As the store's name suggested, its specialty was organic produce, but it also sold fresh meat and seafood. As the automatic doors opened and I stepped in, I felt a surge of irritation at the show for what was obviously a search for wealthy guest shoppers. It seemed to me that the people for whom it would be a big treat to take a chef home were middle-income and low-income shoppers at ordinary supermarkets. The station, however, evidently preferred to have a good chance of shooting in a lavish-looking house with a luxurious, well-equipped kitchen. I consoled myself with the thought that Natural High did have a few advantages. The butcher at the meat counter, a guy named Willie, was the brother of my friend Owen, so at least Willie would get some airtime, and Josh was hoping to stop at a nearby cheese and wine shop run by Owen and Willie's brother Evan.

I found Josh huddled close to Robin in the produce section of the market, where both were scanning for a desirable shopper.

"Found any victims yet?" I placed my hand on Josh's lower back.

"Hey, babe." He grinned and then gave me a quick kiss. Clearly fired up for today's filming, Josh was wearing his white chef's coat from the restaurant where he worked, Simmer, and his gorgeous blue eyes twinkled with energy. Josh usually left his dirty blond hair to its own devices—a look I found adorable—but today he had obviously spent a little time in the mirror styling his waves. As delicious as he looked in person, Josh had managed to look even yummier on TV, as if his enthusiasm for the competition had seeped into the camera. Although he wrapped his arm around me and pulled me in tightly, he continued looking at Robin's clipboard.

"Hi, Robin," I said to the producer.

Robin whipped her long brown ponytail to the side without dislodging her headset. She gave me a curt smile. "Chloe. I didn't know you'd be here today. Nice to see you."

She did so know I was going to be here! "Nice to see you, too."

Robin looked back down at her clipboard and began frantically writing as she talked. "Okay, Josh, so I'd prefer to find a male shopper this time. We've already had three women. And he has to be camera friendly. Since we don't have hair and makeup people, it's got to be someone attractive. And find out about his kitchen. We don't want to end up in some hellhole with cockroaches and no cooking equipment." Robin's sharp voice matched her appearance: a small, pinched nose; perpetually squinty eyes; and pursed lips. She had a very thin, dainty frame, and her no-nonsense clothes fell shapelessly on her body.

Josh and Robin started peering around the store again. When I stepped aside to let them work, I bumped into Nelson, the cameraman, and nearly toppled over.

"Um, hi, Nelson." I stared into the big black lens of his camera, which was pointed directly at me. The light shining from the camera made me squint.

Nelson briefly leaned out from behind the camera to beam at me. "Hi, Chloe."

Nelson, who was in his early thirties, had a prematurely bald head so shiny that I longed to pat his scalp with blotting paper or dust it with talc. His eyes formed two perfect circles, as though they'd been drawn on his face by a first-grader. He was close to six feet tall, and his bulky build must have made it easy for him to carry the heavy camera.

After tucking himself back behind the safety of the camera, he asked, "How are you today? Has school started back up yet?"

"No, I have a few more weeks." My second and final year of graduate school was looming, but I was nowhere near ready to give up on summer. "Oh, I see Digger and Marlee are here. I'm going to say hello."

Josh and his chef friend Digger had enjoyed a friendly rivalry during the past month of taping. The other two chefs were along not just to watch how their competition performed but to serve as sous-chefs if Josh needed them.

"Hey, Chloe!" Digger called out in his husky voice. "What's up, kid?" His curly brown hair was pulled back in an elastic, and his dark skin was even more deeply tanned than the last time I'd seen him. Digger had strong, angular facial features that I found somewhat intoxicating; although he wasn't traditionally handsome, he was masculine and striking. "Has Josh got anyone, yet? We've been here for twenty minutes, and Robin has already rejected four people Josh picked out." Digger cupped his hands to his mouth and called across a bin of red peppers, "Seriously, come on Robin!"

Robin ignored Digger, but I saw that Josh was trying not to smile.

"You know Marlee, right?" Digger gestured to the woman next to him.

"Yes, we met at one of the planning meetings." I held out my hand to the slightly plump woman. "Good to see you."

Marlee let my hand sit in the air. "You, too," she said distractedly. "I wonder who Josh'll end up with this time."

For reasons I didn't understand, Marlee seemed oddly nervous. Today was Josh's show and not hers. Since the last time I'd seen her, Marlee had cut her thin hair into an ear-length bob that did nothing to flatter her round face. Actually, Marlee had a distinct roundness to her entire being; without actually being overweight, she was blah and shapeless, not to mention pasty and bland. She wasn't particularly feminine, but since she worked in a male-dominated industry, maybe she deliberately downplayed her feminine side? I stared at her and prayed that she'd put on makeup before the taping began. She seriously needed color in her cheeks, and I had to peer rather rudely at her to see whether she had any eyelashes at all. Oh, yes! There they were. Would she mind, or even notice, if I pulled out a mascara wand and started coating her lashes?

"Oh, look. He's pointing at someone now." She and Digger craned their heads to get a look, and then Marlee sighed. "Nope. Robin nixed that guy, too. They really better get moving."

Even though it was only a little after four in the afternoon, Marlee was right. Shooting an entire episode would take until at least seven tonight. According to Josh, Robin was particular about nearly everything and liked to reshoot some scenes three or four times, maybe for good reason. After all, she had only one cameraman, and the lighting available in markets and home kitchens had to be less than ideal.

Marlee, I suspected, was hoping that Josh would get another dud shopper, thus improving her own chances of winning the show. Even though *Chefly Yours* was relatively small and underfunded, not to mention imitative, it was still television, and I knew that all three chefs were dying to win the chance to star in the solo series. Marlee was the chef at a small South End restaurant called Alloy, but aside from that, I knew little about her. Josh and Digger had both been reviewed a few times in newspapers, in local magazines, and online, but I'd never read anything about Marlee's restaurant, and I had no reason to think she needed or wanted to win more than the male chefs did.

"Maybe we could help them find a candidate," I suggested to Digger and Marlee.

We headed toward Robin, Josh, and Nelson just as Josh was approaching a well-groomed man in his early sixties. "Excuse me, sir. I'm chef Josh Driscoll, and I was wondering if you—"

Robin practically body-slammed the poor man out of the way. Out of his hearing, I hoped, she hissed, "God, not him, Josh! He's totally wrong! Did you or did you not see his plaid shirt?" She rolled her eyes. "Plaid shirt equals hippie equals crappy TV, okay? And for God's sake, Nelson, why are you filming this?"

"It's reality TV, Robin." He smiled. "This is good stuff

here. This is how you capture moments that create a damn fine film."

Robin's only response was to write yet more notes on her clipboard. Was she grading Nelson as we went along?

"What about him?" I pointed unobtrusively at a college-age guy who was examining a bunch of beet greens. "He looks interested in his food."

Robin shook her head at what she all too obviously regarded as a stupid suggestion.

"Oh, well," I said, "you're the dictator." Oops. "Director! You're the director!"

Robin eyed me suspiciously and crinkled her already crinkled nose.

Just then, a young mother with an infant strapped to her body approached us. "Hey, I recognize you! Are you all from that show—"

Instead of responding to the eager fan, Robin stepped away. Sulking, she said to us, "No, she won't do at all! A man! We need a man. And she certainly doesn't look like a man to me."

The enthusiastic mother was atypical; most people scampered away from us and especially, I thought, from Nelson's bulky camera. I was starting to think that we'd be lucky to find anyone even willing to talk to us; Robin was in no position to drive away interested shoppers. The mother would've been fine, I thought. She and her baby were both attractive, and she had a look of prosperity that suggested the possibility of a snazzy, photogenic kitchen. I gave the mother an apologetic look as she walked away. It was already four thirty, and I thought that by this point Robin would've found any shopper acceptable.

After Robin had rejected four more perfectly normal—and male, I might add—shoppers, her eyes suddenly lit up. "Oh, look, that's the one!" She pointed eagerly at a man entering the store. I couldn't see what made him so special. To me, he looked ordinary: short hair, average height, lean build, brown suede jacket, and delicate round glasses. But Robin, I reminded myself, was the expert; she must know who'd look good on camera and who wouldn't, and she was probably better than I was at guessing the value of the suede jacket and the glasses, which, for all I knew, had cost thousands.

Robin marched confidently over to her selected shopper and pulled down her headset. The rest of us followed. By then, I was convinced that this headset was connected to nothing more than an empty box that she wore attached to her belt. I mean, whom could she possibly be communicating with? Nelson, who was right next to her? The headset, I decided, was a prop intended to make her look official.

"Good afternoon, sir," said Robin, extending her hand to the mystery man, who cautiously took her hand and shook it. "My name is Robin, and I am the producer of a televison show called *Chefly Yours.* We're here today to film an episode of the show, and we'd like to offer you the talents of our chef, Josh Driscoll." Robin shoved Josh in front of her as proof of her statement. "If you'll allow us, we'd like to film you and Josh as he helps prepare a meal for you. Perhaps you have a loved one at home who could use a special dinner tonight? We'll come to your house and give our viewers a lesson in how to prepare high-quality meals in their very own homes." Robin beamed.

"Oh! Uh, I guess that would be okay." He adjusted his small glasses and looked at all of us as we stood expectantly before him.

"Wonderful!" Robin whipped her head around and inadvertently, I assumed, smacked Josh in the face with her long hair. "Nelson? Are you getting this?"

"Yes, ma'am." The cameraman sounded annoyed. "I do know how to use this thing. I am a professional, you know." Nelson turned the camera away from me. I'd been too focused on Josh's potential shopper to realize that I was being filmed. Clearly irritated, Robin reached out and shoved the camera so that it was aimed at Josh. Nelson protested, "This is all part of the reality of the show, Robin. The process, you know? And Chloe's part of this."

I glanced sideways at Nelson, who increasingly felt like a weirdo. "Um, you really don't need to film me, Nelson." I couldn't help feeling flattered that Nelson thought I was camera-ready, but I still found him a bit creepy. I do have to admit, though, that I checked my reflection in one of the store mirrors. Hmm, my red hair could use a hint of styling serum . . .

"And your name is?" Robin prompted the man.

"Um, I'm Leo." Evidently unnerved by the presence of the camera, Leo tucked his head down to glance into his empty cart.

"Wonderful!" Robin practically shouted. "This is Nelson, our cameraman."

"Field operator," he corrected her. "And filmmaker. We've got great color temperature in here, so it's going to be a good shoot today."

Robin sighed at Nelson, introduced the rest of us, and then gave Leo a brief rundown on how the show worked. She explained that for the three chefs, the show was a competition. "Okay, then, Leo. We'll have Josh walk you through the market, and the two of you will select ingredients for your dinner. Then we'll all drive to your house and capture every tiny little detail of the culinary process. Isn't this exciting? Who will we be cooking for this evening?"

"My wife, Francie. She'll be home pretty soon." Leo glanced nervously in Nelson's direction.

Uh-oh. If Leo's wife, Francie, was on her way home, she was presumably dressed and groomed in a presentable fashion. I had the impression that the station preferred to film an episode in which the shopper's stunned spouse or partner looked entirely unprepared to be on television. Ideally, the wife, Francie, would've had a mud mask on her face and rollers in her hair when she discovered that she was appearing in a reality show. I looked at Robin to see whether she was going to nix this shopper, too.

"Well, whether your wife is home yet or not when we get there, won't she be surprised!" For once, Robin was doing her best to be charming. I was relieved that she hadn't tossed Leo into his cart and sent him careening down the aisle before resuming the tedious search for the perfect victim.

Josh stepped in to take over for Robin, who was, I thought, on the verge of frightening Leo into refusing to participate. "Just ignore the camera, okay?" Josh put a hand on Leo's shoulder and guided him over to a display of fresh corn. "So tell me about you and Francie. What do you two like to eat?"

Leo seemed to relax a bit. "Well, you may have a challenge on your hands, Josh. My wife eats meat, but I'm a pesco-ovo-lacto-vegetarian. I eat fish and dairy but not meat. Are you sure you still want me to be on your show? I'm not sure if I'm going to help you win," he said apologetically.

"This is actually going to be great, Leo. I'll get to show the audience how to work around dietary needs," Josh assured him as he examined a perfectly ripe mango.

"I'd like you to make some meat, though, for Francie.

Since I don't usually cook outside my diet, it'd be a treat to have someone cook with her in mind, huh?"

"Excellent. We'll make something for both of you then." I could see Josh's eyes light up as he shifted into his chef mode.

TWO

"WE could do a beautiful pesto that we toss with fresh gnocchi. And serve that with seared scallops for you and some kind of roasted meat with vegetables for Francie. We're almost getting into fall now, so maybe some root vegetables? And how about a gorgeous mixed tomato salad and cheese course? This is a great time of year for fresh tomatoes, so I'd love to use some of those. Check out these yellow pear tomatoes here." Josh reached into a wooden wagon that served as a display for a variety of tomatoes. He proceeded to give Leo and the television audience a short discourse on the joys of tomato season.

"Lucky bastard," Digger said under his breath.

Marlee clicked her tongue. "Yeah, seriously."

"Why is Josh lucky?" I asked the two chefs.

"Josh gets to show off even more now. He's going to

make something awesome even with that pesco-veggie-whatever guy. This is going to make him look good. I'm going to have to find an even better one on my next turn. Maybe someone who only eats flatbread. I can do wonders with flatbread," Digger teased with a smile.

"This blows." Marlee sighed, blew her bangs out of her eyes, and examined her fingernails. For a chef, Marlee certainly had dirty fingernails. I didn't like to think about her handling food in a restaurant kitchen!

"For dessert, what about a peach and raspberry cobbler?" Josh suggested. Leo nodded enthusiastically and helped Josh gather the fruits and vegetables for the meal.

We kept out of the way as we followed Josh, Leo, Robin, and Nelson. From what I could tell, Josh was doing a beautiful job. He chose a variety of ingredients, held foods up to the camera, kept his body from blocking shots, and dealt with Robin's intrusive style better than I would have.

"What about some beet greens, Josh?" asked Robin, reaching for a large bunch. "These look gorgeous."

"Um, maybe—"

"Or arugula? They've got a beautiful selection today." Robin invaded the camera space and handed Josh a plastic bag.

"Actually, we could make a delicious arugula pesto for the gnocchi. Maybe with some Calamata olives in it? And we'll find a good cut of meat for Francie and some seafood for you both. We'll get some nice wine and cheese next door, too."

Leo nodded in recognition. "Sure. I know the place. Um, the only thing is . . . I sort of hate arugula. But Francie will love it, so I think we should make it anyway. I can just have butter on my gnocchi, right?"

"Sure, of course. If that's okay with you, that's what we'll do."

As Leo and Josh worked their way through the produce department, they filled Leo's basket with potatoes, Vidalia onions, heads of garlic, fresh oregano, basil, and parsley, and other items that met Josh's high standards. Nelson followed the pair and managed to keep the camera on his subjects.

So far as I could tell, Robin did nothing except interject unhelpful commands. "Get some radishes!" she ordered. "Those will look great on camera. Remember to look up at the camera, both of you!"

Josh cleared his throat. Then, trying to look simultaneously at Leo and the camera, he said, "Let's head over to the meat counter. When deciding on your pick and cut of meat—"

"Josh," Robin said, "turn your body a bit to the left so Nelson can get the shot. There! Good!" Although Josh must've been ticked off at the interruption, his face showed nothing, but Leo looked like a deer caught in headlights. When Robin had positioned the pair to her satisfaction, she said, "Now, say that again, Josh. About the meat."

Josh uttered three words before Nelson stopped him. "Wait. Sorry. My mike isn't working right." The microphone that protruded from Nelson's camera was covered in a fuzzy sheath. After jiggling the mike with what struck me as unnecessary vigor, he said, "All set. One more time."

Instead of launching into his third attempt to explain how to select meat, Josh said, "Okay, let's talk to Willie, the meat guy here." Josh faced the counter and waved to Owen's brother. "Willie! How are you, my friend?"

Willie looked up from the counter, where he was cutting and breaking down an enormous piece of beef. "My man, Josh! How's it going? And, hey, Leo. How are you? And how's Francie?"

Leo turned to Josh. "My wife and I come here a lot.

We've gotten to know Willie. Well, Francie more than I, since she's the meat eater in the family. But Willie always takes care of her."

"So what's with the entourage today, fellas?" Willie winked at me, wiped his hands on a dish towel, and leaned against the counter.

Josh explained the show and asked Willie for suggestions.

"Well," Willie said, "I know Francie's been eyeing these lamb chops, but I think she didn't know what to do with them. How to cook them exactly. And they're pretty pricey. Worth it, though."

I'd promised myself that I'd keep quiet, but keeping the promise took a lot of effort. How could anyone have absolutely no idea how to cook lamb chops? In terms of culinary challenge, they weren't exactly shad roe or calf brains.

"Dude, those look nice," Digger commented from behind Josh. "Really fresh."

"You're right," Josh agreed. With what I felt sure was no intention of insulting Francie, he said to Leo, "It's hard to ruin a good lamb chop. The worst thing you can do is overcook it, but I'll show you how to avoid that. Okay, Willie, give us a couple of chops for Francie."

Willie selected two from the depths of the refrigerated counter and placed them on plastic wrap on the scale. "So, I'm going to be famous from this show, I assume. If I'd known you were coming, I would've spent a few extra minutes at the mirror this morning." Willie scratched his chin. "Might have even shaved for you."

"You're as pretty as always, dude," Josh said with a laugh. "But we're going to see Evan in a bit to pick up some cheese and a bottle or two of wine. We'll see who's prettier then."

"Tell my brother I'll always win that contest. Hey,

Chloe," Willie called over the counter to me. "How's my soon-to-be sister-in-law doing? She ready to pop yet?"

Willie meant my best friend, Adrianna, who was going to marry his brother Owen in a couple of weeks. Adrianna was eight months pregnant and looked as if she were carrying triplets. As far as anyone knew, there was only one baby inside her, but I was beginning to worry that the one baby weighed forty pounds.

"Well, she's okay. Aside from comparing herself daily to a variety of large mammals and insisting that Owen take over for her and incubate the kid himself. So, you know, she's doing great," I said sarcastically.

"Aw, poor thing. I'll have to give her a call and check in." Willie wrapped the lamb chops in white butcher's paper and passed them to Josh. "Good luck. And tell Francie I send my love, okay?"

"Will do," Josh said with a nod. "Now let's get your fish."

Josh got enough halibut to make a first course for Leo. Then we cruised down an aisle lined with shelves of fancy oils, vinegars, and prepared sauces in imaginatively shaped bottles and jars.

"I've used some of these sauces before." Leo pointed to a series of bottles that bore the pretty green label of an imported brand. "That tends to be how I cook, I guess. With jarred sauces."

As Josh nodded in understanding, Robin nudged Nelson. The signal was unnecessary. Nelson already had the camera on Josh's face, which expressed his passion for helping people to make wonderful food in their own kitchens. "That's true for a lot of people," Josh said. "And it's great that there are high-quality products for when people want to get a meal out quickly. But the downside is that the at-home cook can really miss out on simple, delicious sauces, salsas, chutneys, and marinades, all kinds of things that can be put together with minimal work. As good as some of these products can be, nothing beats the taste and aroma of freshly chopped herbs blended with a fantastic Spanish olive oil. Or a sauce that you've slowly simmered on your stove so you've brought out all the flavors of your ingredients."

Josh and Leo continued making their way through the market, adding products to the shopping cart until Josh was sure he'd have everything he'd need. "I assume you'll have some basic seasonings at your house, Leo?"

Leo nodded. "I think I've got everything you need." He grinned shyly at Robin. Was Leo trying to flirt with Robin? If so, Robin completely ignored him and returned to checking her notes.

All of us finally ended up at a register, where Robin paid. A benefit of being selected for the show was that the station covered the cost of all the food in the cart, including whatever had been in there before Robin and the chef had even approached the shopper. Today, of course, Robin had picked out Leo as he'd been entering the store, so the policy didn't matter, and in any case, most of Natural High's clientele needed no help with food bills. Still, the generous practice spoke well for the station.

"The cheese shop is next," Robin instructed us while simultaneously scribbling on her clipboard. I was beginning to suspect that she followed the David Letterman approach to note taking, which was to say that her notes were nothing more than random scribbles with no bearing on what was happening. "Since it's basically next door, we can just walk over there. Digger and Marlee, you can put the bags in the van for us."

While Robin's back was turned, Digger saluted her and

started pushing the shopping cart. Marlee stayed with him as Robin marched impatiently through the exit door, with Josh, Leo, Nelson, and me hurrying to keep up with her. Everything about her manner and her posture suggested that all of us had been hanging around and wasting time, whereas, in fact, Robin herself had been the sole cause of the delay. Looking back over her shoulder, she had the nerve to call out, "Let's go, people! We're on a timetable here!"

The cheese and wine shop where Evan worked was unimaginatively called the Cheese and Wine Shop. Its setting was no more intriguing than its name. It occupied one of the storefronts in a little strip mall across the parking lot from Natural High. Flanked by a knitting store on one side and a handmade crafts boutique on the other, the Cheese and Wine Shop distinguished itself by displaying a cheerful striped awning that welcomed visitors.

"Welcome! Welcome!" Evan's greeting sounded more affected than genuinely affable. Posed next to a display table that showcased the wine of the month, he had one hand on the table and the other at his waist. I could practically smell calculation in the air. As if to confirm my hunch that Willie had called to give Evan a heads-up, Evan exclaimed, "What a surprise!" After pausing to bestow a toothy smile on everyone, he continued. "And what are you all doing here? Could this be a *Chefly Yours* episode?"

Still trying to keep my vow of silence, I waved to Evan, who, like everyone else in Owen's family, was extraordinarily good-looking—reason to feel confident about the genes that Owen was passing on to his baby. Evan and Willie were a year apart but could almost have been mistaken for identical twins. Evan, however, was a bit bulkier than Willie, probably because Evan was fond of overindulging in the delicious triple-crème cheeses available here.

"And is my friend Leo here the target of all your shenanigans?" Evan's theatrical effort to project made him speak so loudly that Josh and Leo stepped back.

"I am, I am," Leo answered. "I had no idea when I walked into the store today that I would wind up with the services of a talented chef. It's wild." Leo turned to Josh. "I'm a bit of a regular here, as you might have figured out."

Evan shook Josh's and Leo's hands, and then Josh introduced Robin and Nelson.

"Okay, start shooting, Nelson," Robin ordered.

Nelson flicked on the camera's light and moved his eye behind the camera while muttering, "I think I know what I'm doin' here . . ."

Josh nodded and moved to Evan's side. "So, Evan, we're looking for some cheeses to serve after dinner and some nice wines to go with everything. What can you recommend?"

The bright light seemed to have panicked Evan, who began to sweat profusely. "Well, Josh," said Evan, while beaming maniacally into the camera lens, "there are several wonderful choices that I happen to have here." He moved to the counter by the register and pulled out a tray on which eight or nine cheeses, each with a label, were attractively and all-too-conveniently arranged. "Ahem, this is a lovely Tomme de Savoie. And here we have a Serena, which comes from the mountainous Extremadura region of Spain. Oh, and a rich Gorgonzola, which I think should be on every cheese tray— very smooth and creamy. Would you like a sample?" Evan seemed to be loosening up as he eased into his cheese comfort zone, but when he wiped his forehead with his sleeve, I saw Robin wince.

Evan's anxiety made me long to alert Leo's wife, Francie, to the imminent arrival of her husband and his newfound group of television friends. It was five thirty, and I guessed that Leo's wife might be home any minute. I couldn't believe that most people would welcome strangers with a camera into their homes with absolutely no notice. It was easy for me to imagine times when even I, who would drop almost anything for a gourmet meal, wouldn't want *Chefly Yours* descending on my condo. Of course, I didn't have Francie's number and had no way to find it. I didn't even know her last name. The poor woman! And what if she freaked out when we all showed up at her house? What if she ruined Josh's chances of winning? For all I knew, the unknown Francie might toss us out like yesterday's fondue!

Evan cut samples of the powerfully flavored cheese for us all and moved on to a mouthwatering Explorateur. "Decadent and luxurious is how this cheese is best described." Evan cut through the rind to reveal a creamy center. "This is a triple-crème at its finest." He really was nervous! He knew as well as I did that cheeses should be eaten in order from mild to strong. He spread the cheese onto four crackers, and in spite of the competition from the lingering taste of the Gorgonzola, all of us, even Robin, groaned and murmured approval.

Decadent and luxurious indeed! I closed my eyes to savor the rich flavor. The thin, crispy, free-form crackers were perfect. Others might not appreciate the need for a good cracker, but I hated ruining an extraordinary cheese by smearing it on the equivalent of cardboard and then having the whole mess break apart in my hands. Just as bad were the kinds of crackers loaded with seeds, nuts, or spices, textures and tastes that bonked you over the head, obliterating the taste of the cheese. Ick!

Evan gestured around the store at the walls filled with bottles. "Tell me about your meal, and we'll match you up with the right wines. I have a few open bottles that have been breathing for a while, so we can start by trying those."

Josh described the menu, and Evan helped with the choice of wines. My mind wandered. I was more interested in the food than I was in what we'd drink with it. In particular, the little samples of cheese had whetted my appetite for more, and I had no idea how I'd resist absconding with Josh's cheese tray and leaving none for anyone else.

When we'd left the shop, Robin again started giving orders. "I'll ride with Leo so I can fill him in on the release papers he'll have to sign. And you'll follow us. Don't lose me! And we'll meet you outside Leo's house, okay? This is it, people! Are we ready to roll?"

"You bet." Josh clapped his hands together. "This is going to be a fantastic meal, Leo. You're going to be in great hands tonight."

THREE

FOLLOWING Robin turned out to be easy. Leo's house was only a few blocks away. Its appearance surprised me. Fairfield was so uniformly upscale that I'd expected to find Leo and Francie living in a large, beautifully maintained place. As it turned out, their house was a brown-shingled Victorian in decent condition, but the yard, which must once have been attractive, was a neglected mess. My parents run a landscaping business, Carter Landscapes, and I had the strong urge to sic both of them on Leo and Francie. On the upside, the house, much older than the others in the neighborhood, had the charm notably missing from the new construction that dominated the street. I'd waited in the parking lot to make sure that mine was the last car to leave; I hadn't wanted to get there until the rest of the group had arrived. Lingering, I again primped in my rearview mirror, and then locked my purse in my Saturn, took my keys with me, and made my way past overgrown shrubs and weeds to the back door, which stood open. Through the screen door, I saw Josh standing at the kitchen sink.

"There you are," he called to me.

"Sorry." Smoothing my hair and reapplying makeup must have taken longer than I'd calculated.

My first thought on entering Leo's kitchen was that Robin must be having a fit. So much for the theory that Leo's appearance meant that he'd have a fancy, photogenic kitchen. At a guess, it had been updated thirty or forty years earlier, and renovations done since then had been partial. The cabinets were made of a pale synthetic material intended to simulate birch, and the floor was covered in brick-patterned linoleum. The walls were white, as was the refrigerator, but the dishwasher was black, the sink was stainless steel, and the stove a hideous avocado green. Although the room itself was large, there was little free counter space, and the layout had evidently been planned by someone who didn't cook. The refrigerator was far from the sink and stove, and I wasn't sure that it would be possible to open the refrigerator door without smacking the new-looking but awkwardly placed granite island in front of it. I sighed softly. Well, if anyone could work in this space, it was Josh. And at least the range was gas, and at least Josh had a cooperative subject, Leo.

In contrast, Francie, as I assumed her to be, looked less than cooperative. She was a slim, almost scrawny, woman with frizzy waves of dark hair. She stood with her arms crossed while addressing Robin in a high-pitched voice. "It's just that we don't seem to have the best setup here, and . . . well, I just don't know about all this." She uncrossed her arms and waved her hands around almost in the manner of a startled infant. "I'm not, uh, someone who belongs on TV." Then, as if having hit

on an effective argument that stood a chance of driving her unwanted guests from her house, she said with confidence, "I really think you could do better." She ruined the effect, however,
by throwing a pleading glance at Leo.

"Hey, it'll be fun, Francie! Lighten up. I was a little nervous
at first, too, but wait until you see what this chef here, Josh, is
going to make for us. Actually, what he's going to teach us to
make. There's lamb for you. Lamb chops. You love lamb chops.
Come on!" Leo whispered something into wife's ear.

She shrugged and forced a smile. "Well, I guess so. Why
not? I am starving." Francie took off a navy linen blazer and
tossed it on the back of a chair by a small breakfast table.
When she turned to face us, she had a hint of a smile. Although she was not even close to beautiful, she was striking,
with high cheekbones and a strong jaw. With the right
makeup—she wore none that I could see—she'd have looked
distinguished. Now that she'd taken off her blazer, her white
linen shell revealed a surprisingly curvaceous build. "So, what
do I do?" she asked.

Josh already had the cheese selections unwrapped and
coming to room temperature on a plate, and the rest of the
ingredients were spread out across every available space.
Within minutes, Josh, who was used to running a restaurant kitchen, had finished assigning all of us to separate
work areas. Digger, Marlee, and I were given the humble
task of peeling potatoes for the gnocchi. Josh was showing
Leo and Francie how to make the arugula pesto. We potato
peelers were stationed at a small table, and although we
kept bumping elbows, our spirits were good. Josh had had
the foresight to bring a lot of his own kitchen equipment,
including some pots and pans, but Leo and Francie did have
an adequate supply of the basics, including a Cuisinart food
processor.

At the counter near the sink, Josh was teaching Leo to make pesto in the Cuisinart. Standing next to Leo, he was supervising as Leo put the ingredients in the bowl of the machine. "So, we have arugula, pine nuts, garlic, Parmesan cheese, Calamata olives, lemon juice, a little salt, and olive oil. We'll blend this all up and have a fantastic, spicy pesto for the homemade gnocchi."

The loud noise from the food processor almost drowned out Nelson's voice. "Sorry. Sorry. Hey, Josh? Excuse me. Can we do that again, Josh? Something is going on with the camera."

I gritted my teeth. What was Josh supposed to do? Cast some magic spell that would make the pesto ingredients fly apart and reconstitute themselves? Josh was a great chef, but he was a chef. He wasn't Harry Potter.

"Seriously?" Josh glared at Nelson but kept his cool. "Okay, we have enough here to make another batch." Josh emptied the Cuisinart bowl, had Leo repeat the process of making the pesto, removed the container from the food processor, dipped a spoon in, took a taste, and nodded to himself. "A touch more salt, and that's good to go." He handed spoons to Francie and Leo and let them try. Both responded with smiles.

Robin squeezed between Josh and Leo, grabbed the Cuisinart bowl, and angled the pesto toward Nelson. "You have to hold it like this so we get a good view. Here, let's put it in something more attractive." Reaching across the counter, she wrangled a spatula out of a ceramic vase that held cooking utensils and knocked over the vase and its contents. Ignoring the mess she'd made, she grabbed a little hand-painted bowl that sat on a windowsill. "There, here's a nice bowl for the pesto." Nelson lowered his camera and waited until Robin had finished meddling in Josh's business.

When Josh had dutifully transferred the pesto into the pretty bowl, I reluctantly realized that Robin had been right: the reds and oranges of the hand-painted bowl made the pesto look especially green and appetizing. In this instance, anyway, Robin's bossiness was justified.

When the potatoes were peeled and cooked, Josh had Francie and Leo put them through a ricer and spread them out on a tray to cool. The next step, I knew, was to work in eggs and flour. "Make sure your potatoes are nicely cooled," Josh warned, "or you'll cook the egg when you blend it in." With Josh keeping a close eye on the dough, Leo and Francie rolled it into long snakes, cut off small pieces, used forks to make ridges in each piece, and then curved the gnocchi into C shapes.

"Oops, sorry." Nelson careened into me while trying to capture me slicing the peaches for the peach and raspberry cobbler.

"Watch it, Nelson!" Marlee shook her head in disgust at the cameraman's clumsiness.

"Yeah, man," Digger added. "Watch where you're going."

Nelson looked truly apologetic. "I'm sorry. It's crowded here."

"It's okay. I'm fine," I assured Nelson, who was right about the crowding. Although the kitchen was spacious in the sense of being a large room, the work areas were infuriatingly cramped.

"No, you're not fine," Robin informed me. "Nelson, get yourself and your goddamn camera over here. Here, where the chef is cooking the food!" She pointed sharply at the innocent gnocchi. "Zoom in and give me something to work with. Stay on the food until I say otherwise."

Despite Robin's demanding attitude and Nelson's repeated need to reshoot cooking steps and instructions, Josh was able to teach Francie and Leo how to prepare the rest of the meal and how to coordinate the timing so that the separate components of the dinner were ready at the same time. When the gnocchi floated to the top of the pot of boiling water, the lamb chops were perfectly cooked in a nest of herbed vegetables, and the fish was seared to perfection. At that moment, Josh popped the peach and berry cobbler into the oven to cook while dinner was being served and eaten. The cheeses were on a platter, and the tomato salad had been tossed in an aromatic dressing. The cheese and salad course would follow the main course, and the cobbler would be served last.

I was not used to watching Josh cook without being free to sample his delectable creations. Although he'd put me and everyone else to work, I felt stuck at the periphery of the scene. My stomach obviously did, too: it began to growl. When Josh tossed the hot gnocchi into the pesto, I couldn't resist any longer. Catching his eye and glaring at him, I transmitted the message that unless I got some of this food, he was going to have one cranky, miserable girlfriend. I was absolutely ravenous, since it was nearing eight o'clock. As Josh must have sensed, everyone else clearly felt the same way I did. In the chaos of getting plates and serving platters to the table, he let everyone get in a few spoonfuls of food and practically had to swat Robin away from the gnocchi. He also remembered to set aside gnocchi with butter only for Leo. I grimaced when I saw Marlee double-dip her spoon back into the bowl. How uncheflike! Between her dirty fingernails and germ-sharing tasting method, I wondered how this woman's restaurant ever passed a health inspection.

At last it was time to film the dinner scene. The large dining room was painted a deep green that I hoped wouldn't be too dark for the camera. Francie and Leo took their seats on delicate Windsor chairs at a round wooden table beneath what I thought was a fake crystal chandelier. The table was too small for the generously proportioned room and too chunky for the chairs. The piece of furniture that dominated the dining room was a gigantic sideboard with little mirrors and elaborate carving. It seemed to me that the dining room, like the kitchen, had been assembled bit by bit, without any sort of overall plan or theme to guide the selection of elements, none of which had anything in common with any of the others. While I'd been busy in the kitchen, someone had tried to impose eye appeal on the unfortunate dining room by creating an attractive table setting. The matching runner, place mats, and napkins were made of a Victorian-looking fabric with stylized flowers and vines on a black background. The stainless flatware was heavy and oversized—at a guess, the pattern had the word *Hotel* in its name—and each of the two places had two stemmed wineglasses, one large and one small. Someone, maybe Marlee, had opened two bottles of wine, one red and one white, and had placed them on the table. Although I knew very little about wine, I knew that red wine, or at least some red wine, was supposed to be opened ahead of time so that it could breathe. But white wine? And wasn't white wine supposed to be cold? Or at least cool? I didn't ask. Fortunately, as I reminded myself, the show was more about food than about wine; it certainly wasn't supposed to be about interior decorating.

As Josh served Francie and Leo, I noted that he deserved a lot of credit for seamlessly putting together separate dishes for a couple with radically different food preferences. Leo's plate of halibut and buttered gnocchi, Francie's plate of lamb chops and pesto gnocchi, and a platter of roasted vegetables all looked divine. Probably because of the shared vegetables, I had the sense of one coordinated meal, not just a collection of separate items. Leo's willingness to eat the vegetables had surprised me, since they'd been cooked in the same roasting pan as the lamb, as Leo knew. Leo had participated in the cooking, he'd seen the vegetables in the roasting pan, and Josh had even pointed out that they'd been cooked with the meat, but Leo had said that they were fine for him. I'd heard him myself. In any case, now that the main course had been served, the table looked beautiful.

Nelson's camera light shone on the pair of diners. Looking jovial and pleased with himself, Leo poured white wine into his own glass and red into Francie's. Then, just as Leo raised his glass, presumably to make a toast, Robin stopped him. "Wait!" she cried. "We need to get some good footage of the dishes before anyone eats them. Marlee and Digger? Why don't you carry everything back to the kitchen, to the breakfast table, and Nelson can shoot the plates there, where the light's better."

"Sure thing," Marlee said as she handed the vegetable platter to Digger and then removed Francie's and Leo's plates. "While we're at it, we'll sneak a little taste for ourselves from the leftovers in the bowls."

Josh, I knew, would take it as a compliment that another chef wanted to sample his food. My private thought was that Marlee was hungry. I certainly was, and I suspected that everyone else was, too.

Digger sighed as he carried away the platter. "At this rate, the food is going to be dead cold by the time they get to eat it."

He wasn't kidding. It must've taken Nelson ten minutes to film the food that had been taken away, and when it was finally returned and Leo and Francie finally got to take their first bites, Nelson stopped them and announced that they'd have to reenact their first tasting. Poor Josh looked ready to wring someone's neck, and Francie and Leo were exchanging glances of exasperation. Marlee and Digger both looked uncomfortable in some way that I couldn't interpret. Was Josh's competition sympathizing with him? I doubted it. And when Digger suddenly started to beckon Josh, as if he wanted to call him aside to have a word with him, I was furious. This was no the time to chat it up with Josh! This was his big moment! The thought crossed my mind that when Digger and Marlee had carried the food back to the kitchen, they'd concocted some nasty plot to spoil Josh's chances of winning, a scheme that began with getting him away from the table. Fortunately, Josh ignored Digger and, with Robin's unwanted help, rearranged the food on the plates. My heart went out to Josh. He took tremendous pride in everything he prepared. Although the plates now looked appetizing, Josh's hot food must now be lukewarm, if not outright cold.

Even so, once Leo and Francie were at last permitted to eat, Leo raved about his halibut. "This is just spectacular. The fish is cooked perfectly, and I love the sweet crust on it. That's just from the sugar you sprinkled on it?" He took a bite of the gnocchi. "These are heavenly. And the roasted vegetables smell incredible!"

Francie, on the other hand, looked anything but enthusiastic. After she'd tasted her lamb, she grabbed a water glass and took a large gulp. My stomach dropped as I watched her force herself to swallow a few more bites. I looked nervously at Josh, who was staring so intently at Francie that he looked frozen in place. What could possibly be wrong? Even the best chef makes a mediocre dish now and then, but Josh had never cooked anything inedible. Of course, the lamb chops should have been served hot. Maybe the fat had congealed, I told myself. Still, even if the lamb wasn't at its best, it just couldn't be as repugnant as Francie seemed to find it. Francie, I told myself, must be a picky eater, someone who whined and complained about everything she tasted.

"And how's your dish, Francie?" prompted Robin, who had been so focused on Leo that she'd obviously failed to notice Francie's grimacing.

Francie dropped her fork and made eye contact with the camera. "The truth is," she said emphatically, "it's just awful."

FOUR

"FRANCIE!" Leo admonished. "There's no need to be rude."

With a vigorous shake of her head that made her dark, wavy hair fan out, she declared boldly, "It's vile, it's positively disgusting, it's revolting, and I simply can't eat any more. It is by far the worst thing that has ever been my misfortune to taste in my entire life." After a brief pause, she said, looking at Josh, "I'm not trying to hurt anyone's feelings, really I'm not, but something has gone horribly, hideously, dreadfully wrong with this dish."

Nelson lowered the camera.

Leo was seething. "Francie, this no time for your damned theatrics. Do you know how lucky we were to be chosen? We've got a talented chef in our house preparing a gourmet meal for us. Everything I've tasted is better than what we've had at most restaurants, so just chew and swallow. And for once in your life, smile!"

Belatedly, Robin turned her attention to Nelson. What she saw made her blow up. "Nelson, what the hell are you doing?" she demanded. "What we have going on here is action! Emotion! Conflict! What we have here is reality! And where are you? In outer space!"

"Sorry," Nelson said weakly. Clearly, even Nelson's heart went out to Josh.

"Oh, for God's sake, now we have to do everything all over again," Robin complained.

This time, Marlee and Digger took a turn at fussing over the food in what was now a futile effort to make it look freshly plated. Josh stood silent and watched as other chefs tended to his plated dishes.

Meanwhile, Robin chastised Nelson for his incompetence. "Could we possibly get through the rest of the meal without further interruption from you? Hit the On button! Hit it once! Hit it now! And don't touch it again. Is that something you are capable of doing?"

Nelson practically snarled at Robin. "Well, of course—"

"Rhetorical question, Nelson! I was asking a rhetorical question!" Tendrils were beginning to come loose from Robin's once-tight ponytail, as if her fury at her inept cameraman had somehow electrified her brain and escaped through her hair. "And now, for the last time"—she waved at the dinner plates—"let's roll!"

Nelson's light went on.

Francie leaned back in her chair. "I really think I've had enough of this dish."

Leo took a bite of the roasted vegetables and spoke with his mouth full. "Francie, there cannot possibly be anything wrong with your food. Have you even tasted anything? I don't think you have, because if you had, you'd know that it's spectacular." He smiled at Josh and gave him a thumbs-up. Miraculously, Nelson caught the gesture on tape.

Francie, however, was adamant about not tasting another bite of her food. Having watched her more closely than her husband had done, I knew that she had, in fact, eaten some of what she'd been served, but I had no idea whether she was whining about nothing or whether there was actually something wrong with her lamb.

"Absolutely not," she told Leo. "For your information, I have tasted it, and not for anything on earth am I choking it down again."

Josh had had enough. He stepped between the bickering couple and removed Francie's plate. Fumbling for words, he finally said, "I can't apologize enough. I'd be happy to make you something else, something . . . uh . . . if you can you tell me what's wrong with this?"

I seriously thought that Josh might cry. This experience was positively humiliating for him. If he'd been cooking for a private party, he'd have been mortified to serve food that made one of the hosts nearly gag. But this occasion was anything but private! And how many viewers would vote for Josh after watching and listening to Francie? None, I thought. Not one viewer. His chance of winning the competition had just dropped to zero.

"Yes," said Francie, "I can tell you exactly what's wrong. It's bitter beyond bitter." As if she'd failed to make her point, she added, "Horribly bitter! Really very foul tasting."

"The arugula," Josh said hopefully. "The arugula has a sharp bitterness to it."

"No." Francie shook her head and again sent her wavy hair flying. "I'm very sorry, Josh, but that's not it. It's not right. I can't eat this."

Following Robin's orders, Nelson had the camera going. Digger and Marlee both stood rigidly still with their eyes nearly popping out of their heads. The two chefs obviously knew that Josh had completely blown this meal. Neither one looked terribly happy, but they didn't look torn up over Josh's failure, either. I thought I would be sick; Josh looked absolutely crushed.

"There's no time to have Josh make something else. I don't know what to do." Robin bit her lip and seemed momentarily lost. "Well, we'll have to move on. It'll just have to be part of the episode. What happens, happens, I'm afraid." I saw a slight but unmistakable glint in Robin's eye as she savored the prospect of airing this episode of *Chefly Yours*. From Robin's viewpoint, Francie's dramatic condemnation of Josh's food was far better than pleasant murmuring about how delicious everything was. Josh's pain was Robin's idea of great TV.

"Why don't we move on to the tomato salad and cheese course," I suggested. "And dessert, too." I took Francie's plate from Josh's hands, carried it to the kitchen, and braced myself against the counter. *Oh, Josh! What happened?* Maybe he was so nervous that he accidentally added something weird to the food? Or the old oven didn't cook the lamb at the proper temperature and . . . ? No. Francie had complained about bitterness. Overcooked or undercooked lamb chops would be tough or raw or flavorless, but they wouldn't be bitter. Like Josh, I thought of the arugula. At this time of year, it was all too easy to buy lettuce and other greens, including arugula, that had gone to seed and turned bitter. Maybe most of the arugula had been fine, and Francie had somehow ended up tasting a tiny bit that had been ruined by summer heat.

A second later, my dejected boyfriend followed me into

the kitchen but avoided looking at me. "Leo's finishing up his fish," Josh said, "and I'm going to serve the rest of the meal." He swore under his breath and then slammed a pair of tongs into the bowl that held the remains of the gnocchi. "There is nothing wrong with that lamb," he growled.

"Well, why don't we taste it?" I whispered.

Josh looked at me. "Yeah, good idea." He cut a bit for both of us from Francie's plate. "Now, don't think I normally go eating off customers' plates at the restaurant, okay?" He managed a little smile.

Until he tasted the lamb.

"Oh, my God." He wrinkled his face and quickly spat out the offending meat.

"Oh, stop! It can't be that bad." Curious, I sampled a tiny slice. *Bitter,* I realized, was a gross understatement. Gagging, I turned and spat the meat out into the sink, which was, thank goodness, equipped with a garbage disposal, exactly where the vile piece of lamb belonged. I filled glasses of water for us both and did my best to wash out the taste. Francie was, after all, right. The taste was worse than awful. It was hideously and inexplicably dreadful.

"I didn't do that," Josh said softly. "I did not do anything that would make the lamb taste like that. Did I?" He tasted the vegetables from the roasting pan. "These are pretty good. Although it's hard to tell right now with that flavor still in my mouth. How the hell did this happen?"

Here's proof of my love for Josh: in a noble act of self-sacrifice, I risked having that revolting bitterness invade my mouth again. In other words, I tasted the gnocchi with pesto. And again, ahem, used the sink. When I was done, I said, "Oh, hon! The gnocchi with the arugula pesto has the same problem the lamb does. Francie was right. It's that same bitterness." I shook my head. "Not from the arugula or the olives, either. At least, I don't think so. I've had arugula that's turned bitter, but it's not like this. And olives can be bitter, but this is something different, something much, much worse. Josh, what can do this?"

Before he answered, Robin called to him from the dining room. "Josh, we're ready for the next course."

Josh took a deep breath and carried the tomato salad and cheese plate to Francie and Leo. Francie looked hesitant to eat anything that Josh put in front of her, but she did help herself to tomatoes, tasted them, smiled, and offered unmistakably genuine praise. "The flavor and seasoning of the dressing is perfect."

One piece of good footage.

Nelson kept filming as a morose Josh presented the dessert cobbler. Leo again dug in with pleasure and oohed and aahed, but Francie did nothing more than move her spoon toward her dessert plate. The hot peach and raspberry concoction smelled fantastic. Wasn't she tempted to try it? And couldn't she see how miserable Josh looked? Didn't she want to make amends to him for her harsh criticism of the lamb and gnocchi? Not that I could really blame her—the bitterness lingered on my own tongue—but out of love for Josh, I sent telepathic messages to encourage her to speak kind words and help Josh to save face.

"I have to go to the bathroom," Francie announced curtly. So much for my telepathic abilities.

"Please, can you just finish dessert? And then we'll wrap this up." Robin looked desperate to bolt, but she was probably no more desperate than the rest of us were. Every single one of us, I thought, had had more than enough of this episode of *Chefly Yours*.

"We're almost done. I promise," Josh pleaded. He looked ready to sprint out of the house in shame.

"I feel sick." Francie rose from her seat and walked unsteadily from the table.

Join the club! After the whole fiasco, I wasn't feeling too well myself.

Francie staggered out of the dining room into a large front hallway. From where I was standing, I could see her head toward a staircase. Gripping the handrail, she slowly began to make her way up the steps.

"Christ, we're never going to get through this." Digger looked at his watch. "This is like a never-ending day. This blows for Josh, man."

"Yup, but at least it's been interesting," Marlee added.

Robin drew Josh aside and was gracious enough to put her hand on his arm as she spoke softly to him. I hoped she was saying something reassuring. Maybe that the TV station would never in a million years air this horrible episode?

Appalled by everyone's seeming lack of compassion for Francie, who clearly was not just feigning illness, I decided to check on her. I made my way to the front hall and up the stairs. By the time I reached the landing at the top, I could hear gagging and groaning. Following the sounds, I rounded a corner and on the floor ahead of me saw Francie's feet projecting from what was clearly a bathroom. Bright yellow towels hung on towel racks fastened inside the open door. Even before I entered the bathroom, I realized that Francie was horribly sick. She'd obviously been too ill even to close the bathroom door. Besides, the air in the dark hallway reeked. For a second, the taboo against barging into an occupied bathroom made me hesitate, but the dreadful sounds had now stopped, and the silence frightened me.

I stepped into the bathroom and knelt just inside the door. "Francie? Can I help you?" I put my hand on her shoulder. Francie didn't respond. She lay curled up on her side on a yellow bath mat, her hair in her face and her arms wrapped around her stomach. Bodily fluids were spattered on the old white ceramic bathroom fixtures and lay in pools on the cracked tile of the floor. The stench was overwhelming. Holding my breath and fighting nausea, I grabbed one of the thick yellow towels that hung from the door and made a senseless, panic-driven effort to rid Francie of the wet filth that clung to her dark curls and stained her white linen shell. Covering my hand with the towel, I brushed her hair away from her face, and as I leaned in to clean her mouth and cheeks, I realized she was having a terrible time breathing. Before that moment, my efforts had been directed at restoring Francie's dignity, I suppose. The sight of her sprawled on the floor, splattered with her own bodily wastes, had triggered a powerful impulse to clean her up and make her presentable, to spare her the humiliation being seen in this godawful condition. Now, all at once, the gravity of the situation hit me. At a minimum, she was dangerously dehydrated. Without question, she needed immediate help that I couldn't provide. My experience in hands-on first aid consisted of having treated small children with scraped knees. Now, I was facing a life-threatening emergency.

I'd left my cell phone in my purse in the car, and even if I'd been willing to leave Francie alone, I'd have had no idea where to find a phone upstairs in the house. "Josh!" I screamed. "Robin!"

I looked down at Francie, whose jagged breathing frightened me. "Francie?" I whispered. Then with near ferocity, I demanded, "Francie! Francie, can you hear me?" I uselessly dabbed the towel on her face.

Francie made a small, throaty noise and groaned softly. Almost inaudibly, she said, "Oh, shit." Her eyes were barely open, and her skin had a gray tinge.

I heard footsteps and then Josh's voice. "Chloe, is there another bathroom up here? I'm not feeling so great."

"Josh! You need to call nine-one-one! Get an ambulance! Now!" Panic had set in. My own voice sounded distant and unfamiliar. "Get an ambulance!" I screamed.

Looking up, I saw Josh grab one of the yellow towels. Then he retreated to the hallway, where I could hear him being violently sick.

"Oh, God," I whispered to myself. Then, in spite of the nauseating stench, I took a deep breath and bellowed, "Robin! Leo! Help! Call an ambulance! *Help! Help me!*"

Footsteps heralded the arrival of Robin and Leo, and I heard Robin say, "God, it smells awful here," and then, "Josh, what are you doing?"

I was still kneeling on the floor next to Francie. Rising a little, I again pleaded for help. "Call an ambulance! Francie is . . . For God's sake, call an ambulance!"

Instead of responding to the emergency, Leo stepped into the bathroom. "Francie?" he asked. "Francie, get up! You don't want people to see you like . . . We'd better get you to bed. The smell in here is . . . what a mess!" He held his hand to his nose and mouth.

Robin poked her head in and quickly withdrew.

"Chloe," Leo said, "can't you open the window? And help get Francie—"

When I'd first seen Francie, I'd also failed to grasp the reality of her situation. Still, I was furious at Leo. "Never mind the damned window!" I snapped. "Call an ambulance! Now!" I reached and almost punched Leo on the leg. "Go! Call nine-one-one!"

"Chloe, shut up!" Robin called out. "Cut the hysterics!"

"This is an emergency!" I insisted. "Call an ambulance!"

Robin, apparently addressing Leo, said, "Well, now we

know why Francie thought the food tasted bad. She was obviously coming down with a stomach bug. That norovirus thing. Is that what you call it? And she was starting to feel sick."

"Josh?" I called out. "Josh, are you okay? Can you get to a phone? Please! Please call for help!"

Josh cleared his throat. "Yeah, I'm all right now, I think."

I looked down at Francie, whose eyes were now shut. "Francie? Francie?" I rolled her onto her back and shook her. At first she appeared to be unconscious, but when I leaned my ear against her chest, I didn't hear the ragged breathing anymore. "Francie?" I was yelling now, repeatedly saying her name in the vain hope of rousing her. There was no response from her. Nothing. Nothing at all.

FIVE

I practically had to leap over Josh to get out of the bathroom. Then I flew down the stairs, my heart racing and my vision nearly blurred. All I can remember is being hell-bent on getting to the phone that I remembered having seen on the wall near the stove.

When I burst into the kitchen, I almost slammed into Digger, who grabbed me by both arms. "An ambulance is coming," he said. "What the hell is wrong? Is Josh okay? He ran out of here so fast."

"He's sick, too, Digger. I'm really scared," I said. My eyes began to water as I leaned into his chest. "I think Francie is dead." I was almost whispering. "I have to sit down." I was starting to feel queasy myself. Maybe Leo had been right about opening a window. The sickening odor seemed to cling to me. Or maybe fear was wrapping my stomach in knots.

Digger led me to a chair just as Josh entered the kitchen. He now looked more grim than ill, and I thought that I knew why: if Francie were still alive, Josh wouldn't have left her alone.

I found myself sitting next to Marlee, whose presence I hadn't even noticed. She was rubbing her forehead with one hand. Her face was pale and damp. "My stomach is really hurting," she said. "I've got terrible cramps, and I think I might throw up. Is there a bathroom downstairs?"

Digger moved the trash can next to her. "In case you don't make it to one," he said. "I might need it, too. I could hurl any second. I think we've got food poisoning."

"From the way I feel, you're probably right," Marlee agreed. "There's got to be a bathroom down here. Leo?"

For the first time, I noticed Leo, who was leaning against a wall as if propping himself up. He looked frozen in place, and his face was blank.

"Leo!" I said sharply. "Is there a bathroom downstairs?"

He shook himself and pointed to a doorway. "Through there." Sounding like a robot, he added, "I'm going back upstairs. Maybe I can . . ."

"Here, Marlee, I'll help you." Robin took Marlee's hand and led her out of the room.

As I watched them leave, I noticed to my horror that Nelson was standing in the dining room doorway with his face hidden behind his camera.

"Nelson, turn that camera off!" I demanded. "Stop it! This is no time—"

"Cannot do. I'm filming reality here. Raw reality! This is great!"

Glaring at him, Josh said, "Yeah, this is a great, Nelson. It's goddamn perfect."

"Nelson," I said, "the average rock would have more sensitivity than to film us right now. Turn the camera off! Unless you want me to grab it and shove it—"

Josh interrupted me. "There's the ambulance. You hear the sirens?"

"Yes," I said. "Thank God."

I'd somehow expected help to pour in through the back door, but when the doorbell rang, Josh went through the dining room, opened the front door, and took charge of directing the newcomers upstairs to where Francie lay on the bathroom floor. I felt certain that she was dead, but medical personnel and the police could hardly be expected to take my word for her condition, and there still remained a chance, I told myself, that I was wrong. The possibility made me feel guilty: what if I'd abandoned Francie when my presence might have comforted her?

While I could still hear the sounds of feet pounding up the stairs, Marlee reappeared from the bathroom. Her color was worse than it had been before. She had a greenish tinge, and her damp hair clung to her cheeks. "I heard the ambulance," she said. "Chloe, get someone to help me, would you? I'm sick. I'm so sick."

You and everyone else, I wanted to say. What I actually said was, "I'm not too well myself, and neither are—" I broke off. What if Marlee was becoming as horribly ill as Francie had been? "I'll see if I can get someone," I promised. With that, I made my way to the front hall, where the outside door stood open. Through it, I could see more official vehicles than I expected: two police cruisers and two big ambulances. As I stood there wondering how to summon help for Marlee—holler loudly? actually venture upstairs?—a handsome young EMT came bounding down, and at the same time, Josh appeared through the wide doorway to the living room.

"I'm sorry to bother you," I said to the EMT, "but there's someone in the kitchen who wants help. She's sick, too. And so are—"

"I'm going to check everyone out," he assured me, "and then we're probably going to take all of you to the emergency room."

"I'm fine," Josh claimed.

"No, he's not," I insisted. "He threw up all over the place."

"Yeah, I did throw up. I feel okay now, though. I'm fine."

"Josh, you don't know that!" I insisted. "But the one who's feeling really bad is Marlee. And Digger is sick, too."

"Give me a minute," the EMT said.

"We'll be in the kitchen," I told him. "It's in there, through the dining room."

The EMT hurried out through the front door. As Josh and I were on our way to the kitchen, we paused in the dining room to exchange a few words.

"Francie?" I asked.

He shook his head. "They had to do their thing, but . . ."

"I thought so," I said. "Oh, Josh, I was with her when she died. Maybe that's why I feel sick. Maybe I don't have the same thing as everyone else. I can't even tell."

"Hey, we've got to get these guys to take a look at you. Like he said, get you to the hospital."

"Marlee's the one I'm worried about. She looks terrible. Not as bad as Francie was, but I'm scared that she's—"

Josh held a finger to his lips. "Let the EMTs worry about her."

"I have to see how she is," I insisted.

When we entered the kitchen, I was relieved to find Marlee no worse than she'd been before. She was sitting at the table with Robin and Digger.

"Marlee, one of the EMTs will be here in a minute," I said.

Robin spoke up. "I'm really queasy, too. I don't feel right." She was slumped in her seat and was idly fingering her drooping ponytail. "I can't believe this. Is Francie really . . . ?"

Josh nodded. "Yes. Chloe was with her when she stopped breathing."

"Oh, my God, Chloe! Are you all right? Come sit down here." Robin pulled out another chair from the table.

"I'm okay." I still felt weird, but I was too embarrassed to admit that I couldn't tell whether I was sick or terrified.

Just as Josh opened his mouth to start arguing with me, the handsome EMT entered the kitchen in the company of a uniformed police officer, a large, muscular man with a neatly trimmed mustache. Before either of the men had a chance to say a word, Josh put a hand on my shoulder. "Chloe, you're not okay." Addressing the EMT, he said, "You need to take a look at her."

I caught the EMT's eye and gestured to Marlee. "I'll be okay, but Marlee's the one who really needs help."

The police officer's radio crackled loudly. He stepped to the far end of the kitchen and began muttering incomprehensible words. Interrupting the EMT, who was speaking softly to Marlee, he called out, "Where'd you get the food?"

"Natural High," I answered. "The Natural High right near here."

In an effort to be helpful, Josh began to give a detailed description of all the food we'd bought and all the dishes he'd prepared with such enthusiasm. I could hardly listen without crying for him. In the background, I heard heavy footsteps and the sound of the front door opening and closing. For a moment, everyone was quiet, as if we'd tacitly agreed to observe a moment of silence as Francie's body was carried away. My head was spinning, and everything seemed to be simultaneously happening in slow motion and at warp speed. I couldn't think clearly.

I don't know whether the EMT responded to me, to someone else, or to the whole situation, but I clearly remember that he said, "Okay, let's get you all to the emergency room." I also remember that he let Nelson have it: "And turn off that camera!"

Until then, I'd all but forgotten Nelson's existence. Wishful thinking?

"Man, look at it this way," Nelson said. "I'm just doing my job. Pursuing my art, okay? I'm a filmmaker, and I'm not going to miss this. That's what a documentary is about, right? Reality. Whatever happens. No matter what, you get it on film." The glee in Nelson's voice made me feel queasier than ever.

The cop was more effective than the EMT had been in getting Nelson to quit filming. Instead of giving Nelson an order, he did nothing but look at him, raise a hand, point his finger, and utter one word: "You!"

Nelson turned tail and vanished through the dining room.

The next thing that happened was that I stood up and . . . and . . . Well, what I definitely did *not* do was faint. For one thing, as a person who had completed a whole year of social work school and was thus a mental-health professional in training, I couldn't possibly have passed out from anxiety. For another thing, although I'd been feeling sick to my stomach, I hadn't lost any bodily fluids and thus couldn't have keeled over from dehydration. And for yet another thing, I wasn't the swooning type. So, let's just say that one moment I was rising from a chair in the kitchen, and the next moment, the next one I can remember, anyway, I was in an ambulance on the way to the hospital. But not, not, not because I had fainted.

Six

OKAY, so I fainted. The first voice I heard when I came to was Marlee's. "I can't see right," she complained. "Everything is kind of blurry."

The second voice belonged to the handsome EMT. "You with us again, Chloe? You're going to be fine. We're on our way to the hospital, but all that happened to you was that you fainted."

It was then that I became aware of the siren and of the sensation of being in a moving vehicle. To my credit, I didn't ask where I was. In fact, although the interior of the big emergency medical service vehicle looked like my idea of the inside of a space capsule, I knew that I was in an ambulance. "Not me!" I said. "I never faint."

Besides his good looks, the EMT had a sense of humor. He laughed. "Not the type for smelling salts, huh?"

When I tried to sit up, he gently told me to keep my head down for a while, but I succeeded in looking around and saw Marlee on the opposite side of the ambulance. She was rubbing her eyes, and her face looked wet from tears. "What's wrong with me?" she asked in a feeble voice. "With us?"

Although she wasn't addressing me, I answered her. "Something in the house? Like a gas leak?"

To my surprise, it was Josh who replied. His voice came from somewhere toward the front of the ambulance. "It's got to be the food. I don't know how, but it has to." He started reciting a list of everything he'd bought today: "Lamb, halibut, olives, arugula, potatoes . . ."

The comforting rumble of Josh's voice must have soothed me. Although I didn't realize it at the time, I showed two signs of health: practicality and hunger. "I don't have my insurance card!" I said in alarm. "It's in my purse, locked in my car." I had the sense to say nothing about my empty stomach. With one person dead and others ill, this was no time to ask for a snack. Even so, the thought did cross my mind that the hospital probably had a cafeteria or at least a vending machine.

As it turned out, Josh had found my keys and retrieved my purse from my car. Although he grumbled in a sweet way about women and their purses, I was glad to have my belongings with me, especially once we were at the emergency room, which was mercifully uncrowded. By the time we arrived, even my matinee-idol EMT conceded that my case had low priority, as did the nurses responsible for deciding which of us had to be seen immediately and which of us could wait. Although I still felt shaken, I had no physical symptoms at all. Consequently, I ended up in the waiting room with Josh, Digger, Robin, and that damned Nelson, who'd followed the ambulances to the hospital, which was a small one that I'd never heard of before. Marlee, who'd felt increasingly worse, had been hustled into the exam area as soon as we'd arrived. Nelson, camera in hand, was lurking near the entrance. The rest of us were sitting together. Josh and Digger were, as usual, talking about food, but not in the way that chefs typically do.

"Dude, it can't be the food. You know that," Digger tried to assure Josh. "All the stuff you cooked would take time to produce symptoms like this. Food poisoning wouldn't come on that fast and kill somebody. You know as well as I do that it takes, like, six hours at least before you'd get sick. If this was E. coli or something, none of us would be feeling anything right now."

I saw a flash of relief cross Josh's face. "You're right. You're right. I'm just so freaked out, and I can't help feeling like this is my fault somehow. I mean, I fed Francie, and then she died! I don't know everything about food poisoning, but I think there are a few kinds that can produce symptoms in a hour or two. I wish I had my ServSafe books with me," Josh said.

"It's a program," I informed Robin. "ServSafe trains kitchen workers in safe food laws, safe practices."

She spoiled my sense of being in the know by saying condescendingly, "I already know what ServSafe is, thank you very much."

"Josh," I said, "Marlee was saying that she had blurred vision. I've never heard of that being a symptom of food poisoning. That's neurological, isn't it? Blurred vision?" An unwelcome thought occurred to me. What if the problem was not food poisoning, but poisoning? Just poisoning. My stomach clenched in knots. I hoped the doctor who must now be examining Marlee would figure out what she had and would inform the rest of us. "Robin," I asked, "how are you feeling?"

"Been better, but at least I'm not heaving up Josh's food. And you?"

"I'm okay. I'm just shaken up, I think."

I glanced at the desk, only to spot Nelson leaning against it. A second later, a nurse noticed him, too, and in an undertone ordered him to turn off his camera. I couldn't hear her words, but her irate expression suggested that she was threatening fearsome consequences.

I saw Robin smile. "I should hire her." She rubbed her stomach. "So, Chloe, talk to me about something. Anything. Distract me from my screwed-up stomach."

"Well, I'm going to be performing a wedding ceremony in a few weeks."

Robin perked up. "You are? Who are you marrying? I mean, who are you helping get married? That's so cool. How can you do that?"

Although I was a little reluctant to give Robin credit for a good idea, it did take my mind off the present nightmare to think about my best friend Adrianna's wedding to Owen. "All I did was go online, print out an application from the state, and fill out a form. It's called a one-day marriage designation. The application had to be approved by the governor, except that I don't think he has to do it personally. And then I got my Certificate of Solemnization. So now I can marry Adrianna and Owen!" That didn't sound right. Unless I wanted people to think that I was about to commit bigamy, I'd need to work on my solemnization-wording skills. "Well, you know what I mean."

"That is really neat! I didn't know you could even do that," Robin said. "They don't go to church or anything? They didn't want someone more official to preside over their ceremony?"

"No, neither of them is particularly religious, and they're having a smallish wedding. Fifty people or so. And Ade thought it would be more personal if someone close to both of them did the ceremony. They're writing the whole service themselves, vows and all. Of course, I'll do my own piece, too, but it's nice that they can control what they want in and out of the whole thing."

"Chloe?" Josh touched my arm. "They're ready to see you and Robin now. Digger is getting checked out already." Josh's phone rang. "Sorry. I have to take this." When he picked up his call, I could make out a woman's voice on the other end. "I can't talk now," he said. "I'll call you back." He clicked his cell shut. "You ready?"

"Who was that?"

Josh waved a hand. "No one. Just work stuff. Oh, there's the nurse who wants to see you." Josh pointed to a fiftyish woman with a folder in her hand.

The nurse led me into a large room filled with medical equipment and lined with little curtained exam areas. When we reached the area assigned to me and she closed the curtains, I did my best to peek through the cracks to see whether I could see Marlee or Digger and find out how they were doing. Unfortunately, the hospital was all too effective in ensuring patient privacy—I couldn't see anyone at all—but at least I didn't hear any panicked calls for crash carts or loudspeaker announcements of emergency codes, so I assumed that Marlee and Digger were doing okay.

The nurse took my blood pressure and pulse, and shoved a thermometer in my mouth. "So, young lady, tell me what's going on with you." I didn't like the accusatory tone in her voice. And how was I supposed to answer her with my mouth closed?

I made unintelligible sounds with my lips closed until she pulled the thermometer out. "I don't think anything's going on with me. But"—I started to whisper—"I was with the woman, Francie, when she died. I found her on the bathroom floor, and I, uh, I watched her take her . . . well, her last breath."

The nurse squinted her eyes at me. "Her last breath?"

"Yes. I think I'm just unnerved." At normal volume, I said, "I'm upset by the experience. Anyone would be! It was not a peaceful death. She looked like she was in a lot of pain." I looked up at the nurse. "She is dead, right? I mean . . . we heard that Francie was dead." As if the statement were somehow unclear, I said, "We heard that she'd died, but . . ."

The sour nurse stared at me before speaking. "Yes, the woman is dead." She sat down on a stool with wheels and scooted next to me. "Tell me about this party you were at."

"It wasn't a party. Although it did have a celebratory feel at one point, I guess." I briefly explained the concept of the show and told her about the food that Josh had made. "The food was really good, though. Well, except for the lamb, which tasted fine at first. But then later it tasted really bitter and strange. And that dreadful arugula pesto. Ugh."

"So the lamb changed taste as the night went on?" She eyed me suspiciously

"I guess you could put it like that."

"And what else did you people put into your bodies? You know, we can't help you unless we know exactly what's in your system, what it was that you took."

"What I *took* was gnocchi and a bit of the lamb, some vegetables."

"What *substances?*" She didn't bother hiding her exasperation.

"I did not take any drugs! I don't do drugs! I barely even drink anymore now that my best friend is pregnant. I'm supporting her by abstaining from alcohol during her pregnancy. And all the food was from Natural High."

"Natural High, my ass," the wretched nurse mumbled.

"The *market* called Natural High."

I eventually convinced the nurse that no one had snorted, injected, inhaled, or otherwise *taken* or *used* anything except food, and I was allowed to leave.

Josh was in the waiting room. "Everything okay?" he asked.

"Yeah. Either I didn't eat enough of whatever is making us sick, or it's just my nerves that were making me queasy. I'm fine. You look better, too."

"I am. I feel back to normal now. Well, as normal as I get," he teased. He pulled me close for a tight hug. "I guess they're keeping Marlee and Digger. I don't know why exactly. It's not clear if they are admitting them or not. They wanted to hook me up to an IV to rehydrate me, but I told them that was ridiculous. I'll drink some water."

I sighed. "Are you sure? There's no reason to be stubborn about this."

"Look, the last thing I feel like doing is lying down with a needle stuck in my arm all night. I just want to get out of here. I swear to you that I'm totally better."

I didn't get another chance to try to coerce Josh back into the exam room, because Robin's voice began echoing through the room.

"I am not, I repeat, *not* a drug addict!" Robin stormed over to us. "Can you believe this crap? Some idiot back there kept insisting that I must have taken too many prescription pills. Like I was mixing uppers with downers instead of producing a TV show!" She breathed out heavily. "Sorry. I'm just strung out." She turned around and yelled, "And not *strung out* in a drug-related way!"

"So," I said slowly, "I guess we're ready to go?"

"Yes. Where's Nelson? Nelson!" Robin barked.

"At your service." Nelson's tone was so cheerful and his expression so smug that the shine radiating from his damp face and scalp made him appear to be glowing with happiness.

"You need to drive us back to the house so Chloe can get her car. Chloe, maybe you can clean up the kitchen?"

Maybe you can, I wanted to say. Instead, having completed a full year of social work school, I said brightly, "Yes, we'll all pitch in. Robin, what a great idea!"

SEVEN

SO much for the benefits of a full year of social work school. During the drive back to Leo and Francie's house, Robin increasingly complained about her exhaustion, and by the time Nelson pulled the TV van into the driveway, she'd managed to weasel out of doing her share of the cleanup while simultaneously arousing my sympathy for Leo.

"We don't want Leo coming home to that mess," she'd said.

"For all we know, he's there now," I'd replied. "And if he isn't, the house is probably locked up." I'd negotiated the agreement that if we found Leo at home, we'd ask whether he wanted help in cleaning up. If not, Josh and I would leave. If Leo wanted our help or if the house was empty and unlocked, we'd stay. It was more or less a bet that I lost. When we got there, the back door was open, and there was no sign of Leo. My only piece of luck was that Robin insisted that Nelson had to drive her home, so at least he wasn't hanging around filming while Josh and I cleared up the remains of the fatal dinner. I did the dishes while Josh threw out food, took out the trash, and packed up the cooking equipment that belonged to him. Neither of us, however, was valiant enough to don a pair of gloves and scrub the bathroom, which remained a revolting reminder of tonight's tragedy. I just couldn't stomach going back in there. When Leo returned, he'd just have to use another bathroom. Where was Leo, anyway? Someone had said that he'd ridden in the ambulance that had transported Francie—or Francie's body—to the hospital. I hadn't seen him there. Shouldn't he be home by now? Maybe he simply couldn't bear to return home without his wife?

I drove us back to my condo in Brighton. It was a one-bedroom on the third and top floor of what had originally been a large one-family house. My unit had a big bedroom, a small living room, a cramped kitchen, and a tiny bathroom, but I'd never before been so happy to be in the safety of my own little home. Josh made another trip down to the car to bring up the cooking equipment he had so excitedly used only hours earlier, and I put on water for tea. I wasn't much of a tea drinker, and neither was Josh, but I felt chilled and weak, and the idea of tea felt comforting.

Josh returned, placed a cardboard box and his knife bag in a corner of my living room, and collapsed onto the couch. He ran both hands through his hair and held them there, disbelief plastered across his face. "This cannot have happened. This cannot have happened," he kept repeating. He looked up at me with concern. "God, how are you doing, Chloe?"

I put the cups of tea on the coffee table, sat down next to him, and moved in close when he put his arm around me.

He wrapped his other arm around me, squeezed me against him, and rubbed the back of my head. "Not very well," I said in a broken voice as I started to cry. "Oh, Josh," I managed, "I was with her when she died. She couldn't breathe right. And she was lying in her own . . . filth! She must have been in so much pain." I sat up and wiped my eyes. "I can't imagine what killed her. It must be the same thing that made everybody sick, right? I mean, the odds of the two being unrelated are . . . negligible. Zero."

My sleek, black, muscular cat, Gato, jumped onto the couch, positioned himself with his front quarters on Josh's lap, and began purring loudly. "Hi, there, my friend." Josh started patting Gato's shiny coat. That darn cat, who loved Josh to pieces, fended off most of my own attempts to snuggle with him. To me, Josh said, "I'm so sorry you had to watch Francie die. And I'm sorry I wasn't more help. I was feeling terrible, and I don't know that I was thinking all that clearly. What a horrible thing for you to have to go through."

"Josh, I can't shake the image of Francie struggling for air. And her eyes were all glassy and unfocused. What do you think happened?"

"I've got one explanation for this." He sighed. "But it's not good."

"There aren't any *good* explanations, so shoot. Tell me what you think," I said with a sniffle.

"I hate to even think it, but I wonder if Evan or Willie had something to do with it."

Josh's words shook me out of my tears. "What? You think Owen's brothers did this? What on earth—"

"Hear me out." He held out his hand to stop me from telling him he was out of his mind. "You know how Evan and Willie are. They're always pulling practical jokes and goofing around. What if they thought it'd be funny to pull off a joke that ended up on television? To pull one on me? Remember when they stuck a few pieces of fish into the engine of Owen's delivery truck? Once those things started rotting and the smell got into the driver's area, even Owen knew that was not the normal way a seafood delivery truck should smell. They could've messed with the food or the wine to make me look terrible. I don't know what they could've put in the food or maybe in the wine, but it's a possibility."

I froze. Far from hitting me as off-the-wall, the idea struck me as hideously possible. Owen swore that his brothers had always been a lot like Fred and George, Ron Weasley's twin brothers, but that once Evan and Willie had read the Harry Potter books, they'd deliberately modeled themselves on the practical-joking tricksters. Until recently, their antics had simply provided a topic of lighthearted conversation, but as Owen and Adrianna's wedding approached, I'd begun to share Adrianna's fear that Willie and Evan would pull one of their stunts at the wedding, maybe even during the ceremony. I took a sip of tea and thought for a moment. "You know, it seemed obvious to me that Evan knew we were coming to the Wine and Cheese Shop. Willie probably called him to give him a heads-up. Evan had wine bottles open and breathing, and he had that platter conveniently displaying cheeses for you to sample. Do you think he could have put something in the wine? Or on the cheese? Or Willie did something to the lamb?" Oh, God, it would've been just like one of them to lace the food with laxatives to make everyone get sick on camera. But could laxatives have killed Francie? Could an overdose be fatal? Would they cause vomiting, though? I really didn't know enough even to take a guess.

"I'm sure that Willie tipped Evan off," Josh said. "And it

would be just like the two of them to do something. But what? And what could have been so toxic it killed Francie that quickly? And, well, I don't know . . ." He paused and frowned. "The more I think about it, I don't know that they would have done something to make me look *that* bad. I don't know if ruining my episode is really their style. Now, if Evan had given me a wine bottle that had a fake snake pop out when I opened it, that wouldn't have surprised me. But I don't know those two that well."

"Ugh, I hope they don't do anything stupid at Ade and Owen's wedding. It would be just like them to pull some dumb stunt on the day of their brother's marriage." I could just imagine Adrianna's bouquet shooting water into her face or the wedding rings sending jolts of electricity through the bride and groom.

Josh said, "So maybe there was some kind of bacteria in the food we bought. Like E. coli in spinach. Remember that? The arugula could have been tainted with E. coli. We keep hearing about all those food recalls and news reports on people dying from this kind of stuff. And they always say that people with immune problems or chronic illnesses are much more vulnerable than anyone else. We don't know anything about Francie. She could've had an illness that would've made her more susceptible."

"That's true. That must have been what happened, Josh. It's the only thing that makes sense. I guess we should just be glad that we're healthy and that we're not dead, too."

"Yeah, I know. If that's what killed her, though, I still feel responsible. I mean, I chose the ingredients."

"There is absolutely no way you could have known, Josh. There must be other people who bought that food, too. We should probably call the store."

"Yeah, I'll do that tomorrow. Speaking of tomorrow, why

don't you take the day off? It's already almost two in the morning. You've got to be drained."

"That's probably a good idea. I'm sure my parents won't fire me."

During summer break from graduate school, I was working as an assistant to my parents at their landscaping and garden design company. My specialty this summer, rain barrels, tied in neatly with my studies; promoting the use of rain barrels kept me politically and socially active. I'd first heard of them when I'd read an online article. The idea was simple: Large barrels were set under gutters to collect rainwater. A spigot or hose connector was affixed to the bottom of each barrel so that the collected rainwater could be used to fill watering cans or to supply water to a soaker hose. Unfortunately, many barrels were unattractive and came in loud, obtrusive shades of red and green. When I talked to my parents about rain barrels, they said that their wealthy, house-proud suburban clients would totally reject the idea of big, garish barrels no matter how effectively they conserved a limited resource—fresh water. But instead of telling me to forget about ecological friendliness, my parents found a young carpenter, Emilio, who designed and built rain barrels that blended in with the colors and styles of individual clients' houses. My job was to accompany my parents on landscaping consults and push rain barrels into the design equation. I did some neighborhood canvassing on my own, too, but I loathed the door-to-door approach.

"Okay, Carter Landscapes' rain barrel business will have to take Tuesday off." I leaned my head into Josh's shoulder. "Can I come see you at Simmer tomorrow night?"

"You bet. I'll make you whatever you want," he promised.

I loved going to see Josh at the restaurant. Not that I

usually got to spend much time with him there, but his outstanding food made up for his absence. Besides, it was a way for him to be with me, really. He often made me special dishes that weren't on the menu, and those were some of my favorites. Sometimes he played with seasonal ingredients, experimented with dishes he was considering for the menu, or just cooked what he was inspired to make that day.

"Good. Maybe I'll hang out with Ade for a bit tomorrow afternoon, and I'll come in after that. What time are you working?"

"I should get there around nine, I suppose. I have to close, so I'll be there late, but who knows what shape the place will be in after I was gone today?" Josh stretched his arms above his head and gave a long, deep yawn. "This day is officially over, okay?"

Josh and I crawled into bed. "Josh?" I said. "What if it was poison? Not food poisoning, but poison?"

He curled his body around mine and pulled the comforter up high. Even though it was August, we were both shivering. "I know," he answered quietly. "I've had the same thought."

EIGHT

MY mind could have used a good fourteen hours of oblivion, but my body refused to sleep past eight o'clock the next morning. When I awoke, Josh had already left for work. I knew that he must be exhausted. Even so, since he was going to be at Simmer tonight to cook me the dinner he'd promised, he'd be working a brutally long day. I brewed a pot of coffee and called my mother to let her know I wasn't coming to work today. I didn't feel ready to tell my parents about Josh's nightmare of a TV episode yesterday, so I simply said that I had a cold. In fact, I sounded so raspy that it took almost no effort to make myself sound sick.

"Chloe, you poor thing. Aren't those summer colds the worst?" My mother was so full of sympathy that I felt a pang of guilt about my lie. "Why don't I stop by later with some tissues and soup? Or, better yet, why don't you come and stay with us for a few days, and we'll take care of you?"

I was touched by my mother's offer to nurse me back to health, but even if I'd been sick, I'd have refused. I loved my parents to pieces, but it would have been impossible to get any real rest with my mother popping into the guest bedroom every five minutes to take my temperature and feed me hot broth. I'd have had to return home to recover from recovering.

"No, thanks, Mom. I'm really fine. It's just a cold. I should be much better tomorrow."

"Well, don't worry about tomorrow, either. I think it'll be a slow day around here. I'll call you if we need you. While I have you on the phone, are things looking all set for Adrianna's shower on Saturday?"

"I think so. I've heard back from almost everyone."

I couldn't believe that it was only four more days until my best friend's combination wedding shower and baby shower. Both the shower and wedding itself were going to be held at my parents' house. I'd been determined to host Adrianna's shower myself, but it would've been impossible to squeeze more than a few people into my little condo. And the wedding? Owen, who was working as a fish purveyor, was living off the commissions he made from selling seafood to restaurants, and Adrianna had just stopped working as an independent hair stylist. Consequently, the two parents-to-be were barely able to pay their bills. Owen's parents simply didn't have the money to help them, and Adrianna's mother, Kitty, had suggested that they go to City Hall for a quick service. Kitty was less than thrilled about the order in which her daughter was getting married and starting a family. Adrianna's father had vanished when she was very young, and she had no grandparents or other family members with the money or the desire to help finance her wedding.

So, a few months earlier, when it had become clear that Owen and Ade were stuck, I'd secretly approached my parents, who not only had offered to host both events at their house but were paying for practically everything. One reason for their generosity was that they knew and liked Owen and Ade. Another was that they understood how important my friends and their unborn baby were to me. A third was what felt like moral outrage at Adrianna's mother's nasty, stingy attitude. "We can afford to do it," my father had assured me, "and so we will! The wedding will be beautiful. And," he'd added, "if Adrianna's mother doesn't like it, she can sit in the back row and glower."

Once the plan was in place, I invited the bride and groom to dinner at my parents' house in Newton, where my mom and dad surprised Adrianna and Owen with their offer. Ade and Owen were completely overwhelmed at my parents' generosity, and each had thanked my parents so frequently and profusely that my dad eventually started joking about rescinding the offer if the two wouldn't shut up. Fortunately for my parents' bank balance, Adrianna and Owen wanted a fairly small, simple wedding rather than one of those over-the-top affairs with a full band, a bridal party of twenty, an expensive photographer, and an exorbitantly priced reception hall. My friends would never have asked my parents to pay for a gigantic, pricey wedding, which wouldn't have been Ade and Owen's style, anyway.

Ade's mother was flying in from Arizona on Friday, the day before the shower, and would be staying for over a week—in other words, until after the wedding. Although my parents were footing the bill for the shower and the wedding, Kitty had done nothing but complain about how much everything was costing her. Adrianna and Owen had had a hard time convincing Kitty that there was no room for her in their tiny apartment, which barely had room for the two of them—the nursery was a converted closet—and they'd suggested that Kitty skip the shower and just come to the wedding. Eventually, Kitty had decided to stay at a hotel for the week, but not without asking, "Do you have any idea what that's going to cost me?"

Thank God that Ade had my dad and mom, Jack and Bethany Carter, to act as substitute parents!

"So," my mother said, "Josh still can't cater the shower, right?"

"No. He got Gavin to give him the day of the wedding off so he can cater it, but Gavin wouldn't give him another Saturday, too." To maintain the illusion of illness, I pretended to blow my nose.

"Well, darn it, Josh works so hard at that restaurant! You'd think that this Gavin would have the sense to keep his executive chef happy. Anyhow, we can handle the food. The shower won't be that big. Is Adrianna excited?"

"Very. Mom, she is so overwhelmed by everything you and Dad are doing for her. Thanks again." My parents' help meant as much to me as it did to Ade and Owen.

"Of course. We'd do anything for them. With the baby coming in a few weeks, the last thing they need to worry about is trying to pay for a wedding. And I can't stand the idea a tiny civil ceremony with no real celebration to go along with it. We wouldn't have it any other way. So let's talk food!"

We finalized the menu for Saturday's shower. I hung up feeling guilty for feigning a cold, but if I'd told my mother about Francie's death, we'd've had a whole long conversation that I didn't feel like having right now. And all this wedding talk was so fun! While making all these plans over the past few months, I'd spent my fair share of time fantasizing that I was planning my own wedding to Josh. Not that I was expecting an engagement anytime soon, but it seemed like marriage could be a possibility for the two of us.

As soon as I'd put down the phone, it rang again. I looked at the caller ID window and saw the dreaded words *Private Call*. Answering the phone when caller ID had picked up no information about the incoming call was risky: for all I knew, I'd be stuck talking to someone who'd coerce me into responding to a long survey about tile cleaning products or about my infomercial-watching preferences.

"Hello?" I said tentatively.

"Hi. Why aren't you selling rain barrels? Do you want to come over?" Phew. It was Adrianna, whose new number was still unlisted. I'd have to get on her about having her number published, or I'd be missing a lot of calls.

"I'm playing hooky. Yeah, let me just throw on some clothes, and I'll be over soon."

When Ade and Owen had moved in together last spring, I'd been glad that their apartment was within walking distance of my place. Today, I actually wished that Adrianna lived a bit farther away than she did, because a good, long walk would've helped shake off some of yesterday's tragedy. I tossed on a pair of gray yoga pants (not that I actually *did* yoga) and a white top, and yanked my hair into a ponytail. Knowing that Adrianna wouldn't have any caffeinated coffee, I filled a travel mug with my own and left to see my incredibly enlarging friend. On the way, I resolved not to make any more jokes about how many babies she was carrying. *Quads? Are you sure it's not at least triplets?* Well, I'd try very hard not to. The last time I'd made a joke about multiple births, she'd thrown a stuffed bear at me. Next time it could be something painful, like a bottle warmer or a diaper bin.

Like me, Ade and Owen lived on the top floor of a house.

Trudging up the stairs to their place, I once again lamented the steepness of the steps my friends would have to manage with a baby. Now, while she was pregnant, Ade needed to stop for a break when she climbed the stairs, but once she had a baby or toddler in her arms, the staircase would become perilous. At least the apartment looked attractive. It was minuscule but charming, with hardwood floors and original molding around the doors and windows.

I knocked on the door while simultaneously opening it and announcing my arrival. "Ade?"

The heavenly smell in the apartment made me suspect that Adrianna was once again cooking. Now that Ade had stopped work, she was doing the whole nesting thing: she spent most of her time organizing and reorganizing the apartment, baking decadent cakes with elaborate icing, and putting together scrapbooks using strange craft tools I'd never seen before.

"Hi, Chloe. Come in," my friend called.

I stepped into the hallway and into the bright living room–kitchen area. All I could see of Adrianna was her backside popping out from the open door of the refrigerator. "Yeah, I know. I'm cooking again. But wait until you see what we're having."

"No complaints from me," I said happily, peering into a pot on the stove. "What are you making?"

"I already baked a coffee cake, and now I'm starting the artichoke and spinach eggs Benedict with a spicy hollandaise sauce on croissants. And potatoes with rosemary, onion, and garlic. It's going to be bang-up." Ade emerged from the depths of the fridge, her arms loaded with half its contents. Her blonde hair cascaded down her back in soft curls. Even hugely pregnant, she was stunning. Her face was bare of makeup, and she wore black stretch pants and an oversized tank top over a sports bra, but she still looked better than anyone else I knew.

"Look at you!" I practically squealed. "You've become so domestic and cute!" The change in Adrianna was incredible. The prepregnant Adrianna never appeared in front of anyone without makeup. As for cooking, she'd been the queen of takeout—high-end takeout, admittedly, but take-out nonetheless. Not that I objected: a warm, comforting meal was just what I needed to soothe my nerves.

"Shut up. I'm not domestic, and I'm certainly not cute. Have you seen my feet?" She kicked a leg out for my view-ing pleasure. "I mean, I haven't seen my feet in weeks, but I imagine they are monstrous, swollen blobs. Grab a mixing bowl for me, will you?"

I complied and then helped her to mix spinach, artichoke hearts, mayonnaise, sour cream, garlic, mozzarella, and Parmesan cheese. She poured the concoction into a ceramic baking dish that I popped into the oven. While the oven door was open, I got a glimpse of the aromatic potatoes that were crisping beautifully.

"Now the hollandaise sauce," she said.

I watched in awe as Adrianna heated a double boiler and began melting butter. This from a woman who adored food as much as I did but who, until now, had had zero cooking skills!

"Here, separate the eggs for me." She pushed the carton toward me.

"Yes, ma'am!" I dutifully began cracking eggs, separat-ing yolks and whites, and tossing the shells into the sink.

"Oh, so I want to hear about Josh's filming yesterday, but get this," Adrianna began as she cut a lemon for the sauce. "Owen called me earlier and said that someone from the De-partment of Public Health went into Natural High and

Evan's cheese shop first thing this morning to investigate a serious case of food poisoning. How gross is that?"

"Oh, God, really?" When I turned from the sink to look at Ade, I broke the yolk from the egg I was trying to separate. "Well, I can't say the filming went smoothly." Gross understatement.

"Why? What happened? Josh didn't panic and burn everything, did he?"

I handed Ade the bowl of egg yolks and watched as she mixed them with an electric beater. "No," I yelled over the din, "he didn't do anything wrong. But the guest's wife died during dessert."

"She cried? His food was that bad? Screw her. Who cries over a dessert?"

"Died, Adrianna! Died!" My loud voice filled the room when Ade abruptly turned off the mixer.

"Someone died eating Josh's food? I guess she did get screwed." She started adding small portions of the egg to the melted butter and lemon. "Did she have a heart attack or something?"

"No, I wish," I answered. "Not that I wish she'd had a heart attack! It's just that . . . that the situation is complicated."

I told Adrianna all about yesterday's events as she finished making the hollandaise, which was now spiked with hot sauce, and began to poach four eggs. "Francie died while I was with her. She looked horrible, Ade. She was so sick. And it happened so fast. Right in front of me." My stomach clenched in knots, and I tossed my head as if trying to shake out the image of Francie dying on the floor of that filthy bathroom. "Ade, I have to know what happened to her! I was right there, and I couldn't do anything to help her. I *didn't* do anything."

I was ashamed of not having made some sort of heroic effort to revive Francie. At a crucial time, I had completely frozen; in the worst possible way, I had let Francie down. The ugly thought came to me that since I'd done it once, I might do it again. I was Adrianna's backup birth coach! What if Owen was unreachable when Ade went into labor? And I was the only person she had to depend on? Owen's fish truck could break down, his cell could be out, and I would be Adrianna's sole support. Some help I'd be! To judge from my reaction to Francie's crisis, if Adrianna relied on me to help her through labor, I'd stare dumbly while she pushed a human being out of her body. I had to get it together! There was no way I was going to fail my best friend.

"Chloe, it doesn't sound like there was anything to do. She was obviously incredibly sick. Whatever killed her, killed her very quickly. I can't imagine anyone could have saved her." Ade ladled the eggs from the simmering water and began assembling our plates. She scooped the melted artichoke and spinach mixture onto the croissants and placed an egg and hollandaise sauce on top of each. "So you think it was food poisoning? That's why the health department wanted to talk to the stores where the food came from?"

We carried our plates to the coffee table in the living room, which also served as the dining room. "I guess," I said. "I don't know what else to think. The police were there, and they didn't . . . well, they didn't do much of anything." Although I couldn't entirely dismiss Josh's speculation about Evan and Willie, I avoided telling Adrianna that her fiancé's brothers might have perpetrated a prank with a very unfunny outcome. "Now that I'm saying it out loud, it does seem weird that the police just assumed it was food poisoning and didn't want to investigate any other possibilities. Even Josh and I wondered for a minute whether Francie had been poisoned. Whether all of us had been poisoned, really." In spite of the unappetizing topic of conversation, I was still able to savor Ade's cooking. The delicious eggs were exactly the comfort food I needed.

"I bet I know," Ade said as she stuffed her mouth full of the outstanding if unorthodox Benedict. "Look at the neighborhood you were in. Who the heck gets killed in a wealthy upper-class town like Fairfield? Plus, when the cops showed up, most of you were sick to some degree. I watch cop shows, you know, and it's the job of the first police officer on a scene to determine if it's a crime or not. At first glance, it definitely looks like food poisoning, so I guess he felt he had no reason to think of it any other way. See, the good thing about being pregnant and slothlike is that I've been reading tons of mysteries and watching TV. It's paid off, don't you think? So who would want that poor Francie dead?"

"I have no idea. I don't know anything about her. But after watching what she went through as she died, I want to know what killed her. Or who killed her. No one should have to die like that." I shuddered. "What else did Owen say?"

"He said he talked to Willie, and Willie told him that everyone at the store was furious because, of course, no one wants to be blamed for selling nasty food, right? What business wants that kind of notoriety? I guess they had to yank a bunch of stuff from the shelves, and it's causing a big stir there. If I walked into an expensive market and saw employees pulling tons of food, I'd turn around and walk out. And Evan is closed for the day, now, and since it's his store, he's losing money while they check out everything he's selling. A reputation for selling deadly food could destroy his business."

I took a deep breath and blew it out. "Let's change the subject," I said with as much cheer as I could muster. "Let's talk about the wedding."

"Chloe, you're traumatized and depressed." Adrianna said matter-of-factly. "I'm sorry you and Josh had to go through all of this. Let me take care of you." Ade picked up a piece of croissant and wiped the plate with it before popping the last bite in her mouth. "The best route to feeling good is looking good. So I'm going to do your hair. A run-through for the wedding, okay?" She stood up as gracefully as she could. "I need the practice so I don't lose my touch before I have to do my own hair. I'll do your hair the way I'm going to do mine. So try to look like me."

I almost shoved a couch pillow under my shirt but didn't want to risk one of Ade's mood swings. I cleaned up the kitchen and helped myself to some freshly baked coffee cake while Adrianna gathered her styling tools. Although the temperature in the little apartment felt comfortable to me, Ade decided that the thermometer that read a mere seventy-two degrees was horrendously inaccurate, so she cranked up the air conditioner while I huddled under a blanket. "Besides, the AC will dry out the air in here and make for better hair," she insisted. "Now, go stick your head in the sink and then sit in front of me. And this reminds me. Tell your mother I'm doing her hair, too. I don't want to take the risk that she might stick something weird in it. Seriously, I love Bethany to pieces, but I really don't want her wearing one of her craft projects on top of her head."

This wedding had become a Carter family affair. I was performing the ceremony, my mother was to be Adrianna's matron of honor, and my father was walking the bride down the aisle. Josh was doing double duty. Besides serving as Owen's best man, he was catering the reception. Digger was going to help in the kitchen, but I had no idea how Josh was going to coordinate the food preparation while simultaneously being a member of the wedding.

We watched *Veronica Mars* on DVD while Ade began blowing out my hair. "Oh, ick, Chloe! Look at your roots!" My highlights had grown out enough to horrify the bride-to-be. Consequently, after my hair was thoroughly dry, she started covering my head with foils and lightener. "And you need a trim. Your hair has got no shape left in it."

I resigned myself to sitting in one spot for the next few hours while Adrianna brought my hair up to her wedding standards. After toying with a variety of complicated updos involving curls and twists pinned to my scalp, Adrianna decided on a looser, more flowing style with gently shaped curls that would work beautifully with her simple veil. When the predicted hours had finally passed and I was finally allowed to look in the mirror, I was speechless. I'd almost forgotten about the veil affixed to my head. I'd never before worn a veil, and I have to say that all of a sudden, I was a princess! I was about to start twirling when Ade saw me wide-eyed in the mirror. "Don't get all dopey on me now. Let's get through *my* wedding first. You look like a lovesick puppy."

"It's just so fun to wear a veil. There's really no good excuse for wearing a veil except for when you're a bride, so let me enjoy myself for two minutes. Please?" I was *so* not taking off the veil. A short headband piece that had been wrapped in bright white material was affixed to the top of my head, and sheer layers of fabric fell to just below my shoulders. I looked at my reflection and imagined myself traipsing down the aisle, headed toward wedded bliss with my chef.

"All right," she agreed. "But don't get anything on it."

I crossed my heart with my finger. "Promise. Hey, I'm going into Simmer for dinner tonight. You want to come?" I leapt up and down the narrow hall, letting the veil fly out behind me, while Adrianna shook her head at my lunacy.

"No, thanks. Owen is going to be home soon, and I want to take a nap, and then we're finally going to put the crib together."

The baby's room was actually a walk-in closet with a window and a radiator. Once a crib was in there, it would occupy so much space that there might not be room for an adult to stand. To get the kid into the crib, Adrianna and Owen would be able to open the door and toss the baby in. But how would they ever get the baby out?

"Come here," Adrianna said. "Let me do your makeup, too, and then you'll really knock Josh's socks off tonight."

I reluctantly let Ade remove the veil. By the time she'd painted my face with M•A•C cosmetics, I was ready for this in-home salon to close. I hugged her good-bye, thanked her for the spectacular job she'd done on my hair, and rubbed her belly.

I went home and admired my newly blonde-streaked hair in my own mirror. My scruffy clothes looked silly with my fancy hair and makeup, but I didn't care. Adrianna had certainly cheered me up and distracted me from dwelling on Francie. And tonight I would see Josh! I tried to take a short nap, but visions of Francie danced unpleasantly in my head. The ringing of the phone rescued me from the atrocious images. Caller ID showed my favorite number.

"Hi, Josh," I said happily into the phone. "How's it going there?"

"Good. Good," he answered. "Um, how are you?"

"You know, as well as can be expected after yesterday."

"So . . . what else is going on? You know . . . you doing anything?" Josh sounded strange.

"No," I answered hesitantly. "Josh, is something up?"

"What? Oh, no. It's just, um, do you want a cat?"

"A cat? No, not really. I already have Gato. Why? Do you know someone giving away a cat?"

"Sort of. Yeah. This guy is giving away this Persian cat, and . . ." Josh's voice trailed off.

"Spit it out, Josh."

Josh coughed. "When I went out to get a coffee on my break, I walked past this guy outside the T station who was stopping people and asking them if they wanted a cat. He stopped me, too. He said he just broke up with his girlfriend and moved, and he didn't want the cat anymore, so he was trying to give it away."

"Josh, I'm sure someone will take it. Especially a Persian. Or he'll take it to a shelter."

"Maybe," Josh said skeptically.

"Josh?"

"Yeah?"

"Josh, did you take the cat?"

There was a long, long pause. "Yeah."

I sighed. As much to myself as to Josh, I said, "You took the cat." Turning practical, I asked, "Where are you? You didn't bring it into the restaurant, did you?"

"No, I'm sitting in my car behind Simmer, and it's in a cat carrier next to me."

"Oh, my God." Josh was hardly ever at his own apartment. He certainly wasn't there enough to take care of another living creature. In other words, I knew whose cat this was going to be.

"Chloe, I asked the guy what he was going to do with the

cat if nobody took it, and he said he was going to throw it in the river! The Charles River is only a few blocks from here, and I think he was serious." Josh was talking a mile a minute now. "He was a totally normal-looking guy, too, which was weird, but he said it was his ex-girlfriend's cat, and they broke up, and he didn't want to deal with it, and so I took it. Her, actually. She's a girl. And she is so beautiful. She's got white fur and orange ears, and she's just sitting here looking at me, and I feel so bad for her."

I was momentarily torn. On the one hand, I was irritated with Josh for taking in this strange cat that would end up with me. On the other hand, I felt overwhelmed with appreciation of how sweet and adorable my boyfriend was. How many men would even have stopped to listen to some idiot on the street trying to give away a cat? And Josh hadn't just listened but had gone on to rescue the cat from her heartless owner.

"Do you know how old she is? Has she been to the vet?" I asked.

"He said she's not even a year old. And I don't know if she's been to the vet, but I sort of doubt it. Her fur is all matted, Chloe, and she looks so scared and sad. I had to take her."

I smiled. "Of course you did. Should I come get her?"

"I guess I could take her to a shelter if you don't want—"

"No!" I cut him off. "We are not taking her to a shelter. Do you know how overcrowded those places are? Who knows what would happen to her! I'll come get her."

I was suddenly excited. In the wake of Francie's death, I suddenly had a new pet, a rescued cat to smother with love. I kissed my quirky black cat, Gato, and did my best to explain to him what was about to happen. "Now listen, mister.

Someone is moving in with us, and you're not going to like her right away. I accept that. But I expect you to be on your best behavior nonetheless."

Gato rubbed his head against my cheek, swatted my hair, and then ran off. Maybe a feline companion was just what he needed.

NINE

I flew down Newbury Street into the heart of Boston, my heart racing with eagerness at the prospect of meeting my new housemate. I pulled into the alley behind Simmer and parked next to Josh's car.

"Hi, babe." He grinned sheepishly at me. "You're the best."

"No, you're the best. I love that you saved her from a Sopranos-style death. Let me see her!" I demanded happily.

Josh reached into his car, lifted out a beige plastic cat carrier, and gently lowered it to the pavement. I bent down, peered through the little wire door of the carrier, and found myself looking into the round blue eyes of a small white cat with a darling little smooshed-in face. Eager to get a better look and also eager not to get scratched, I asked, "Do you know if she's friendly?"

"Oh, yeah," Josh said with a smile.

Careful to avoid giving the little cat the chance to escape, I eased open the wire door and tentatively reached in. After giving the cat a few seconds to adjust to the presence of my hand, I stroked her face. When I reached in and gently touched her back, my hand encountered a heartbreaking combination of thick mats and palpable bones. "Oh, Josh! The poor cat!" I said angrily as I removed my hand and closed the carrier door. "Look at her fur! She's never been groomed. And she's starving. What kind of monster would do this? That bastard!"

"I know. I know. That's why I had to take her. But look at her gorgeous blue eyes! She's so sweet, too, Chloe. I took her out and let her walk around in my car, and she let me hold her. She even started purring a little bit." Josh's eyes were glistening. "So, you'll keep her?"

"Yes, I'm going to keep her! This poor thing has had a rotten life so far, and we're not going to let anything else happen to her. Ever! I'll take her to the vet and get her checked out and make sure she's okay."

"I'm really sorry, but I have to get back to work. Gavin is going to kill me as it is for taking such a long break. I'll still see you tonight, though, right?" Josh handed me the cat carrier and kissed me, lingering just a bit. "Thanks, Chloe." He turned and bounded up the back steps to the restaurant.

"Hey, Josh," I called, "what's her name?"

"The jerk didn't say. But she told me her name was Inga." He grinned and disappeared into the restaurant.

I lifted the carrier up to eye level and looked into those amazing blue eyes. "Inga, huh? It actually suits you. Come on, Miss Inga, let's get you out of here."

I called Gato's vet as I maneuvered my way through the downtown traffic. Once I'd given the receptionist a capsule version of Inga's story, she agreed to have the vet see the cat right away. As much as I wanted to take little Inga home immediately, I knew it would be unfair to Gato to expose him to whatever bizarre cat disease the neglected Inga might be carrying. And if she had fleas? Well, neither Gato nor I wanted them.

An hour later, Inga and I arrived at my Brighton condo. Aside from being severely underweight and in need of spaying, Inga seemed to be fine. When the vet had subjected her to shots and had taken a blood sample for tests, she'd peed all over the vet's assistant and squirmed so much that she'd pulled out one of the needles and spattered herself with blood. The tests were still being run, but for the moment, she was given a clean bill of health, and I'd been told that it was safe to take her home.

When I arrived in my apartment, opened the carrier door, and released Inga, Gato acted downright furious. He took one look at Inga, put up his hackles, leapt to the top of the fridge, and positioned himself in his favorite pissed-off Halloween-black-cat stance. I sat the frightened Inga on a towel in my lap and tried to work on getting the knots out of her fur. After only a few minutes with a metal grooming comb, I gave up. Her body was covered in matted snarls that almost seemed to grow like tumors from her skin. I imagined that she must be terribly uncomfortable; I knew how I'd feel if some mean person were yanking my hair twenty-four hours a day. "You will have to go to a groomer tomorrow, my little friend." Unready to get up and explore her new home, Inga remained motionless in my lap.

I ran my hand across the top of her head and scratched under her chin, the only places without tangled clumps. "I couldn't help Francie, but I can help *you*." The little cat rewarded me with a small purr. In spite of a disapproving glare from Gato, I offered Inga a small dish of his dry cat food. When she had eaten hungrily, I carried her to the living room, flicked on the television, and held her until it was time to get ready to go out for dinner.

Newbury Street, where Simmer was located, isn't just any old ordinary Boston street. Especially around Simmer, near the Boston Public Garden—home of the Swan Boats and the setting of *Make Way for Ducklings*—it's lined with art galleries, high-end clothing stores, fancy cafés, and trendy restaurants. On my graduate-student budget, I couldn't afford the outfits that would've let me be mistaken for one of the beautiful people who spent money on Newbury Street, but I did change into something more worthy of Simmer's fancy location than the hanging-around-and-grooming-a-cat clothes that I had on. In other words, I wore black. Because I was hesitant to leave Inga alone with my cranky Gato, I'd put her in my bedroom with food, water, and a litter box, and shut the door. I wouldn't be gone all that long, and I hoped that she'd eat and take a good nap while adjusting to her new, safe home.

Then I drove downtown and scanned the street for a space. Parking in this congested area of Boston was always a challenge, but it was a bit easier on a Tuesday night than it would've been on a Saturday night. It had been a while since I'd eaten at Simmer, but with Josh's work schedule what it was, visiting him at the restaurant was sometimes the only way to catch a glimpse of my overworked chef. I had Inga to thank for the rare chance to see him twice in one day. Since the parking garages and lots in the area were breathtakingly expensive, I'd gotten good at spotting legal spaces on the street, at finding spots on side streets, and at squeezing my car into miniature spaces. Tonight I snagged a place around the corner from the restaurant. I had to pin myself between two BMWs, but getting an actual metered space at all was a good sign.

The patio outside Simmer was packed, but inside there were only a handful of customers. Although Josh said Mondays and Tuesdays were typically slow nights at most eateries, I found it disheartening to see the large room so empty. The tiled floors and the warm colors of the walls softened the angularity of the modern light fixtures, the square tables, and the high-backed chairs. The room's earth colors were welcoming, and I was pleased to see candles lit on each table and in sconces on the walls. Keeping candles in stock and replacing the ones that burned down was a challenge. Simmer used dozens every day, and no one who worked there wanted to add candle duties to the already long list of tasks to be done daily.

I waved to the hostess and helped myself to a seat at the bar. I wished that Ade had come with me. Eating out alone was lonely, but if I'd stayed home, I'd have moped in front of the television by myself watching Bret Michaels in reruns of *Rock of Love*.

The general manager, Wade, strolled behind the bar and checked for empty bottles. Because Wade was salaried, he often ended up working the bar so that the owner, Gavin, didn't have to pay another employee. "Hey, Chloe. I haven't seen you here in a while. You here for dinner?"

I nodded. "You know I can't resist Josh's cooking." I smiled, partly at the thought of Josh's feeding me and partly at the sight of the elaborate gel work formed by Wade's dark hair. Wade's hair was always a sight to gawk at, if not to admire. Today, he must have taken extra time to sculpt the poofy clumps that sat high off his scalp. Still, since Wade spent as much time working out at the gym as he did styling his hair, I couldn't complain about how he looked in the fitted black T-shirt that was standard for Simmer employees.

Wade handed me a menu, and I scanned the familiar items. At one time or another, I must have tried everything on the menu, but I never tired of the food. Besides, in addition to the standard dishes, there were specials that Josh ran a few times a week. They were always wonderful, but tonight I was hungry for two of my favorites from the regular menu, the crab and corn fritters that came with a lemon-cilantro aioli, and a Caesar salad with homemade dressing. Josh's Caesar dressing was based on egg yolk and anchovies. I could practically drink it by the bucket. He also offered a less fishy—and very popular—version for those who didn't like the strong anchovy taste, but I preferred the powerful version.

Wade took my order, brought me a lemonade, and told me that Josh would be out in a few minutes. As I watched Wade shine glasses with a towel, I started wondering what Josh had told his coworkers about the filming yesterday, but my thoughts were interrupted by Gavin Seymour's unhappy voice.

Simmer's owner was glaring angrily at a server. Gavin was in his late thirties, quite handsome, and dressed exclusively in clothing purchased from the high-end shops on this street. His usually toned physique looked neglected, though, and even his overpriced outfit couldn't hide that. "Now what is it?" Gavin demanded of a quivering young male server. "Can't we ever get anything done around here without a problem?" Gavin stormed away from the server and beckoned to Wade.

Before responding to Gavin's summons, Wade rolled his eyes and imitated Gavin. "Now what is it?" he echoed with an exaggerated whine.

Although Gavin caught my eye, he otherwise ignored me and, after speaking briefly to Wade, he disappeared into the kitchen.

I turned away and glanced uncomfortably at Wade, who was again polishing glasses.

"Don't worry about Gavin. He's all worked up tonight. Everyone is trying to stay out of his way today because he's in such a salty mood. I guess some guy from the Department of Public Health came in to talk to Josh." Wade shrugged.

If DPH was wandering around Simmer, the staff must know something about the disastrous *Chefly Yours* episode. "What did he want with Josh?" I asked.

"I guess to find out more about the food he'd made for the show. I was sorry to hear about that, by the way. Really sucks. Anyhow, Josh told Gavin that the issue had nothing to do with Simmer, but Gavin has been insisting all day that if it has to do with Josh, then it has to do with Simmer. 'I'm not interested in excuses, Josh,' is what Gavin must have hollered twenty times." Wade again mimicked Gavin and waved his hands around in no-no gestures. "Whatever. Gavin will get over it. Everyone is just trying to steer clear of him today."

Josh appeared with a plate of the deep-fried corn and crab treats. "Hi, babe," he said, kissing me on the cheek. Josh looked more worn-out than usual but, as always, he was putting on a happy front for my benefit. Flipping a dish towel over his shoulder, he covered half of a huge food stain on his once-white chef's coat. "How is Inga?"

I briefed Josh on the vet visit and explained that Inga would need some serious time with a cat groomer, who, I hoped, would get out the mats in Inga's coat without shaving her entire body. "She's had enough humiliation for one lifetime. I couldn't bear to see her with no fur."

"I'm just glad she's alive and not at the bottom of the Charles," Josh said. "Oh, guess who called me today?"

"Who?" I asked through a mouthful of fritter. I loved the fritters, with the crispy batter fried to perfection on the outside and the gooey, creamy crab mixture on the inside. Heaven on a plate.

"Two calls, actually. Robin and then Leo."

I nearly choked. "What did they say?"

"Well," he began, perching himself on the stool next to me, "Robin is insisting that the series won't be affected by what happened. She says we'll just tape another episode." He raised his eyebrows in doubt. "I don't know how she thinks this isn't going to be a problem. I mean, word is going to get out about Francie, the show, and me. No one is going to want me to go to their house after hearing that I'm the one who killed Francie—"

"Josh! Don't say that. You know that's not how it was." I put my hand on his and gave a good squeeze.

"I know, I know. Obviously I didn't kill her, but I'm going to be associated with her death, and that's less than appetizing, so to speak. So it's not going to be smooth sailing." He paused. "Maybe if the television station makes a public statement? If we can really clear up what happened, then things might blow over for the show. I don't know." Josh exhaled deeply. "Oh, and then Leo called the restaurant an hour ago to get your phone number."

I wrinkled my brow. "He wants to talk to me?"

Josh nodded. "He said he wants to talk to you about Francie. I hope it's okay, but I gave him your number."

Ugh. If Leo wanted to hear about Francie's last moments, what could I possibly tell him? "Yeah, that's fine."

"There's more. He told me that it turns out that Francie had definitely been poisoned and that the police are involved.

So it wasn't food poisoning. It wasn't something I did or bought. I knew that, but it's a relief to have it confirmed."

"So she *was* poisoned! What was it?" I nearly shouted. "This means Francie was murdered for sure. Who did it? Have the police talked to you?"

"Leo didn't say what the poison was. He said that the police are investigating who could have done it. A detective called me earlier, and I'm going to talk to him tomorrow morning, but I'm pretty much in the clear since practically every second of that day is on film. And I don't have any motive. So I'm not worried."

Josh might not be worried, but I was—and would be until Francie's murderer was locked up in a cell. Why would someone murder Francie? And during Josh's cooking episode?

"I have to get back to the kitchen. Gavin made me send home all the hourly employees, so I'm alone except for Santos tonight. I'll go make your salad and get that out to you in a few minutes. Love you." Josh kissed me again.

"I love you, too."

I took a big drink of my lemonade and tried to process what I had just learned: Francie had been poisoned. Someone had intentionally killed that poor woman and let her die a painful, grotesque death. I shivered. Lost in thought, I jumped at the sound of a dish breaking behind me.

"Your job isn't that hard. It's quite simple, really." Gavin's voice echoed throughout the restaurant as he marched across the floor. "Pick up dishes. Take them to the kitchen. Seriously, it's not tough. Break another dish, and I'll take it out of your check."

I spun around on my stool. Standing before Gavin was a young Brazilian busboy who held a plastic tub filled with dirty dishes. The busboy hung his head while Gavin continued his tirade.

"Do you know how much those dishes cost? Do you? Clean up this mess and get out of my sight."

Aha! I finally got it. To my surprise, I realized that Gavin was drunk. I could hear it in his voice. Josh's boss wasn't normally my favorite person, but he and I had no problems with each other, and he had always been pleasant to me. According to Josh, Gavin could be tough to work for, but Josh had never mentioned anything like what I was seeing and hearing now. Yelling at a busboy? Creating a drunken scene that was bound to drive customers away? Never. Or never before.

"Like I was saying," Wade said as he refilled my lemonade, "best to stay out of Gavin's way today."

After what I'd just witnessed, I was hardly going to get *in* Gavin's way. Avoiding him was evidently going to be easy, since he was continuing to ignore my existence. When he appeared a few seats down from me at the bar and leaned over the counter to grab some lime slices for his drink, he barely looked my way before dropping lime into his cocktail and again disappearing.

"What's going on with him?" I asked Wade.

"Oh, you know, typical owner bullshit." He spoke while he adjusted his gelled hair in the mirror that walled the back of the bar. "Josh must have told you some of it, though, right? Gavin has been hanging out here after hours with customers, drinking free from the bar, going home with college girls, snorting a little here and there. He's become a pain in the ass."

What? I'd heard none of this from Josh. And using cocaine? Stupid, stupid. "No wonder he's so moody, then, huh?"

Wade leaned against the bar. "No kidding. We can always tell when Gavin's been here late at night, because we open the restaurant to find dirty glasses, spilled drinks, half-finished beers. Then we have to clean the place again after the night crew already did it. It's disgusting. Plus, Gavin is losing money on all that alcohol he's drinking, and then he complains about having to reorder more liquor. I just ignore him."

A waitress brought out my Caesar salad, but it was hard to enjoy it as much as I usually did. In fact, it occurred to me that most of what I was being served tonight was one piece of bad news after another. What happened next confirmed that impression: Gavin popped out of the kitchen, again summoned Wade with a gesture, spoke to him for a few seconds, and then slumped down at the end of the bar and pulled out his cell phone. Wade returned to me with an apologetic look on his face. "I'm sorry, Chloe, but Gavin is making me give you a bill for your dinner. He says he's tired of his staff bleeding him dry."

I'd never before paid for dinner at Simmer. Gavin had never expected me to pay. And it wasn't as though I were in here every day ordering lobster and foie gras. All along, from the time Simmer had first opened, I'd assumed that Gavin knew how hard Josh was working to make Simmer a success and that Gavin saw my occasional meals as a small symbol of thanks. Hah! Apparently not.

I finished my salad, thundered off the stool, slammed my purse on the counter, and pulled out some cash. Gavin showed zero reaction, but Wade absolutely refused the tip I tried to give him.

"I always tip, even when the food is free," I protested. "Wade, please!"

Although Gavin was still at the far end of the bar, Wade spoke softly. "Not tonight. Consider it my apology for Gavin's behavior."

"If Gavin continues acting like this in front of customers,

pretty soon he's not going to have any." I thanked Wade again, grabbed my purse, and rushed out of Simmer.

Josh always painted a pretty picture of everything about the restaurant, but over the past few months I'd been learning more and more about the downside to life at Simmer. Despite Gavin's early promise that when Simmer began to do well, Josh would do well, there'd been no improvement in Josh's brutal schedule or in his pay. On the contrary, although Simmer had now been open for eight months and had, I thought, done very well, it seemed to me that Gavin's demands on Josh were becoming more extreme and more unfair than ever. I wondered how long Josh would put up with his increasingly impossible boss.

TEN

I spent Wednesday morning at home going over rain barrel orders, of which there were a surprisingly large number. Considering that this summer had been my first attempt at jumping into the world of sales, I was pretty pleased with how many barrels I had sold. Of course, I hadn't done it alone. Each time my parents landed a new landscaping job, they sent me to meet with the client to suggest the addition of an environmentally responsible rain barrel to the project.

Because my parents ran an eco-friendly company, many of the clients were receptive. These were people who lived in Boston's wealthy suburbs, where environmentalism was just beginning to influence landscape design and maintenance. Many of them had seen Al Gore's film and were aware of the environmental impact of traditional landscaping and lawn care. Noise pollution was impossible to miss. There were days when I went to my parents' house and found that we could barely have a conversation over the roar of the leaf blowers and gigantic lawn mowers that attacked the neighbors' yards. Those machines guzzled gas. And then there were the ubiquitous sprinkler systems that sprayed water on every available surface, including sidewalks and streets, at preset times, even during torrential rainstorms.

My parents discouraged large, water-hungry lawns. They encouraged clients to plant shrubs and flowers that could survive with minimal watering, to install solar lighting, and even to make compost. As much as possible, Mom and Dad used recycled materials and herbal pesticides and herbicides. Fortunately, Jack and Bethany Carter's switch to green design had been good for their business. Environmentally friendly gardening did not come cheap, but in their affluent area, homeowners could afford to go green.

And I was enthusiastic about something related to school! I'd spent my first year of social work school frustrated, irritated, and lost. My uncle Alan had stuck a clause in his will that required me to get a master's degree in anything in order to receive my inheritance. The requirement, which had originally felt outrageous, was finally beginning to make sense. I'd been floundering through my early twenties, and it turned out that forcing me into school was the kick I needed to get me focused. Although a lot of the students at social work school were exclusively interested in one-on-one counseling and mental health, the school pushed us to get involved in what was called "organizational social work," a field that included politics and larger social issues that trickled down to affect individuals on a daily basis. I'd discovered this summer that the one-on-one therapy tricks I'd acquired this year were incredibly helpful in talking with landscaping clients about their plans. Using my newfound people skills, I engaged clients in discussions about water conservation without sounding like an annoying, pushy salesperson who was just trying to make money.

I leafed through the pending jobs. A few of the clients were going to have prefab rain barrels installed and didn't mind the large green plastic containers that would catch water from the gutters. Most clients, however, were going to have our new carpenter, Emilio, build encasements to cover the unsightly barrels. I hadn't yet met Emilio, but from what I'd heard, he could do just about anything. In particular, he worked with eco-friendly materials and was skilled at making the barrels blend in with a house and its garden design. I was meeting up with my mother and Emilio later at my parents' house, after I dropped Inga off at the Fancy Feline, a nearby cat groomer. The owner, Glenda, had promised me on the phone that she'd try to preserve as much of Inga's fur as possible.

As I was reviewing the rain barrel projects that needed to be installed first, the phone rang. I reached behind me and blindly picked up. "Hello?"

I heard a man clear his throat. "I'm trying to reach Chloe. Chloe Carter."

"Speaking," I said as I scanned the installation requirements for a house in Needham.

"Oh, hi. Chloe, this is Leo. From the other day." He spoke unsteadily.

I dropped my papers. "Leo. My . . . my gosh, how are you?" Under normal circumstances, I don't go around saying *my gosh*. The circumstances of Francie's death had, of course, been anything but normal. "I mean, how are you holding up?"

"I guess I'm doing the best I can. I'm not sure if the shock has worn off yet."

"Well, I'm awfully sorry about Francie. I don't even know what to say. Of course you're still in shock. Josh said you might call. Is there something I can help you with?"

"Actually, there is. You were with Francie upstairs. You were the last person to see her before she lost consciousness and then . . ." His voice trailed off. "I am just wondering what she might have said. Did she have any . . . ? Did she . . . I don't know. Did she say anything?"

I shut my eyes and tried to invent something comforting or profound to pass along. In truth, Francie's last words had been "Oh, shit," whereas it seemed to me that her poor husband needed her to have said, "Tell Leo I love him," or, "It's okay. I've lived a long, wonderful, fulfilling life with the man I adore." Not only would Francie's actual last words fail to ease Leo's sorrow, but who in her right mind would want to be remembered for Francie's real exit line?

I racked my brain for what to say to Leo. The first thing that came to mind was what Oscar Wilde had reputedly said on his deathbed: "Either that wallpaper goes or I do." I sighed. The walls of the fatal bathroom, so to speak, hadn't even had wallpaper, and if they'd been covered with some ghastly palm-and-flamingo pattern, Leo would hardly find solace in learning that Francie had departed this life while expressing discontent with the home they had shared. It suddenly came to me that someone—who?—had sat bolt upright on his deathbed and demanded, "Who is that?" Francie had been far too weak to sit up and had shown no sign of perceiving the approach of the Grim Reaper. Even so, I went ahead and attributed the words to her.

"She said that?" Leo asked dubiously. "Wasn't that what Billy the Kid said?"

Damn. "Maybe she was quoting him. Or maybe she imagined she'd been shot." I did my best to backpedal. "She wasn't terribly lucid. And of course, I didn't know her well. Maybe she was making a joke." There. That put a positive spin on it!

"Francie had many . . . many good qualities. But a sense of humor really wasn't one of them." Leo paused. "Maybe she was asking who poisoned her? Or asking who you were? Or who Death was?"

"Well, if Billy the Kid was serious, I guess that she might've been, too. But, yes, she certainly might have been asking who poisoned her." I took the opportunity to gather information. "Leo, do you know what the poison was?"

"I'm told that it was something called digitalis. That's what the autopsy showed."

I talked with Leo for a few more minutes but managed to hang up before I had to lie about anything else. Thank God he hadn't asked me whether Francie had suffered. I wouldn't have been able to tell him the truth about that, either: that she had indeed suffered an excruciating, humiliating death, a death that was apparently the result of digitalis poisoning.

What was digitalis, anyway? I had a half hour before I had to go to my parents' house to meet with them and with Emilio. I Googled *digitalis* and quickly scanned Web pages for information. According to the first few pages I read, digitalis was a drug used mainly to treat congestive heart failure and some arrhythmias. Could someone with access to the food have added digitalis to one of the ingredients or dishes? Did anyone with access to the food have a heart problem? Everyone was too young for heart failure, I thought, and I'd noticed no one who seemed less than healthy. An arrhythmia? That condition might not be obvious. But what did I know? I was in social work school rather than medical school. I did know that Owen and his brothers had grandparents who lived near Boston. Maybe one of them was taking digitalis? It would've been just like Willie or Evan to swipe some of a grandparent's medication to use in playing a practical joke.

I called Adrianna under the pretense of asking about Saturday's wedding shower and baby shower and also about the wedding itself.

"I think we're in good shape for the wedding," she said. "Josh is doing the food, we have our dresses, the music will play over the speakers, and we've solicited various people to take pictures for us. No way would I pay some professional photographer five grand for a wedding album. With everything you can do to digital pictures on the computer, I think we'll end up with great photos. And the shower is all set, too. I told your mom I wanted to keep it pretty simple and low-key. I'll have enough to worry about with my deranged mother in town. I think the brunch idea was perfect. That way it won't turn into an all-night event with everyone drunk and dancing on couches."

"Will Owen's mother be there?" I asked in my most casual voice.

"Yeah, his mother, grandmother, a few cousins, I think. Grampa will be at the wedding. Why?"

"Just wondering. I know he has a big family."

"You're not kidding. Owen's mother, Eileen, isn't totally happy about everything, but he thinks she'll come around. The family as a whole is pretty relaxed, but Eileen is more traditional and still not completely rooting for me. The rest of them are all so excited about the baby that I'm afraid I might not even see my own kid for the first year. They've all got plans for holidays and birthdays, and they're fighting over who gets to take the kid to Disney World first. Nut jobs," she said, but I could hear the affection in her voice.

"That's great, though, Ade. Your baby is going to have so

many people in his life that love him. Or her. I can't believe you haven't found out if it's a boy or a girl!"

"Yeah, Owen's losing his mind over that, but I want to be surprised. All I care about is if the baby is healthy."

"Of course," I agreed. "You don't have any reason to worry though, right? Is there, you know, any family history that you need to worry about?"

"What do you mean?"

"Oh, you know . . . diabetes, heart disease. Anyone in the family with a condition like that? Anything treated with medication?"

"What? Are you saying my baby is going to be born with a congenital heart defect? What a sick thing to suggest!"

"No! No!" I was backpedaling again today. "I'm sorry! I didn't mean that at all. It's just, don't they ask you family history stuff when you get pregnant? I didn't know if there was anything you were worried about."

"Oh. Well, no. There's nothing. Not that I know of. Everyone in Owen's family seems to live well into their nineties. They're all healthy as horses. What the hell is wrong with you?"

"Seriously, Ade. I'm sorry. I really didn't mean to alarm you." God, I was an idiot. "I know your baby is going to be the most gorgeous, healthy, bouncing baby in the world. I don't know what I was thinking."

I hung up feeling appropriately mortified; I had really messed that up. In simply trying to find out whether Evan or Willie had had access to heart medication, I'd unintentionally suggested that there might be something frighteningly wrong with Ade and Owen's baby.

Especially after that fiasco, I wasn't about to call up everyone who'd been present at the filming to inquire about family health histories. Besides, the only person there I knew well enough to interrogate was Josh, who would be willing to answer any weird, prying questions I might ask but who would never, ever have poisoned food he was preparing. He'd never met Francie before and had had no reason to kill her. And if—inconceivably—he ever did decide to murder someone, he'd use a gun or a knife or any other weapon except the food in which he took such pride. I'd met Digger before the filming, but I knew him only as one of Josh's chef friends. When I'd been with Josh and Digger, they'd traded anecdotes about restaurants where they'd both worked and about the local restaurant scene. It was possible, I guessed, that Josh knew something about Digger and his family. Not that I was aching to prove that Digger was a poisoner! But Francie's death had been no accident. Furthermore, her killer had been willing to risk having any of the rest of us eat the poisoned food and die, too. Some us had been sick. For the first time, it occurred to me that the murderer had benefited from having people besides Francie get sick. When the police and the EMTs had arrived, it had been easy and natural for them to assume that the cause of Francie's death and other people's illness was food poisoning. I had a vivid image of Josh and me as we'd cleaned up the kitchen. Unknowingly, we'd been tossing out evidence! But the food wasn't the only evidence. That annoying Nelson had had his camera going almost every second. Who had his film now? Nelson himself? Robin? Or maybe the police?

I called Josh while I was in the bathroom putting on makeup. Besides wanting to see what I could learn about Digger, I wanted to hear Josh's voice.

"Yup?" Josh sounded as if we'd been in the midst of a conversation.

"Hi, honey. It's me."

"What's up, babe?"

"Not much. Inga is going to the Fancy Feline later to get cleaned up. And I just wanted to thank you for dinner last night. Everything was delicious, as always."

"Anytime. You know that."

Josh clearly didn't know that I'd paid for my dinner, and I wasn't about to break the news to my overstressed chef that Gavin was no longer letting him comp food. "Hey, I heard someone from the health department was in to see you yesterday. How did that go?" Leaning against the basin, I practically had my face in the mirror as I tried to apply mascara without dropping the phone. Driving isn't the only thing it's risky to do while having a phone conversation. Applying makeup has its hazards, too. I should probably get a hands-free phone for the bathroom.

"Oh, fine. He asked me a lot of questions about the fresh herbs that I used on Monday. What kinds I bought, did I use them all, did I use anything from Francie and Leo's house? Questions like that. Stupid questions, if you ask me, because there is no way anything I used was tainted. I told him the truth about everything, since obviously I have nothing to hide. I assume he's going to go check out Natural High and pull some of their produce and herbs, though. Hold on a sec." Josh must have covered the phone because I heard a very muffled *I told you not to dress the salads now because they'll be wilted by lunch. Come on!* Then Josh said to me, "Sorry, I'm back. Hey, has a detective called you yet? "

"No. Did someone call you?"

"Actually, a detective showed up while the health department guy was here. He made me run through every detail of the day. Nice guy, but I had to repeat the same answers three times while I was trying to work. He may call you, too, and I assume he'll talk to everyone else who was there."

"Josh, did the detective tell you . . . Josh, what killed Francie was digitalis. It's a heart medicine. She was poisoned. Leo called me, and he told me. So, I hope they'd want to talk to everyone there. Do you know if they have the video footage? I was thinking there might be some useful evidence on there."

"The cops do have it. They made sure I knew they had it, and they reminded me I better be telling the truth, since they had a detailed record of the day."

So much for getting my hands on the video. I changed the subject. "Is everything going all right at Simmer? Gavin seemed to be in a bit of mood last night."

"Yeah, just the usual bs around here. It's all good."

"Seriously? Because it seems like things have been pretty rough for you there. I know Gavin has been riding you pretty hard about food and labor costs, and you're still working such long days—" I started.

"Look, I don't want to talk about this, but trust me. Everything's going to work out."

"If you say so," I said with some doubt. "Hey, it was good to see Digger the other day. Except for the circumstances, I mean. How's he been doing?" I asked.

"Good. Same old grind at his restaurant, too, but I think he's doing great."

"Oh, good. I guess I thought he looked a little off the other day," I hinted. "Even before everyone got sick. Kind of pale."

"Pale? Well, you know us chefs. No one gives us a day off to go relax in a hot tub or lie in the sun."

"I just thought maybe he wasn't feeling well. Maybe a virus." I cleared my throat. "Or a heart problem."

"What are you talking about? Digger doesn't have a

heart problem, you kook." I recognized the sound of a pan hitting the professional-sized gas range in Simmer's kitchen.

"Oh, good. Is there anyone in his family with a heart condition? Maybe he should be careful about—"

"Are you out of your mind?" Josh started laughing. Meanwhile, I poked myself in the eye with the mascara wand, smearing dark brown goop all over my eyelid. "I don't know what you're up to, but Digger is the same as ever, and I don't know the slightest thing about his family. Is this about this poison? The heart medicine? Whatever you're doing, you're not being subtle. So, what's going on?"

"Um, nothing. Forget it. I don't want to talk about it yet."

"Chloe? Spit it out."

"Then tell me what's going on at Simmer," I countered.

"Fine." He laughed again. "We'll call it a draw."

"Agreed."

"Give Inga a kiss for me, and tell her I said good luck at the groomer's."

I shut down the computer, gathered my client files, and got Inga into her carrier. On the way to my car, I repeatedly assured Inga that everything she was about to endure was for her own good. Once we got to the Fancy Feline, the owner, Glenda, confirmed what I'd been telling Inga; Glenda was as horrified as I was about the state of Inga's coat. "What monster did this to you, sweetheart?" Glenda asked as she gently examined the little cat. But Glenda had goods news: she thought that she'd be able to shave off the mats rather than Inga's entire coat.

I apologized to Glenda for the blood and urine that remained on Inga. I'd done my best to get the mess out, but I'd wanted to avoid hurting or frightening her; I was playing good cop, and Glenda was stuck playing bad cop. When Inga was back in her carrier, I poked a finger through the grated door and wiggled it at her. She looked pathetic and scrawny.

"I promise I'll come back for you. I promise." I wiped tears from my eyes as I left the shop.

ELEVEN

TO avoid feeling overwhelmed by my sympathy for Inga, I spent the ten-minute drive to my parents' house cursing the clumsiness of my efforts at detection. As social work's answer to Nancy Drew, I was a flop. The official investigators, however, weren't exactly a success, at least so far, and they'd presumably known the autopsy results longer than I had. Furthermore, they weren't motivated the way I was: I was the one who'd seen Francie suffer the effects of the poison, and I was the one who couldn't get that image out of my head. So, instead of scaring Adrianna about her baby's health and instead of asking Josh ridiculous questions about Digger's cardiac status, I needed to cool down and apply my powers of rational thought. For example, Josh had said that the person from the department of health had asked about herbs. Was there some reason to suppose that the digitalis had been added to the herbs that Josh had used? Or was there some other connection between digitalis and herbs? I'd scanned only a few of the Web pages that my Google search had produced. I'd return to the task when I got home. In the meantime, I decided, I'd do my best to avoid discussing Francie's murder with my parents. Their house was going to be my safe harbor. My happy place.

My parents' white Spanish stucco house did look happy— or at least improbable and whimsical, belonging as it did in Santa Barbara, California, rather than where it actually was, in Newton, Massachusetts. I let myself in the front door and found my mother and a young man huddled over the dining room table. My mother, Bethany Carter, was decked out in virtually every piece of hideous jewelry she owned, and she owned a lot. I could never reconcile my mother's good horticultural taste with her astoundingly awful taste in almost everything else. Despite the vile adornments, my mother was a pretty woman, and not the tiniest wrinkle had appeared on her face, so I had high hopes for aging well. She'd recently cut her hair into a wash-and-wear style that fell in soft waves around her face and had colored it a chestnut brown to erase the four gray hairs that had dared to grow on her head.

Hearing me enter, she popped her head up. "Chloe, come meet Emilio. Emilio, this is my daughter, Chloe."

Whoa. Happy place, indeed! Emilio was hot. Not just good-looking or handsome but downright hot: sexy, rippling biceps, broad chest, dark skin, and a strikingly gorgeous face. Think Mario López meets John Stamos. All coherent thoughts flew out of my brain, and I stood there thunderstruck and mute as I fought off the mental video I'd inadvertently created of a tan, sweaty, half-naked Emilio playing beach volleyball to the *Top Gun* soundtrack.

Miraculously, my knees did not buckle out from under me as I stepped forward to shake Emilio's hand. "Hi, I'm Chloe," I said breathlessly. "Oh, my mother already said that. It's nice to meet me. You! I mean you! I already know me. Myself. I know myself, of course. Ha-ha!" I laughed idiotically. "Should we talk about rain barrels?"

When Emilio the God smiled, dimples appeared. As if this guy needed any more alluring physical traits! "It's really nice to meet you, Chloe." Although my mother had told me that Emilio was Colombian, he sounded totally American. If he'd had a Spanish accent, I'd have been totally gaga. "I heard you've drummed up a lot of business this summer," he continued. "I'm ready to get going on this with you."

"Yes, I'm ready to get going on you, too." *Oops.* "On the projects!" I said quickly. "I'm ready to get going on the rain barrels!" One hot guy, and I fell to pieces. *Get it together, Chloe!* I already had a good-looking boyfriend. But there was no denying that Emilio was more than drool-worthy.

Okay, I just wouldn't look at him.

"So," I started as I sat down next to Emilio and across from my mother, "Anna Roberts is our first client. She's going to have three rain barrels installed, and she'd like them to be enclosed in a rounded rock wall to match the existing rock walls she has in her yard." I handed Emilio the photos I'd taken of the house and grounds. I relied heavily on my digital camera for these projects, because my drawing skills were limited to stick figures, and sloppy ones at that. "Do you think you can come up with some sort of top to go with this? Maybe a wooden one that would coordinate with her deck? And something environmentally friendly, of course."

Emilio nodded enthusiastically. "Absolutely. I could do bamboo, for instance. That's a great wood to use because it's an easily renewable natural resource. There are also really beautiful materials made from recycled plastics that I could use. I can show Mrs. Roberts a few options and let her decide."

"Perfect."

My mother went into the kitchen to get us some lemonade, and I pulled out the next client's specifications. "So, Emilio, my mother told me that your family owns a large nursery and garden center nearby. My parents do business there. You came back to Boston after college?"

Emilio flashed his dimples. "That's right. One of my interests at Princeton was environmental studies, and after I graduated, I spent a year working with my family at their business. I did a lot of work on their property, finding ways to save energy and turn their business green. We actually won a local award from the Small Business Association." More dimples. "Then I spent a few years interning with an architect in Boston and learning about green design. It's amazing what can be done now with eco-friendly design. It used to be that anything made from recycled products was . . . something you wouldn't want to look at. But not anymore. So I wanted to bring some of what I'd learned back to my family's business and keep them on the cutting edge. The problem is still the initial investment costs, though. The people who can afford to install things like wind turbines and solar panels aren't the people who need four-dollar electric bills."

Handsome and politically conscious to boot. I could be in trouble.

I nodded in agreement. "You're right. We really need to get energy-efficient structures into low-cost housing areas. We need to get costs in the reach of the middle class. I think over time we'll see the costs come down, but for now it's the wealthy who are benefiting from these kinds of resources."

My mother returned with tall glasses of iced lemonade.

As she set a glass down in front of me, I noticed a hint of makeup on her usually bare face. Ah! Apparently my mother wasn't immune to Emilio's looks, either—hence her overzealous display of jewelry today, too. I was feeling a bit guilty for admiring Emilio, but knowing that my happily married mother wasn't resistant to his charms made me feel better. There was nothing wrong with looking, right?

Look but don't touch! Look but don't touch! I repeated in my head.

"Chloe, did you know Emilio's family is from Colombia? He's been a great translator for me. My Spanish is quite rusty. Last month I asked Fernando and Matias to dig an ocean in the Marberrys' backyard."

Emilio waved away my mother's compliment. "Glad to help, Mrs. Carter. Listen, I hate to rush us here, but I just moved into my new apartment. I'm right by the Hynes T stop, near Newbury Street and Mass. Ave. It's a cool location, even if the apartment is pretty small. Anyhow, I've got loads of work to get done there, and I'm hoping to finish unpacking today so I can start building tomorrow. Can we run through the other projects?" An apologetic Emilio looked hopefully at us.

"No problem," I said. "There are four more, and they are all pretty straightforward."

Fifteen minutes later, when we'd run through the last of the clients, Emilio left to finish his unpacking. "It was nice to finally meet the carpenter you've been talking about. He seems nice," I said casually to Mom.

"Yes, and isn't he positively gorgeous?" my mother said exuberantly.

"Mom!"

"Well, he is. There's no denying it. No harm in admiring, is there?" She took a sip of lemonade and skimmed over the schedule for constructing the rain barrels. "I guess he and his girlfriend just broke up, and he moved out of the apartment they shared. I'm sure it won't be long until he finds someone else, though."

"Probably not," I agreed.

"Are you and Josh doing all right?"

"Yes, we're fine," I said quickly. "Why would you even ask that?" I glared at her.

"Just checking. Emilio is a great catch, that's all. Don't misunderstand me, Chloe. I adore Josh, and I think you two have a wonderful relationship. It's just that I know how much he works, and I imagine that must take a toll on you. It's hard enough for couples who've been together for years, but you two have only been dating for a year. His schedule must present some challenges." Mom rose from her seat and picked up our glasses. "And that damn restaurant world is not the most conducive place for cultivating a romance, right? Josh is under tremendous stress a lot of the time, and I just hope you're not getting shortchanged in the relationship."

"I'm not. Everything is okay, Mom. I'm used to his schedule, and we always manage to find time for each other." At least we *tried* to find time for each other.

"Oh, did I tell you that Emilio and a couple of his cousins are going to help out at the wedding? They're going to carry out food, serve drinks, that sort of thing. I thought we'd need a few extra sets of hands, especially people who aren't in the wedding and aren't guests. Maybe Emilio can help Josh with the food, too."

Emilio and Josh. Josh and Emilio? An interesting combination. I shrugged my shoulders. "I think Josh will be fine. Digger will be here to help him out." Digger was not only Josh's friend, of course, but a chef who could be counted on to put out delicious food. Besides, I had no visceral reaction whatever to Digger, whereas the prospect of having Josh work next to the hunky Emilio was all too . . . visceral, let's say. "But we could definitely use Emilio's help with all the other work that will need to be done that day. Anyhow, I've got to get going. I have to go pick up Inga."

"Who is Inga?" my confused mother asked. "A new friend from school?"

I laughed and explained how Josh had rescued the white cat from death by Charles River. "She's at the groomer's right now. I'm just hoping the owner there didn't have to shave all her fur off."

"Josh is an angel, isn't he?" Mom said warmly.

I had to agree. Josh was an angel. I felt scummy for even noticing Emilio. Would Emilio ever save a pitiful cat from death? His dedication to finding solutions to a multitude of environmental crises might save the world, but I couldn't say for sure that he'd have rescued Inga.

But I did want to think so.

TWELVE

"HERE is Miss Inga!" Glenda beamed as she lifted the cat carrier onto the counter. "She looks like a whole new cat, doesn't she?"

She truly did. Even peeking through the grated door, I could see she looked clean and beautiful. "I told you I'd come back, little girl, didn't I?" I cooed to my cat.

I swear that there was gratitude in Inga's big blue eyes. Sticking a finger into the cage for her to smell, I felt her touch me with her wet nose. Then she rubbed her head against my finger.

"How was she, Glenda? Was she a monster?" I was sure that Inga had peed all over the groomer as she had the vet, but I was wrong.

"She was fine. No trouble at all. I think she knew I was trying to help her. Those were some nasty mats she had, but

I managed to just shave off the clumps and let her keep the rest of her coat."

"Thank you so much for fitting her in today. How much do I owe you?" I reached for my purse. Even though Glenda gave me a discount because of Inga's escape from death, I still shelled out a hefty sum. But my money bought me a clean cat no longer tormented by mats that yanked at her skin. As if to celebrate Inga's rehabilitation, Glenda had tied a silly pink bow between the little cat's ears. I waved thanks to Glenda and drove Inga back to my condo.

When we got home, Gato was sitting on the couch, but one look at Inga sent him back to the top of the fridge to mope. I knew that he'd come around in a few days, but I hated to see him even crankier than usual. Gato normally ate dry food, but I kept a small reserve of canned food for special occasions and bribes. I opened a can of salmon and chicken, dumped it in a bowl, and placed it on top of the fridge in an effort to cheer my boy up. Gato didn't share my opinion that the cat food smelled like garbage. On the contrary, it elicited a steady purr. As Gato scarfed down his meal, I reached up to pet his shiny black coat.

Then I went to my bedroom, which was the largest room in my small condo and hence doubled as a work space for school and for my summer job. Sitting at my desk, I checked my e-mail, sorted through a few messages about rain barrels, and decided to do another search for information about digitalis.

Wham! Digitalis was a genus of perennial plants, the most common being foxglove. As the daughter of two horticultural experts, I should have known! In fact, my parents would've been horrified to realize how little botanical information I'd absorbed over the years. In particular, I liked the common names of plants and had never bothered to learn botanical names. So, digitalis was a stranger, but foxglove was an old friend. I'd always adored the tall, spiked plants with their showy, tubular flowers.

Digitalis in the form of foxglove was obviously much easier to obtain than was digitalis in the form of a prescription medication. In fact, as I read about foxglove, I had to wonder why such a dangerous plant was positively all over the place: offered in seed catalogs, sold at garden centers, and grown in backyards. Every part of the foxglove was poisonous, and especially toxic were the leaves from the upper stem. The symptoms of having ingested foxglove were identical to those that Francie had shown. Furthermore, it had a strong, bitter taste. So that was why Josh's arugula pesto and lamb had tasted so putrid! Dear God, all of us who'd tasted it could have died! I remembered how sick Josh had been. It was a blessing that in vomiting up everything in his system, he'd rid himself of most of the poison.

Damn. Instead of pestering people about possible cardiac conditions, I should have been asking about gardening. My questions about heart problems and family health histories had been awkward and unwelcome, but gardening was an ordinary topic that was easy to introduce in a casual conversation. My mother was always saying that gardening was the most popular hobby in America. Had anyone present at Leo and Francie's house pursued the hobby?

Evan and Willie shared an apartment. I hadn't been there, but they could be growing foxgloves in pots on a balcony or in a yard, and they might well not have realized how lethal a practical joke involving digitalis could be. Leo and Francie's house had some kind of a disheveled garden, but I hadn't really paid attention to it except to notice that it was a weedy mess. Foxglove was a biennial rather than a perennial. In its first year, it produced leaves, but it didn't blossom until its second year. Then, I thought, it died. But it self-sowed. In other words, if someone had planted foxglove in Leo and Francie's yard a long time ago, the descendants of the original plants could still be growing there. Although it was obvious that neither Francie nor Leo had been maintaining the garden, Leo might have known all about foxglove and might have known that it was growing right outside his house. Murders were often family affairs, weren't they? They were on TV. So Leo had to be a suspect. What's more, the rest of us had just met Francie. What possible motive could Robin, Marlee, Digger, or Nelson have had for killing her? None, so far as I could tell. Except possibly Nelson? Not that the cameraman had had anything personal against Francie, but he'd certainly been the weirdest person there. He'd kept spouting off at the mouth about the power of reality television, and he'd ghoulishly kept filming when Francie had fallen ill and after she'd died. He'd even tried to film the aftermath of the poisoning in the ER. Could Nelson have killed Francie only to have "reality" to film? If Nelson was, in fact, the murderer, he probably hadn't cared which of us died. Maybe he'd even been disappointed to have only one victim. Sick thought, yes, but especially as a social-worker-to-be, I knew that there were sick people in the world.

I remembered something else potentially important. When Josh and I had both sampled some of the food before it had been served, there had been nothing wrong with it. But when we'd tasted the same food after Francie had complained so forcibly, it had been horrible. In between those two times, there'd been chaotic activity. The food had been served, returned to the kitchen, and served again. The scene at the dinner table had been filmed and filmed again. Everyone, or almost everyone, had had the opportunity to contaminate the food with poison. Marlee and Digger had handled the food when Robin and Nelson had accompanied them to the kitchen to reshoot the plates. Leo had had his hands all over the food, hadn't he? To complicate matters, it seemed possible that the digitalis had been added either to what was originally on Francie's plate or to one of the bowls or pans used to replenish her plate before the dinner-table scene was reshot.

It's typical of me that the thought of food, even food loaded with a fatal toxin, made me hungry. I was in the kitchen getting myself a snack when the phone rang. "Hello?" I managed between bites of garlic-stuffed olives. I really needed to go food shopping.

"Hi, Chloe. This is Robin. From the TV show."

"Robin. Hi. How are you?" I couldn't imagine why Robin was calling me.

"Fine. Fully recovered. Well, I'm fine considering the hellish week it's been. The station is having a fit about what happened. They're trying to spin it in a way that doesn't get our show off the air forever. It's a nightmare, actually. But the reason I'm calling is that I wanted to find out more about this wedding ceremony you're performing for your friend. Angelica, is it?"

"Adrianna. Adrianna and Owen."

"I thought I might be able to do a piece on getting a license to perform a wedding ceremony. It's such a fun idea that a friend of the couple can officiate. After Monday's disaster, I'm trying to find other pieces to do for the station in case they yank the chef series. This wedding business sounds like a great human interest story. I was thinking that we could film the wedding, if your friends don't mind. But maybe they already have a videographer."

On their budget, Ade and Owen most certainly did not have a videographer. My parents had mentioned the possibility, but there was no way that my friends would accept more than my parents were already paying for. Adrianna and Owen did, of course, want a video of their wedding, but all they intended to do was to shove a recording device into a guest's hands and hope for the best. "Robin, that would be wonderful," I said. "I'm really excited about doing this wedding. Ade and I have been friends for ages, and I just adore her. And Owen is a good friend of mine, too. I know they'd love to have you film their wedding. I don't even have to ask."

"Listen, I have to run, but how about we meet for dinner tomorrow? Have the bride and groom come with you, and I can talk to you more then about how you got licensed. I'll bring Nelson, and we can talk about filming the wedding."

Although I wasn't dying to spend an evening with that creepy Nelson, I was eager to find out more about him. What's more, sometime during the dinner, it would be easy to slip in a subtle reference to gardening and to find out whether Robin or Nelson had a garden.

"Okay," I agreed. "I'll have to run the idea by Adrianna and Owen first and make sure it's okay with them, but I'm sure they'll love it. Where do you want to have dinner?"

"Why don't we meet at Marlee's restaurant? Alloy, it's called."

"It's in the South End, isn't it?" So were dozens of other trendy restaurants.

"Yes. Tomorrow at seven? The food is fantastic. Very contemporary. You'll love it."

The choice of Alloy didn't surprise me, since Marlee was one of the chefs in rotation on *Chefly Yours*. I assumed that her food must be good. She was, after all, competing against Josh and Digger, both of whom I knew to be talented. "That sounds great. I'll see you there."

I scrounged around in the kitchen for something else to eat and came up with nothing good for dinner. Too bad I wasn't meeting Robin tonight.

I called Adrianna and explained Robin's idea for filming the wedding. "It wouldn't cost you a thing, and you'd have the entire day on tape. Isn't this cool?"

"That sounds really nice. Please tell Robin we accept her offer. But I'm not eating at Alloy, I can tell you that. I have a client who ate there once, and she said it was the worst."

The real reason for Adrianna's refusal suddenly occurred to me. "My treat," I said casually. Not that I had all that much money! But Ade and Owen had practically none.

"No, it's not that, Chloe. Really, she said that it was pretentious and snobby, superexpensive, and the food was nasty."

"Oh," I said, disappointed. If I was going to shell out money for a pricey dinner, I expected the food to be delectable. I hoped that Ade's client had lousy taste buds.

"Didn't you read the Mystery Diner's review a few months ago? He totally panned the place. Said it was one of the worst restaurant experiences he'd ever had. Not only was the food a disaster, but he wrote that it was dirty and probably broke every health code in the book."

The Boston Mystery Diner, who wrote a popular column for a local paper, was genuinely mysterious: nobody knew who he was. Josh told me that restaurant staff around the city were forever wondering, worrying that the patrons on a given evening included the elusive reviewer.

"I'm surprised he wasn't sued," I said. "I didn't see that one, but you know how unfair some of his reviews are. He said Pinnacle serves a revolting basket of fried clams, and I think it's the best seafood place in Boston."

"True enough," Ade agreed. "Can you imagine what an

awesome job that would be? Eating in restaurants with no one knowing who you are? And eating everywhere and having the paper pay the bills? I'd do that job in a heartbeat."

"Join the club. You sure you don't want to talk to Robin yourself?"

"No. I'm sorry, Chloe. I can't eat at that place after what I've heard. Besides, I'm too huge to leave the house. I'll probably end up having the baby in my apartment because they won't be able to push me out the doorway."

"Very funny," I said. In spite of Adrianna's joking and protestations, I remained half convinced that her real reason for refusing to come with me to Alloy was money. Or money and pride. I was sure that she already felt indebted to my parents and wanted to avoid feeling like an object of my charity. She was not, in fact, totally housebound. And Alloy was surviving in the South End, where competition among restaurants had to be ferocious. How bad could it really be? "Do you have any requests for how the wedding is filmed?" I asked. "Anything you want me to pass on to Robin or Nelson?"

"Tell them not to film my goddamned mother. I just know she's going to be difficult, and I don't need a visual reminder of her stinky attitude when I watch that video twenty years from now. If they accidentally get her on tape, have them put one of those blurry circles over her face and remove her voice from the audio. What's today? Wednesday? She's coming in on Friday, so the countdown to doom has officially started."

"Don't worry about her. There'll be enough people around to keep her under control," I assured Ade while reminding myself to designate someone to head the official Kitty Patrol.

I hung up and searched the Web for reviews of Alloy. The

ones I read were far from fantastic. A local arts and enter-tainment magazine called Alloy's food "undeveloped and mundane" but admitted that the dishes were helped by the bountiful use of fresh herbs. The reviewer was not ready to dismiss Alloy and hoped that time and experience would improve this little restaurant's fare. Online customer reviews were mixed, with some people raving about simple ingredients and dramatic presentations, and other people complaining about small portions and an overemphasis on elaborate style at the expense of flavor.

I looked up Alloy on Boston's Mayor's Food Court, a Web site that was, I thought, a bane to restaurants and a great boon to consumers. Posted on the site were the results of every Boston restaurant's health inspections, and not just general results, either, but details about every violation, no matter how minor. According to the home page, "The Mayor's Food Court provides consumers with current infor-mation about Boston's restaurants so that they can make in-formed decisions about where they will eat." In other words, I could make an informed decision not to eat at Restaurant X, which was infested with rodents and cockroaches, and rou-tinely stored food at temperatures meant for growing a plethora of bacteria.

I have to admit that out of curiosity, I'd looked up Sim-mer a couple of times. Because Josh was an absolute fanatic about keeping his kitchen sterile and up to code, I'd never found any violations. As I soon discovered, Alloy, on the other hand, had been repeatedly cited for improper cooling of cooked or prepared foods, unsound equipment mainte-nance, toxic items not properly labeled, and evidence of—ewww!—rodents.

All I could think of was the Monty Python sketch about rat tart. Still, I absolutely couldn't cancel the dinner. One point of it was to get a free professional wedding video for Adrianna and Owen. Another was to ask about gardening and thus to find out who might be growing foxglove. The third point was frivolous: being in a "human interest story," to use Robin's phrase, would be a hoot. Being in? Well, as the official solemnizer, I wouldn't just be in the story, I'd be one of the stars. So rat tart or no rat tart, and Nelson or no Nelson, I had to go. I wondered whether Nelson would have his camera at the restaurant. From what I knew of him, I had to assume that yes, he would, so I'd better dress accordingly. Never having been the subject of a human interest piece before, I wasn't sure exactly what was involved, but if I was going to discuss my role as a one-day solemnizer at a wedding ceremony, I presumably shouldn't wear a tube top and stilettos.

I tried to reach Josh on his cell at Simmer but just got his voice mail and didn't feel like leaving a message. I parked myself on the couch, ordered in Thai food, and lamented the crummy schedule that kept Josh chronically exhausted and separated him from me.

While washing down yum nuah and drunken noodles with a few bottles of beer, I dealt with a phone call from the same detective who'd questioned Josh the other day. With my mouth half full of food, I reeled off my account of Francie's death to a man who sounded less interested in figuring out who had killed Francie than he was in learning where he, too, could get good Thai food. In his view, was her horrible death just one more murder? Or maybe the authorities felt hopeless about solving the crime. If so, I could understand why. After all, the crime scene had been compromised, and a great deal of the evidence had been destroyed.

"You know," I said, punctuating my words by jabbing my fork in the air, "I heard that digitalis is what killed

Francie. That's foxglove. It's a common biennial. I hope you're finding out who does and doesn't have a garden. I, for one, don't. I live in a condo. There's a yard, but it's just a lawn, really, with no flowers."

"Ma'am, I really can't comment on the investigation, but we're doing everything we can," the disembodied voice said unconvincingly.

"I watched that woman die, and let me tell you, it wasn't a pretty sight." I took a big swig from my beer. "And why didn't that police officer think something fishy might be up when he got to the house and there was a half-dead woman and a bunch of other people sick and vomiting all over the place, huh? That was a mistake, wasn't it?"

Okay, my alcohol tolerance was negligible, presumably because in a show of solidarity, I'd had almost nothing to drink since Adrianna got pregnant. With Ade out of commission—she was the only girlfriend I ever went to bars with—abstaining from alcohol had been an easy sacrifice. Somehow the lure of the beer that Josh kept in my fridge had sucked me in tonight, and the alcohol was hitting me hard.

Even so, I answered as many of the detective's questions as I could, but I knew almost nothing about the people who'd been at Leo and Francie's. The exception was, of course, Josh. I'd never seen either Francie or Leo before, I knew Digger only through Josh, and I'd met Robin, Marlee, and Nelson only a few times. I hung up and polished off the spicy beef salad.

"Damn detective," I said to Inga, who was perched on a windowsill, eyeballing my noodles. Inga licked her paw in response.

I heard a thud as Gato leapt down from the fridge and casually strolled into the living room as though he hadn't been hiding out for the past few days. He gave Inga the hairy eyeball and hissed spitefully before hopping onto the couch and curling up a foot away from me. I reached over, patted him, and whispered, "That's a start, buddy."

THIRTEEN

THURSDAY was a day of rain-barrel activities: re-searching designs that I could pass on to hunky Emilio, re-turning phone calls from potential clients, and preparing written materials on the environmental benefits of watering gardens with rainwater. I was pretty pleased with the pamphlet that I came up with to pass out to clients. I gave my-self extra credit for printing it on recycled paper. I was building an e-mail list, too, so that we could keep clients posted on new developments in the exciting world of rain barrels without using more paper than necessary.

I worked steadily, with hardly any interruptions, and by early evening I was starving and ready for my dinner with Robin and weirdo Nelson. The grilled cheese and tomato sandwich that I'd eaten for lunch hadn't satisfied this gour-met girl, and I was really hoping that the fare at Marlee's restaurant would be better than the Boston Mystery Diner claimed.

I showered, dried my hair, and stood disgruntled in front of my closet, unable to find anything I was in the mood to wear. Then I remembered that I still had a bag of Adrianna's prepregnancy clothes to root through. In spite of my loyalty to Adrianna, I dreaded the inevitable day when her fabulous clothes would once again fit her, and she'd demand their return. In the meantime, I was making the most of the goods. Until now, I'd been wearing her summer things, but it was relatively cool this evening. In almost no time, the fall clothes that had been stashed in a large bag in my front closet were strewn all over my bed, and within minutes, I was wearing a brand-new outfit. Ade's pants were a mile too long for me, so I opted for a camel-colored wrap skirt that could've been meant to be long and an off-white scoop-neck top. I pulled on some nylons and shoes, and feeling like a crazy cat lady, ordered Gato and Inga to behave themselves. Then I left for Alloy.

On-street parking in the South End can be tough to find, but I lucked into a legal spot about a block away from Alloy—a block away according to Google Maps, anyway. Still, I had a hard time finding Alloy, mainly because I expected it to occupy one of the charming old brick town houses that are typical of the South End. In fact, the outside of the restaurant was so modern that I couldn't even figure out how to enter the building. Large metal-framed glass panels covered the face of the eatery. Peering in, I saw Robin and Nelson seated at a stainless-steel table off to the left. Robin was talking on her cell phone but caught my eye and waved. I casually waved back and pretended to inspect the architecture. The glass panels all looked the same to me, and I could not for the life of me determine which one was the entrance. No welcome signs, no door handles, no overhead awning! Metal light fixtures that hung equidistant from one another across the length of the restaurant facade provided not a hint about where to enter the restaurant. I walked slowly to my right and watched Robin's face pinch in confusion. I then headed left and, in desperation, ran my hand along the side of the building in hope of discovering a tactile clue about how to get in and have dinner here.

Aha! I touched a barely noticeable keyhole and pushed. What was presumably the door hardly moved, so I gave a kick and, at last, found myself in the interior of Alloy, which was so hard to break into that it should have been named Fort Knox. If the food was as crummy as the reviews claimed, maybe the owners were deliberately trying to keep customers out.

Finding no hostess up front to greet me, I simply joined Robin and Nelson at their table. "Hello," I said but was unable to take a seat because there were no more chairs at the table. "Oh, I guess I better ask for a chair." I whirled around to find a staff member to help me.

"No, Chloe, you have a seat. There's a stool under the table," Robin explained.

Indeed, hidden beneath the table was a backless stainless-steel stool. Doing my best to hide my surprise, I pulled it out. "I see. How . . . modern."

Who the heck wanted to eat while sitting on a cushionless, backless metal stool? First I'd been unable to come in, and now I didn't want to sit down. The entire room was so heavily decorated in metal that I wondered whether I should have worn the Tin Man's outfit out to dinner. Perching on the stool, I silently vowed to avoid alcohol tonight lest I get off balance and tumble off my seat.

"So," Robin said with a bright smile, "Marlee should be

out any minute. As soon as she gets a break." I looked at Robin's beady eyes and was struck by the realization that she quite strongly resembled a hedgehog: a cute, delicate little body that you just wanted to pick up in your hand and cuddle. Except that I knew what a nasty bitch she could be while directing a shoot.

Despite the unusual and, I thought, unfriendly decor, Alloy was about three-quarters full of diners. I suspected that the would-be patrons who'd have made up the fourth quarter had been unable to locate the door.

"How are you, Chloe?" I barely recognized Nelson without his camera pointed in my face. His plaid golfer's cap, which concealed his bald spot, seemed to violate Alloy's unofficial dress code, which evidently called for trendy formality. And the hat made it unattractively obvious that Nelson's ears were three sizes too big for his head. I was glad that I'd raided my cache of Ade's fall outfits. "You doin' okay after what happened with Francie?"

"I'm all right, I guess. Still in a state of shock, I think, but I'm okay." I really did not want to rehash the details of that fatal day. Besides, to ferret out anything incriminating about Robin or Nelson, I'd need to use subtle methods; I couldn't just blurt out the questions I actually wanted to ask, such as whether either one of them had murdered Francie. Thankfully, we were interrupted.

A waitress approached our table to deliver menus. She held up a pitcher of ice water. "Would you like me to refill your drinking vessels?"

Our *drinking vessels*? You had to be kidding me. But the pretentious phrase was oddly appropriate: the cylindrical metal tubes that sat on our table certainly were not glasses. "No, thank you. I'm fine," I said while sucking in my cheeks to hide my smile.

The waitress poured water for Nelson and Robin while she robotically recited the specials. "Alloy uses herbs that the chef grows in her own garden. All of our dishes are complemented by fresh herbs. Tonight we have a cucumber soup made with organic cucumbers, crème fraîche, and homegrown dill, and garnished with a spiral of lemon zest." She looked down and flicked a piece of lint off her apron. "Then there's a farm-raised chicken leg encrusted with fresh herbs and roasted with a mélange of organic mushrooms and topped with a truffle foam."

Are the herbs fresh? I wanted to ask. *Could you tell us one more time?* I also refrained from asking whether it was only the *leg* of the chicken that had been raised on a farm, whereas the rest of the bird had grown up elsewhere. And no way was I going to eat *foam*. I'd seen enough *Top Chef* episodes to know that gastronomic foam meant a substance that looked like spit. The waitress left the table without so much as a nod.

Robin raised her glass. Whoops! Pardon me. Robin lifted her drinking vessel. "Cheers to the wedding!" She took a sip and opened the menu. "Let's take a look at what else Marlee has for us." Addressing me, she advised, "Sometimes it's best to order off the menu."

The menu had such long, grandiloquent descriptions that it was all I could do to decipher what was actually being offered. Also, I had the sense that I was reading a culinary version of the "The Twelve Days of Christmas": nearly every dish included numbers: *Six Clams Simmered in White Wine and Five-Herb Garlic Butter*, *Two Slices of Pork Loin Seared and Served with a Three-Potato Gallette*, and *A Tower of Four Shrimp with Seven Seasonal Vegetables*.

"*Fiiiive golden rings!*" I sang in my head.

Because I wasn't sure whether Robin was paying for dinner, the high prices had me scanning the menu for the cheapest items. Furthermore, the reports on the Mayor's Food Court had left me leery. Under no circumstances did I ever go out of my way to order a dish garnished with food-borne illness—*Salmon with Salmonella*, let's say, or *Sole on a Bed of E. coli Spinach*—but now, a few days before Adrianna's shower, I especially wanted avoid the risk. I decided on the cucumber soup and roasted cod. As I decoded the description of the fish, the dish had something to do with pureed chickpeas and, needless to say, a mountain of fresh herbs.

"So I gather that fresh herbs are the theme of this restaurant, huh?" I asked the table.

"Absolutely," Robin answered.

"I wonder how Marlee finds time to garden? Considering that she must work here all the time."

"Oh, she's an avid gardener. And the herbs are very important to her."

Hmm. An avid gardener who might grow more than just herbs? "Does either of you garden?"

Nelson shook his head. "Nah. I don't care about flowers and all that. I've got a small apartment with no yard, anyhow."

"Same here," Robin said. "I've got a black thumb when it comes to flowers. Not that my apartment has a yard or a balcony, even, but I can't keep so much as a houseplant alive. I forget to water them. Marlee!" Robin stood up and smiled as Marlee made her way through the dining room.

The female chef looked even pastier than the last time I'd seen her, and her soiled white chef's coat did nothing to flatter her stocky figure. "I heard you were out here, Robin." Marlee tucked her short hair behind her ears, a move that only exaggerated her round face. I caught sight of her dirty fingernails and desperately prayed that she was cooking with gloves on. "I'm so glad to see you. Hi, Nelson. Hi, Chloe. I have to get back in the kitchen, but I wanted to say hello and let you know that I'll send food out for you, so don't bother with the menus, okay? I'll pop out again if I can." Marlee smiled curtly and waved.

Robin reached under the table and pulled a yellow notepad from her bag. "Now, I want to talk about the process of obtaining permission to solemnize a marriage. This is going to be a great piece. We're not filming today, because I want to run the story by the station first, but they're just going to love it."

Phew! So I'd continue to be spared Nelson's camera. I went over the simple process of solemnization with Robin, while Nelson munched on a green bread stick that, according to Robin, was flavored with pureed fresh thyme.

"Adrianna is really excited at the idea of having her wedding filmed," I said. "If it weren't for you, the only footage she'd have would be from a home video camera, and the result would be shaky images and bad lighting. With the baby coming so soon and the shower this weekend, this is one less thing she needs to worry about."

Robin's eyes lit up as I talked. "So, wait! Adrianna is giving birth soon after the wedding?" She looked at Nelson.

"Cool. Now I'm really interested in filming the wedding. Maybe she'll go into labor! Talk about good film." Nelson's eyes brightened, probably in the hope that Adrianna's water would break in the middle of her vows.

"Well, we must film the shower then, too! What an exciting time for your friends, Chloe. And maybe I can use some of the footage of the shower in the piece on solemnization. This will be wonderful!"

"Sure. I guess that would be okay with Adrianna." I

made a mental note to add two more people to the guest list for Saturday. "And Adrianna will still have a few weeks before she's due. So," I said lightly as I eyed Nelson, "let's plan on filming the shower and the wedding and *not* the delivery on the same day." As if Nelson's hopes could induce labor! Still, I had the superstitious sense that his greed for dramatic events to film could jinx Adrianna.

Robin's cell phone rang shrilly. When she pulled it out of her purse, its color—metallic hot pink—should have told me that she had no desire to use it unobtrusively. Foolishly, I expected her to turn it off. Instead, she not only answered but spoke loudly. "Hello? What? I can't hear you. Speak up. This isn't really a good time. Not now." Although the people at the next table glared at her, Robin kept talking. Meanwhile, Nelson and I sat in uncomfortable silence, unable to converse even if we'd wanted to over Robin's noisy phone call. She finally snapped her phone shut.

Food began to arrive. Mindful of the Mayor's Food Court, I looked nervously at my plate as I inspected its contents for signs of improper storage or rat poop. Finding nothing noticeably wrong, I picked up my fork and stared in disbelief: the fork had only two tines. I looked at Robin and Nelson, and then glanced around at other customers who were eating. Was I the only one who found it completely bizarre that we were expected to use this *prong*? Evidently so. Reconciling myself to impaling my food or possibly balancing it, I turned to a dish that Marlee had sent out, a shrimp tower of sorts that initially resisted the attack I mounted with the not-a-fork. After a couple of failed efforts, I had to use my fingers to yank out a rosemary spear that elevated the shrimp above a mountain of thick brown mush almost covered in what appeared to be grass clippings.

Although the shrimp were terribly overcooked, I managed to chew and swallow a few bites, but I nearly choked on a small prongful of grass.

"It's got a kick to it, huh?" Robin handed me my water. "That's the jalapeño Marlee puts in her mushroom and sprout puree."

"Very unusual," I sputtered.

Robin's cell phone went off again, and she began another loud exchange. A male server approached our table. "Ma'am? I need to ask you to turn off your phone." He pointed to a prominent sign on the wall requesting that all cell phones be turned off in the restaurant.

"Oh, all right," Robin said sharply to the server. "Shit, I'll go outside." She made quite a display of stomping across the floor and rolling her eyes as she marched out of the restaurant. At least she found the exit. I made a mental note of its location. Looking embarrassed, the server left the table.

"Just you and me, Chloe." Nelson chomped happily on the vile food. "I've been hoping to get a chance to talk to you. Maybe we can find some time to talk on Saturday at the shower."

Eeek! To cut Nelson off, I signaled the server who had asked Robin to leave. She'd been so rude to him that I felt compelled to apologize, as I couldn't do in her presence. "The sign about not using cell phones is pretty clear," I said. "I'm sorry for what happened."

He shrugged his shoulders. "Friend of the chef. That's how it is. Thanks, though. Excuse me, I have an order to bring out."

Nelson was gazing at me with strange intensity; he almost seemed to be in a trance. In what I intended as a startling tone, I said, "I didn't know that Robin and Marlee were friends. I thought they just knew each other from *Chefly Yours*."

"Oh, yeah. They've been good friends for a while. Robin wants to keep that quiet, though, because she doesn't want it to look like she's playing favorites on the show."

Well, Robin most certainly *was* playing favorites! And having a chef friend of hers in the competition was bad enough, but keeping the friendship secret was even worse. Granted, Robin couldn't control the number of viewers who actually called in to vote for each chef, but for all I knew, she could falsify the voting results. What if Marlee ended up winning the show because Robin had tinkered with the numbers?

I was fuming. It ticked me off to realize that Josh could lose to a chef who served such disgusting food at her restaurant. In the single episode that Marlee had done, the food had looked better than the revolting stuff I'd eaten tonight, but Josh's cooking was incomparably better than Marlee's, and his on-camera personality outshone Marlee's by light-years.

Nelson's hand slithered across the table toward mine. I swiftly yanked my hand away while desperately looking around for Robin. Mercifully, she was on her way back to her stool.

"Sorry about that. That waiter is an asshole."

I pushed my food around on my plate and watched in awe as Robin polished hers clean. Nelson ate all of his food, too, but he struck me as someone who'd be unable to discriminate between a dinner at a run-down roadside shack and one at La Tour d'Argent. When the entrées appeared, I repeated the process of pushing my food around and managed to ingest only a tiny portion of the lavender-and-oregano-infused salmon that Marlee had chosen for us. Chosen for us? Inflicted on us, I should say.

To avoid Nelson's ogling, I shifted around to face Robin and concentrated on giving her a detailed description of the wedding plans. Robin sounded delighted to have the opportunity to produce Adrianna and Owen's wedding video and assured me she'd edit the footage down and set it to whatever music the couple wanted.

"Another delicious meal!" Robin pronounced as the waitress cleared our plates. "After that, I think I'm too full for dessert tonight."

"I agree. Stuffed. I'm absolutely stuffed." The last thing I wanted was cilantro-scented ice cream or whatever other vile dessert Marlee would send out. I was already brainstorming about where to stop on the way home to buy an edible dinner.

"Would you like to go see the kitchen? I know Marlee wouldn't mind." Robin put her napkin down and gestured to the depths of the restaurant. "Nelson, we'll be back in a minute. Here's my credit card. Will you get the check?"

"I'd love to see Alloy's kitchen," I said cheerfully. I went on to thank Robin for treating me to dinner. Thank God I hadn't paid out of my own pocket for that terrible meal.

A restaurant kitchen was no novelty to me—I already knew the ins and outs of Simmer's—and I was less than eager to examine the source of dishes that had made me gag, but I could hardly say so to Robin, who was Marlee's friend and who was footing the bill. Still, a visit to Alloy's kitchen would give me the chance to see for myself whether there were any signs of all those code violations I'd read about. There presumably wouldn't be rodents or insects in sight, but I was so used to Josh's exceptionally sterile kitchen that I should be able to detect iffy conditions in Marlee's.

As it turned out, no experience was required to spot unhygienic areas in Alloy's kitchen. Chicken pieces lay uncovered on a plastic cutting board, their juices running onto the counter and floor. The floors were wet and filthy, and the one drain I could see was covered in gray gunk. In contrast to the minimalist metallic dining area, the entire kitchen had an air of chaos. I did notice a spray sanitizer, but its nozzle hung over containers of chopped vegetables that sat on a long stainless counter. The soap dispenser over the sink was empty, its drip spout clogged. I shuddered to think of the bacteria that must already be growing in my poor gut.

"How was your meal?" Marlee rounded the corner from behind a high shelf that held teetering pots and pans. "Not too shabby, was it?" She smiled at what she assumed to be her outstanding culinary skills. She wiped her forehead with a dish towel and then slapped it onto the counter, where it landed in the chicken juice.

"Brilliant, again, Marlee," Robin chirped.

"Thanks. Business has been up and down." Marlee shrugged and examined her filthy hands with no visible alarm. "What're you going to do, right? I just do the best I can and put out a great product. Anyone who wants to complain can get out."

"Thanks so much, Marlee," I said politely, resisting the impulse to douse her with a bottle of sanitizer. "And, Robin? I'll give Adrianna your number so she can call you tomorrow and talk to you about the shower." I couldn't wait to escape. "I should get going," I said. I gave Robin quick directions to my parents' house and said good-bye.

As I turned to leave, I noticed a large corkboard by the doors to the dining room. Pinned to it were the usual permits and postings from the state, but what stuck out was the Boston Mystery Diner's damning review of Alloy. The article was covered in black marker: a large X ran across the typeface, and "Eat Me!" and "Screw You!" were printed in angry letters at the top of the page.

Most noticeable, however, was a gleaming, stainless-steel knife that had been plunged into the center of the review.

FOURTEEN

I spent most of Friday afternoon and evening at my parents' house, and I was back there again at nine on Saturday morning to finish the preparations for Adrianna's shower. I'd already finished some of the work: the table linens had been washed and ironed, the white dishes set out, the flowers arranged in vases. The candles were ready to be lit. Fortunately, an eleven o'clock shower meant brunch: it was much easier for three amateurs to do brunch food than it would've been to cook and serve lunch or dinner. Dad was going to be kicked out of the house when the guests started to arrive, but for now he was busy arranging a fruit platter.

"Why did I get stuck with the fruit platter when there are four boxes of perfectly delicious pastries I could be setting out?" My dad eyed the white cardboard boxes tied with red and white string.

"Jack, you cannot be trusted with the pastries. That's why you're in charge of cantaloupes and kiwis." My mother walked across the kitchen with a tray of bagels, cream cheese, lox, red onions, and capers. "I'll try to save you some tiramisu if you promise to stay away until after the girls have gone. Chloe, watch your father," she instructed me as she disappeared into the dining room.

"Dad? What does Mom think she's doing with that *thing* on her head?" I was referring to a silk-flower headpiece my mother wore.

"Ah, yes." He cleared his throat. "That's her latest craft project. She seems to believe that floral headwear is going to be the fashion hit of the year." He spoke with amused resignation.

I shook my head in disbelief. "She looks like she's going to a Maypole dance." I'd have to make sure that she didn't accessorize with that monstrosity on the day of Ade's wedding. "Dad!" I yelled. "No!" I practically had to tackle my father, who had grabbed a pair of scissors and was on the verge of breaking into the pastry boxes.

"Oh, all right. Some help you are," he teased. "I did my dumb fruit platter, so I'm going to get out of your hair and go to my yoga class. Did Mom tell you about it? It's wonderful! Watch this."

Dad raised his arms while teetering awkwardly on one foot. Even while he was striking a ridiculous pose, I had to admire how muscular my middle-aged father was. He still had a full head of hair, most of it gray, and with his fit build and those Paul Newman blue eyes of his, he was quite a handsome man.

I laughed. "Okay, Dad. Go work on your chakra or whatever, and we'll see you later."

Dad grabbed a gym bag and blew me a kiss. "I'm trusting you to snatch a few of those treats for me."

"Hey, Dad?" I stopped him. "Thanks so much for everything you're doing for Adrianna and Owen. Especially walking her down the aisle. It means a lot to her. And to me."

"You got it, kiddo. We love those two. It will be an honor for me to stand in for her father." He smiled and went out the back door.

I mixed up a yogurt dip for the fruit platter and then put puff pastry shells in the oven to bake. They'd eventually be filled with a sweet cream filling and topped with strawberries.

At about quarter of eleven, when I was finally finishing up, my mother answered the doorbell and let Robin and Nelson in. Ushering them into the kitchen, she said, "Chloe, your friends are here."

Not friends, exactly.

"You'll never believe it," my mother exclaimed, "but Robin and I know each other!"

Nelson, hiding behind his camera, panned to my face.

I said, "Oh, really? How?"

"Robin produced a show on gardening at a house where your father and I had designed the landscape. Small world, isn't it?"

"That was what? Two years ago?" Robin asked.

"I think so," Mom agreed.

"Come on, Nelson," Robin said. "Let's get some footage of the rooms and the decorations." She directed her cameraman to the dining room. Robin wore a bright floral dress, and an eighties-inspired wide white belt hugged her small waist. She stomped away with Nelson, and her skirt flounced decisively.

A few minutes later, at five before eleven, the doorbell rang again, and I welcomed Naomi, who'd supervised my school internship during the past year, into the living room. When Naomi engulfed me in her usual bear hug, I had to blow her long braids out of my mouth. Since I'd known her, Naomi had chosen a version of the Bo Derek hairstyle; her entire head of hip-length hair was braided into chunky strands.

Naomi barely knew Adrianna, but Adrianna had so few female friends that I'd had to pad the guest list. Including men wouldn't have worked, since almost all of Adrianna's male friends were ex-boyfriends. The women who disliked Adrianna were fools. They envied her looks and were put off by what they saw as her haughty manner. Little did they know what a loyal, generous person she really was. In any case, Naomi belonged at the shower and at the wedding because she'd written the letter of recommendation for me that was required by the commonwealth before issuing a Certificate of Solemnization. Attesting in writing to my "high standard of character," as the instructions phrased it, had made Naomi feel intimately involved with everything about Adrianna and Owen's wedding and procreation. Among other things, she'd mistakenly gained the impression that Adrianna and Owen were following her advice about what she called "alternative birthing" methods. Naomi, who was a big fan of the alternative, the natural, and the New Age in all its forms, had had a long conversation with Adrianna about the benefits of acupressure, hypnosis, water birth, and guided imagery during labor. It was typical of Naomi to have misinterpreted the gasps of horror that Adrianna emitted during the discussion as exclamations of enthusiasm. In reality, Naomi's arguments in favor of drug-free birth had done nothing except fuel Ade's desire for a super-strength epidural.

"What an exciting day!" Naomi was glowing with enthusiasm. "Wait until you see the gift bag I have for our mother-to-be! It's full of aromatherapy oils that promote relaxation during labor. And all sorts of other goodies! In a bag made from natural hemp, I should add. Just like my dress." Naomi spun around, sending her braids flying horizontally off her head while showing off her clay-colored pinafore. I ducked before I got smacked in the face but complimented her on her politically correct attire. "What a beautiful house!" she exclaimed after her three hundred sixty–degree spins.

My parents' stucco house did look wonderful. In keeping with Adrianna's fall theme, my mother and I had run red, orange, and brown ribbons along the traditional Spanish archways that ran between rooms on the first floor. Last year, my parents had refinished the wood floors in the large living room and had put in terra-cotta and decorative hand-painted tiles in the dining room to enhance the style of the house. The walls had been painted in soft earth colors, and at times I felt as if I were actually in New Mexico instead of in a Massachusetts suburb.

Adrianna arrived dressed entirely in hot pink, her nails painted to match her above-the-knee maternity dress and her chunky shoes. "I swear on my baby's life that I'm going to kill my mother," she hissed into my ear as I hugged her.

Adrianna was soon followed by her mother, Kitty, who appeared to be in deep mourning. She wore a black pantsuit with no accessories except a watch that she was already checking. Her badly tinted blonde hair hit her shoulders, where it rolled under in a perfect curl. Her expression suggested a combination of dissatisfaction and grief. Despite Kitty's funereal garb and air, it was hard to miss her incredible figure and easy to see where Adrianna had gotten her modelesque looks.

"Chloe, it's lovely to see you. Where shall I put this?" Kitty held up a white gift bag.

"I'll take it. It's wonderful to see you, too." Knowing that Kitty did not like to be touched, I leaned in and gave her air kisses. "I know my mother is eager to catch up with you. Why don't you go find her in the kitchen?"

"Wonderful, darling." Kitty brushed past me to seek out my mom.

I went to shut the door and nearly slammed it in Owen's face. "Owen? What are you doing here?"

Poor Owen's disheveled appearance made me suspect that Kitty had put him through the wringer since her arrival yesterday. No matter what, Owen was always incredibly handsome, but today his black hair was messy, and his fair skin had a sickly pallor.

"I drove Ade and Kitty here. I can't leave Adrianna alone with that woman! Please let me stay." His expression was pitiful.

"No, you can't stay, dummy. This is a shower just for the girls. I promise I'll mediate the Kitty situation. Ade will call you when it's over."

"But what if—"

"It'll be fine," I said as I shoved the groom-to-be out the door.

I introduced Robin and Nelson to Adrianna and then left the three of them to discuss the video.

Next to arrive were Owen's mother, Eileen, his grandmother, Nana Sally, and his cousin Phoebe. Moments later, two women from Simmer showed up: Isabelle, a shy young cook whom Josh had taken under his wing, and Blythe, a waitress. My sister, Heather, who had let herself in the back door, deposited a gigantic box on the coffee table. Heather had curled her hair into a mass of Shirley Temple ringlets. As usual, Heather was vibrating with such energy that she made the rest of us look like slugs. The mother of a one-year-old and a five-year-old, Heather always looked as if she'd just emerged from fourteen hours of sleep followed by a trip to a spa.

"Give me a hug, Sis." Heather wrapped me in her arms and held me tight. "So I hear that young Emilio caught your eye. Any chance you're finally done with Josh?"

I pushed her away and glared at her. "Don't start," I warned her.

"Don't get all pissy. I'm just asking."

Unlike my parents, Heather was anything but a fan of Josh's. Her idea of the perfect man for me was a money-maker who had gone to a four-year college and who worked a traditional job with regular hours.

"Well, stop asking," I snarled. "And today is about Adrianna, anyway, not about me. Or Josh. So we are not getting into it now."

She smiled sneakily. "But Emilio is hot, isn't he?"

I couldn't help grinning back. "Well, duh!"

I didn't notice Nelson until he quickly turned his camera away. The exchange with Heather was a segment that would have to be edited out of the final video. I hoped, of course, that there would be few such segments. But at least the video would show that a satisfying number of people had attended the shower. Desperate for guests, I'd expanded the list by including a couple of my fellow students from social work school, Julie and Gretchen, who must have been bewildered about why they had been invited to a shower for someone they didn't know, but who showed up nonetheless.

The guests helped themselves to plates of food from the dining room. My parents had sprung for champagne, which was poured, served, and sipped by most of the guests. Adrianna avoided it, of course, as did I, but Owen's grandmother, Nana Sally, compensated for our abstemiousness by quickly drinking her first glass, refilling it, downing that one, and then getting yet another refill. "Mother, go easy!" I heard Eileen whisper.

Kitty sat down next to Eileen on the living room couch and nibbled on a shortbread cookie. I sighed, hoping that they'd manage to converse without bashing the wedding. In particular, I hoped that Eileen would refrain from voicing her belief that Adrianna had tricked Owen into marrying her by getting pregnant. Nelson and Robin stood a few yards from the couch with the camera focused on the two women. If my fears were realized, here was another segment that would have to be edited out. Alternatively, maybe Robin could replace the audio throughout the tape with music, thus obliterating forecasts of marital doom.

"Chloe?" Adrianna handed me a cup of tea. "Who are those girls over there?"

"Oh. Um, well . . ." I faltered. "That's Gretchen and Julie. You remember them, don't you?" Raising my cup of tea and taking a sip, I tried to act as casual as possible. In other words, I tried to avoid having Ade realize that she had never even seen either of them before. "They were so happy to hear about your wedding and the baby that I just had to invite them."

"Uh-huh." Ade looked at me doubtfully.

"Come on! Let's open presents."

I signaled to my mother, who joyously clapped her hands and addressed the entire group. "Everyone? Let's all gather over here while our guest of honor opens her gifts."

The older women sat on the couches, while most of the

younger women seated themselves on the floor around the coffee table. I reserved a big, soft, upholstered chair for Adrianna.

"I'm never going to get out of this seat," Ade said as she sank into the deep pillows.

"Open this one first," I ordered, handing her my present. Adrianna unwrapped my gift and looked totally boggled.

"It's a BabyBjörn," I had to explain. "You strap the baby to your body and voilà! Hands-free! Like a backpack for your front. I got the leather one so you'd be the most fashionable mommy out there."

"This is so cool!" Ade beamed happily. "I really think I'm going to like this. I'm still learning about all this baby stuff. I've never even heard of this."

Next she opened a box packed full of small baby items, gifts from my sister, Heather, who said, "I know these might not look exciting, but they're all things you'll use. See? Teethers, rattles, baby blankets, bottle brushes, onesies, wipes. Seems boring, but they'll be useful." My niece, Lucy, was one, and my nephew, Walker, was five. Heather prided herself on having nearly every conceivable baby and child gadget ever invented.

"Wow, Heather. This is amazing." Ade rooted through the gift box, her eyes wide with interest at all these never-before-seen infant supplies. "This is so thoughtful of you. Thank you."

Adrianna had never been one to fawn over babies—worse, she'd actually seemed to dislike children—and her surprise pregnancy had thrown her for a good loop. Early on, I'd given her some books about pregnancy and about baby care, but I was far from sure that she'd read them. Owen was the one who'd hurled himself into stocking up on kid paraphernalia. Only as Ade opened the baby presents with little apparent recognition of everyday baby items did I understand how hard it was for her to come to terms with the prospect of motherhood. The gifts were, I thought, giving her the boost that she needed to get through to the end of her pregnancy; the fun stuff was a better choice than my books had been. Remarkably, Adrianna even looked interested in Naomi's aromatherapy oils and in the big inflatable ball that Ade was supposed to sit on during major contraction time. Cousin Phoebe and Nana Sally jointly gave Ade a Baby Jogger stroller that looked as if it could be propelled over rock-strewn mountains without jostling the child, and Gretchen and Julie from my school were generous enough to give a stranger three adorable unisex baby outfits. Shy Isabelle and Blythe the waitress had put together a collection of board books for babies that would endure hours of the kid gumming and chewing the hard pages.

I handed Ade the gift from Owen's mother. Unwrapped, the package turned out to contain a voluminous white cotton nightgown with a high ruffled neck. Staring at this chaste garment, I realized that it should have had a prominent monogram that read Not Adrianna. Ade shot me a look out of the corner of her eye, and I refrained from laughing out loud.

"This is lovely, Eileen. Thank you." Ade spoke politely.

"Isn't it?" Eileen said cooly. "You can think of me every time you wear it."

"Yeah, every time I return to the convent," Ade muttered in my ear as she noisily scrunched up the wrapping paper.

Adrianna had seen what I'd missed: the nightgown was suitable for a nun and must have been chosen to keep Owen as far away from Adrianna as possible. Dream on, Eileen!

Adrianna could wear a chicken costume, and Owen would still find her the sexiest woman in the world.

"I'm sure it will be beautiful on you when you lose all the weight you've put on, dear," added Kitty, passive-aggressive as ever.

I hurriedly put Kitty's gift in front of Adrianna. "Now, your mother's present."

When Adrianna had removed the wrapping paper, I could hardly believe my eyes. Or maybe I just didn't want to believe what I was seeing. To Adrianna, to her own daughter at this wedding and baby shower, Kitty had presented a cheap-looking basket that held a small assortment of cheese balls and dried sausages. Bad? Bad enough if the basket had been new, but the terrible gift had already been opened: one of the sausages was obviously missing.

"Thank you, Mom," Ade croaked.

My heart broke for her. Of all the stupid, meaningless, idiotic gifts to give to a daughter on any occasion! But now? Oh, I was furious. Goddamn it. Kitty soared to the top of my official shit list. So what if Adrianna was pregnant before her wedding? Couldn't her own mother have the decency to fake understanding? Kindness, generosity . . . and even love? Evidently not!

Robin reached out to push Nelson's camera down. Amazingly, for all the cameraman's greed for his notion of reality, he actually looked sympathetic.

Adrianna's eyes were glistening. Before she had time to shed tears, I put the presents from my mother in front of her. One was in a big box on the coffee table, the other in a long, wide package too bulky to lift off the floor. I knew what Mom was giving Ade and saw the lavish gifts not just as expressions of celebration but as tokens of the maternal devotion that Ade's own mother withheld. Adrianna opened the Cuisinart food processor and then a fancy high chair with an adjustable seat, a dishwasher-safe tray, and all sorts of decorative doodads, baubles, and bells.

Kitty leaned over for a better view of my mother's gifts. "My, how extravagant."

Adrianna pulled herself up from the chair and gave my mother an enormous hug. Ade was not one to get sappy or weepy, but I saw her wipe her eyes.

Naomi's voice rang through the room as she happily leaped off her seat. "Hasn't this just been a touching display of female bonding? Really, the power of a group of women coming together to celebrate the impending arrival of another life!" She placed her hands on her chest. "My heart is overwhelmed with the love in this room."

I smiled at Naomi, who was totally oblivious to the family drama that had just transpired. Although this couldn't be the first baby or wedding shower that my supervisor had ever attended, I suspected that it was rare for her to find herself in a gathering of women not associated with some sort of political movement.

Nelson was standing five or six yards from Naomi with his camera fixed on her. He briefly peered around the camera to gaze at her with such clear interest that I spotted an opportunity, pounced on it, and pushed him in her direction. As far as I knew, Naomi was still involved with her boyfriend, Eliot, who owned a gallery on Newbury Street right near Simmer. Still, it wouldn't hurt to have Naomi see that other men noticed her.

"Why don't you go interview Naomi?" I suggested to Nelson. "I'll bet she'd give you some really good material to include in the video."

Nelson responded immediately. He practically skipped

across the room to position himself smack next to a surprised Naomi.

I cleaned up wrapping paper, moved gifts into one area of the living room, and then helped my mother to replenish the supply of coffee and pastries. When I returned to the living room and took a seat, Nana Sally was narrating a tale about Owen's brothers, Evan and Willie. From the look on Cousin Phoebe's face, I gathered that this sort of recitation was a family ritual.

"Hee hee!" Nana Sally shrieked. "And remember when those two set up that skateboard ramp for Owen?" She had a fit of laughter. "Owen was fifteen, but he still could barely stand on the skateboard without falling off. Love him! But athletic he is not. Well, Evan and Willie built a ramp and told him it would be easy as pie for him. They got poor Owen standing on the skateboard at the top of a hill, and then the pair of them sent him flying down onto this ramp contraption that they'd thrown together out of old plywood. I don't know how Owen managed to get all the way to the ramp without falling off, but he did. As soon as he hit the top of the ramp, he fell crashing down!" Nana Sally again squealed with laughter. Covering her eyes with a napkin, she finished the story by saying, "Those damn kids had rigged the ramp to crumble when Owen hit it!"

Eileen crossed her arms and frowned. "It wasn't funny, Nana. Owen still has a scar on his forehead from that incident. Four stitches, he needed!"

Ade perked up her head. "Owen told me he got that scar from a fistfight he had in ninth grade."

Phoebe took a turn at storytelling. "Then there was the time those two rascals balanced a bucket on top of the door so it would fall on their dad's head," she said. "Remember that?"

I chimed in. "That doesn't sound so bad. It's an old trick. Did they fill the bucket with water or something?"

"No!" Nana giggled. "Rocks!" She exploded into uproarious laughter.

Rocks? The prank didn't strike me as the least bit funny. In fact, both of the supposedly hilarious practical jokes sounded cruel and dangerous. Nana Sally's and Phoebe's stories, far from convincing me that Willie and Evan were harmless pranksters, fueled my theory that Owen's brothers could have perpetrated a horrible joke that had turned deadly last Monday. I hated to have Adrianna's shower end on such an ugly note.

By the time Owen arrived to pick up Adrianna and Kitty, Ade looked exhausted. Owen loaded the gifts into the car and did his best to be polite to Kitty, who issued nonstop criticism disguised as advice.

"Owen, I don't understand why you're putting the bags in the car first," she said. "You ought to start with that overpriced high chair." Kitty shook her head as she spoke. It seemed to me that she might as well have come right out and voiced the opinion that her daughter had chosen to procreate with an idiot.

"Thank you for that very sage advice, Kitty. I'll reload the car in the proper manner." Owen winked at me and picked up the last of the gifts.

"I can't thank you enough for all for all of this, Chloe." Adrianna engulfed me in a hug. I rubbed her back with my hands as I squeezed her.

"I'm so sorry about your mom, Ade," I whispered. "I don't know what in the world is going on with her."

"What's going on with her is that she is a bitch." She pulled back from me. "It's just the way it is. She's done nothing but complain since she got here. The hotel is crappy, she hated the restaurant we went to last night, and she is one hundred percent put out that she has to stay in town for the week until the wedding. Believe me, I'm put out by it, too. And the kicker? My due date is a major pain in her ass. She has herself in knots because the birth might interfere with a work conference she has in Chicago. I informed her that no one invited her to the delivery room anyhow, and after that, we had a particularly obnoxious exchange. What are you going to do, right?" Adrianna waved her hand in the air. "I'm going to go home and inhale some of those aromatherapy oils Naomi gave me. Maybe they'll actually work."

Before the tipsy Nana Sally was helped to the car by Phoebe, she slipped me an envelope for Adrianna and Owen. "Give this to the proud couple at the rehearsal, okay? I don't want Kitty and Eileen to know about it." Nana Sally kissed me sloppily on the cheek. "You're a good friend, Chloe."

When everyone had left, my mother started on the dishes while I cleaned up the living room. Under a napkin on an end table I came across the distinctive cell phone that Robin had used at Alloy, the metallic hot pink phone that was as loud and obtrusive as her phone conversations had been. I tucked it in my pocket to take home.

"Well, that went pretty well, don't you think?" My mom threw a dish towel over her shoulder and somehow managed to get it caught on her Maypole hair wreath. "Oops, there we go." She untangled the towel and surveyed the room. "Looks like we're all set in here."

"Aside from Kitty, it was perfect." I couldn't bring myself to mention Nana Sally and Phoebe, who'd done their share, too. "Adrianna looked really happy. You and Dad have been amazing to her, and I know how much she appreciates you guys."

"Our pleasure, Chloe. With a mother like that, Adrianna needs all the support she can get. Oh, before you leave, I have a bag of clothes to donate to that women's shelter you volunteered at."

"Haven't you done enough good in the world today?" I teased. "Now you're just showing off!"

FIFTEEN

WHEN I got home, I hauled the bag of clothes up to my apartment and put it in the living room, where it served as a reminder of what a lovely person my mother was: kind and generous to her family, her friends, her daughters' friends, and even to the strangers at the women's shelter; considerate to everyone; respectful of privacy; and, in short, the kind of fine human being who would return someone's forgotten cell phone without so much as thinking of turning it on and exploring its contents. Bad luck for Robin that it hadn't been my mother who'd found her phone. I should've been calling the shelter to arrange to drop off the clothes, but first things first: I turned on Robin's cell, plopped down on the couch, and started scrolling through her list of contacts. Inga settled in next to me and began purring melodiously. I stroked her with one hand as I tapped through names on the phone.

One stood out: Leo.

Unless Robin knew Leonardo DiCaprio, I had a strong suspicion that this Leo was Francie's husband and not a famous movie star. Because Leo's number was still stored on my own caller ID, it took me all of thirty seconds to confirm that Robin's Leo was, in fact, Leo the widower. When had Robin added Leo to her list of contacts? On the day of the filming? In other words, on the day of his wife's murder? Or could Robin have known Leo before the show?

Leo. Hmm. As I knew from carefully studying thousands of TV shows, murderers were often spouses or lovers, so unless Francie had had a lover, Leo should have been the prime suspect from the beginning. Did the police agree? Did they watch as much TV as I did? And what about motives? What about love and money? Maybe Leo had wanted to get rid of Francie because he had a lover or because he stood to inherit oodles of cash when Francie died. As to access to digitalis, for all I knew, he had foxglove growing right in his weed-choked garden. Under other circumstances, I could have gained access to his yard by trying to sell him a rain barrel, but as it was, I couldn't very well call him up and say, "So sorry your wife died a grisly death, but would you like to conserve water by recycling rain?"

Still, I could follow him to see whether he did anything suspicious. Such as? I didn't know exactly. But there was nothing wrong with my keeping an open mind. And how hard could it be to tail someone? I was too wiped out from Adrianna's shower to set out on a spying expedition today, but I resolved to pursue the investigation the next morning.

I checked my messages. There was a brief one from Josh to ask how the shower had gone. He said that tonight he was again working late and working an early shift on Sunday, but could he come by in the late afternoon? I returned his call and left him a voice mail saying that unless he showed up tomorrow, I was going to kidnap him from Simmer and, like some sex-starved cave woman, drag him back here. I was on my way out, I said, to buy a loincloth, a club, and a bone for my hair, so he'd better watch out.

Early on Sunday morning, I drove to the warehouse in Waltham where my parents stored equipment and supplies. They did most of the landscape design and planning work from home, but the rest of the company ran out of the second location, which was only a twenty-minute drive from my place. The deep red building gave the impression that a tornado had dropped a barn in the middle of Waltham, and the stacks of hay and the smell of garden manure only fueled that fantasy. I can't say that I was a fan of the manure aroma, but I did love the smell of hay and soil and the sawdust aroma from Emilio's lumber. I parked my Saturn in the small parking lot, let myself into the building through a large red door, and got the keys to the oldest of the five vehicles used for deliveries, a beat-up gray Chevy van with seats in the front and all sorts of shovels, rakes, and hoes in racks on the walls of the rear. The other two vans were new, as were the two pickup trucks. As I drove toward Leo's house, the stick shift gave me a hard time, and I regretted my choice of the beat-up gray van, which I'd picked because it was the smallest of the vehicles and would presumably be the easiest for me to maneuver. As it was, although I'd driven the gray van a few times before, everything about it felt unfamiliar, and I hated having to rely on the side-view mirrors. Whoever had driven it last had left half-empty coffee cups in the holders. With each passing mile, the trip seemed more and more like the stupidest idea ever. I was hardly Veronica Mars. But by the time I'd decided that the whole undertaking was a mistake, I'd passed the Natural High market and was almost at my destination.

I parked the van a few houses down from Leo's place and sank into my seat. Vans used for real surveillance had equipment such as listening devices rather than gardening implements, but I had eyes and ears, I reminded myself. Besides, the old van really did belong to a landscaping company, and if anyone questioned my presence, the Carter Landscapes logo on the side of the van and the garden equipment would show that I was who I said I was. Few landscapers would be working on a Sunday morning, of course, but I could always claim that a resident had been stricken with a crisis of environmental conscience and desperately needed information on rain barrels.

I felt like an idiot sitting there parked on the street, periodically looking at a clipboard I'd found on the passenger seat and wrinkling my brow in false concentration as I read and reread my parents' pamphlet on their company. An hour after my stakeout began, Leo finally drove his car out of his driveway and zoomed to the end of the street. No one else was visible in Leo's car, so unless someone was flattened on the floor, Leo was alone. Following him proved to be nothing like what I'd seen in movies and on TV, probably because the streets were almost empty and because he wasn't going very far: I just stayed a block behind him and trailed him to a large chain supermarket.

Disappointed that I hadn't caught Leo pulling over to burn evidence or stopping to engage in a scandalous love affair, I debated about whether to get out of the van and follow Leo right into the supermarket. Feeling disappointed, I decided that the risk of being seen was just too high, so I stayed in the van and waited for him to emerge from the market. I consoled myself with the thought that I couldn't be missing much: the probability was slight that he was having a clandestine amorous encounter among the cabbages, the steaks, or the cartons of milk.

After thirty minutes, I reconsidered: Leo still hadn't appeared. Then my hopes rose when I caught sight of a police cruiser in a side-view mirror. I watched excitedly as it slowly passed by. Maybe Leo was about to be arrested! Eager to witness the capture of a murderer, I stuck my head out the window, but the cruiser moved past the entrance to the store and continued along.

A few minutes later, Leo exited the supermarket and pushed a full shopping cart to his car, where he transferred his shopping bags to the trunk and got into the car. The only vaguely suspect action he took was to fail to leave his cart in one of the designated areas, but irresponsibility with regard to shopping carts obviously didn't prove him guilty of true crimes. As he backed out of his parking spot, I started up the van's engine and shifted into reverse. Before I'd even put my foot on the gas, however, I was stopped by the presence of a police cruiser right behind me. The lights were flashing. Seconds later, that first cruiser was joined by a second one.

A uniformed officer slowly approached and through the open window of the van said, "License and registration, please."

I smiled brightly at the officer, who looked old enough to be my great-grandfather. I prayed that my winning grin would send him away. "Is there a problem?" I asked as I fumbled through my purse. What was I thinking? Of course there was a problem! Why else was this cop talking to me? I handed him my license, shuffled through papers and maps in the glove compartment, found the registration, and passed it to him. I couldn't be in that much trouble since this officer looked so ancient and scrawny that I had a hard time picturing him chasing down violent, gun-toting criminals. I could probably knock this man over with one push of my pinky finger.

Without even examining the registration, he wrinkled his wrinkles and said, "This vehicle had been reported stolen."

Crap.

I hate the kind of robotic pretense at politeness that's more offensive than honest rudeness, and that's what I got. It took twenty minutes to straighten out the mess, but the officer did eventually call my parents, who convinced him that I hadn't stolen a beat-up van that no one would even dream of stealing. Giving up on Leo for the day, I left to exchange the supposedly stolen van for my Saturn. On the way, I called my mother and fed her an improbable tale about scouting out neighborhoods where people might be interested in rain barrels.

"You're not even working this week, Chloe," my mother said with exasperation. "You have the week off to help with the wedding. And the next time you take one of our vans, you'd better let us know!"

"Promise." I said. And meant it! I wanted never again to face the kind of public humiliation I'd just experienced.

"While I have you on the phone, I had a call from Robin. She thinks she left her cell phone at our house."

"She did. I have it."

"Chloe! Why haven't you let her know? She is a producer for a television station, and I'm sure she needs it back. What is going on with you?"

"Nothing. I'll call her as soon as I get home."

I hung up feeling grumpy and frustrated. While learning nothing about Leo, I'd pissed off my mother. When I reached my condo, I dug up Robin's home number and left her an apologetic message saying that I had her cell phone and would be happy to return it anytime. Then I cleaned the apartment and spiffed myself up for Josh's arrival. The first half of the day had stunk, but maybe the evening with my boyfriend would compensate.

Sixteen

WHEN Josh arrived, I threw my arms around him and kissed him deeply. When we finally came up for air, he said, "Well, it's nice to see you, too."

I ran my hands through his hair and looked into his blue eyes. "I was beginning to forget what you looked like. You're very cute, you know that?" He did look cute. Cute and tired.

Josh pulled me with him as he collapsed on the couch. "You're not so bad yourself." He snuggled me into his body and shut his eyes.

I sighed inwardly. Maybe if I let him take a nap, he'd perk up.

Josh's phone rang. He growled and sat up. "Now what do they want? I've been gone twenty minutes!"

When Josh wasn't at Simmer to supervise, the staff routinely called him about supposed emergencies. Despite having a strong sous-chef, Snacker, the restaurant seemed practically unable to function without Josh. Our romantic moments were forever being interrupted because someone couldn't find the order sheets or because the stove wasn't working properly or because the produce bill hadn't been paid or . . . The list was endless.

"Oh, it's not them," Josh said, meaning his staff. To me, he said, "Hold on, I have to take this." He stood up and walked into the kitchen as he talked. "Hi, this is Josh Driscoll."

I trailed after him and wrapped my arms around his waist. I could make out the sound of a woman's voice coming from the phone.

"Yeah, that sounds good. Can I call you back, though?" Josh sounded strange. Embarrassed, maybe? "Okay, thanks." He hung up.

"Who was that?" I asked.

"No one. Don't worry about it. I'm going to take a shower, if that's all right." He loosened my arms from his body and slipped his phone into his pocket.

"Sure. What do you want to do for dinner? I could make something, if you trust me to feed a chef of your caliber."

"Actually I'm meeting up with Digger later."

"Oh," I said, unable to disguise the disappointment in my voice.

"It's just kind of a guy thing tonight. That's all." Josh went into the bathroom and ran the water in the shower while I sat dejectedly at the kitchen table. "Are you upset?" he called from the shower.

I poked my head into the bathroom. "Kind of. I mean, I feel like I've hardly seen you." After a pause, I said, "That's because I *have* hardly seen you."

It was quiet for a moment, and then Josh spoke. "I guess it would be all right if you came."

Irritated, I said, "I don't want to be a third wheel or anything."

Josh pulled the curtain back and peeked out. "You won't. I want you to come." He puckered his lips and blew me an exaggerated kiss.

I blew a kiss back and planted myself on the toilet seat to talk to him. How pathetic is that? I was so desperate for time with my boyfriend that not only was I going to barge in on his guys' night out, but I was stalking him while he took a shower.

"So how has work been?" I asked. "I'm getting the impression that there have been a lot of problems recently." Problems? If a restaurant's dining area is noisy, and the service is a little slow, and a couple of menu items are unavailable, there are problems. If the owner is meandering around drunk in front of the patrons and using cocaine with them after hours, there aren't just problems with the restaurant, there's a catastrophe in the making. But I deliberately used the weak word.

"Ah, just the usual crap."

"Obviously Gavin's been cranky and difficult lately, but I can't tell how bad things are for you there."

"It's nothing, okay? And like I told you, Robin told me we can just film another episode for the TV show, so that won't be a problem either. She's just going to pretend it never happened."

I didn't inform Josh that I, at least, intended to remember that the murder certainly had happened. Furthermore, since I was sure he'd disapprove of activities such as driving around in a stolen landscape van tailing a suspect, I said nothing about my morning's adventure.

"Josh, you know you can talk about work with me if you want. Maybe I could help you," I suggested.

"Lay off, okay?" Josh sighed audibly. "It's fine. Leave it alone."

"Fine." I shut the bathroom door and let him finish his shower. Maybe he'd wash off some of his grumps.

This was hardly the romantic start to the evening that I'd hoped for. Something was up with Josh, but I didn't know what. And who was that woman on the phone? I'd heard Josh deal with a lot of calls from Simmer. This hadn't been one of those. Josh would never cheat on me, would he? If not, why was he was getting secret calls from unknown women? But this was clearly not the right time to push him on the subject of her identity; although I hadn't tackled him about her, we were already verging on the seriously irritable.

While I was changing clothes, I heard Josh turn the water off and then heard him talking. He had his phone in the bathroom with him, and I couldn't help sticking my head into the hallway to eavesdrop.

"Dig? It's me. Just FYI, Chloe is coming out with us. So just don't say anything, okay? Cool. We'll see you there in an hour."

Don't say anything about what? I didn't like Josh's odd behavior one bit, but I had to trust him not to keep anything important from me. I'd just have to suck it up and act maturely; he'd talk when he was ready.

"Babe? How's La Morra sound to you?" When Josh opened the bathroom door, he looked totally normal, as though he hadn't just made that cryptic phone call to Digger.

"Good. I love that restaurant."

While I finished getting ready to go out, Josh spent twenty minutes snuggling Inga and cooing to her. "Who's so pretty now? Who is all clean and cute and gorgeous? Aren't you lucky to be living here with Chloe instead of with that nasty shithead who starved you and didn't brush you? We won't talk about what might've happened to you, okay? Gimme a kiss." I heard goofy kissing noises coming from the living room.

Josh and I got to the restaurant a few minutes early and were seated at a table near the bar, where we had a view of the semiopen kitchen. La Morra was a northern Italian restaurant on Boylston Street in Brookline. Wood beams ran across the ceiling, and the wood tables were set with colorful place mats and white dishes rimmed with a warm yellow. The staff at La Morra were consistently warm, and the whole restaurant had a wonderfully cozy and rustic feel to it. Also, as I knew from previous visits, the food was fantastic. My mood improved the second we sat down.

"S'up, kids?" Digger's rough voice echoed across the restaurant.

We waved to him, and then Josh stood up to shake his hand. Digger leaned in and gave me a kiss on the cheek before grabbing the seat next to Josh.

Our waitress welcomed us, handed us menus, and took our drink orders. The menu here began with cicchetti, which were preappetizers, little mouthfuls of amazingly delicious snacks. Digger, who was working at a small tapas restaurant in the South End, was bound to become a fan of these small dishes.

I looked up from the menu. "We have to get the Tuscan meatballs with porcini and prosciutto. And also the fried risotto balls."

"Fried olives, too," Josh added.

"Nice!" Digger agreed. "And then for antipasti, we're getting the savoy cabbage salad with pomegranates, hazelnuts, and bagna càuda." The bagna càuda was a strong anchovy and garlic dip that I could practically drink. "Do you guys mind sharing the soup?"

The lobster soup with spaghetti squash and toasted pumpkin seeds was another of my favorites. I certainly didn't mind sharing a bowl with Josh and Digger.

Josh added his request. "And I pick the shaved sunchoke salad with pickled mushrooms and frisée."

We spent a few more minutes deciding on main courses before placing our order and returning the menus to the waitress.

"Digger, you've recovered fully from Monday's fiasco, I hope?" I asked the chef.

"Tough as an ox." He thumped his chest with his fist. "I could've used a few days off from work though, so maybe it's too bad I got better so quickly." He grinned slyly.

"Why? What's going on there?"

"Ah, it's a wreck. The servers suck, and they're totally obnoxious. Every night they let the orders sit out until they're practically bone cold, and then they get sent back. It's crap, I tell ya! I can't even believe I'm off tonight. I've worked the past two weeks straight, except for last Monday, and the goddamn owner is on my case about keeping food costs down." Digger took more than a sip of his wine. "Did you see the Mystery Diner's write-up about us? Frickin' hated the place. Hated everything about it. The food, the decor, the staff. Everything. And you know what? He was half-right, too. The service is awful, and the customers get treated like shit."

Digger's colorful language reassured me that he'd recovered from any digitalis poisoning that he'd had.

"I didn't see that review." Josh furrowed his brow. "Your food is great. What could the reviewer find to pick on?"

Digger shrugged. "The usual stuff. This was too oily, that was underseasoned, this wasn't spicy enough. And my favorite? The portions are too small. It's tapas for Christ's sake! Obviously the portions are small!"

"That's not fair." Josh shook his head. "Some of these reviewers . . ." His voice trailed off.

I had to agree. "I saw that Marlee and Alloy got a pretty nasty review from him, too. That one might have been on target, but it was still vicious."

Digger continued. "That dude is one mean son of a bitch. Do you know how much power reviewers have? People come into a restaurant and say they read a great review, and so they wanted to try us out. Nobody comes in and says, 'Hey, I just read a crappy review of this place, but I thought I'd give it a shot anyhow.' The Mystery Diner may have been right about the service, but not about the food. And I'm not just saying that to be cocky. The food really is good. That Mystery Diner should be strung up, if you ask me." Digger took another drink and then looked sheepish. "Sorry. But you know what? Bad reviews happen. And the review didn't single me out. The reviewer just hated the whole place. It's part of the business, and it makes the good reviews all the better. Still, I'm not gonna say it doesn't sting like a bastard when I read the awful ones."

"And then you get blamed for it, right?" Josh gave Digger a knowing look. "The owner rides you for a bad review and takes all the credit for a good one. What're you going to do? That's the life we chose." Josh lifted his glass in a sarcastic toast.

"Actually, I'm looking for another job. *That's* what I'm gonna do. When things reach a certain low, we chefs have to move on and find something better. There's only so much punishment I can take on a daily basis, you know?"

"Wow," I said, stunned that Digger was thinking about quitting. "Do you have any leads?"

"A couple. I got a headhunter I use. Actually I gave—"

"The food is here," Josh cut in.

The waitress set down the cicchetti we'd ordered. I inhaled the aroma and couldn't wait to taste the meatballs. As I knew from a previous visit, when I'd practically interrogated the server about the meatballs, they had been seared and then simmered in the oven with white wine. I popped one in my mouth. Heaven!

Inevitably, we talked about the murder. Digger hadn't known about the digitalis found in Francie's system. "It's a heart medicine," I said. "It comes from a flower. Foxglove. Don't some people garnish dishes with flowers?" I bit into a risotto ball.

"Ugh, yeah. Nasturtiums and shit. Ick." Digger blew a raspberry. "I've never done that, have you, Josh?"

Josh shook his head. "Nah. That was sort of trendy for a while. Some flowers are edible, but I never got into that. Seriously, nobody wants to eat a flower."

I'd had nasturtiums in salad that had been pretty good, but I felt unqualified to argue flavor with two chefs, so I kept quiet.

Digger pointed his fork at me and spoke with his mouth full. "Flowers belong in a garden or in a vase, if you ask me. Just don't make me grow 'em for you. I've never touched a garden in my life."

By the time I finished my entrée, lasagna con coniglio brasato (braised rabbit and crispy polenta lasagna with shaved raw mushrooms, thyme, and gremoulata), I was so stuffed that I didn't know whether I'd be able to eat dessert. As usual, though, my appetite returned quickly, and I managed to squeeze in a ricotta cheese tart with Marsala sauce.

When Digger went to the bathroom, Josh reached across the table and took my hand in his. "I'm sorry I was so snappy earlier. Really."

Since Josh looked so genuinely apologetic, I squeezed his hand back. "How early are you working tomorrow?"

"Not that early." Josh winked at me.

SEVENTEEN

"IT'S not possible that I got bigger since Friday!" Adrianna's yell shot through my phone's receiver. "What in heck made me think it was a good idea to alter my own wedding dress?"

"I don't know," I said helplessly. "I wish I could do your alterations, but I'm not particularly adept with a needle and thread. Do you want me to come over anyway and see what I can do?"

Adrianna had bought a discount wedding dress for herself in a much larger size than she normally wore. The supposed point was to alter it to fit her pregnant shape.

"Yes, I want you to come over and help! Can't you hear the anxiety in my voice? Get over here!"

I told Bridezilla I'd be over in a few minutes.

Even though Josh and I had more than made up the

previous night, things between us still felt strained. That stress, combined with the experience of having Francie die in front of me and my so-far-unsuccessful investigation of the murder, left my spirits low. I worried that my mood might rub off on Adrianna. She was already nervous enough about the wedding, the baby, and her future in general, and it was supposed to be my job to calm her down. I'd need to muster every ounce of cheer I could.

As I was about to head out the door, Robin called. "I'm so glad I caught you. I really need to get my phone back. Can I stop by and get it this afternoon? Around three?"

"Absolutely." I gave Robin my address and directions, and promised to be home.

When I arrived at Adrianna's, she had her wedding gown half on. It was inside out, and most of the material was gathered around her middle, where her waist had once been.

With despair on her face and in her voice, she said, "I can't deal with this right now, Chloe. I can't."

"Calm down. Let me help you."

I pulled the front of the dress up over her chest, which had practically doubled in size, and tied the halter top around her neck.

"No one told me I was going to get Pam Anderson boobs," she seethed. "I look trampy. I can't wait to hear what my idiot mother has to say about it."

"Here," I said handing her a box of pins. "Start pinning and stop whining. You can do this. Just pin and sew, okay?"

"Okay." Ade started pinning the sides of her dress. I helped in the spots she couldn't reach. "This is not exactly the image I had of how I was going to look on my wedding day," she said with a sniff.

"What? You didn't picture yourself beautiful? Stunning? Radiant?"

"No," she barked at me. "Stressed out, bloated, huge, and busty like a porn star."

"Ade, stop," I said firmly as I pinned the hem. "Everything is going to work out perfectly."

"Your mom has her dress all set, right? And your dress is ready?" I nodded, petrified about how she might have reacted if I'd said no! Ade continued. "I have to call today to confirm the arrangements for renting the tables, chairs, and linens. Oh!" She snapped her fingers. "And I have to finalize the flowers." She exhaled deeply.

"I'll do all that for you. Just give me the numbers. You don't need to do anything except finish the dress and then rest. My mom is taking care of the tent, and the company is going to set it up on Thursday afternoon. You'll be able to see it Friday at the rehearsal dinner."

The rehearsal itself was going to be a quick run-through rather than an elaborate, formal affair. My dad, with the best of intentions, had promised to grill dinner. It was remotely possible that he'd fulfill his promise without charring everything.

I spoke with pins clamped between my lips. "And I want you to try to keep Kitty from driving you insane. Where is she, by the way?"

"I'm trying to keep my distance from her, so I sent her off to Faneuil Hall to do the tourist thing. And there's enough shopping down there to keep her occupied. Who knows? Maybe she'll find another smoked sausage basket for me."

"I'm so sorry about that, Ade." I moved to the front of her dress and continued pinning, doing my best to keep the hemline straight.

"I shouldn't have been surprised. I should be used to my mother by now. But it does hurt. I'm pregnant and getting married, and I need my mother. Or, rather, I need a less insane mother. Kitty is never going to be who I want her to be, so there's no use trying to change her. I don't have the energy for it anyhow. Bless your parents for taking such good care of me. And you, too, of course." Ade looked down at me and smiled.

"I'd do anything for you. You know that." I smiled back.

When I left, Ade was running her dress through the sewing machine. Although she seemed to have relaxed a little bit, I was reluctant to go. But I had to get home to meet Robin and return her cell phone. I still hadn't thought of a way to ask her whether she'd known Leo before the filming without accusing her of rigging the show and also, of course, without revealing that I'd explored her cell phone. Once I got home, I hurriedly scanned through her phone again in search of recently dialed or received calls. Everything had been erased; there were no call records. The absence meant nothing. I routinely erased all of my own calls.

Following the directions I'd given her, Robin knocked at my back door, which opened to a wooden fire escape that doubled as a miniature patio. "Hello?" She cupped her hand over her forehead and peered through the window.

I opened the door. "Hey, Robin. I bet you'll be glad to get your phone back. Come on in."

"Sorry about this. I can't believe I left my phone at your parents' place. It's been driving me crazy not to have it."

"Here, grab a seat. Pardon the clothes everywhere. My mom gave me a ton of stuff to donate to a home for women in transition. It's a temporary place for homeless women to stay while they're trying to find jobs and housing. My mom gave me some great stuff that could be worn on interviews." I'd spread everything out on the couch. Feeling embarrassed about the mess, I started folding the outfits and putting them neatly in bags.

Robin's eyes lit up. "That's a wonderful idea. You know, Leo could probably use some help in clearing out Francie's belongings. I'm sure that the last thing he feels like doing is going through all of her clothes. Maybe he'd want to donate them to this women's place."

"You've been in touch with Leo?" I asked casually.

"Obviously I called him to offer my condolences. I guess there isn't going to be a funeral. He said maybe a memorial service later. I'll give you his number." Robin took a scrap of paper from her purse and jotted down Leo's home number. "I'm sure he'd appreciate some help. Sort of a grisly process, I'd think, going through your dead wife's clothing." Robin grimaced.

"I'll definitely give him a call. Thank you."

It distressed me to realize that poor Francie was going to disappear. No funeral? And nothing more than the possibility of a memorial service? In no time, I thought, it will be as if Francie had never existed. But the possibility of going through Francie's clothing did offer the hope of learning something—anything!—about her murder.

As soon as Robin left, I called Leo, who picked up after a few rings. His voice sounded raspy and weak.

As I explained why I was calling, I felt grateful for my social work training. "I'm sorry if this is premature on my part, but I've done some volunteering at a shelter that helps homeless women to find jobs. Do you think that Francie would have liked the idea of donating her clothing? I just thought I could be of some help to you. Maybe you're not ready, though."

"You know what? I do like that idea. I've been trying to figure out what to do around the house. Do I throw out anything that reminds me of her? Do I keep the house set up as though she were still here? No one gives you an instruction manual that tells you what to do when your wife dies. But this feels right."

"Do you suppose that I could come by tomorrow morning?" I tried to suppress my excitement at the prospect of getting to peek around his house.

"Sure. How about nine o'clock?" Then he asked the last question you'd expect to hear from a grieving widower: "Uh, by the way, not that it matters, but do you know if these donations are tax deductible?"

"Yes," I said. "Yes, they are."

EIGHTEEN

I drove to Leo's house on Tuesday morning, my energy fueled by two large cups of coffee and a zest for snooping. This time, I parked in his driveway and checked out the yard: an overgrown privet hedge thick with maple saplings, a few rhododendrons and azaleas, a couple of peonies clinging to life, and—damn!—nothing even remotely like foxglove. If there'd been foxglove here, the police would have found it by now, wouldn't they? Yes, almost certainly.

I opened the trunk of the car and grabbed a cardboard box and the garbage bags I'd brought for Francie's clothing. Feeling superstitious, I avoided the front door, the one through which Francie's body had been carried, and went to the back door. I rang the bell and waited several minutes for Leo to answer.

"Chloe. Hi. Excuse my shirt. It never occurred to me to

learn how to do laundry. Isn't that stupid?" Leo looked dreadful. His eyes were puffy, his hair unruly. His shirt was not only dirty but buttoned wrong. Had he relied on his wife to align buttons and buttonholes? Once I'd entered the kitchen, it was clear that laundry was far from the only kind of housework left undone. Every surface of the kitchen was piled with dirty dishes, empty and half-empty take-out containers, newspapers, junk mail, and tons of other debris, including four grocery bags that hadn't been unpacked and, scattered all over the floor, what must have been at least two pounds of coffee beans. Leo waved his arm around. "Sorry about this. I had no idea how much Francie did around the house."

"Really, it's no problem. I don't know what to say after what you've been through. I'm glad I can do something," I said in my best social worker voice. "Why don't you show me where Francie's closet is, okay?"

"Sure. It's up here," he said as he started for the stairs. "But I've got to warn you. Avoid the bathroom where, uh, where Francie, you know . . ." Leo stammered. "The police spent hours up there, but they didn't . . . It hasn't been cleaned. Can you believe that? It's their job to find out what happened to my wife, and they leave that filth in there for me?"

As if it were a police job to scrub the bathroom for him! Leo might reasonably want to avoid sanitizing the area himself, but couldn't he have hired a cleaning service? Or some sort of company that specialized in hazardous waste? It was obscene that the mess had been sitting there for over a week now. Was Leo just going to seal off the bathroom forever? I tried to remember the exact words I'd used in offering Leo my help. I prayed that I hadn't been foolish enough to tell him that I'd do absolutely anything. As we passed through the dining room and the front hall, I noticed yet more litter as well as the need for dusting and vaccuming. The mess seriously detracted from what was otherwise a beautiful house. The multitude of large and brightly colored art pieces on the walls were so cheery that I momentarily forgot this was the scene of the crime.

"Leo," I said speedily, "there are companies that can be hired to clean anything. I can help you find one, if you like."

"Really? That would be wonderful. I just haven't known what to . . . Here you go." We entered the master bedroom. "Thank God there's another bathroom off the master suite. That's Francie's closet." Leo pointed to an oversized walk-in closet with sliding doors that were partly open. "Please, take anything you think these women could use. Francie has enough clothes to outfit a hundred homeless women. I'll be back in a minute." Leo left the room.

Because of the condition of the rest of the house, I was surprised to find the bedroom tidy. Amazingly, the bed had been made, and Leo had taken care to arrange the bright blue bedding and pillows to resemble a guest room at a Vermont inn. Expensive off-white Berber carpeting was stain-free, and the four windows that let bright light into the room gave it a fresh, unsullied appearance.

Leo's promise to be right back suggested that he intended to stay while I gathered Francie's clothes. Since I couldn't order him to leave so that I could tear the house apart looking for clues, I had to make the most of my time. Leo's return would require me to go through the closet. Consequently, I took advantage of his absence to peer under the bed, where I found nothing but a few dust bunnies, and to take a quick look at the night tables, on each of which sat a small lamp. The table on the left-hand side had nothing else. The second night table had, in addition to the lamp, an empty bottle of mineral water, a box of tissues, a clock radio, and a stack of magazines, with a recent issue of the *New Yorker* on top.

Afraid of getting caught, I turned to the closet, which was jammed full of women's clothes. Every one of its many shelves, drawers, hangers, and shoe racks was occupied by some item of clothing. Tall boots and plastic storage containers teetered at the edge of the top shelf; I resolved to keep an eye out for falling objects. I set down my cardboard box, shook out a garbage bag, and started to remove clothes from hangers. Francie had had a large wardrobe in a narrow range of colors and styles. The predominant shades were brown, beige, and gray. The boldest color was dark navy. Many items were conservative pieces from Talbots. I was learning nothing that would contribute to my amateur investigation, but the good news was that many of Francie's things would work perfectly as interview outfits for the women at the shelter. I folded simple sweaters, blazers, and dresses and collected at least twenty-five pairs of nondescript dress shoes.

Toward one end of the heavy wooden rod that supported the hanging clothes were several large zippered plastic clothing bags. Unzipping one, I was nearly blinded by color. The outfits in this bag were radically different from everything else I'd seen. Yanking the bag open, I fingered through a slinky pink outfit, an ugly flower-print dress, a series of short skirts, and even a man's suit. I unzipped the next bag and found additional outfits as outrageous as those I'd just examined. I stood on tiptoe and pulled down a printed storage box that turned out to contain hats. Checking another box, I found high-heeled shoes, brooches, eyeglasses, and scarves, all in styles radically different from the dull, conservative look of the clothing displayed openly in the closet. Yet another box contained wigs: long hair, short hair, curly hair, blonde, brunette—you name it, and Francie had a wig for it. I sat on the floor of the closet surrounded by a mound of bizarre . . . outfits? No, not outfits. Costumes. These had to be costumes. But why? Why had Francie been dressing up as other people?

"Francie's little secret." Leo's voice made me jump."I guess I should have warned you," he said. "The things in the boxes won't work for the homeless women, will they?" He produced an almost hysterical-sounding laugh. "Or maybe they will! Oh, what the hell does it matter now?" Leo tossed his hands up as he spoke. "Maybe you'll think it's funny. What the heck! Francie wrote restaurant reviews. You may have heard of her. The Boston Mystery Diner? She got the idea for the costumes from Ruth Reichl. You know that food critic from the *New York Times*? Francie made reservations under false names, and she'd go to dinner all gussied up in one of these outfits. Sometimes I'd go with her. I've got some, uh, costumes, I guess you'd say, too." Although I tried to keep my face neutral, my expression may have been what prompted him to add, "She wanted to do fair reviews and not get recognized as a reviewer every time she walked into a restaurant."

Francie? Francie, of all people, was the notorious Mystery Diner? Unbelievable! And fair reviews? Those I'd read had been ruthless, unforgiving, and cruelly unfair.

"Wow," I said. "I had no idea. For some reason I'd always assumed that the Mystery Diner was a man. Everyone does, I think. I don't know why. Wow," I said again.

"She was the most prominent food critic in Boston. She was very astute and had high standards, so her praise meant a lot to local restaurants."

Praise? I wanted to ask. *What praise?* Well, maybe in reviews I hadn't seen.

"Please, Chloe," Leo continued. "Don't tell anyone." He spoke earnestly, even urgently. "Francie was proud of what she did and so proud of not being recognized. She took her job seriously, loved what she did, and there's no reason to spoil her game now."

"Of course. Sure." I nodded.

Nothing about Leo's statements or demeanor even began to hint at any comprehension of how violently his wife was hated in the restaurant community. As far as I could tell, he believed that Francie's reviews had been admirably honest, and he failed to comprehend the damage and devastation they had inflicted on the hardworking staff of the restaurants she had trashed.

As quickly as possible, I finished packing the clothes I wanted and left behind the wild costumes. No woman at the shelter needed to set off for a job interview sporting a neon dress and a blonde wig or, heaven forbid, a man's suit; the shelter did not encourage employment in prostitution, nor did it seek to promote cross-dressing. Before I left, I thumbed through a phone book that Leo dug up, copied down the numbers of a few cleaning services that could take care of the bathroom situation, and left Leo the task of making the calls.

During the entire drive home, I puzzled over the revelation that Francie had been the Mystery Diner. I'd previously seen Francie as a harmless, innocent victim. In contrast, the Mystery Diner's reviews I'd read had been downright vicious. Of course, I hadn't looked at the Mystery Diner's complete works, so to speak; maybe from time to time she'd lavished praise on a chef. And I was baffled by Leo's apparent obliviousness to the impact of the reviews and the anger they generated. Or was he playing dumb? And if Leo had murdered his wife, why was he keeping her secret identity a secret? The Mystery Diner's reviews had provided many chefs and restaurant owners with a potential motive for murder. If the Mystery Diner had torn Josh to pieces, I'd have felt like killing her myself! Why wasn't Leo pointing the finger of suspicion at the restaurant people whom Francie had enraged? Why wasn't he deflecting suspicion to people who'd hated her?

Marlee had a defaced copy of the Mystery Diner's beastly review of Alloy pinned up in her kitchen. Someone, probably Marlee herself, had stabbed that review with a knife. Digger, too, had had a rotten review. His attitude was more mixed than Marlee's; he seemed torn between anger at the review and acceptance of it as an inevitable part of the restaurant business. Still, Francie's reviews had excoriated both Marlee and Digger, both of whom had had the opportunity to add digitalis to the food that Francie had eaten. According to Leo, Francie's identity as the Mystery Diner was a secret. Oh, really? Just how secret had her secret been? Leo had revealed it to me readily enough. Had he told others during Francie's lifetime? Had she?

Robin. Yes, if Robin had had a prior relationship with Leo, he might have told her that Francie was the Mystery Diner, and Robin absolutely could have passed that information on to her good friend, Marlee. What's more, Robin could have let it slip to Marlee that Leo was going to be the shopper chosen for the filming of *Chefly Yours*. If so, Marlee would have known ahead of time that she'd be in Francie's kitchen and would thus have the opportunity to poison food that Francie, the despised reviewer, would eat.

I peeled into my parking space, left the clothes in the car, flew up the stairs to my condo, rushed to the computer, and searched for Francie's reviews online. I'd only glimpsed the review posted in Alloy's kitchen; I hadn't really read it, in part because the knife sticking out of the center had distracted me. The review I found on the Web was worse than I'd imagined, far worse than merely scathing. As I read it, one damning sentence after another hit my eye:

What is meant to be a sleek and artful presentation is instead an exercise in pretension . . . Each dish is comprised of unsightly lumps; not only do these lumps not relate to one another in any conceivable way, but each is inedible on its own . . . Despite the chef's effort at contemporary plate arrangement, I found the microgreen and herb-stem garnishes unattractive; far from whetting my appetite, they destroyed it. My roasted chicken had what appeared to be a small branch poking out of its thigh. I appreciate fresh herbs as much as the next diner, but there is no need to overwhelm a guest with what amounts to piles of shrubbery . . . The service? Worse than what one would expect at a fast-food joint . . . The trio of beef was enough to convince this reviewer that I would rather stick kabob skewers in my eyes than return to this restaurant.

Good God! What a horrible review! And, unfortunately for Marlee and Alloy, it was all the more horrible for being accurate—or at least consistent with my own experience. Perhaps the Mystery Diner's reviews—Francie's reviews—had, after all, been fair, just as Leo had claimed. Mean and nasty, yes, but on target. Still, it would have been possible to critique Alloy honestly yet tactfully, whereas Francie had clearly prided herself on snarky, savage reviews that titillated readers and sold newspapers.

But the piece on Alloy might be an aberration. Consequently, I looked up Francie's review of Digger's restaurant. After tearing apart the whole notion of small servings and declaring tapas to be a lame excuse to overcharge patrons for the supposed novelty of minuscule plates, the review went on to blast the quality of the food. It was one thing for a chef to hear that the service was poor or that restaurant was unacceptably noisy, but to attack the taste of the food was to hit a chef where it hurt. In contrast to the review of Alloy, this one didn't ring true. Although I'd never been to the tapas restaurant where Digger worked, all the meals that he had ever cooked for me had been delicious. The Mystery Diner had made some direct assaults on Digger. For example:

> *Whoever cooked the smoked sausage with olives and tomatoes should throw in his knives and not even bother returning to culinary school. In the opinion of this reviewer, the dish was a pure insult.*

Ouch! Digger had given me the impression that the review was a harsh critique of the restaurant as a whole and not a personal attack on his skill as a chef. In reality, Francie had slung insult after personal insult at Digger. She'd called him, among other things, an "untalented fool" and an "ordinary hack." My close reading made me question Digger's apparently mellow attitude about the review. Maybe Digger had simply been saving face. Still, at La Morra, Digger had repeatedly referred to the Mystery Diner as "he" and had given no indication that he knew the reviewer's true identity. Plus, Digger had seemed genuinely clueless about gardening.

Stinging with empathy for chefs who'd been Francie's victims, I struggled to be unbiased. Digger was Josh's friend and therefore my friend. Marlee was not. Even when I took my bias into account, it remained true that Marlee was the one who'd shown outward hostility to the Mystery Diner. Hard though I tried, I couldn't shake the image of that knife in the corkboard.

NINETEEN

AFTER reading those beastly reviews, cooking was the last thing I felt like doing. For all I knew, Francie's spirit might appear in my kitchen and criticize my efforts! But Adrianna and Owen were coming for dinner to go over the wedding ceremony. They were writing their own vows—at least they were *supposed* to be writing them—and I'd put together some ideas for the rest of the ceremony. All of a sudden, I felt a sense of urgency: unless I finalized my part, I'd find myself standing in front of an expectant crowd and babbling incoherently about the joys of marriage.

I ran out to the store and returned with everything I needed to make a simple pasta salad. My recipe had two big advantages: it was easy, and it produced one of the few pasta dishes I'd ever made that tasted even better the next day than it did when it had just been cooked. It consisted of fettuccine tossed with shrimp, avocado, red onion, tomatoes, Calamata olives, fresh basil, balsamic vinegar, olive oil, and Parmesan cheese. Francie's ghost failed to materialize while I cooked, so I felt confident that I hadn't offended the dead. I set aside the shrimp and the pasta, which would be cooked just before the dish was served, and I mixed the other ingredients.

When Ade and Owen showed up at seven, one look at Adrianna told me that she was seriously annoyed with her husband-to-be.

"What's up? Why are you making that face?" I asked.

"You won't believe what Owen has done!" Ade turned to her fiancé. "If you think there's any chance that we're using those vows—"

"She's really overreacting," Owen protested before Adrianna could finish. "I just wanted to mix it up a bit. You know, do something untraditional. We don't want a formal, stuffy wedding ceremony, right? So I came up with something unique!" Owen handed me a folder that contained a sheet of paper with handwritten vows.

I eyed him suspiciously and braced myself. Owen's idea of untraditional or unique was most people's idea of crazy. I dragged a kitchen chair into my small living room and let Ade and Owen take the couch. Ade sat on one side of it with her head tilted and resting on her hand, while Owen sat at the opposite end of the couch with his hands solemnly folded. Despite the separation between the two of them, I could see that Adrianna was muffling a smile.

I skimmed through Owen's proposed vows. Oh no! "Seriously?"

Serious was exactly what my question was not. As if there were any possibility that I'd deliver these lines! Incredibly and ridiculously, Owen had composed wedding vows à la Dr. Seuss:

> *Do you take Ade as your bride?*
> *Will you stay loyal and filled with pride?*
> *Will you love her all your life?*
> *Even in times of marital strife?*
> *Will you take out the weekly trash,*
> *And provide for her some ready cash?*
> *Is it your wish that I proclaim,*
> *That she shall take your given last name?*

I couldn't bring myself actually to read the rest. Instead, I ran my protesting eyes down the sheet of paper. After catching sight of an especially hideous rhyme—something about a wedding ring, wanting to sing, and making Owen feel like a king—I gave up. Staring at Owen, I said, "I'm looking at you now, Owen, and you look like a perfectly normal human being, but it turns out that you are not." Owen, in fact, looked not only normal but even handsomer than usual. Maybe Ade's pregnancy glow had rubbed off on him. His cheeks had a rosy tint that brightened his fair complexion, and his black hair could've been primped by a *GQ* stylist. In case I'd failed to make my meaning plain on the first try, I said, "You're an idiot, Owen. I love you, but you're an idiot."

"Hallelujah!" Ade shouted and clapped her hands. "A voice of reason!"

"Come on, it's funny. Don't you think it's funny?" Owen pleaded.

"A wedding ceremony is not supposed to be funny," I instructed. "You don't have to use the traditional vows, but no way in hell am I reading this." I crumpled up the paper and flung it at his head.

"Yeah, and what was that business about giving me cash?" Ade demanded. "You don't talk about money in a ceremony. Or trash, for that matter."

"Okay, okay, I give in! But it's a happy occasion. I want everyone to have fun."

My voice suffused with the authority vested in me by the Commonwealth of Massachusetts, I said, "This is the first and probably only wedding at which I'm going to officiate, and I'm not going to make a freak out of myself by reciting a bunch of dumb rhymes." Fortunately, although I hadn't expected anything quite so preposterous as Owen's doggerel, I wasn't caught off guard. Suspecting that both Adrianna and Owen were more attached to the idea of writing their own vows than they'd be to the process of composing them, I'd done my wedding-vow homework and consequently was able to hand them copies of material I'd assembled from Web sites and written myself. "What about these?"

"I don't want that business about obeying the groom in there," Ade said as she reached for the papers.

Owen's face brightened. "Maybe we could put in a vow of *dis*obedience. I will never do anything Ade tells me to do!"

"You better watch it," Ade warned him. "Your frivolous attitude is making me worry. Did you get your tux yet? I swear, Owen, if you got some garish tuxedo in loud colors, I'll scream."

"I wouldn't do that." To my ear, Owen sounded all too serious. "I got the boring black one like you told me."

I'd have bet good money that Owen was lying, but Ade apparently believed him, and she didn't need to be more riled up than than she already was. As she read the vows I'd put together, Ade kept nodding, and even Owen agreed that although my suggestions didn't rhyme, they would work.

"Do you trust me to put together the service?" I asked them.

"Yeah, we do," Owen rubbed Ade's back. He looked at her and wiped the tears from her cheeks. "Babe, it's going to be a wonderful day."

I said, "Good. I'll do the whole wedding service, and all you'll have to do is repeat after me." Adrianna still looked stressed out, but at least she'd moved close to Owen and was leaning against him. "Relax," I said. "There's nothing to worry about. This is all fun stuff going on, okay?"

I cooked the pasta and the shrimp, and tossed them together with the vegetable mixture. As we ate dinner in the living room, we talked food.

"How's the menu coming?" Owen asked.

"Oh, I almost forgot! The food is going to be out of this world! Even though it's still August, I know you wanted a fall menu, so Josh is going to put out an amazing spread with that in mind."

"I know I'm a pain, but I always wanted to get married in the fall, and since that won't work out," she said, patting her belly, "we can at least eat like it's fall. I'm probably driving Josh crazy."

I brushed aside her worries. "Not a big deal. You know how Josh loves a challenge. He's going to do an extravagant pumpkin stew cooked in a pumpkin, a salad with dried cranberries and maple vinaigrette, tenderloin medallions, a roasted rack of lamb with grape-chili jam and goat cheese sauce. What else? I can't remember it all right now, but you'll love it."

"Sounds amazing," Owen said happily.

"Josh is off on Friday to prep all the food. I think he's coming here to do it. I'll actually get to spend some time with him, so it'll work out for well for me."

I sounded more optimistic than I felt. When Josh was here, he'd be in his chef mode, and we'd have no real conversation. Still, it would be good to be together, and our shared focus on the wedding might restore our relationship.

I sent Ade and Owen off with the promise of a beautiful ceremony with vows that didn't rhyme. After cleaning up the kitchen, I spent an hour at the computer writing the service and quit only when I was so tired that my fingers started typing in Dr. Seuss style. I collapsed in bed with the intention of sleeping in the next morning. The prospect was shattered by the sound of feet pounding on my front door.

TWENTY

"CHLOE? Let me in!"

I glanced at the clock. What the heck was Josh doing here at eight a.m.?

I flung back the sheet and forced myself to stagger to the door. "Hi, honey," I managed sleepily. I rubbed my eyes and stared in confusion at Josh. My boyfriend had evidently kicked my door because his arms were full of trays and containers covered in plastic wrap. A small cardboard box was teetering off the top of the pile, and I grabbed a squirt bottle just as it began to fall. "What are you doing here? Oh, my God! Is today Friday?" I really was not awake yet. Panicking, I thought, *Oh, no! It's the day before the wedding!*

"No, no. It's Wednesday. I just got the rest of the week off, and I thought I'd start cooking for Saturday. I've got a ton to prep, and my kitchen is a wreck." In my opinion, the

191

entire apartment that he shared with his sous-chef, Snacker, was a chronic disaster area, but I didn't say so. "The goddamn stove broke again, and Snacker left a huge mess in there. Seriously, there's no way I'm doing his dishes again, and he's working at Simmer while I'm off, so who knows when they'll get done. Can I use your kitchen?"

"Yeah. Of course." I plodded into the kitchen and set the squirt bottle box on the table. "Coffee. I need coffee."

I worked on brewing a pot of caffeine while Josh returned to his car for more food. I was psyched to have Josh here but totally surprised that Gavin had given him so much time off. Josh was lucky to get one day a week. Maybe Gavin had finally come to his senses and realized how badly he'd been treating his gifted and hardworking chef. Josh had had no vacation time whatsoever since he'd started at the restaurant last year, and Gavin must have realized that Josh was about to crack. Oddly enough, even though Josh would be cooking like a madman for the next few days, I knew that he was looking forward to catering the wedding. Chefs! For me, a vacation meant blue skies, burning sun, sterling ocean, fruity cocktails, and skimpy bathing suits, but Josh wasn't the type to lounge around on a beach and do nothing all day. What did he do when he finally had time off? Cook.

"Okay, I have to make the pasta and then marinate the vegetables for the strudels . . ." Josh said to himself as he checked off a mental list on his fingers.

"What kind of pasta are you doing?" My question was vital. I could probably live on pasta alone.

"A butter-poached lobster on tagliatelle with a yuzu pesto and mushrooms." Josh moved his eyebrows up and down and then winked at me. "You like the sound of that one?"

"Amazing," I said, echoing Owen. "Except, what on earth is yuzu?"

"Japanese citrus fruit. Sour. You'll love it."

"Strudels. What's in those?" I craned my head to get a look into my chef's containers.

"Grilled vegetables rolled in puff pastry. Fantastic." Josh clapped his hands. "All right! Outta my kitchen!" he ordered in a joking voice. "I've got a million vinaigrettes to mix up."

"Yes, sir."

"Oh, wait. Here. Can you charge my cell phone for me?" Josh handed me his cell and charger. "Thanks, babe."

I went into the bedroom, plugged in Josh's phone, and worked on Ade and Owen's ceremony. Who'd have guessed that writing a wedding service would be so difficult? At the end of two hours, when my script for the wedding was in pretty good shape, I decided to go snoop in my kitchen to see what Josh was up to.

"Yum. What's in that?" I sniffed a tray of vegetables that were marinating in an aromatic mixture.

"Not telling." Josh grinned. Then he snapped his fingers. "Oh, damn. I forgot to pick up the beef tenderloin and the duck breasts I ordered. That was dumb. I'm going to run and get them. Back in a few." Josh kissed me and ran out the door before I could even say good-bye.

I was proofing the ceremony when Josh's cell rang. In case the call had something to do with food for the wedding, I answered. "Hello?"

"Ah, yes, is Josh there?" The woman spoke with a heavy French accent.

"No, he should be back soon. Can I take a message for him?"

"Er, yes. Tell him Yvette called. He has my number."

"Sure. I'll tell him." I clapped the phone shut.

Who the hell was Yvette? On the night we'd been at the

emergency room, Josh had had a call from a woman. The other day when he'd been here, he'd again had a call from a woman. He'd certainly never mentioned Yvette to me. I hated the knots that were forming in my stomach. When Josh returned, I didn't give him the message. He was keeping some kind of secret from me, but I wasn't up for having it revealed right now.

Besides, I had my own secrets.

"Look at this beauty!" Josh gleefully held out the large beef tenderloin. "And the duck breasts are beautiful. I'm going to do those in a red wine and orange sauce. I'm on fire today!"

I had to agree. Josh was in the cooking zone I'd come to know so well: all of his creative juices were flowing, and he was reveling in an endorphin rush.

His phone rang again. I ran to my bedroom, grabbed it, checked caller ID, and returned to the kitchen. "It's Robin," I said. "You want to take it?"

"Sure." Josh wiped his hands on a dishcloth and took the call. "Hey, Robin. What's up?'

I shamelessly eavesdropped on the conversation. Without even hearing what Robin had to say, I could tell that she was slathering on the praise and making grand promises. "Really? Thanks so much . . . Good, good. I'm glad . . . Excellent news . . . You think? Wow!" Josh hung up and turned to me. "Guess what? Robin called to tell me that we're going to film the next episode on Tuesday. That's a relief."

Reluctantly, I said, "Josh, I found out something kind of strange."

"What?" Josh began finely chopping a pile of herbs.

"It turns out that Robin and Marlee are friends. Good friends. It seems pretty likely that this supposed competition is rigged so that Marlee will win." As much as I hated to dash Josh's hopes of winning his own TV show, I had to tell him.

Josh stopped his knife work and stared at me in confusion. "What?"

"Josh, I know. I understand. It's rotten. It's unfair. It's messed up. And not that anything would make it all right, but let me tell you that Marlee's kitchen is filthy, and her food sucks. And on top of all that, I think she's the one who killed Francie."

"Marlee? Mousy Marlee is a killer? You're crazy."

"Josh, Francie was the Mystery Diner." I let that sink in for a minute. "You should see what she wrote about Alloy."

I filled Josh in. In particular, I told him about the defaced review posted in Alloy's kitchen.

Josh was skeptical. "First of all, Chloe, even if Robin and Marlee are friends, it doesn't mean that she's necessarily going to win. It's up to the viewers who vote. And second, I don't think that anyone who was part of the show killed Francie. For a lousy review? Chefs are used to crummy reviews. It happens to all of us, and we don't all run out and kill the reviewer. If we did, there'd be a trail of evil-reviewer bodies spread out across the country. I still think it was one of Evan and Willie's stupid pranks that turned deadly."

In the spirit of full disclosure, I recounted the stories I'd heard at Ade's shower. In describing Evan and Willie's unfunny practical jokes to Josh, I again started to worry about their guilt.

"You see? That's what I'm talking about," Josh said. "Dropping rocks on someone's head? Sending their brother skateboarding toward a death trap? Owen is lucky he survived growing up in a house with those two."

"God, you don't think they'll do anything at the wedding, do you?"

"Well . . ." Josh spoke slowly. "I talked to Owen the other day when he dropped off Simmer's seafood order."

"And?" I said, panicking.

"He told me that Evan and Willie have been threatening to show up at the wedding with shotguns. You know? Shotgun wedding."

"What? They'd better do no such thing! The last thing those two nutballs need is to get their hands on shotguns. Does Ade know about this?"

"No, and you're not going to tell her. Owen said he'd convinced them not to do anything stupid like that on his wedding day. It'll be fine."

My lovingly crafted script for the wedding service made no provision for any such vile interruption. What if they made good on their threat? They'd catch hell from me, but I had no idea how I'd give them hell without ruining the wedding. As for Adrianna, she might just turn the shotguns on them.

By late afternoon, Josh, having finished the preparations he could do three days before the wedding, was crashed out asleep on the couch while *The Usual Suspects* DVD played on the television. To avoid awakening him, I went to the bedroom and spent an hour and a half on the phone confirming wedding arrangements. The white tent would be set up tomorrow, Thursday, and then the tables, chairs, linens, china, glasses, and silverware would be delivered on Friday. The order for champagne, wine, liquor, and ice was set, as was the delivery on the day of the wedding, when the floral decorations, bouquets, and boutonnieres would also arrive.

My fridge was brimming with gourmet food and fresh ingredients. I rooted through the produce, decided that Josh could spare a few items, and made a quick trip to the local seafood store to pick up a bag of mussels for a simple but aromatic mussel bouillabaisse. Josh was still snoozing when I returned. I thinly sliced green and red peppers, fennel, and onions, and then quartered a few tomatoes and began sautéeing the vegetables in butter. I added tomato paste, wine, and garlic, and let the mixture cook for ten minutes. The smell was already wonderful, and when I added clam juice, it got even better. I turned the heat down a bit to let the pot simmer. About an hour later, when Josh woke up, I tossed in the mussels and a pinch of saffron. An advantage of having a chef boyfriend who cooked in my kitchen was that Josh routinely left interesting spices and seasonings, including luxury items like saffron.

When the mussels opened, I dished out large bowlfuls for both of us and was pleased to get a compliment: "These mussels rock, babe." But when we'd finished eating, Josh fell back asleep on the couch, so I crawled into bed by myself.

On Thursday morning Josh continued with his wedding preparations, but my own wedding duties meant that I couldn't stay to smell his latest creations. When I was about to leave, the two cats sat poised on the small kitchen table, following Josh's every move in the hope that he'd drop a piece of meat.

"Inga, Gato, and I have this all under control. Don't you worry about us!" Josh was slightly manic today. Waving an oversized wooden spoon around, he announced, "Inga is in charge of cutting the pasta, and Gato will supervise her."

"That's reassuring. What are you working on this morning?"

Josh checked his prep list for the wedding. "Tabouleh, fruit chutney, celery root soup, butternut squash puree, fennel puree, and pickled peppers. That's just to start. Easy stuff, though."

Leaving Josh to cook and, evidently, to train cats as

sous-chefs, I went to a boutique in Brookline to pick up my dress and my mother's. Adrianna had wanted us to choose our own dresses, and she hadn't wanted us in traditional bridal-party wear, so we were saved from having to sport pastel satin with poofy sleeves. I was wearing an adorable silk taffeta sleeveless dress in a soft shade that the salesperson referred to as "chocolate." The dress had a fitted bodice, a scoop neck, and a pleated skirt. My mother had picked out a classically tailored suit in periwinkle blue with a beaded shell in a darker blue to go underneath. A wedding-party miracle: outfits we would wear again!

Instead of returning home, I decided to deliver our wedding finery to my parents' house. Otherwise, I'd have risked leaving our beautiful things behind on the wedding day. When I pulled up to my parents' house, the sight of the gigantic white tent being erected in their yard made the wedding vividly real: Adrianna honestly was getting married! Filled with excitement, I grabbed the garment bag from the car and practically skipped over to my mother, who was standing outside supervising the tent crew.

"Look at this!" I cried. "The tent is going to be fantastic!"

"The tent is fine. It's the yard that's the problem," my mother growled.

I glanced around, looking for dead shrubs or insect-infested plants. "What are you talking about? The yard looks great."

"No, it doesn't look great. It's late August, and almost everything is past its bloom time. I should have planted more late-blooming flowers when we decided to host the wedding here. Dammit!" My mother crossed her arms and continued to survey her garden with dissatisfaction. "Dammit!" she repeated.

"This event isn't actually a garden tour, Mom. It's a wedding. And we've got plenty of floral arrangements coming. It'll be fine."

"No, it won't be fine. Everything out here is shabby and blowsy."

My poor mother was funneling all of her anxiety about the wedding into unhappiness about her lovely yard. In a way, I couldn't blame her. None of us had thrown a wedding party before. "Well, we do have our outfits," I said. "I just picked them up. I'm going to put them in the house." I gave my mother a hug. "Please don't worry. This wedding is going to be perfect."

TWENTY-ONE

ON Friday, the day before the wedding, I awoke to a scene of devastation. Entering the kitchen in search of coffee, I stared in horror at the apparent evidence that the explosive force of a small bomb had hurled cooking implements and food items everywhere. The bomb had a name: Josh. My boyfriend, in full cooking mode, was preparing a salmon mousse while simultaneously parcooking large pieces of meat on the stove top.

"How's it going, Josh?"

"Good. Good, I think. Thank God your father is grilling dinner tonight."

"We'll see if you thank him later. Dad has the enthusiasm, if not the skill."

By braving the wreckage of the kitchen, I managed to make coffee. As soon as I'd had a cup of it, I got ready to leave for my parents' house, where Ade and I were going to spend the night. Ade had insisted that even though the word *traditional* described nothing about the wedding, she still wanted to spend the night apart from Owen. Furthermore, she was determined that on Saturday, he wouldn't see her before the ceremony.

I packed a bag with almost every one of the hundreds of beauty-supply items I owned as well as with my digital camera and with clothes for tonight's rehearsal and dinner. Later in the day, I would pick up Adrianna and return to my parents' house with her.

"Josh, are you going to be able to handle all of this yourself?" I wrinkled my brow as I watched oil splatter out of a Dutch oven.

"Trust me, babe," Josh said with a wink. "I'm in my element here. I guarantee everyone will be blown away. Besides, I'll have help tomorrow. Digger will be there to deal with the kitchen during the ceremony while I'm standing up there with Owen. And that Emilio kid'll be there, too, right? Your mother said he was going to do whatever we needed."

Emilio. Yum. I shook all thoughts of that hottie out of my head. "Okay, then. I'm off. I guess I'll see you tonight."

"Catch you later, hon." Josh didn't stop to give me a hug or a kiss.

I arrived at my parents' house just as a delivery truck was pulling in. The chairs, tables, dishes, and glasses were there right on time. The white tent was fully set up now, too, and looked incredibly elegant. Things were coming together! Even the weather was cooperating. Today was quite hot, but the forecast for tomorrow promised temperatures in the mid to low seventies and, thank heaven, clear skies.

"Mom?" I called as I entered the living room and dropped my bags on the couch.

"Chloe? Is that you?" Mom poked her head out of the kitchen. "We have an emergency."

Oh, no! By foolishly telling myself that everything was coming together, I'd jinxed the wedding. Grimly, I asked, "What's going on?"

"Come look at this." My mother's voice was shaking.

I followed Mom as she led the way through the house to the front door and across the lawn to the tent. At the entrance, she came to a dramatic halt. *"This,"* she said with disgust, "is where Adrianna will appear! *This* is where the bride will enter! Can you believe it?"

"What the heck are you talking about?"

"Chloe! It's dismal! And barren! We need plants. More plants. Lots of greenery! I need you to run down to the nursery and get . . . plants! Lots of them!" With the frantic air of someone boldly averting disaster, she gave me directions to the nursery, which emerged as the one owned by Emilio's family. "Take the van. It's here, fortunately, so that will save you some time. Charge whatever you get to our account there. And splurge! Go nuts! I want tons of plants."

"Mom, the flowers are arriving tomorrow—"

"I know that! But this tent is mammoth, and we're not going to have it look empty. Get plants with height! And lots of blooms! Hanging plants, too! Run!"

My mother was having a floral breakdown.

I was in no mood for an argument. Consequently, I refrained from challenging her insistence that the tent looked desolate and was thus in dire need of the help that plants would provide. Fortunately, the van parked at the end of the driveway was one of the new ones rather than the old gray rattletrap that had unhappy associations. Unfortunately, however, the nursery was only a few miles from the house; I'd have preferred a long respite from my mother's frenzy.

Nursery turned out to be a misleading term for Emilio's family's sprawling, impressive garden center, which had eight large greenhouses and a main building with a garden-supply store, as well as two or three big outdoor areas devoted to trees, shrubs, and small plants of all kinds. I found a wagon and began strolling the aisles of the first greenhouse in search of plants that would appease my mother—in other words, horticultural tranquilizers. Knowing my mother as I did, I avoided anything that would have to be planted in the ground. It would have been just like Mom to decide that the whole family had to spend the rest of the day and night digging holes and planting shrubs.

"Chloe?"

I whipped around to see Emilio before me. "Hi," I gasped. "I'm looking for plants," I added stupidly, as if there were thousands of other reasons for pushing a wagon through a greenhouse.

"Do you need any help?" Oh, those darn dimples.

I explained my mother's instructions, and Emilio nodded. "Sure. Why don't you come with me. I can help you."

Can you ever, Emilio.

He added, somewhat disappointingly, "We've got a bunch of new fall plants in terra-cotta containers."

Within minutes, we'd made so many selections that we needed a second cart. "I can't believe I've never been in here before," I said as I admired the many healthy plants. "This is a wonderful nursery."

"Thanks. Let's check over here, too. We've got tons of perennials and biennials that are seriously discounted because it's the end of the season. They're in pots. You won't have to sink them in the ground. Some of them are in bloom. Not all, but some."

"Let's take a look," I said. "My mother will have a fit if

I show up with yellow mums like the ones in the supermarkets."

I followed Emilio into another greenhouse where, just as he'd said, there were bargain-priced perennials and biennials, some flourishing, some rather battered. I browsed the aisles and stopped in front of a group of low, green plants with some tired-looking old leaves mixed with bright new growth. I didn't have to read the labels to recognize foxglove. Foxglove! Digitalis! Lots of it, all cheap, all readily available to absolutely anyone. Oh, and all deadly, of course. Well, so much for finding out who did and didn't have a garden. Anyone, including an apartment dweller, could have bought the plants that were the source of the poison that killed Francie.

"Emilio? Have you been selling a lot of this foxglove?"

"Probably not. Most foxgloves bloom in the spring. They're not at their best right now. Look at them. But I'm not sure. I'm not always here at the nursery. Why?" he asked with curiosity. "Bethany won't want them. Your mother wants a show. For the wedding tomorrow. Not something that'll bloom next year."

"I know," I said. "It's . . . there's just something I'm wondering about. Do you think we could find out from somebody else who works here?"

Emilio had been nowhere near Leo and Francie's house on the day of her murder, of course; he couldn't possibly have had anything to do with it and was obviously not a suspect. Even so, I couldn't bring myself to admit my reason for wanting to know who'd bought foxglove. I could barely imagine how I'd phrase my purpose. *Well, Emilio, I'm leading a secret life as social work's answer to Nancy Drew.*

Happily, he didn't demand an explanation. All he said was, "Yeah, I guess I could ask my cousins." Emilio waved to a young man across the greenhouse who then approached us. Emilio began speaking rapidly in Spanish. The only word I understood was the one repeatedly spoken in English: *foxglove*. The young man kept nodding his head. Then he smiled at me and left.

"He says that they've sold lots of foxglove to lots of Americans," Emilio reported with a smile. "I don't suppose that helps you."

"I wouldn't say it narrows the field, but thanks anyway." I'd run out of time to pursue my investigations. I had to get the plants back to the house, and I had to pick up Ade. "So my mother said I could just charge all this stuff to her account," I said.

"Of course. I'll write it up."

Many hundreds of dollars later, Emilio offered to help me load the plants into the van. As we worked, he said, "I guess I'll see you at the wedding tomorrow."

"Yeah, I hear you and your cousins are going to help out. That'll be great."

"Hey." Emilio placed a potted sedum in the van and then posed charmingly with one arm against the sliding door. "I was wondering if you might want to get together sometime. After the wedding, of course. I thought I could take you out to dinner. There's a new little French restaurant on Exeter Street. In the Back Bay, near my apartment."

Oh, God. I wished that my immediate thought were something other than what it was. I should have been thinking that there was no way on earth that I'd ever be interested in anyone but Josh. As it was, all I could think was that this was an adorable, smart, socially and environmentally conscious guy who worked regular hours and . . . Hold it! The weirdness between Josh and me certainly didn't mean that I should accept Emilio's offer. Or did it? No matter what,

I couldn't just keep standing there staring at him. Mustering up the courage to respond, I said, "I'm flattered. I really am. But I have a boyfriend. Josh. He's the one doing all the cooking tomorrow."

How could my mother have failed to mention Josh when she'd asked Emilio to help? A simple statement—"My daughter's boyfriend is catering the wedding"—would have been sufficient. When things got uncomfortable tomorrow, it would be my mother's fault.

"I'm sorry. I didn't know." Emilio shrugged. "I had to try. I just got out of a relationship, and I thought I should take a stab at dating again. Let me know if anything changes."

I drove away. I wished that Emilio hadn't asked me out, and I wished that I hadn't hesitated. I exhaled deeply. After checking my watch, I decided that instead of going directly to my parents' house, I should pick up Adrianna on the way. After four tries, I finally parallel parked the van on Ade's street. Climbing the stairs to her apartment, I wondered, as I had many times before, how a humongous pregnant lady made it up these steps every day. I let myself in only to be greeted by the unmelodious sound of Kitty's voice.

"Is that what you really want to wear tonight? All right. If you think that's appropriate, be my guest."

"Mom! I swear on my baby's life that if you don't shut your—"

"Hello?" I called cheerily, hoping to abate some of the tension. "Where is the bride-to-be?"

"Chloe. Thank God." Adrianna emerged from the bathroom with a major scowl planted on her face. She wore a clingy yellow top, a white knee-length skirt, and sandals with three-inch heels. I loved it that Ade hadn't spent her pregnancy shrouded in oversized outfits. Her clothes hugged her beautiful curves and celebrated her pregnancy. In my opinion, Kitty had no reason to criticize Ade.

"Hello, Chloe." Kitty's smile was forced. "Adrianna, I just think that you could find something less . . . revealing than that outfit. You are a bride, after all. You could be less obvious."

"Less obvious? You mean I'm supposed to make it less obvious that I got knocked up before I was married?" Adrianna sounded incredulous. "You think I can hide my pregnancy? You think I'd want to? Say it, Mom. Just say it! *You* want to pretend I'm not pregnant. *You* want me to play the part of some virginal bride, right? Well, tough."

"Adrianna Zane! How dare you!" Kitty had turned an alarming shade of red. Her lips were tightly pursed.

"How dare I what? How dare I say what you're thinking? You hate that I'm pregnant. You hate Owen, and you probably hate me." Despite her raised voice, Adrianna looked remarkably calm for someone who was duking it out with her mother. "I cannot deal with you right now. I can't change how you feel and how you treat me, but I don't have to put up with it."

Kitty stood frozen, aghast at her daughter's brutal frankness.

"Chloe, I'm packed and ready to go. Mother, you can let yourself out. I'll see you tomorrow if you can drag yourself to the wedding. But I want you to leave right afterward. I don't want you around after the wedding, and I don't want you around when I give birth. Come on, let's go."

I picked up Adrianna's bags, she carried her wedding dress, and we bolted. We said nothing until we were seated in the van.

Ade managed to buckle her seat belt and then took a

look around the plant-packed van. "This is not exactly the glamorous limo ride I was expecting, but thanks for getting me."

"No problem. I thought a limo might be too pretentious and clichéd. A van packed with greenery hit me as celebratory without being excessive or trite."

"Good thinking."

I did a forty-point turn to get us out of the tight parking space. "You okay?"

"Yup. I'm quite okay. Actually, I'm fantastic." Ade smiled broadly. "I'm ready to get married, Chloe. I'm really ready. Kitty can suck it!" she cheered.

"That's my girl!" I yelled happily. "Kitty can suck it!"

TWENTY-TWO

"LOOK at the tent!" Adrianna's eyes lit up with happiness as I pulled the van to the front walkway. "It's just beautiful, isn't it, Chloe?"

"It's gorgeous. The ceremony is going to be amazing. Let's go put our things in the guest bedroom, and then we'll look around."

When my father opened the front door for us, he was humming Wagner's "Bridal Chorus."

"Oh, here we go." I rolled my eyes.

"I love it. Keep up the music, Jack." Adrianna hugged my dad.

"Can you believe this weather?" he exclaimed. "I'm going to sit out on the deck tonight and do some meditation. Did Chloe tell you I've become addicted to yoga?"

"Dad, not now!" I said, exasperated.

Mom entered the living room. "Did you get everything we need? Oh, hello, Adrianna. Isn't this fantastic? Chloe, where are the plants? Did the nursery have what we need? Jack, start unloading the plants from the van. Bring them all into the tent."

While my father obediently headed for the van, I calmed my mother down by informing her that I had enough foliage to fill four tents. Ade stifled a yawn. I took the wedding gown from her arms and asked, "Do you want to lie down for a bit while we unload the plants?"

"I think I should. I feel like I'm ready to burst."

Mom put her arm on Ade's and fired off ten or twelve questions one right after the other, including: "What has your doctor said? Does she think you're getting close to delivering? Are you having Braxton Hicks?" My mother, I suspected, had consumed one espresso too many today.

"Um, actually, I skipped my appointment this week and rescheduled it for next week. Owen and I aren't going anywhere for a honeymoon, so he'll be around to go with me." Ade saw my mother's alarmed face. "Honestly, Bethany, I feel fine. I really do. I'm just tired, that's all."

"If you say so. Make yourself at home in the guest room, and come and join us when you've gotten some rest."

My parents and I spent the next few hours moving all the nursery purchases from one place to another in the tent. Astonishingly, my mother was eventually satisfied. The ceremony would take place on one side of the tent, where white folding chairs were set up for the guests. The other side of the tent already had some tables and chairs in place. Fifty or so people made for a fairly small wedding, but additional tables would have to be added once the ceremony was over. Long tables covered in white tablecloths were ready for Josh's food. Another table would serve as the bar.

Adrianna roused herself in the late afternoon. To my relief, she looked thoroughly refreshed and even energetic. Nodding at a monstrous blue box that she held in her hands, she announced, "Nail time, ladies!"

My mother and I let Ade paint our fingernails in a shade called Sheer Tutu Pink. Meanwhile, my father prepared the grill for tonight's dinner. I called Josh, who muttered something about "crazy lamb" and "stupid pot's too small." Otherwise, I got barely an intelligible word out of him except a promise to be at the house for the rehearsal.

Josh and Owen arrived in Owen's refrigerated fish truck, which held some of the food that needed to be stored at my parents' house. "Your fridge is filled to capacity, Chloe," Josh said, "and this stuff I won't need until tomorrow."

"How is everything coming?" I asked.

"We're in good shape. Risotto is ready, squash puree is done, soup is ready. Everything. It's all good. Dinner will be fantastic tomorrow."

At six thirty, the wedding party assembled in the tent. I stood at the front of the aisle, flanked by two empty white podiums. Tomorrow, they'd hold floral baskets. Owen, Ade, Mom, Josh, and my father all sat before me in the white chairs while I went over the ceremony.

"Tomorrow," I said, "the guests will mostly seat themselves, but Evan and Willie will be here to act as ushers if needed." Owen had refused to have either of his brothers in the wedding party; he'd maintained that the risk of their misbehaving was simply too great. "Owen, come stand right here. Don't fidget, pick your nose, touch your hair, or otherwise move unless I tell you. Stand there and watch the back of the tent for your bride. Mom and Josh, when the music starts, you will walk down the aisle together, followed by Adrianna and Dad. Let's do that now." The music would be provided by nothing fancier than my MP3 player hooked up to outdoor speakers.

The members of the wedding rushed to their places, and then Josh looped my mother's arm through his and escorted her down the aisle. "Now Adrianna and Dad . . . Good. Dad, you kiss Ade's cheek, pass her off to Owen, and sit down. Wait! Owen, *you* don't kiss her now!"

"Sorry, sorry." Owen beamed. "I couldn't help myself!"

I continued. "The music will stop, and I'll begin the ceremony. That part is a secret until tomorrow, so all you need to know is that at some point I will get to the vows and ask you both to repeat what I say. And, Owen, let me dash your hopes right now. There is no rhyming. Then I will pronounce you husband and wife. *That's* when you get to kiss. Then Mom and Josh walk back up the aisle, followed by the bride and groom. That's it."

I received a small round of applause for leading such a quick rehearsal, and all of us moved to the patio by the grill. Because tomorrow would be so busy, tonight's dinner was simple: Dad was grilling chicken, and Mom had made a big salad. Josh, I could tell, was having to struggle to restrain himself from taking over at the grill. Inevitably, Dad was singeing some of the chicken pieces.

I filled a paper plate for Adrianna, who was seated next to Owen. "You got your tux, right?" I asked.

Owen nodded. "All set. I picked up mine and Josh's today."

"Can I see them?" Ade spoke nonchalantly, but I knew that she wanted to make sure that Josh and Owen would, in fact, be dressed in black and not blue.

"They're back at the apartment. I didn't want to leave them in the fish truck and take the chance they'd smell like seafood."

Adrianna looked surprised and impressed that Owen had had the foresight to avoid smelling like fish during their wedding. I felt skeptical. I didn't expect him to go out of his way to stink of seafood, of course. Still, I didn't trust him to present himself appropriately and wouldn't trust him until tomorrow when—if—he was actually standing next to me fully outfitted in the conventionally handsome attire he'd sworn to wear for the wedding.

"I'd like to make a toast." Owen rose, helped Ade out of her chair, and lifted his glass of beer into the air. "To Jack and Bethany. Before we head into the inevitable chaos tomorrow, we both want to let you know how unbelievably grateful we are to you both. You are giving us exactly the kind of wedding we want."

Ade continued. "Owen and I didn't want a formal, stuffy reception, and this dinner-party style you've put together is really us. You both know that my father is out of the picture and that my mother is not exactly the mother I would have handpicked. You two have made us feel like part of your family, and we will never forget that. And Chloe? I couldn't ask for a more loyal, special friend. I love you."

Owen wiped his eyes and put his arm around Ade. "I'm so sorry about your mother," he whispered. She nodded and lifted her lemonade. "To the Carter family!"

We all clinked glasses and traded mushy hugs and kisses.

"There is one more treat for you two," I said as I handed Owen the envelope Nana Sally had slipped to me at the end of the shower.

"Whoo hoo!" Owen yelled. "We're going to the Ritz! Nana Sally is sending us there for our wedding night." The groom did a goofy little dance that involved weird hip thrusts and snapping fingers.

Ade giggled and then managed to settle him down. "God,

I've always wanted to go there. That's going to be fantastic! Oh, and Jack and Bethany, we have something for you."

The bride and groom handed my parents a gift-wrapped box. My father was busy burning chicken, so it was my mother who opened the package and lifted out a hand-blown glass vase.

"I know it's not much," Adrianna said, "but we thought you'd like it."

"It's simply beautiful. You shouldn't have," my mother said as she admired the vase.

"Chloe, we have something for you, too." Owen gave me a piece of paper that had been rolled up and tied with a pink ribbon.

I slid off the knot and unrolled what looked like an official invitation. I read the page and looked up at my dear friends. "Are you sure?"

Ade and Owen nodded. "Absolutely."

"What does it say?" my father asked.

I cleared my throat and grinned. "They want me to be their baby's godmother."

TWENTY-THREE

THE next morning, I turned over in one of the twin beds in the guest room and looked at Ade, who was still asleep in the other bed. The bride-to-be was curled on her side, her mouth open, drool making its way down her chin. Her hair had tangled itself into such a Medusa-like mess that I decided to force her into the shower the second she woke up; if she got a look at herself in a mirror, she'd start her wedding day by freaking out.

The ceremony was at four o'clock, and it was already nine thirty. How had we slept so late? I could hear dishes clattering downstairs, and I knew that the household must be bustling with wedding preparations.

Ade snorted and woke herself up. "I'm getting married today, aren't I?" she said, stretching her arms.

"That's the plan." I got up and sat on the edge of her bed.

She rubbed her belly. "Baby, how about you move that elbow off of my bladder, okay? It's quite annoying."

"Can I feel?"

Ade nodded. "Go ahead. The baby doesn't move around as much now because it's so squished in there, but you can feel a knee. Right here." She placed my hand on the side of her stomach, and I felt something hard against my hand. "At least I think it's a knee. Might be some other body part, but there is definitely something pushing on my bladder, too."

"I know this sounds ridiculous, but I cannot believe that there's a little person in there. Right there!" I leaned in and whispered to her stomach. "Baby, it's Auntie Chloe here. Please move around so that your mommy doesn't spend the day needing to pee. Okay?"

We waited silently, hoping that the baby might actually respond to the request. Ade shook her head. "Nothing. This kid isn't budging. Maybe after I get up and walk around. Help me up."

By rolling and pushing, I got Ade out of bed. Then I walked her to the bathroom and got her into the shower without giving her the opportunity to see herself in the mirror. "I'll go get you some breakfast, okay?"

"That would be great. After that, we should get started on our hair. That's top priority, so we don't run out of time later."

"Gotcha." I tossed on my overpriced but adorable Juicy hoodie and pants, pulled my hair into a ponytail, and headed downstairs to the kitchen to see what I could find to feed Adrianna. With all the wedding food in the house, I wondered whether there were any breakfast possibilities at all.

Josh was already in the kitchen. With him were the cousin of Emilio's I'd met yesterday at the nursery and another dark-haired guy who looked so much like the first that he had to be a relative. Both of Josh's assistants were busy slicing their way through a mountain of vegetables. Josh himself was buried in the fridge, pulling out one container after another. "Morning, beautiful!" he chirped.

"You're hard at work already, huh?"

"Yup. This is Alfonso and Héctor, Emilio's cousins, who are helping me with everything."

I waved at the two cousins, and both smiled warmly at me. I was glad that Josh spoke Spanish—or at least spoke what he called "kitchen Spanish," enough of the language to communicate his culinary needs. "I met one of them, Alfonso, when I was picking up all those plants for my mother, but I didn't get his name. So Emilio is here, too, I assume?" Not that I was itching to have Josh and Emilio in the same room.

"Apparently, but I haven't run into him yet. He might be out in the tent helping rearrange the six thousand plants and setting things up outside."

I grabbed a box of cereal, a gallon of milk, and some bowls and spoons and headed back upstairs to deliver breakfast to the bride.

"Chloe, you're up. Is Adrianna awake, too?" My mother stopped me as I was starting up the staircase.

"She's in the shower. She wants to do our hair as soon as possible. Sound good? Is everything going all right so far?"

"Mostly. I had to send Emilio to go pick up the flowers. The store messed things up. He should be back within an hour. Other than that, I think we're on track."

"Where's Dad?" By now, my mother must have put him to work.

"Oh . . . um . . ."

"Dad," I said. "My father. Your husband. Jack. The man who burns chicken."

"Chloe, I know who Jack is. He's around somewhere. Don't worry about him. Just tell me when Adrianna is ready for me."

Since Ade was still in the shower, I left the breakfast supplies on the dresser and made the beds. When I went back downstairs, Robin and Nelson were quarreling in the living room. "That film belongs to me, Nelson!" Robin was glaring at her cameraman. "You weren't supposed to make a copy of it. The police were the only ones who should've seen it." Robin's dark hair was yanked tightly off her face, and her beady eyes were bulging in anger.

"The camera belongs to me, and you don't need the film anyway," Nelson shot back. "It's not like the station is going to be airing the footage from that day, are they? Josh's *Chefly Yours* episode was scrapped, so who cares?"

"Listen to me," Robin snarled, "your job is to film the series. Since you filmed that episode for me, the film was and is mine, and since that footage obviously isn't going to become part of the series, you shouldn't have a copy."

"That's exactly why I have a copy, Ms. Director! It's not part of your rip-off show, so I can keep it!" Nelson's raised voice was echoing throughout the room.

The last thing Ade needed was to overhear a nasty argument. "Could you two keep it down, please?" I said sharply.

"Sorry," said Robin, looking appropriately ashamed. "Look, we'd love to film Adrianna while she's getting ready. Is she upstairs?"

"I really don't think she'll want you up there." I certainly didn't. On inspiration, I said, "Adrianna is a very private person. She's thrilled that you're going to film the wedding, but she'd rather you focus on food preparation than on . . . bride preparation. Why don't you go into the kitchen and tape Josh while he's cooking?"

"Perfect! Nelson, let's go."

Nelson raised his camera and aimed it at me. I sighed inwardly but said nothing to him as I led the pair back to the craziness of the kitchen. A glance told me that Nelson would practically be filming a crowd scene. Josh and Emilio's cousins were still at work, Digger had arrived and was scraping out pumpkins for the baked pumpkin stew, and my mother was rushing around pointlessly moving platters from counter to counter and probably driving Josh bonkers. I just had to get her out of his way soon. But what really hit was the presence of an uncomfortable number of people who'd been around on the day of Francie's murder: Josh and me, obviously, as well as Digger, Robin, and Nelson. And Willie and Evan would be here soon, too. How had Adrianna's wedding turned into a reunion of homicide suspects?

"Does everyone know each other?" my mother asked. Without waiting for a response, she began introductions, each of which included a short bio. "Digger is the executive chef at a delightful tapas restaurant. He's going to be Josh's right-hand man today."

Sweat glistened in Digger's curly hairline. He gave a gruff "Yo!" to the room as he set a stainless-steel tray on a counter.

"And Robin." My mother gestured to the cable-TV director, who was busy trying to get Nelson to move the camera off me. "Robin did a splendid piece on gardening a few years ago. She not only featured our landscaping business but also filmed part of that show at the nursery owned by Emilio's family, the one where these two assistants work." When Mom pointed at Emilio's cousins, I noticed that Héctor was staring intently at Robin.

My mother continued her spiel. "Next is Alfonso, currently in charge of inventory and ordering at one of my favorite nurseries. He doesn't speak English, so thank goodness we have Josh and Emilio here to translate. Where is Emilio, by the way? He should've been back by now."

As if on cue, Emilio entered the kitchen. "I'm here. Sorry that took so long." He was holding an open box filled with flowers. I couldn't wait to get a better look at the flowers. Ade had ordered deep orange roses for the bouquets. Even from across the kitchen, I could see how beautiful the color was.

"Oh, good," my mother said. "Everyone, this is Emilio. Emilio, this is Robin, Nelson, and Digger. Of course, your cousins and Chloe you already know."

When Emilio smiled at me, I did my best to remain cool as I smiled politely back. I wished Nelson would get that silly camera off me.

"And this is Josh Driscoll," my mother said, pointing to Josh, who finally set down the knife he'd been using to slice mushrooms.

Josh wiped his hands on his apron. He looked up, ready to greet Emilio, but all of a sudden, his face hardened.

Emilio looked momentarily confused and then started to speak. "Oh. It's you. We've, uh, we've actually met before—"

"That's right. We have met before, you goddamn bastard!" Without warning, Josh rammed his way through the mob of people in the kitchen, reached Emilio, came to an abrupt halt, drew back a fist, and punched Emilio squarely in the jaw. The first punch was powerful, but before Emilio had a chance to recover from the blow, my chef socked him again. Hard. Emilio spun sideways, and as he fell to the ground, he dropped the flower box and sent the bouquets and boutonnieres flying everywhere.

I was flabbergasted and furious. "Oh, my God! Josh, what are you doing?" I reached Josh and grabbed his arm before he could haul off and hit Emilio again. Somehow,

Josh must have discovered that Emilio had asked me out. Who would have told him? How on earth had he found out?

"You want to know who this is?" Josh looked at me with fury in his blue eyes. "This is the asshole I took Inga from. This is the creep who was going to throw that cat in the river."

TWENTY-FOUR

"WHAT?" I yelled in disbelief. "What!"

Emilio had managed to rise to his feet, but I marched up to him, shoved both hands against his chest, and knocked him back down.

"You sicko!" I screamed. "You get out of here! Get out of here now, before I grab one these knives and cut your throat, you fiend! You were going to drown a poor, helpless little cat! *My* poor, helpless cat! Get of here right now before I knock you senseless and drag you to the bathtub and hold your head underwater and see how you—"

While I was in the midst of my tirade, Emilio scrambled to his feet. Clutching his jaw, he crushed Ade's flowers as he backed out of the kitchen. Everyone who remained was frozen in place, but poor Héctor and Alfonso looked more dazed than anyone else. As Josh began explaining the situation to them in Spanish, I explained in English.

"Good God!" my mother said, shaking her head. "Well, we simply can't have *him* here. Good riddance! What kind of monster would do that to a cat? And Emilio of all people! I never would have guessed. Never!" She paused and said, "And to think that he went to Princeton!"

Digger's muscular hands began forcefully yanking seeds from the pumpkin. "Seriously. What a scumbag!"

Robin remained silent but scurried to pick up the mass of flowers that had fallen to the floor.

I took a deep breath. I couldn't help but feel that the gods were conspiring to ruin what was supposed to be Adrianna's perfect day. But Inga, I reminded myself, was, after all, safe; Josh, my Josh, had snatched her from Emilio's clutches. "Okay," I said, "let's all just calm down. Adrianna is going to lose it if she finds out that there was an actual fistfight at her wedding. Or almost at her wedding. Although, I suppose it was more of a clobbering than anything else." I grinned at Josh, who winked at me. I mentally kicked myself for having given Emilio a second thought.

"Yeah, and I got it all on film!" Nelson whispered excitedly.

I didn't have time for Nelson and his obsession with so-called reality. "Mom, let's get out of the way and get upstairs so Adrianna can start on our hair."

We were on our way to the stairs when I heard my name called. Turning around, I saw Héctor walking toward me.

"Chloe," he said in a heavily accented voice.

"Yes? Héctor?" Despite all the time I'd spent trying to teach myself the language from online sites, my Spanish was pretty bad. "Mom, I'll meet you up there."

Héctor began speaking so rapidly that I couldn't even begin to guess what he was trying to tell me. What's more, I really had to get upstairs to be with the bride. "I'm sorry, I'm sorry," I apologized. "Josh. Go see Josh. He'll understand. I have to go."

My mother and I found Adrianna in front of the full-length mirror on the inside of the closet door in the guest room. She was wearing a robe and had her hair bound up in large rollers.

"My matron of honor! And my solemnizer! Is that even a word?" Even with a crazy mountain of curlers on her head, Ade was all glowy and adorable.

With tremendous formality, I announced, "We are here and at your command. Who's first?"

"You are, Chloe. Go shower, and I'll get you started. And then Bethany."

By the time our hair was done, it was midafternoon. Mom's hair had been parted on the side and flatironed straight. My highlighted red hair had been slathered in serums and styling creams to prevent any dreaded frizziness; I now had a gorgeously soft and smooth mane that Ade had blown dry with a gigantic round brush that gave me plenty of height at the roots and curl at the ends. I really needed to practice my blow-drying skills so I could duplicate this result myself. Ade's blonde hair fell in soft curls down her back, and the front was pulled away from her face by the veil I'd worn while prancing around her apartment. My mother and I had on our wedding outfits, but Adrianna hadn't yet put on her gown.

"I have to go check on your father and make sure he got out the, uh, well . . . nothing! I'll be back in time for the ceremony, Adrianna. Don't worry!" Mom rushed out of the room.

"I haven't seen Jack all day, have you?" Ade asked with a

hint of concern. "I hope your dad will appear in time to walk me down the aisle."

"He wouldn't miss it. Not a chance. I'm sure everything is fine." I watched while Adrianna did her makeup. "Are you nervous yet, Ade?" I took some pictures of her with my digital camera while she peered at herself in the mirror.

"Not at all. Especially because my mother knows she isn't allowed to see me until the ceremony. The last person I wanted to spend time with today was her. I'm just so glad I have you and your mother with me while I get ready. There! My makeup is done." She turned to me, and her eyes lit up. "I think I should put on my dress."

We unzipped the white gown from the garment bag, and I helped Adrianna to step into the dress. When I zipped up the back, I was quite relieved to find that the fit was perfect. "Let me look at you."

I stood in front of my best friend and clasped my hands to my mouth to stifle my choked gasps. The crisp white material was fitted over her chest and tied halter-style at the nape of her neck. Adrianna had altered the dress so that it fell softly against her belly and accentuated the beautiful shape of her late-pregnancy body. Gentle gathers of fabric made up the skirt. Her wedding dress was simple, with no lace or huge bows: just clean, flowing lines. I felt overwhelmingly happy that Kitty wasn't here to make snide comments about Adrianna's decision to wear virginal white.

I grabbed a tissue and dabbed my eyes. "You're breathtaking, Ade. You really are." I started maniacally snapping pictures. I looked at my watch. "It's getting close. Oh, we almost forgot the flowers! I'll go find the bouquets. And then I have to get all my papers for the ceremony."

"Okay. I'll just be here."

I couldn't leave Ade by herself. My dad was going to

walk her down the aisle, but she needed a woman to wait with her. "Don't worry. I'll send someone up to sit with you. Give me a hug."

"Watch the dress." Ade shrieked as I leaned in. We hugged gently, not wanting to crinkle our dresses or ruin our makeup.

"I'll see you on the aisle." I opened the guest room door and stepped into the hall.

"Oh, screw it. Give me a real hug." Ade held her arms out.

I raced to my friend and squeezed her tightly. "This is it."

TWENTY-FIVE

I had to find someone to stay with Adrianna while we dealt with last-minute details. In so many ways, Ade really was alone: she had almost no women friends, her father had disappeared, and her hostile mother was worse than none. If she waited by herself, she was bound to feel painfully solitary. My mother was her matron of honor, but this was Mom's house, and she was mobbed right now. I looked out the front door and spotted my sister. No, Heather wouldn't do; she couldn't open her mouth without criticizing someone or something. Although Heather wouldn't intentionally hurt Adrianna, she might blurt out something thoughtless and stinging. Besides, she and her husband, Ben, were busy trying to keep their kids from ruining their fancy outfits. And they did look adorable; one-year-old Lucy was wearing a poofy pink dress and white Mary Jane shoes, and five-year-old Walker had on a navy suit. I had visions of them serving as flower girl and ring bearer at my own wedding. Romantic visions of Josh and me riding off into the sunset momentarily distracted me. I shook off my fantasies and continued looking for an appropriate person to stay with Adrianna.

Owen's relatives were impossibly difficult, and Kitty was obviously out, too. Then I saw Naomi and her boyfriend, Eliot, on the front lawn, admiring the tent. Aha! Naomi was, well, Naomi. New Age, corny, touchy-feely, yes, but Naomi was absolutely genuine, and she was sweet, supportive, and reliably kind. "Naomi!" I waved her over. "I need a favor."

For the wedding, Naomi had fastened her dozens of braids with turquoise beads that matched her long garment, which appeared to be an actual sari draped in some non-Indian manner. On her feet were what I recognized as brand-new tan suede Birkenstocks. On the positive side, Naomi said that she'd be more than happy to stay with Adrianna until my mother could officially begin her matron-of-honor duties. "Chloe," she said with her usual enthusiasm, "I brought a copy of the letter of reference I wrote for you. The one I sent to the secretary of state's office. I thought Adrianna might like a copy for her wedding album. Here, I'll read it to you."

Keeping one eye on Naomi, I used the other to look out the front door for arriving guests.

"This is my favorite part," Naomi said happily. "'Chloe Carter has a remarkable soul, and I offer up my sincerest hope that she be allowed to unite her two friends—'"

"Son of a bitch!" I screamed.

"Well, that's not very nice, Chloe." Naomi crinkled her nose at me.

"Not you, Naomi. Owen." I pointed to the groom, who stood outside talking to Josh.

Josh looked positively dashing. More than dashing. Regal. As Adrianna had requested, he wore a black tuxedo. Owen was another story. His neon purple tuxedo and matching top hat were, in all probability, visible from outer space.

I stomped over to the groom. "I swear that you'd better be kidding, Owen."

The petrified-looking Owen was on the verge of tears. "I don't know what to do, Chloe. I rented this one and a black one. This was the joke one, and I was just going to wear it for a while before the ceremony. But the rental place didn't get me my black tux. They sent Josh's, and when I looked in the bag yesterday, I saw the black and figured everything was in there. Ade is going to kill me!"

"We could just spray paint you," Josh suggested flippantly.

Oh, my God! This had to happen now, at the last minute! I moved to the entrance to the tent, looked in, and saw that many of the guests had already arrived. Ade would flip out if we ran late. Since Dad wore jeans almost everywhere, the only suit he owned was the one he was wearing. Besides, he was smaller than either Josh or Owen. One of the guests? I could hardly charge up to one of the men and demand that he immediately exchange his suit for a purple tuxedo.

"You are a stupid, stupid man, Owen!" I put my hands on my hips. "Switch. You'll have to switch. Josh, put on that horrible purple thing and give Owen your tux."

The boys started to protest, but I held up my hand. "We have twenty-five minutes until the ceremony. There is nothing else to do." I yanked the horrible top hat off Owen's head. "But nobody is wearing this."

As I stormed off to locate the flowers that Emilio had dropped when Josh punched him, I realized that Nelson had been filming the entire tuxedo fiasco. Remembering Robin's quarrel with Nelson, I resolved to participate in the editing of this film and to get my hands on any copies that Nelson might make. Adrianna was damned well not going to be exposed to Nelson's vision of so-called reality.

I brushed past the cameraman and was heading toward the kitchen when I caught a glimpse of my father, whom I hadn't seen all day. He was scurrying through the living room. On his head was a baseball cap, of all things. "Dad! Dad! Where have you been?" Then his appearance registered on me. "What on earth happened to you? What is that black stuff all over your face?" I pulled off the baseball cap. "And your hair? And your hands? Dad!"

"It, um, well, it seems to be tar. Tar. In fact, that's what it is. Tar."

I stared helplessly at my father. Struggling to control my voice, I said, one word at a time, "Tell. Me. What. Happened."

"Well, after everyone went to bed last night, I thought I'd take a scotch up to the second-floor deck and relax. You know, look at the stars, be one with the earth. My yoga teacher suggested we meditate outdoors. I thought it would be great. I wanted to commune with nature, so I lay down on the deck. Then when I tried to get up, I realized I was stuck."

I shut my eyes. This supposed deck above the living room of my parents' Spanish colonial revival house was, in fact, a roof, a large, flat area surrounded by a stucco wall. No one really used the roof, which had leaked badly and stained the living room ceiling until my parents had finally had it coated with tar.

I glared at Dad. "And it was hot yesterday, so the tar heated up and started to melt. And now you are covered in it."

Dad nodded and suppressed a laugh. "I think I took off all the hair on my body when I finally got myself up."

"You were naked?" I hissed.

"Yeah. That's the best way to meditate. At first I thought I was glued to the deck, and when I managed to get loose, I crawled into bed, and now the sheets are ruined. Your mother is pissed, let me tell you. She tried pouring olive oil on me to get it out, and that helped a little bit. There was a lot of tar in my hair, but I fixed that. I took a pair of scissors and cut it out."

"That would explain the jagged spikes jutting out of your head." Had all the men around here gone crazy? In desperation, I slapped Owen's purple top hat onto my father's head. "Here. Wear this. I don't know what to say to you except that you are a big dope. Go put on your suit and be ready to walk Adrianna down the aisle in a few minutes. I have to go find the flowers."

On the dining room table sat the box of flowers. Because of Robin's efforts, some of the blooms had survived the Josh versus Emilio outbreak. If you looked closely, you could see that some stems were crumpled and that there were fewer orange roses than there should have been, but it was far too late to buy new flowers. I caught Naomi just as she was coming down the stairs in search of Adrianna's and my mother's bouquets. "Whatever you do, don't say anything to Adrianna about what Owen is wearing. Or *was* wearing. Or what . . . Just please keep her calm and happy."

I couldn't help noticing that Naomi herself was a lot calmer than I was. All of her yoga, herbal remedies, acupuncture, and other alternative practices and preparations were apparently more effective than I'd ever imagined. "Don't worry about a thing, Chloe," she said with a beatific smile. "Adrianna and I are having a significant bonding experience."

I hurried to the kitchen to retrieve my script for the ceremony from my purse. Digger was now in charge, and under his supervision, Alfonso and Héctor were beginning to plate appetizers on serving trays. I retrieved the typed pages and nearly collided with Nelson, who was evidently trailing me again. Well, if he was filming me, he'd inevitably capture Ade and Owen as they said their vows. In any case, I had no time to argue with him now.

"Chloe. Chloe." Héctor tapped my shoulder.

"Yes. What is it, Héctor?"

Again he started speaking in Spanish that I couldn't follow. I shook my head in confusion. Then I caught the word *foxglove*.

"Wait! Say it again. I don't understand. I'm sorry."

"He's saying something about Americans buying flowers," Digger explained. Digger and Héctor exchanged words for a moment. "Oh, okay. He wants you to know that one of the Americans who bought foxglove plants is here today. She has brown hair in a ponytail. The woman with him." Digger pointed to Nelson. "He means the director. Robin."

Robin, who had been to the nursery while making the gardening film that had involved my parents. Robin, who lived in an apartment without access to a garden or balcony and who'd said that she had no interest in plants. Robin, who'd thus had no horticultural reason to buy foxglove. Robin, who had been present throughout the filming of the reality TV episode, including the entire time in the kitchen. Well, this was the worst possible moment to take in the implications of this new information, never mind to act on it. For Pete's sake, I had a wedding ceremony to perform!

"Foxglove," Digger said. "Isn't that—"

"Yes, but never mind," I said. "Not now!"

As I was hurrying through the dining room on my way to the tent, I ran into my mother as she headed upstairs. "Mom?"

"What is it, Chloe? I've got to get your father so we can start the ceremony."

"I know. Quick question. One second. When Robin did the gardening film, were there any references to poisonous plants? In particular, did you talk about foxglove?"

Mom shot me a look of exasperation. "I don't know why you want to discuss this now, but, yes, as a matter of fact. The film was mainly about flower borders and included talk about the toxicity of many common ornamentals, including foxglove. What a thing to ask when you're supposed to . . . Chloe, get going!" My mother hurried up the stairs and called over her shoulder. "Take your place, Chloe. The music is playing already, but Josh has the remote, and he's going to start the processional when you're ready."

I exhaled deeply and made my way out the front door and toward the tent. Josh, in ghastly purple, stood just outside the entrance with Owen, who looked even handsomer than usual and was dressed exactly as Adrianna would want. As I took my first step past the masses of potted plants I'd bought at the nursery and into the tent itself, Josh, right on cue, changed the music. Flanked on either side by wedding guests, I felt suddenly awed by the responsibility that the Commonwealth of Massachusetts had granted me, and as I walked down the aisle, my knees shook. Flashes from cameras blinded me, and I was afraid that I'd trip over Nelson, who was a few feet in front of me as he walked backward down the aisle, his camera trained on me. When I finally stood before the guests, my stomach lurched. Owen's father was seated in the front row with Phoebe and a few other cousins. Two chairs in that row had been left empty for the mother of the bride and the mother of the groom, Kitty and Eileen, who would be ushered in by Willie and Evan. The prospect of facing Kitty did nothing to calm me. I cursed myself for ever having agreed to perform this ceremony. Who did I think I was? Why had the Commonwealth of Massachusetts ever agreed to give me such power? But by then, Josh and Owen had joined me. They were standing to my left, facing the side of the tent.

Nelson had now moved toward my right, his camera still fixed on me, but at least he was not blocking my view of the aisle and the entrance. Eager to get the ceremony under way—desperate to get it over!—I stared at the opening of the tent, through which Eileen and Kitty should now be entering with their escorts. My hands were shaking so hard that the papers I was clutching rattled loudly.

Instead of escorting in Eileen and Kitty, Willie and Evan abruptly stepped into the tent by themselves. Staring at them in horror, I nearly dropped my papers. Those two idiots had actually brought shotguns! Monsters! They were doing what they'd threatened, supposedly in jest. No! Absolutely, positively not! In an emotional turnabout, I suddenly felt entitled to the central role I was playing today. I was, after all, the minister-priest-rabbi-justice-of-the-peace figure here. It was I who possessed a Certificate of Solemnization issued by the Commonwealth of Massachusetts. Therefore, I, Chloe Carter, was in charge!

In my most swift yet dignified manner, I marched to the tent entrance, faced the miscreants, and backed them out of the tent. "No way!" I growled at Evan and Willie. "If you do not get rid of those guns this second, I'll shoot you my-self!"

TWENTY-SIX

MY muted voice must have rung with the authority of the governor, the secretary of state, the attorney general, the head of the state police, and every other Power—with a capital *P*—in the Commonwealth of Massachusetts, because the brothers immediately obeyed me. Pointing at the potted plants, I whispered, "In there!" Mercifully, there was enough foliage to conceal the weapons. Lurking a couple of yards behind Willie and Evan were Eileen and Kitty, who had clearly been enablers, if not actual coconspirators. With a little smirk on her face, Eileen said, "Now, Chloe, the boys were only—"

"It is no joke," I whispered. With that, I pivoted around and tried to stroll casually back to my spot before the guests. I smiled and then nodded to Evan and Willie, who, deprived of their shotguns, escorted Eileen and Kitty to their seats and then took their own. My mother was the next to make her way down the aisle. By comparison with Eileen and Kitty, she seemed like an angel, and as Nelson recorded her progress, I was pleased that he was managing to point the camera at someone other than me.

My father and Adrianna appeared at the entrance, he with the ludicrous purple top hat balanced on his head, she the ultimate beautiful bride. Glancing at Owen, I saw that he was frozen in awe. I'd been dreading the moment when Adrianna caught sight of Josh's outfit, but I'd underestimated her: she took one look at him, a vision in purple, and giggled the entire way down the aisle. My father's coordinating hat must have prepared her for subsequent silliness. Dad led her to our little group and sat down.

Adrianna and Owen turned to face me. I locked eyes with my best friend. She tipped her head toward Josh, then toward my father, then down at her slightly battered bouquet, and rolled her eyes. We grinned at each other, and I relaxed.

"I want to welcome you all. We are gathered here to celebrate one of life's great moments and to add our loving wishes to the words that will unite Owen and Adrianna in marriage." My hands did not shake, and neither did my voice. By the time my mother and Owen's father read poems, I was thoroughly enjoying myself.

Then I began the exchange of vows. "Owen, repeat after me. I, Owen, take you, Adrianna, to be my wife, my constant friend, my faithful partner in life, and my one true love."

When Adrianna slipped the simple silver ring on Owen's finger, I got choked up and had to pause before the pronouncement. Adrianna and Owen held hands tightly and waited for me.

"By the authority vested in me by the Commonwealth of Massachusetts, witnessed by your friends and family, I have the pleasure to pronounce you husband and wife. You may now seal your vows with a kiss."

And did they ever. Their kiss went on for so long that the guests had to begin a second round of applause. The newly married couple finally parted lips and made their way back down the aisle.

Because this was a small and informal wedding, Adrianna and Owen had decided to forgo the traditional receiving line. They didn't vanish for professional photographs, of course. Rather, a lot of guests surrounded the couple and snapped pictures outside the tent. Josh wrapped me in his arms, whispered, "Great job, babe," and then ran off to the kitchen to help Digger and Emilio's cousins with the food. I had my picture taken with Adrianna and Owen and accepted compliments from guests about the ceremony.

Héctor and Alfonso arrived with trays of hors d'oeuvres, and champagne began to flow. The chairs that had been in rows for the ceremony were moved to make room for extra tables, and within minutes, guests were mingling merrily in the tent and munching on delicious food. I sampled a baby creamer potato with salt cod brandade and Osetra caviar, and then tried Maine lobster with shaved daikon, Thai basil, and pink peppercorn vinaigrette. Outstanding!

I dragged Adrianna away from the crowd for a moment to explore the buffet table, where more appetizers awaited us. "You must be starving."

Adrianna nodded vigorously. "Famished. God, look at all this! I can't believe Josh pulled it off."

I took a small plate and filled it with butternut squash puree topped with shrimp, arugula, and radish, and drizzled with a brown-butter vinaigrette. I took a taste and groaned happily. Individual servings of celery root soup were topped with small pieces of seared foie gras, pickled apples, celery leaf, and truffle honey. The soup was indescribably delicious. Next I tasted grilled tuna served with couscous tabbouleh and tropical fruit chutney with mint tarragon dressing. I was able to identify mangoes, pineapple, tomatoes, and red onion in the delectable fruit chutney but couldn't figure out what else was in this creation. I'd have to ask Josh. When I heard guests raving about the food, I swelled with pride at my boyfriend's accomplishments. Ade and I scarfed down food and then got whisked off to have more pictures taken. Every member of Owen's family had a camera, and every single person insisted on taking plenty of shots.

I barely had a moment to ponder what I had learned about Robin and her knowledge of the lethal foxglove. Just when I thought that I finally had a minute to devote to working out what had happened, large chafing dishes with piping hot entrées began to appear on the tables. Ade and Owen served themselves, and I followed, piling my plate with medallions of beef with cognac; duck in a red wine and orange sauce; vegetable strudels; and a green salad with maple syrup dressing and dried cranberries. I eyed the lamb with grape-chili jam and goat cheese, and the incredible pumpkins that had been roasted with Gruyère cheese, mushrooms, crème fraîche, and bacon. A large chafing dish held a tempting tagliatelle with lobster, yuzu pesto, and exotic mushrooms. Another dish featured a whole snapper with pickled peppers, chorizo, and fennel puree. I knew I'd be back within a few minutes to refill my plate.

I sat down next to Adrianna. "Are you happy with everything, Ade? I can't believe you haven't strangled Josh or my father for wearing those crazy clothes."

Adrianna chuckled. "Well, I was a bit taken aback when I saw Jack and that flipping ugly hat, but he pulled it off and showed me a head of hair full of black goo. He looked so pathetically sorry that I couldn't be mad at him. As for Josh? Well, I'm pretty sure Owen is responsible, but I can't be mad at him today, can I."

"He did try, Ade. I swear! I guess there was a mix-up—"

"I'm not worried about it. I'm having a wonderful time. You were amazing up there, Chloe, and the ceremony was beautiful." Ade wrapped an arm around me and squeezed. "Another wonderful thing is that my mother has yet to speak to me today. I couldn't be happier!"

Josh, having freed himself from the kitchen for long enough to sit down, took the chair next to Owen's. "The food is coming out awesome, huh? Everything good for the happy couple?"

Adrianna and Owen both nodded enthusiastically.

Throughout dinner, people clinked their glasses with silverware, thus prompting Owen and Ade to kiss repeatedly. Naomi, her boyfriend, Eliot, and my sister, Heather, joined us at the table.

Heather happily dug into her plate of food. "Ben is chasing the kids around, so I get a few minutes to actually sit down and eat. Will wonders never cease?"

Heather and Naomi began a debate about natural childbirth. "Listen, Naomi, I know you are trying to help Adrianna, but I have two kids. Drugs are a godsend."

"I'm sure Adrianna will do what's best for her and the baby." Naomi winked at Adrianna as though the two were pulling one over on Heather. "Speaking of which!" Naomi rose from her chair and, raising her glass, accidentally submerged one of her long braids in her champagne. "I'd like to make a toast. To Adrianna and Owen, on the impending arrival of the fruit of their union!" Naomi removed her hair from her glass and took a long drink.

My parents and Josh made loving toasts, as did Owen's

father and Nana Sally, both of whom welcomed Adrianna to the family. Kitty made the best toast of which she was capable: none at all. I watched to make sure that Nelson was filming all of the speeches, as he was, probably because Robin stayed right by his side and kept muttering directions and scolding him for not following all of her orders. At one point, their bickering began to escalate, but Robin had the sense to shoo Nelson out of the tent to finish the spat.

I went back to the buffet table to help myself to the lamb. Then I set my plate down and filled a small bowl with the incredible roasted pumpkin stew. I took a spoonful of the stew. Heaven! Rich, gooey, and cheesy. As I ate, I walked slowly along the edge of the tent to survey the scene and fix it in my memory. As I was wondering whether Robin and Nelson would be able to resolve their differences for long enough to finish filming the wedding, I heard Nelson's voice and then Robin's. The two were no distance from me; only the fabric of the tent separated us.

"You're getting the angles all wrong, Nelson, and—"

"I swear on my mother's life, Robin, if you don't shut up and let me record this thing how I want, I'll blow your dirty little secret. How'd you like that, huh?"

"What are you talking about? You don't know anything." Robin was seething.

"Oh, yeah? I know about you and Leo Loverboy. So, now what do you have to say for yourself, Ms. Director? I bet a lot of people would be interested in that. You two have been going at it for months. And having him be the chosen shopper for the show was no accident. You set that whole thing up. So shut your trap about what I film."

TWENTY-SEVEN

WHOA! The conversation stopped me in my tracks.

Robin and Nelson reappeared in the wedding tent, but I lingered at periphery of the crowd. Robin had been having an affair with Leo. Even though she had no garden, she had bought foxglove, which was not a houseplant. Because of the gardening film she'd made with my parents, she'd known of the nursery where she'd bought the plants and known of their toxicity. It was she who'd chosen Leo as the featured shopper; she'd engineered his participation and thus, of course, Francie's. Once in the house with Francie, she'd poisoned food that Francie but not Leo would eat. Robin must have prepared the plants in a way that made it easy to slip the poison into the food that Josh had served to Francie. According to what I'd read about foxglove, every part of the plant was so toxic that the preparation would have required no skill. And if others, too, were poisoned? Robin hadn't cared. If others got sick, or even if they died, so much the better! Francie's death, instead of appearing to be a deliberate murder with Francie as the victim, would pass as an accident—in other words, exactly what the police officer saw it as when he arrived at the house. What's more, after Francie's death, it had been Robin who'd arranged to have me remove Francie's clothing from the house; Robin had used me to eradicate the traces of her lover's ex-wife.

Had Leo known of Robin's plan? Had he known that he'd be the *Chefly Yours* shopper and that Robin was going to poison his wife during the filming? Or had he realized only after Francie's death that his lover had murdered his wife? Suddenly, my focus shifted to my own safety. As soon as Robin saw the wedding footage, she'd see and hear the exchange between Héctor and me that Digger had translated. She'd learn that I'd been interested in the purchase of foxglove and that Emilio's cousin had identified her as the buyer. She'd immediately conclude that I was piecing together the elements of the murder.

But I couldn't spoil Adrianna's wedding reception. Despite Josh's eccentric tuxedo, my father's tar fiasco, Josh's fistfight with Emilio, the consequent damage to the flowers, and Evan and Willie's attempted shotgun prank, we had avoided ruinous catastrophes; the ceremony had been beautiful; Adrianna and Owen were now, in fact, married; the food was even more delicious than I'd expected; and the reception was lively and joyous. I would simply have to wait until the bride and groom had left for the evening before I called the police and told the entire story to a detective. Robin hadn't yet seen the film and couldn't watch it while

Nelson was still shooting. Therefore, no one was in immediate danger. I retrieved my plate and returned to the table to finish dinner. Josh had vanished. In his place sat Kitty.

"You know, darling," Kitty began, leaning in to speak to her daughter, "I talked to my friend Rhonda the other day. She wants a divorce, the poor thing. Horrid man she married, really, and I can't blame her. But she says she'll never leave him because he's got all the money, and they don't have a prenup. I guess you two won't have that problem. You know, fighting over money. No need for a prenuptial agreement if there's nothing to fight over!"

"Kitty, would you like anything else to eat?" I said in a panic.

"No, thank you, dear. I'm not even sure what half of the food is."

Bringing up divorce and money at her daughter's wedding was bad enough, but insulting Josh's food? Now she had really crossed the line! I saw Ade inhale and exhale through her nose and will herself to ignore her mother.

As dinner wound down, coffee and dessert plates arrived on the buffet tables. Digger and Alfonso lined up row after row of martini glasses filled with a mixture of crumbled ladyfingers, limoncello, and mascarpone, and topped with fresh raspberries. The bright yellow of the lemon liqueur and the red of the berries looked cheerful and celebratory. As for the ladyfingers, I could eat those spongy delicacies by the dozen. In other words, the dessert was bound to be right up my gastronomic alley. A tray of figs poached in champagne, vanilla, cinnamon, and lemon zest arrived with a pitcher of cream. How was I going to make room for everything? Somehow or other, I'd find space.

"Oh, Chloe, look! Here come the cupcakes!" Adrianna pointed to one of the buffet tables.

Ade had decided that what she wanted instead of a typical wedding cake was a cupcake tower fashioned from Sprinkles brand cupcakes. Josh had ordered mixes in red velvet, dark chocolate, and vanilla and had baked a hundred and fifty cupcakes that he'd iced this morning and arranged in a tower. Josh and Héctor entered the tent, both supporting the tray of tiered cupcakes.

"How fun is this!" Ade said happily.

"This was the coolest idea, hon." Owen rubbed his hands together. "Let's go cut the cupcake, my blushing bride."

"Cupcakes," snorted Kitty. "Whoever heard of such a thing! Childish, I call it. How are they going to cut a cupcake?"

I rose from my chair. "With a knife."

Nelson and Robin followed the couple to the buffet table. I kept a keen eye on Robin to make sure that she didn't get close enough to sprinkle the Sprinkles with poison. The bride and groom choose one cupcake from the top of the tower and held the knife together as they split the cake in two. I cheered as Ade frosted Owen's nose with her half and then *awwwed* as they shared a gooey kiss. I caught Robin forcing Nelson's camera away from me and back onto Ade and Owen.

When the couple took their seats, Robin threw her hands on her hips. "Nelson, I've had it. You are totally incompetent! Give me the damn camera, Nelson! I mean it!"

"Yeah, right." In showy defiance of Robin, Nelson slowly played the camera back and forth over the crowd.

I felt certain that this time, Robin and Nelson wouldn't take their fight outside, and I was equally sure that they wouldn't make peace on their own. To prevent an ugly scene, I stepped in. "Stop it!" I ordered in an undertone. "Both of you! Come over here." I herded the pair out of the tent and stopped just outside the entrance. I didn't relish having to chat it up with Robin, but I had no choice; I couldn't allow the two of them to make a spectacle of themselves at the reception. "What the heck is the problem now?"

Ignoring me, Robin resumed her attack on Nelson. "Get this straight. I am making this film. Me! I am in charge. It's not about whatever pretty girl you happen to feel like looking at. I'm the producer and director. You're just the cameraman. I'm the brain, you're the eyes, and that's all you are. You shoot what I tell you to. Got it?"

Nelson leaned forward. "Maybe the film *was* yours, but it's mine now. And my film is much more interesting than yours would have been. I'm an artist, and you're nothing but a third-rate, unoriginal, imitative, small-time hack!"

Robin laughed condescendingly. "You're nothing but a technician. If you think that you are *ever* going to be a filmmaker, you're dreaming. You don't have the talent. As a cameraman, you're barely adequate!"

"Oh, Robin." Nelson spoke all too calmly. "I warned you. You have no idea what I have on film. I have so much! A great shot of you buying foxglove not too long ago. I bet you'd love that little sequence, my dear. It's all right here, baby." Nelson sneered and patted the camera that he held at his side. I had to wonder about his claim. Wouldn't he have downloaded that footage?

But Robin failed to share my doubt. She made a mad grab for Nelson's camera. He, however, held it in a firm grip. I was furious! Josh had been more than justified in punching Emilio, and he'd done it in the kitchen before the wedding, not just outside the tent during the reception. Now, I wasn't about to tolerate a physical altercation

"Cut it out!" I demanded.

Robin drew her leg in and then swiftly kicked Nelson

smack on the kneecap. Nelson yelled out in pain, and as he fell to the ground, Robin wrestled the camera from his hands. While Nelson was clutching his knee and swearing, Robin jabbed at the camera in what seemed to be an inept effort to locate the part that held the recording.

"You two are totally out of control!" I whispered angrily. "And don't you dare ruin the wedding footage," I warned.

"Stay out of this, Chloe. It has nothing to do with you." Robin turned the camera upside down and began trying to pry out its innards.

Nelson snorted. "Actually, it has a lot to do with Chloe. Chloe was asking questions about—"

I cut him off. "There has to be a way to work this out."

"Leave me alone!" Robin raised her voice. "Mind your own business, Chloe. And your boyfriend's, too. I happen to know a lot more about Josh than you do, so maybe you should pay a little more attention to him and less to me."

"What are you talking about?" I asked, completely confused and momentarily distracted. "What do you know about Josh?"

Robin halted her fiddling with the camera and looked smugly at me. "I know he's not the chef at Simmer any longer. He quit. The new chef there is his supposed friend, Digger. Digger starts tomorrow. Marlee told me. You know how quickly restaurant gossip flies around."

Robin had to be out of her mind. "You don't know what you're talking about, Robin. Josh would have told me if he'd left Simmer. And there is no way Digger would take Josh's job. It's an unwritten rule that you don't take your friend's job, no matter what the restaurant."

"How dumb can you be? You know these chefs. They all want to be stars. Digger wouldn't hesitate to take a job on

Newbury Street, even if it ticked off his good buddy. God, Chloe, you don't know anything." Robin laughed heartily.

Nelson stood up, his knee apparently not permanently damaged. "On the contrary. Chloe knows quite a bit. In fact, she knows everything she needs to about you, Robin. She knows about Francie. And the foxglove. She must be waiting for this wedding to be over to call the police. Isn't that right, Chloe? Just wait until my movie hits the Internet."

Robin's face blanched.

I'd underestimated Nelson. All along, he'd known that Robin had killed Francie, whose agonizing death had registered on him as nothing more than a sort of twisted docudrama. As I was staring at Nelson, Robin, camera in hand, bolted toward the street and her car. Dammit! She was welcome to whatever evidence the camera held, which was not the only evidence of her guilt. Among other things, Héctor, Nelson, and I could testify. But that camera was valuable: it held the only recording of Adrianna's wedding! And I was not about to let Robin destroy irreplaceable images so precious to my best friend. I took a few steps back and grabbed one of the shotguns that Evan and Willie had stashed in the plants by the entrance to the tent. I knew that those shotguns weren't loaded, of course. But Robin didn't share my knowledge.

I assumed my best gun-toting stance, or what I imagined that a gun-toting stance should be, and hollered at Robin. "Stop or I'll shoot!" Those words from my mouth? Whoever would have thought?

A second later, I heard a shot and saw Robin fall to the ground, facedown. Blood quickly stained the back of her shirt. She lay still.

But I hadn't fired the gun. I hadn't so much as brushed the trigger with my finger.

I whipped around and saw Nelson with the second shotgun still aimed at the immobile Robin. Thank God I hadn't accidentally pulled the trigger myself. Why were these guns loaded? Willie and Evan, I realized, hadn't just intended to march in with the shotguns. They'd planned to discharge the weapons!

Guests began pouring out of the tent. "Call an ambulance!" someone shouted. "I'm an EMT. Get out of the way."

A young man, a friend of Owen's family, pushed his way through the crowd and knelt down next to Robin. I turned and stepped away. Almost everyone at the reception took out a cell phone and dialed for help.

"Baby?" My chef had materialized next to me. I almost drove my head into his chest.

"Josh. Where is Ade? More importantly right now, where the hell are Evan and Willie?" I was beyond furious; I was livid.

"They're over there." Josh gestured behind him. "What happened?"

As we wove our way through shocked guests, I did my best to explain how Robin had ended up with a bullet in her back. At the same second when I located Owen's brothers, ambulances, fire trucks, and police cruisers began to arrive. I paid no attention to the emergency vehicles; rather, I concentrated on Evan and Willie, who at least had the minimal decency to look appalled at the consequence of their aborted and unfunny prank.

"What were you thinking?" I demanded. "Arriving at this wedding with shotguns was bad enough, but *loaded* shotguns? What if Heather's kids had found them?"

Evan was the first to brave my wrath. "We were planning on firing a resounding volley into the air at the end of the wedding ceremony. It was going to be very dramatic."

"Dramatic? You were going to shoot off guns in the tent? Endangering our lives? Not to mention puncturing the tent! You two are the stupidest, most—"

"Chloe, I need your help." The voice was Adrianna's.

I felt terrible. Poor Adrianna must be a wreck. This was supposed to have been the perfect day she'd dreamed of. And now this! To my surprise, however, Adrianna looked remarkably happy for someone whose wedding had just become a crime scene.

I put a hand on her arm and said, "I'm so sorry about this. About everything! What can I do to help you? This is just terrible. First Josh punched Emilio, and then the flowers got wrecked, and then . . . Well, it goes on and on."

Adrianna spoke with unusual force. "Chloe, I need you to focus." She grabbed my shoulders and squared me in front of her. "Chloe, my water broke."

Twenty-Eight

I stared at Ade. "Your what did what?"

The exasperated bride put her hands on my cheeks and pulled my face an inch away from hers. "My water broke. Meaning, my water broke, and I'm going into labor!"

"What?" I practically hollered. "The baby is coming now? Oh, my God. Oh, my God." I frantically looked around for I didn't know what. Something! Should I find Ade's hospital bag? Rush her to the hospital? And there was that pesky matter of the swarm of policemen roaming the grounds . . .

"Chloe, get me out of this dress before it's ruined. And then you can go find Owen. Crap, I wanted to go to the Ritz tonight." She scolded her belly. "You couldn't have waited another twenty-four hours?"

I rushed Adrianna upstairs to the bathroom and helped her remove her dress before any icky things got on it. "Okay, you get changed. I'll go grab one of those EMTs downstairs and find Owen." I hung the wedding dress back in its garment bag and zipped it shut.

"You will do no such thing!" Ade glared at me. "If you tell those guys, they'll send me to whatever hospital they want, and I want to go to Brigham and Women's like I planned and have my own doctor. I know that I have to go soon since my water broke, but I doubt this baby is going to fall out of me in the next few minutes. Oh, and for Christ's sake, don't let my mother know what's going on!"

"Gotcha!" I said. "I'm on it. Are you in pain? Do you need anything?"

"No, I'm okay for now, but I don't expect that to last, so you better find Owen. And one more thing," Ade started as she yanked a shirt over her head. "Care to explain the gunshots, screaming, and sirens downstairs?"

"Um, not really. Don't worry about anything! It's all under control. Gotta run!" I dashed out of the bathroom in search of Adrianna's new husband.

I found Owen in the chaotic crowd outside. The groom was still tearing into his abashed-looking brothers for their outrageous behavior at his wedding. "Shotguns? I mean, come on!"

"Owen!" I yanked him out of the crowd before someone tried to question me about the shooting. "Adrianna is having the baby."

"I know she's having the baby. I can't very well do it, can I?" Owen looked irritated with the shambles left of his wedding reception.

"No, dummy. She is having the baby now! Come on. You two have to get out of here and get to the hospital."

Owen's face blanched. "Now? What about the Ritz?"

"Your wife said the same thing. Come on."

I had taken two steps with the stunned Owen behind me when Naomi materialized in front of me. "The baby is coming now! Wonderful! Let me help. I know I can be of assistance in this impending event!"

"Actually, you can help. Go find Adrianna's mother, Kitty, and engage her in conversation. Anything will do, but just don't let her know that her daughter is in labor. Adrianna wants her out of the picture."

Naomi nodded in understanding. "Yes, that woman's aura is filled with negative energy, and she should not come near a woman on the verge of bringing new life into the world."

"Stay with her for about ten minutes and then sneak around to the side of the house and take my car. You can drive Owen and Ade to the hospital, and I'll be there as soon as I can. My keys are in my purse in the kitchen."

"Of course. Tell Adrianna to picture a delicate blue iris. Trust me, these imagery techniques work wonders in managing pain." Naomi rushed off into the crowd calling, "Kitty? Kitty? There you are! Let's talk about the experiences you'll have as a mother-in-law and grandmother."

"Okay, Owen, Ade is upstairs in the bathroom. I better go talk to the police officers, so just run, and I'll see you two as soon as I can get out of here."

"You want me to go up there alone?" Owen looked petrified.

"Yes! Stop looking so freaked out! You're not the one facing hours of painful contractions, so just get yourself together. Go!" I shoved Owen toward the house and approached the group of officers who were busy sorting out who in the hysterical mob knew anything of importance. I located Josh with one of the uniformed cops, a paunchy, mustached man who looked happily surprised to be working on a night when something dramatic had happened in the typically dull suburb of Newton.

"Here," Josh said to the officer. "This is Chloe Carter, and I think she has some information." Josh swung an arm around my shoulder and pulled me in. "Evan and Willie are under arrest, and their parents are already headed down to the station. Can you fill this officer in on what you know about Robin and Nelson? Can you believe that dopey Nelson shot her?" Josh shook his head and pointed to the street. I saw Nelson handcuffed and being led to a cruiser.

Despite my desire to come off as an insightful crime fighter in my own right, I gave an uncharacteristically terse and abbreviated version of what I knew and what I had overheard. Robin and Leo had staged the shopping trip so that he would be the chosen shopper, and Robin would have an opportunity to poison Francie. I didn't know whether Leo had known about the murderous part of the plan or not, but I did know that he had failed to mention to anyone that he'd been having an affair with Robin.

"Is Robin dead?" I asked hesitantly.

"Nope," the officer said, running his hand over his mustache. "Not yet. Can't tell what kind of shape she's in. Now, miss, let's go over everything you saw again."

Argh! I just wanted to get out of there and get to the hospital. I reminded myself that there was no way I would actually miss the birth, since Ade would presumably be in labor for many hours. But I did want to be there for her during her labor, so I decided the best thing to do was to reiterate my story as thoroughly and patiently as possible and avoid further questions.

Josh stayed with me until I was done. Then I hurried him into the kitchen. I didn't want to waste time talking with my family or anyone else right now. "Ade is in labor, so

I have to leave in a few minutes. Can you cover for me? They don't want anyone to know right now since Kitty is a horrid pill, and Owen's family is a bit busy trying to bail their other two sons out of jail."

"Absolutely. How exciting! I bet Ade and Owen are disappointed about not going to the Ritz tonight, though—"

"Would everyone stop saying that?" Honestly, who gave a rat's ass about the Ritz when a baby was on the way? "Listen." I took Josh's hand. "Robin was seriously unbalanced."

"Obviously. I'm just glad no one else got hurt tonight."

"Yes," I agreed. "She's deranged. And she told some horrible lies. Not just to cover up that she had poisoned Francie. Robin even tried to get me to believe things about you."

Josh looked quizzically at me.

I continued. "She had the audacity to try to convince me that you quit your job at Simmer and that Digger was taking over for you."

There was an uncomfortably long pause. Robin, I realized, had been telling me the truth.

"Josh?"

He sighed and looked around the room. "Yeah, it's true. That's why I've had so much time off in the past few days. It just got to be too much, Chloe. Gavin is off his rocker, and he's impossible to work for. I told Digger the job was his if he actually wanted it. I've been looking around for other jobs. I have a headhunter named Yvette." That explained all the phone calls Josh had been getting from a woman. "She actually found me a great job. In Hawaii. A private chef for a family there, Chloe. Great pay and free housing in their guesthouse. And they travel all the time. They said you could come with me, too." Josh finally looked at me. "I'm flying out of Boston in a few days. What do you say, Chloe? Do you want to move to Hawaii with me? Do you?"

TWENTY-NINE

"THIS simply must be the most gorgeous baby in the world." I gazed down at the newborn I held tightly in my arms. A blanket swaddled the tiny baby, and I could not stop staring at the little one's perfect features and healthy pink glow. "Patrick, huh? It's a great name."

"Isn't he perfect?" Adrianna beamed from her hospital bed. "I'd read so many stories about babies coming out with misshapen heads and blotchy faces, so I'd prepared myself that my kid might look awful for the first few days, but Baby Trick is too handsome for words."

"Baby Trick?" I giggled.

"Yeah. Isn't that cute?" Adrianna's hair was pulled off her face in a high ponytail. She'd changed out of the unflattering hospital gown into a pair of yellow silk pajamas. Considering that she'd given birth only forty-eight hours ago, she looked spectacular enough to remind me of the celebrities who appeared on the cover of *People* magazine showing off their newborns.

By the time I'd finished giving my umpteenth rendition of events to the police officers and detectives on the night of the reception, I'd arrived at the hospital to find Adrianna in full-blown labor. Naomi had stayed with Ade and Owen until I got there and had refrained from scowling when the anesthesiologist had stuck a needle in Ade's spine to deliver a good dose of medicine. Owen and I had held Adrianna's hands as she pushed; Owen had managed not to faint, and I had managed not to cry (too much) as baby Patrick entered the world.

"Thanks for spending so much time with me in the hospital. I can't wait to get out of here. Owen slept at home last night, but he should be back here in an hour or so to pack us up and take us home. I can't wait to get Patrick into his new house." Ade adjusted her pillows and winced, still sore all over from the delivery. "So fill me in on the rest of my reception. I missed all the drama with that nutball, Robin." Ade stifled a yawn.

"Robin is still in the hospital. I guess the bullet missed any major organs, and she'll be facing murder charges when she recovers. Nelson is being charged as an accessory after the fact. It seems that the night of the murder, while we were all on the way to the hospital, he made a copy of the video footage from that day's filming. All the footage was on a hard drive on his camera, and he transferred a copy to his laptop and was planning on cutting it to make his own reality episode with the more grisly scenes. And I'm sure he could have sold it for a ton of money, too. With all these weird TV shows and Internet video sites, he might have become a big deal." I shook my head in disgust. "Speaking of the reality show, that chef who runs Alloy? Marlee? Her restaurant was shut down by the health department late yesterday. One of her employees ratted her out about some serious violations, and the health inspector came out and closed the restaurant for repeated failures to correct critical violations of the State Sanitary Code."

Ade wrinkled her face. "Ick. I told you not to eat at that restaurant!"

"I don't think anybody will be eating there again."

"Speaking of closings," Adrianna started tentatively, "Owen said Simmer is closed. He called the guy who is covering his deliveries this morning and heard that the doors are locked, the lights are out, and no one is returning calls. What's going on?"

"Oh. Well . . . it seems that Gavin has a major cocaine problem. Really major. Not only was he using money from the restaurant to fund his habit, but he had become a real ass to work for. A few of the employees staged an intervention, and Gavin is now in rehab. He had to close the restaurant and is selling the business to try to salvage whatever he can financially." Obviously Digger wasn't going to be taking over as the executive chef there.

"What?" Ade's exhausted eyes widened in shock. "What about Josh? What's he going to do? Maybe he can get a job with better hours, and you two will get to have a normal relationship. Maybe this will be for the best, Chloe."

"Hmm, maybe." I felt my eyes start to well up. I did not want to have this conversation now. "So, Baby Trick it is." I gently rubbed Patrick's soft cheek with my thumb. "I'm in love."

"You're already in love with Josh. But I guess he won't mind sharing you with my little guy." Ade rolled over in bed and lay on her side, staring at her child in my arms, her eyes heavy with exhaustion.

"No, I don't think Josh will mind. Especially since he's not here."

"I'm sure he'll come by later."

"No, actually. He won't. He went to Hawaii." I cleared my throat. "Moved to Hawaii, I should say."

Josh's invitation to move with him had confused me. Adrianna, Owen, and Patrick needed me, and I needed them. And I had my second year of social work school upon me, and I was finally starting to feel connected to the work I was doing. But Hawaii with Josh would be . . . well, Hawaii with Josh. Paradise. Double paradise.

"Chloe, what are you talking about? What do you mean he—"

"Ade, I need to talk to you." My voice shook as I spoke. Patrick's face became blurry through my tears. "Ade, I don't know what to do. I just don't know what to do."

RECIPES

Roasted Rack of Lamb with Grape-Chili Jam and Chèvre Sauce

Angela McKeller, Cookbook Author and Show Host
Atlanta, Georgia
www.kickbackkook.com

Serves 4

> 1 rack of lamb, 8 chops
> ½ cup grape jam
> 2 serrano peppers, seeds removed and chopped
> ¼ cup red wine vinegar
> ⅛ cup chèvre (goat cheese)
> ⅓ cup sour cream

Preheat oven to 450°.

Score the fat on top of lamb meat, making shallow crisscross knife slashes, but do not cut into the meat of the lamb. Cover the ends of the bones with foil to prevent charring. Sear the lamb by placing the rack of lamb in the oven, fat side down, in a shallow baking pan for 10 minutes. Then reduce heat to 325° and roast according to your preference using the following chart:

- An additional 15 minutes per pound for medium-rare; meat thermometer should read 145° after resting.

- An additional 20 minutes per pound for medium; meat thermometer should read 160° after resting.

- An additional 25 minutes per pound for well-done; meat thermometer should read 170° after resting.

Remove lamb rack from oven and tent pan with foil to rest for 10 minutes.

While lamb is resting, combine jam, peppers, and vinegar in a blender and blend well. Transfer jam mixture to a saucepan and warm the sauce over medium-low heat. Do not boil! (That would render a sauce too thick for use.) When sauce begins to produce a light steam, remove from heat.

In another saucepan, combine chèvre and sour cream over medium heat. Stir well until smooth and then remove from heat.

Remove the foil from the lamb, place meat on a cutting board, and cut between each chop so that you have 8 individual chops. Place two chops on each plate and top with 3 tablespoons of the grape-chili jam. Drizzle lightly with the chèvre sauce; using a squeeze bottle of some type gives a lovely presentation. Serve with your favorite sides.

Spinach and Artichoke Eggs Benedict with Spicy Hollandaise Served with Rosemary, Garlic, and Onion Breakfast Potatoes

Angela McKeller

Serves 8

Eggs Benedict

1   8-oz. pkg. frozen, chopped spinach, thawed and
    well-drained
1   14-oz. can quartered artichoke hearts, drained
    and chopped
½   tbsp. minced garlic
2   cups mozzarella cheese, grated
1   cup Parmesan cheese, grated
1   cup sour cream
⅛   cup mayonnaise
8   large croissants, halved and toasted
16 poached eggs

Preheat oven to 350°.

Combine first 7 ingredients. Bake in a ceramic or glass oven-safe dish until completely melted into the consistency of a dip. Spread each half of croissant with a heaping tablespoon of spread. Top each croissant half with a poached egg and top with 2 tablespoons hollandaise sauce (recipe follows).

Hollandaise Sauce

12 egg yolks
4 tbsp. butter
1½ tsp. lemon juice
Tabasco or Crystal Hot Sauce

Beat egg yolks together. Melt butter in a double boiler (water softly boiling) with lemon juice. When melted, slowly add egg yolks (equivalent of about one yolk at a time) so as not to scramble the eggs. Stir constantly until very hot and serve. Add salt to taste if needed. Give a quick dash of hot sauce on the finished dish for visual presentation and a bit of a kick.

Breakfast Potatoes

1½ lbs. red-skinned potatoes, well-rinsed, cubed with skin on, and placed in a zipper baggie
2–3 tbsp. olive oil (more if needed)
3 tbsp. chopped fresh rosemary
1 tsp. minced garlic
1 sweet yellow onion, finely chopped

Preheat oven to 400°.

Place all of the ingredients in the baggie with the potatoes. Shake *very* well to coat potatoes with the other ingredients. Place on large cookie sheet sprayed with cooking spray. Do not layer or pile the potatoes; have one even layer. Bake for 45 minutes or until brown and crispy on the outside and tender on the inside. If they don't brown enough during baking, use a kitchen torch for a few seconds over the potatoes just until they are crispy and browned, and serve with Benedict.

Pumpkin Stew in a Pumpkin
Anne and Michel Devrient
Semur-en-Auxois, France

Serves 4–6

1 *medium sugar pumpkin*
1 *large onion, diced*
3 *tbsp. unsalted butter*
2 *cups fresh bread cubes, cut into 1" cubes from a French loaf*
2 *garlic cloves, minced*
3 *cups mixed fresh mushrooms (button, portobello, chanterelle, oyster) cleaned, stems removed, sliced ¼" thick*
  Salt and pepper to taste
3 *cups Gruyère cheese, grated*
4 *strips cooked bacon, crumbled*
1 *container (7–8 oz.) crème fraîche or ½ pint heavy cream*

Preheat oven to 200°.

Cut the top off of the pumpkin as you would if you were going to carve it for Halloween. Scrape out the seeds and loose pulp, being careful not to remove the pumpkin flesh itself, since pumpkin is the basic flavoring of this dish. Save the top of the pumpkin, which will be placed back on during cooking.

In a large skillet, sauté the onions and 2 tablespoons of the butter over medium heat for a few minutes, and then add the fresh croutons and toss. Stir and cook the croutons for another few minutes and then add the garlic. Toss the mixture and cook until the croutons begin to brown. Add more butter as needed to keep the mixture from drying out. Set aside.

In a separate pan, sauté 1 tablespoon of butter with the mushrooms. Cook until the mushrooms have released their juices and begun to reabsorb them. Season with salt and pepper. Set aside.

To assemble the pumpkin for cooking, put in layers of the bread mixture followed by a dash of salt and pepper, then a layer of the grated cheese, a layer of mushrooms, a bit of the crumbled bacon, and a thin layer of crème fraîche or heavy cream. Keep layering until the pumpkin is filled. End with a layer of cheese.

Put the pumpkin lid back on. Set the filled pumpkin in a casserole dish that will support its sides. Fill a roasting pan with 2 inches of water, and place the pumpkin, in its casserole dish, in the water. Bake for about 3 hours, checking from time to time, until the pumpkin pulp is getting soft enough to spoon up.

To serve, gently remove the pumpkin from the water bath and place on a large platter. Scrape out some of the pumpkin flesh with a large, sturdy spoon as you dish out each bowl.

Salad with Maple Syrup Vinaigrette

Meg Travis

Ipswich, Massachusetts

Serves 4–6

Salad

> Salad greens, approximately 1 head of lettuce for
> every 3 people
> 1 small log of goat cheese, crumbled (Make sure you
> buy goat cheese that's been salted. My favorite is from
> Vermont Butter & Cheese Company)
> 1 package of dried cranberries or Craisins
> ½ cup pecans, toasted and chopped

Mix together and toss with the maple syrup vinaigrette.

Maple Syrup Vinaigrette

> Sea salt and freshly ground black pepper to taste
> 2 tbsp. balsamic vinegar
> 1 tbsp. Dijon mustard
> 2 tbsp. grade B maple syrup
> 1 tsp. dried sweet basil
> ½ cup olive oil

Whisk together the salt, pepper, and balsamic vinegar until the salt dissolves. Stir in mustard, syrup, and basil. Whisk constantly while drizzling in oil: the dressing will form an emulsion and thicken. Refrigerate until ready to use. Bring up to room temperature before serving, since the olive oil will harden in the fridge. Makes roughly ¾ cup.

Polpette (Tuscan Meatballs)

Josh Ziskin, Executive Chef at La Morra
Brookline, Massachusetts
www.lamorra.com

Serves 8–10 as appetizer

½   loaf bread, cut into large cubes
3   cups milk
1½   cups dried porcini mushrooms
5   lbs. ground beef
2   cups Parmesan cheese
¼   lb. prosciutto, thickly sliced and diced
4   eggs
3   cups flour
3   cups white wine

Soak bread in milk until it is fully absorbed. Soak porcini mushrooms in water until hydrated and clean. Remove and chop. Mix the next 4 ingredients, and then add mushrooms and bread. Mix well. Roll into desired-size balls. Flour each ball, and shake off the extra flour. Sear in a pan on all sides until light brown. Add wine until it comes halfway up the side of the meatballs. Put in oven and bake at 400° until cooked through, approximately 15 minutes.

RECIPES

Arancini (Fried Stuffed Risotto)
Josh Ziskin

Serves 8–10 as an appetizer

1	yellow onion, diced fine
4	tbsp. cooking oil
1	pound Arborio rice
½	cup white wine
1	quart water or chicken stock, warm
4	tbsp. butter
½–¾	cup grated Parmesan cheese
	Salt to taste
2	oz. Italian meat (salami, capicola, etc.)
6	oz. smoked mozzarella or Fontina cheese
2	eggs
	Flour for dredging
2	cups bread crumbs
	Oil for frying

Sauté onion in oil until translucent. Add rice and cook for 3 minutes until rice is coated in oil. Add wine and stir until absorbed. Add warm water or chicken stock, 2 cups at a time. Rice should absorb liquid each time before the next amount is added. Repeat until rice is fully cooked through. Add butter, Parmesan cheese, and salt. Stir until fully incorporated.

Lay mixture flat on a sheet pan until fully cooled. While rice mixture is cooling, dice Italian meat and cheese into ¼" dice. Beat eggs and place in a bowl. Place flour in a separate bowl. Place bread crumbs in another bowl.

When rice mixture is cooled, moisten hands. Pick up about 2 ounces of rice and create a cup shape in your hands. Add meat and cheese mixture inside cup, and close rice around mixture to form a ball. Once all aroncini are formed, roll each aroncini in flour, then egg, and then bread crumbs. Refrigerate for ½ hour. Deep-fry aroncini in oil until golden brown and warm through.

Warm Pasta Salad

Jessica Conant-Park
Manchester, New Hampshire

Serves 4

1	lb. pasta, preferably fettuccine
½	small red onion, thinly sliced
1	avocado, cut into ½" bites
1	container grape or cherry tomatoes, or 2 plum tomatoes, cut up
½	cup (or a good handful) Calamata olives, pitted and roughly chopped
1	bunch fresh basil, roughly chopped
½–¾	cup good-quality olive oil
¼	cup balsamic vinegar
1	big squeeze lemon juice
	Salt and pepper to taste
16–20	large frozen or fresh shrimp, peeled and deveined or 1 lb. chicken cutlets
	Other: olive oil, salt, pepper, sugar, and Parmesan cheese

Start cooking the pasta while you prepare the vegetables.

Mix all the vegetables and basil with the olive oil, balsamic vinegar, and a big squeeze of the lemon. Toss in a good pinch of salt and pepper. When the pasta is ready, mix it with the vegetables and dressing.

Heat a sauté pan with a splash of olive oil over medium-high heat. When the pan is nicely heated, add the shrimp or chicken. If using shrimp, cook for about 45 seconds to 1 minute per side until perfectly pink and cooked through. If using chicken, season both sides of the cutlets with a generous sprinkling of salt, pepper, and sugar. Sear on each side until golden brown. Don't move the cutlet around too much while it is cooking, because you want the sugar to give a wonderful caramelized crust.

Toss the shrimp or chicken in with the pasta salad and serve with Parmesan cheese. I prefer this dish with lots of dressing, so add more olive oil or balsamic vinegar if you like.

Medallions of Beef with Cognac Wine Sauce

Nancy R. Landman, President and CEO
Great Cooks & Company and Great Cooks at Home
Indianapolis, Indiana
www.greatcooks.biz

Serves 8

Tenderloin

2 tbsp. butter
2 tbsp. olive oil
1 beef tenderloin, trimmed
Salt
Fresh pepper
1 cup beef or veal stock

In a skillet, heat the butter and oil until butter sizzles. Sauté the tenderloin on all sides; if the fats aren't hot enough, the meat won't sear. Season the beef with salt and pepper. Finish cooking the meat in a 350° oven until desired doneness, approximately 20 to 25 minutes.

Deglaze the skillet with beef or veal stock. Reserve these drippings for sauce.

Cognac Wine Sauce

2 tbsp. butter
1 tsp. chopped shallot
1 cup red wine
2 tbsp. Cognac
1 cup beef or veal stock
Herbs and spices to taste (salt, pepper, thyme, bay leaf)

In a saucepan or skillet, heat 1 tablespoon butter. When hot, add chopped shallot, and sauté. Add red wine, Cognac, stock, herbs, and spices. Reduce mixture to ¼ cup and check seasonings. Add deglazed drippings from tenderloin. Add remaining 1 tablespoon butter bit by bit to finish sauce, whisking continuously.

Turned Vegetables

12   large Idaho potatoes, cut in half crosswise
12   large fresh carrots, cut in half crosswise
¾   cup clarified butter
½–¾ tsp. crushed dried rosemary
      Salt and fresh pepper to taste

Prepare turned vegetables: Carve or "turn" the vegetables into 7-sided ovals. Steam the vegetables until three-quarters done. Heat clarified butter with rosemary. Sauté vegetables until done. Finish with salt and pepper.

To serve: Slice beef and serve on warmed plates or platter on top of sauce. Garnish with sprigs of fresh herbs and turned carrots and potatoes.

Champagne-Poached Figs with Heavy Cream
Nancy R. Landman

Serves 8

1   bottle dry champagne or sparkling white wine
      Zest of 1 lemon
1   cup sugar

½   *vanilla bean*
4   *3-inch cinnamon sticks*
24–32   *ripe, fresh figs, preferably purple*
        Heavy cream for serving
        Fig leaves for garnish, optional

In a large saucepan, combine champagne or wine, lemon zest, sugar, vanilla bean, and cinnamon sticks. Bring to a boil and cook for 5 minutes. Reduce heat.

Add figs and poach over low heat until tender but not shapeless, 20–30 minutes. Transfer the figs to a serving dish.

Reduce poaching liquid to 1½ cups. Remove vanilla bean and cinnamon sticks. Pour sauce over figs. Serve at room temperature with heavy cream. Garnish with fig leaves if desired.

Magret de Canard Barbara

Barbara Seagle
Brookline, Massachusetts

Serves 4

⅓   *cup water*
2   *tbsp. sugar*
2–3   *navel oranges, sliced*
        Unsalted butter
        Four boneless duck breasts, skin and fat layer intact
        Salt and pepper to taste
⅓   *cup red wine*

Combine the water and sugar in a sauté pan and cook over medium heat until the sugar dissolves and the liquid comes to a simmer. Add the orange slices and cook over medium-high heat until the oranges are soft and caramelized to a deep brown color. Swirl in the butter at the end of the cooking. Set aside.

Score the fat side of the duck breasts in a crisscross (diamond) pattern right through the fat layer, but not cutting the meat. Salt and pepper the breasts lightly on both sides. Heat a sauté pan over a medium-hot fire and add the duck breasts fat side down. They will sizzle and smoke. An amazing amount of fat will be rendered off. Cook on the first side for about 10–12 minutes. Most of the fat layer will be gone, but some should be left. Turn the breasts and cook another 10 minutes. Timing will vary depending on the size of the breasts, but they should be a nice deep rosy pink. Do not overcook. Remove to a serving platter or plate.

Pour off all the fat from the pan and add the orange mixture and red wine. Cook this mixture down until slightly syrupy. Add the duck breasts and heat through, basting with the sauce.

Slice the breasts across the grain at an angle into thin slices and arrange in a fan on each plate. Place an orange slice or two beside the breast and top with a dribbling of sauce. Voilá!

Mussels Bouillabaisse

Raymond Ost, Chef and Co-owner of Sandrine's
Cambridge, Massachusetts
www.sandrines.com

Serves 6

6 *large tomatoes, quartered*
2 *green peppers, julienned*
2 *red peppers, julienned*
2 *fennel bulbs, julienned*
2 *Spanish onions, julienned*
½ *lb. butter*
4 *cloves garlic, crushed*
2 *cups tomato paste*
4 *cups white wine*
1 *gallon fish stock or clam juice*
3 *lbs. PEI mussels*
1 *pinch saffron*
 Salt and pepper to taste

Sauté the tomatoes, peppers, fennel, and onions in the butter until tender. Add the garlic, tomato paste, and white wine, and cook for 10 minutes. Add the fish stock or clam juice and simmer for 1 hour. Add the mussels and saffron, and simmer until the mussels open. Add salt and pepper to taste.

Grilled Tuna Served with Couscous Tabbouleh, Tropical Fruit Chutney, and Mint Tarragon Dressing

Raymond Ost

Serves 6

Tuna

6 6-oz. *center-cut tuna steaks*
Olive oil
Sea salt
Black pepper

Brush tuna with olive oil and season with sea salt and pepper. Grill for 2 minutes on each side over medium-high heat for medium-rare doneness.

Tabbouleh

1 *box couscous (small grain)*
3 *plum tomatoes, chopped*
2 *bunches flat parsley, chopped (not too fine)*
1 *red onion, chopped*
½ *bunch scallions, chopped*
Juice of 1 lemon
½ *cup olive oil*
6 *sprigs lemon verbena (optional) for garnish*
Salt and pepper to taste

Cook couscous as directed on box. Cool completely. Add the rest of the ingredients and mix well. Season with salt and pepper to your liking.

Dressing

1   cup olive oil
    Juice of 2 lemons
1   tbsp. Dijon mustard
4   cloves garlic, chopped
½   bunch mint, chopped
1   bunch tarragon, leaves only
2   roasted red peppers (seeded and skinned)

Whisk ingredients together and set aside.

Tropical Fruit Chutney

1   pineapple, peeled, cored, and diced
2   mangoes, diced
1   red onion, diced
2   tomatoes, diced
½   bunch mint, chopped
½   bunch chopped parsley
       Juice of 2 lemons
2   tbsp. honey
4   cloves of garlic, chopped
½–1   small habanero pepper, chopped (Note: These
       peppers are extremely hot. Please wear gloves when
       handling. Use pepper sparingly.)

Mix all ingredients together and macerate for 24 hours.

To Serve

Make a bed of tabbouleh, place a tuna steak on that, and top with a few tablespoons of the fruit chutney.

Drizzle the dish with dressing and add lemon verbena for garnish, if you like.

Celery Root Soup with Foie Gras, Truffle Honey, and Pickled Honeycrisp Apples

Chef Erik Battes, Chef de Cuisine at Perry Street
New York, New York

Serves 6–8

Celery Root Soup

2   *large celery roots*
6   *tbsp. butter*
2   *shallots, sliced thin*
12   *oz. chicken stock*
    Salt, to taste

Peel and cut celery root in even, large dice. Melt the butter in a pot over medium heat and sweat the shallots until tender. Add the celery root and the chicken stock and cook until the celery root is completely tender. Puree in a blender and season to taste with salt.

Pickled Honeycrisp Apples

1   *cup champagne vinegar (or white wine vinegar)*
½   *cup sugar*
2   *Honeycrisp apples (or other crisp, juicy apples), peeled and cut into small dice*

Combine the champagne vinegar and sugar in a pot. Bring to a boil and then cool down. Cover the diced apples with the vinegar and sugar mixture (pickling solution) and let sit for at least 30 minutes. The pickled apples should hold for about 2 hours.

Glazed Celery Root

¾ *cup butter*
3 *tbsp. water*
  Salt, to taste
1 *celery root, small dice*

Combine butter and water in a pot and cook over high heat until the liquid becomes homogenous and creamy. Season the butter and water with salt to taste. Add the celery root and simmer gently until tender. Remove from heat and reserve.

Seared Foie Gras

Foie gras, 1-oz. piece per serving
Sea salt, coarse
Black pepper, coarsely ground

Heat a dry pan until aggressively hot. Place the foie gras in the pan and cook on one side until it is 85 percent cooked. Then flip the foie gras, cook for 15 seconds, and then remove from the pan. Season immediately with the coarse sea salt and black pepper.

To Serve

Celery leaves, picked from the center of the head
Truffle honey or regular honey*

Place a spoonful of the glazed celery root into the center of a bowl. Then top with a seared piece of foie gras. Top the seared foie gras with the pickled apples and some celery leaf. Drizzle the truffle honey all around the bowl. Pour the soup into the bowl table side.

Seared Shrimp with Butternut Squash, Brown Butter Ginger Vinaigrette, and Rocket Arugula

Erik Battes

Serves 4–6

Shrimp

20–30	*extra-large shrimp (5 shrimp per person)*
1	*tsp. chili flakes, ground*
5	*tsp. star anise, ground*
5	*tsp. salt*
	Olive oil

Season the shrimp with the chili flakes, star anise, and salt. Sauté in a smoking-hot pan with a small amount of olive oil until just cooked.

* You may also use an herb-flavored honey (rosemary or thyme) or you can drizzle a bit of truffle oil on regular honey.

Brown Butter Ginger Vinaigrette

¼ *cup butter*
1 *tbsp. ginger, brunoise (small dice)*
2 *tbsp. shallots, brunoise (small dice)*
1 *tbsp. rice wine vinegar*
1 *tbsp. lime juice*
2 *tbsp. soy sauce*

Cook butter in a pot until the milk solids turn dark brown. Combine all of the other ingredients in a bowl and whisk in the cooked butter. Be sure to include all of the milk solids with the butter. Reserve warm.

Butternut Squash Puree

Butternut squash, halved and seeded
Salt
White pepper
Olive oil
2 *tbsp. butter*

Rub the butternut squash with salt, pepper, and olive oil. Cover with foil and roast on a sheet tray at 350° until tender. Scoop out the cooked squash. While hot, puree the squash in a blender until completely smooth. When ready to serve, combine 1 cup of the butternut squash puree with the butter. Work with a rubber spatula in a pot until combined. Adjust seasoning with salt.

To Serve

Arugula, wild lettuce mix, or both
Red radish, julienne

Lay down a line of butternut squash puree on a plate, and then set the seared shrimp on top. Combine the arugula or lettuce with a small amount of radish julienne, lightly dress with the warm brown-butter vinaigrette, and place in a tight pile right next to the shrimp on the plate.

Butter-Poached Lobster with Yuzu Pesto Tagliatelle, Honshimeji Mushrooms, and Shiso

Erik Battes

Serves 4–6

Lobster

1 *half-pound lobster per person, alive*
Salt
Cayenne
Butter

Remove the lobster tails, claws, and knuckles while lobsters are still alive. In a large pot, boil water and season with salt until it tastes like the ocean. Add the lobster tails and cook for 2½ minutes and immediately put into ice water to cool. Add the claws and knuckles, cook for 9 minutes, and put into the ice water as well. Once cool, crack open the shells and remove the intact lobster meat. It should be 75 percent cooked. Season with salt and cayenne pepper, and put into a sauté pan with ½" of melted butter. Cook in a 200° oven for 8 minutes or until completely opaque.

Yuzu Pesto

¼   *cup yuzu juice (available in most Asian markets) or lemon juice*
½   *cup pine nuts, toasted*
4   *cloves garlic*
¼   *tsp. dry chili flakes*
½   *cup olive oil*
1½ *tsp. salt*

Combine all in a food processor and process until the mixture is mostly smooth but still contains some texture.

Shiso Puree

15 *shiso (Japanese mint) leaves, or mint or basil leaves*
½   *cup olive oil*
1   *tsp. salt*

Cook the shiso, mint, or basil leaves in a pot of rapidly boiling water for 45 seconds. Remove from the pot and immediately put into ice water. Remove from the water and squeeze as much moisture as you can out of the shiso leaves. Combine the shiso with the olive oil and salt and puree in a blender on high until the mixture is smooth. Chill immediately.

Mushrooms

1   *cup honshimeji mushrooms (or other mushrooms such as trumpet, clamshell, oyster, beech, or cremini), cleaned and bases trimmed*
2   *tbsp. shallots, brunoise (small dice)*

2   tbsp. olive oil
1   tbsp. water
     Salt
     White pepper

Combine all in a small pot and cook covered over medium heat until the mushrooms are tender.

To Serve

1–1½ lbs. cooked tagliatelle (or any other long pasta)
     Grated Parmesan cheese

Toss the pasta with yuzu pesto and the cooked mushrooms, and place in a serving bowl. Top lightly with some shiso puree and Parmesan. Serve the lobster on top of the pasta.

Sautéd Red Snapper with Spanish Lomo, Pickled Baby Bell Peppers, and Fennel

Erik Battes

Serves 4

Snapper

4 6-oz. portions of American red snapper, skin on
     Salt
     Espelette or cayenne pepper, ground
     Grapeseed oil

1 tbsp. butter, unsalted
1 sprig of fresh thyme

Season the snapper liberally with salt on both sides. Season with Espelette or cayenne pepper to taste on the flesh side only. Score the skin side three times with a sharp knife. Heat a pan with ⅛" of grapeseed oil over high heat until it has just begun to smoke. Place fish skin side down and press down immediately with a spatula until the skin relaxes and sits completely flat. Turn down the temperature to medium, and cook until the fish is 85 percent done. Add a tablespoon of butter and a sprig of thyme to the pan, and baste the flesh side of the fish with a spoon until done.

Pickled Peppers

1 lb. orange and yellow bell peppers
  Olive oil
  Salt
  White pepper
6 oz. Japanese rice vinegar
6 tbsp. sugar
3 sprigs of fresh thyme

Remove the tops and seeds of the peppers and toss in olive oil and season with salt and white pepper. Roast in a 375° oven until the skin starts to separate from the flesh of the pepper. Do not overcook. Place in a bowl and cover with plastic wrap to steam until cool. Peel the skins off of the peppers and cut into 1" dice.

Combine the vinegar, sugar, and thyme in a small pot and bring to a boil. Pour the vinegar mixture over the peppers and let marinate for at least 2 hours.

Fennel Puree

> 1 *large fennel bulb, top and core removed*
> 2 *tbsp. butter*
> 1 *tsp. salt*

Slice the fennel thinly and cook over low heat with the butter and salt. Once the fennel is completely tender and translucent, puree on high until smooth.

To Serve

> 1 *oz. Spanish lomo (or chorizo), fine julienne*
> 2 *oz. of the pickled peppers*
> ½ *tsp. fresh thyme*
> 1 *tbsp. butter*
> *Espelette or cayenne pepper, ground*

Sauté the lomo or chorizo in a dry pan until it is completely crispy and rendered. Do not drain the fat. Add the pickled peppers, thyme, and butter, and cook until glazed. Season lightly to taste with Espelette or cayenne.

Place 1½ ounces of hot fennel puree on a plate, place the cooked fish on top, and finish with a spoonful of the glazed pickled peppers.

Crab and Corn Fritters with Lemon-Cilantro Aioli

Chef Bill Park
Manchester, New Hampshire

Makes 12 fritters

Fritters

½   tbsp. butter, melted
6   ears corn
¼   onion
½   cup flour
½   tsp. baking soda
½   tsp. kosher salt
¼   tsp. black pepper
⅓   cup milk
1   egg
1   lb. crab claw meat, fresh or canned
    Canola oil for frying

Mix all ingredients together and form into equal-size balls, roughly ¼ cup each. Heat a deep pan with about an inch of oil over medium-high heat. Cook the fritters until browned on all sides. Fry in batches so that you don't overcrowd the pan. Set on paper towels.

Lemon-Cilantro Aioli

1   cup mayonnaise
½   tsp. lemon juice

1 *tbsp. lemon zest*
2 *tbsp. cilantro, chopped*
¼ *tsp. white pepper*
¼ *tsp. salt*

Mix all ingredients together and serve with fritters.

Mascarpone and Limoncello Dessert

Dwayne Minier, Personal Chef
Boston, Massachusetts
www.minierculinary.com

Serves 4

8 *ladyfinger cookies*
1 *cup mascarpone cheese*
1 *tsp. lemon zest*
2 *tsp. limoncello (lemon liqueur)*
1 *tbsp. powdered sugar*
2 *tbsp. freshly squeezed lemon juice*
1 *cup raspberries*

Roughly crumble 2 ladyfingers into each of 4 martini glasses and set aside. In a bowl, whisk together the mascarpone, lemon zest, limoncello, powdered sugar, and lemon juice until thoroughly combined.

Gently spoon cheese mixture on crumbled cookies and top with fresh raspberries.

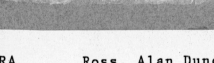

THE MEDICINE OF

ER

THE MEDICINE OF

ER

OR, HOW WE ALMOST DIE

ALAN DUNCAN ROSS

AND

HARLAN GIBBS, MD

BasicBooks
A Division of HarperCollinsPublishers

To my father, Irving.
Medicine was always your third son.
You continue to make us all proud.
—A.D.R.

To my parents, Manny and Phyllis, whose
inspiration led me into medicine, and to Debi,
Jessica, and Spencer, whose love keeps me going
during the crazy times in the ER.
—H.G.

CONTENTS

PART III
LAUGHTER AND TEARS

The Golden Hour

I t is Christmas Eve. A time to be with family, to celebrate peace on earth, goodwill toward men. You're on your way back from a party, happily humming along to carols on the radio. You stop for a red light. It's 11:00 P.M. Suddenly a man appears in your headlights, a gun in his hand. Pointing the gun at you, he comes around to your window and demands the keys to the car. You instinctively go for the gas. Before your foot even reaches the pedal, you feel a crushing pain. You open your mouth in a desperate attempt to draw a breath, but your lungs won't fill with air. You reach for the door in a blind panic. An instant later, you feel a numbing cold just before you succumb to darkness.

Lucky for you, someone has seen the whole thing and called 911, kicking the Emergency Medical System (EMS) into action.

The action will take the form of a race, the emergency response personnel (paramedics, doctors, nurses) pitted against your wounded body, spiraling down to the final peace of death. But overshadowing this race will be another, this one against time— one hour of it, to be exact. In emergency medicine, this slim margin of the first 60 minutes is revered as the **golden hour**. The people who are trying to save your life can make no mistakes, waste no moments, take no opportunity to do anything a second time to get it right. Everything done or undone within this hour weighs heavily in the life-or-death calculus.

The clock started ticking the moment the bullet ripped through your flesh. Although your immobile body, lying stage front, will be the focus of the play, you have no lines, no stage directions to follow. You're unconscious, and all that is about to happen to you is beyond your control.

Three minutes after the attack, two paramedics, dispatched by the 911 operator, bear down on the crime scene. A crowd has gathered—many people feel a morbid curiosity about strangers who are injured or dying. For others, the sight of a person facing imminent death kicks in the heroic side of human nature. So it is for the paramedics 15 times a day, every day of the year.

Police forces back the crowd to make way for the paramedics, and the first one to get to you spots blood oozing from a dime-size hole in your chest. Immediately, he feels for a wrist pulse and, turning to his partner, says, "still alive." Barely. Seven precious minutes have passed since you were shot. Death is already around the first turn, and the emergency team is still in the blocks.

If the paramedics want to have any chance of winning this race, they are going to have to make up for lost time. Massive demands are about to be made on them, testing their skill and speed, both mental and physical. But first, they need to "scoop and run" if you are to have a prayer of making it as far as the ER. With lightning speed, they place a rigid collar around your neck (to avoid paralysis, in case you have a spinal injury), wrench you from your car, strap you onto a gurney, and position you in the back of the ambulance.

Inside, they must stabilize your death spiral. It's a heavy responsibility. These fierce, well-conditioned professionals rise to the challenge with the ABCs of life support. *A*irway. *B*reathing. *C*irculation. Since we don't manufacture oxygen in our bodies, and because the brain must have oxygen to manage our life-support systems, the paramedics' first job is to reestablish a flow of oxygen from an outside source to the brain.

First order of business: airway. *Clear an airway that allows life-saving oxygen to flow into the patient's lungs.* One of the paramedics checks your mouth. No blood, and nothing to obstruct your breathing. But your breaths are shallow, and this triggers the second rule of life support: breathing. *Make the patient's lungs work properly, allowing oxygen to get into the bloodstream.* The other paramedic moves the stethoscope across your chest. He shoots a look at his partner. "No breath sounds on the left side," he declares.

Both men know what this means. *No breath sounds* indicates that the bullet, like a pin popping a balloon, must have pierced and collapsed the left lung. Your chest is filling with blood instead of air. To ensure that your one good lung gets enough air to allow oxygen to reach the brain, they will have to assist you with your breathing. Acutely aware that time is short, they choose the fastest way possible, **intubation** (in ER lingo, "tube 'im"). This is the simple task of inserting a tube into a patient's trachea, or windpipe. The paramedic opens your mouth, peels off the sterile cover of a long polystyrene tube, and skillfully works it down your throat and into your trachea in seconds. Then he quickly attaches a bag (called an **ambu-bag**) to the end of the tube and forcefully squeezes the bag, sending air flowing into your chest. He is breathing for you. With each squeeze of his fist, life-preserving oxygen fills your right lung. He glances at his watch: 11:13.

The other paramedic is already taking your blood pressure. "60 over 40," he whispers. That's low (**hypotension** is the term for low blood pressure), probably due to the blood loss from the gunshot wound. **BP** (blood pressure) measures how well blood circulates through your arteries. The heart contracts, sending blood gushing into your bloodstream and throughout your body, raising the blood pressure to a high level known as the **systolic** pressure (the top number of the BP). When the heart relaxes, the pressure drops to a low level, known as the **diastolic** pressure (the bottom number).

Sufficient pressure is needed to send blood into the body, providing oxygen. If there is a leak in the system and a lot of blood is lost, the systolic pressure starts to drop. When the pressure drops too low, not enough oxygen gets to the brain. A systolic blood pressure of 60 is low, too low for you to live much longer.

Since the paramedics can't plug the leak, they do the next best thing, the third tenet of life support: circulation. *Ensure that the patient's blood has enough pressure to circulate adequately and carry the oxygen to the brain.* There's only one way to do this: use **IV** (intravenous, or directly into the vein) fluids, which will introduce new fluids into the blood to make up for the loss of volume through the leak.

Already fifteen minutes into the golden hour, the paramedics will have to do it on the run. One of them vaults into the driver's seat, cranks the engine, and pulls out onto the road, while his partner swiftly inserts the IV needle into your right arm.

This may sound like a routine task, but imagine trying to thread a sewing needle while sitting in the back of a bumpy truck doing 50 miles per hour and you'll have some idea of the skill it takes to pull this off. Now imagine doing it during a **Code 3** (highest priority), with lights flashing and sirens blaring. Finally, imagine that the eye of the needle is hidden from view—for that's how it is with an IV: the paramedic can't punch just anywhere, but must find the target under the skin. He's done this a thousand times before, and he slips the needle right into your vein. He grabs a bag of **saline** solution (salted water) from a rack on the sidewall, hooks it up, and lets it rip. Then he repeats the procedure with the left arm. Now, saline solution—the temporary substitute for lost blood—flows into both arms, filling your veins with fluid. Your blood pressure starts to rise. Your pulse strengthens. The first lap is over, and the medical team is back in the race.

It is 11:18. The wailing siren trumpets the ambulance hurtling through city streets toward the nearest Level 1 **trauma center**— an emergency room with a trauma surgeon on duty 24 hours a day. The paramedics know that in order to control the bleeding, you will need emergency surgery on your chest. The driver is already on the radio alerting the ER to your impending arrival.

The burly general clerk for the emergency department picks up the radio call at the reception desk. "Five minutes, people. **GSW** to the chest," he blurts out, using the abbreviation for "gunshot wound" and setting an irrevocable chain of events into motion in the ER. One of those special-mission rooms, like the poker room at a casino or mission control at NASA, the ER has its own peculiar kind of high-stakes energy.

The senior physician, the big cheese of the ER, captain of the medical team that will receive you (on the show someone like Mark Greene), stands within earshot of the clerk. Very much in charge, he rallies his troops: "Get the respiratory therapist, call the chest surgeon, and let's get Trauma Room 1 ready. **Stat!**"

"Stat" is one of these special code words that embrace the spirit of the place where it is spoken and the people who speak it. From the Latin *statinum,* it means "immediately," and it captures the essence of emergency medicine. For those who work in the emergency room, stat is the air they breathe.

And so it is that the ER team gathers—stat! Two nurses are responsible for monitoring your blood pressure, pulse, IV fluids, and medications. A respiratory therapist is responsible for controlling your airway and breathing. And since this ER is a teaching hospital (just like County General on the TV show), a sprinkling of medical students will help with the necessary and sometimes unexciting chores termed "scut work," such as running your blood samples to the lab. And last, but not least, a surgeon will be needed to repair the internal damage caused by the bullet.

11:20 P.M. The ER is crowded. In the waiting area, the TV blares, a baby cries, a homeless man moans, a family sobs. Amid the cacophony, you come crashing through the doors of the ambulance entrance on a gurney.

The ER physician, there to meet you, your own Mark Greene (we'll call him Mike Gray), hustles alongside the paramedics. Out of breath, they run through the hallway gasping to him, "GSW to the chest, last BP was 80 over 40, no lung sounds on the left. IV's been running wide open." This means that the faucet-type valve controlling how much fluid is entering your body is open as far as it can go. Then, like sprinters passing the baton, the paramedics pass you on to the trauma room team for the remaining laps of the race. Their job is done.

Now it is up to a new crew to bring you into the final stretch. With less than 40 minutes of your golden hour remaining, you're dying from a bullet lodged in your chest. Dr. Gray and the ER staff are your last line of defense between a lousy Christmas and eternity.

High-tech equipment shares cramped quarters with IV solutions, medications, and instruments. The only person in the room not moving, under the bright lights, is you. A frenzy of staffers swarm over you—at least ten hands grabbing forceps, needles, scissors, tubes, within easy reach of a specially prepared table—working in unison under the stewardship of Dr. Gray. His calm voice and demeanor, like that of an airline pilot flying through turbulence, reassures the staff that he's in complete control of his craft.

Those who know their job need little direction and are already at work. The respiratory therapist has to keep the *A* and *B* (airway and breathing) of life support in check. He is already at the head of the bed, squeezing the ambu-bag that now provides your one inflated lung with oxygen.

The nurses monitor vital signs (heart rate, blood pressure, body temperature, and rate of breathing), prepare you for procedures, and carry out Dr. Gray's orders. The charge nurse in the

ER, not unlike Carol Hathaway on the show, is already cutting into your blood-soaked shirt with a pair of large scissors. Another nurse checks the IV lines to make sure they are flowing properly. The charge nurse cuts away the rest of your clothing. She has taken care of countless trauma patients in the past and can remember times when a second wound was overlooked because patients were not undressed and adequately examined.

A nurse places three sticky, hardened, quarter-size gel electrodes on your chest and speedily attaches them to wires connected to the cardiac monitor, a miniature television screen above your head. It shows the rhythm of your heart. Beep . . . beep . . . beep. . . . For every precious beat, there is a corresponding squiggly line on the monitor; a computer counts and displays the number of beats per minute. The beeps sound much too close together, and the charge nurse looks up at the screen to check this number; your heart is beating faster than the lambada. And that's not good. She turns to Dr. Gray and says, "Tachycardia."

Tachycardia, or rapid rate, occurs when the heart needs to beat faster in order to get more oxygen to the brain. It can occur for a lot of reasons, but for you, it's because you have lost a lot of blood. The heart needs to pump faster and harder to keep the remaining blood in your body circulating to the brain.

"Great," Dr. Gray sarcastically acknowledges the nurse.

But he is already listening to your chest through his stethoscope. "No breath sounds on the left," he announces, confirming the earlier observations made by the paramedics. And in this situation, no breath sounds can mean only one thing.

"Pneumothorax," he announces. Your lung has collapsed, and blood and air seeping into the chest cavity are preventing it from reexpanding. The lung needs to be re-inflated, both to help your breathing and to help control the bleeding.

Dr. Gray looks up at the clock on the wall . . . 11:26. The golden hour is passing quickly, and he knows he has to accelerate his team if they are going to cheat death on this one. He announces that you need a chest tube.

He makes an incision on the upper left side of your chest and inserts a plastic tube directly inside your chest cavity. He hooks up the tube to a suction device and begins to remove the excess air and blood. Seconds later, your lung re-inflates.

Dr. Gray rips off his latex glove and turns to a nurse. "Order six units of O-negative blood, a chest X ray, and a CBC—stat." Type O-negative blood is sometimes called the universal donor, because it can be given to any patient without the need for time-consuming cross-matching. In life-threatening cases, O-negative will buy some time while a sample of the blood is typed and cross-matched. The X ray is done in the ER department, and will show whether the chest tube has been positioned correctly inside your chest. The **CBC**—complete blood count—tallies up the number of red blood cells, white blood cells, and platelets and will tell the team, among other things, just how much blood you have lost.

It's 11:35. You're stable. Dr. Gray hurries across the hall for a pit stop while he has the chance. Less than a minute later he is on his way back when he meets up with Patrolman O'Reilly, someone like *ER*'s Al Grabarsky. A frequent visitor, the cop, like his fellow officers, must file a report on any victim of a crime or traffic accident. He looks behind the curtain, taking in the gruesome tableau of you with plastic tubes woven into your torn flesh. He lets go of the curtain and turns back to Dr. Gray. "Just sittin' at a red light and—boom—carjacked!" he says. "I just don't get it."

"We see shooting victims every night of the year. What don't you get?"

"It was a fourteen-year-old punk with a .38. Got four squad cars chasing him right now."

"The family here?" Dr. Gray asks. The cop nods.

"I probably should let them know—" Dr. Gray is interrupted by a nurse pulling back the curtain. She nods to the officer and then says to the doctor, "I need you in here! BP's down again to 60."

Just as your doctor and his team are moving along at a nice clip, they suddenly find themselves losing ground once more in the race for your life. Dr. Gray runs back into the trauma room as the nurse continues: "Neck veins are distended [swollen], and

I can't hear heart sounds." She doesn't have to say anything more. Dr. Gray and everyone else in that room know that they are losing you.

It's not a lung problem. This time it's your heart. Your symptoms suggest that the **pericardium,** the sac around your heart, is filling with fluids—**cardiac tamponade.** The sac whose job it is to protect the heart from harm is now its mortal enemy.

Picture it like this. Imagine your heart is your hand and the pericardium is a thick protective rubber glove tied at the wrist. Suddenly, your hand starts to bleed profusely. The space between your hand and the glove fills with blood. The glove expands to make room for the fluid building up inside it. Now suppose the rubber glove is nearly impossible to break. The pressure continues to build, but around your hand . . . until it chokes the blood supply altogether. Worse, the pressure fights against the expansion and contraction—the beating—of the heart muscle. When the blood from a wound fills up the sac to the point where the heart can't beat, you're about to pack it in.

"Where the hell is the chest surgeon?" Dr. Gray shouts.

The charge nurse responds matter-of-factly, "He should be here in five minutes."

"He'll be dead in five minutes," he says as he looks up to the wall clock. It's 11:48. Only twelve minutes left of the golden hour.

Dr. Gray has only one choice: a last-ditch effort to reverse death from again taking the lead. He can count on one hand the number of times he has opened a patient's chest with a **thoracotomy**—the Roto Rooter of cardiac emergency plumbing—and actually saved a life. (This is a procedure we've seen Mark Greene or Peter Benton do on the show often.) It's your only chance of making it to the **OR** (operating room).

He grabs a scalpel and cuts horizontally along your chest, creating a 10-inch incision that extends from the breastbone on the left side all the way to your armpit. The incision is deep, cutting through the muscles between the ribs. He then takes a large metal rib spreader, inserts the device between two of your ribs, and spreads the ribs wide enough apart to get both of his hands into your chest cavity. He can see your heart—life—beating below his fingers. The sac around your heart bulges from the blood that has seeped into the pericardium.

With a pair of scissors he cuts into the sac, and the blood that had been trapped around your heart gushes out. The pressure is instantly relieved, and your heart begins to beat more forcefully. But he sees that blood is still oozing from your heart. A piece of the bullet has pierced its right side, creating a small hole, about the size of the tip of his smallest finger.

Instinctively, he pokes his pinkie into the wound and stops the flow of fluid, like the boy who put his finger in the dike. "Gotcha," he exclaims, watching his finger pulsate up and down with the beating heart.

"Blood pressure is 90 over 70," the charge nurse yells. "The OR is ready. What do you want to do?"

"Let's go!" With his finger in your heart, Dr. Gray, along with his team, carefully guides you out of Trauma Room 1. The golden hour is nearly over, and it looks as if the ER team has won another one against death—fair and square.

As the team rushes the gurney down the hallway toward the OR and over the finish line, they beam with pride. Tonight a human life—your life—has been saved. A precious triumph, indeed. For you, it will be a lousy Christmas and, considering what awaits you in your recovery, maybe a lousy winter. But for the men and women of the ER, it's as if they just won the gold!

PART

I

A Cast Holds
Together More Than
a Broken Leg

CHAPTER ONE

The Helping Hands Without an MD

The EMS, Nurses, Physician's Assistants, and Clerks

Let's talk about the cast of *ER*. Does Anthony Edwards—a k a Mark Greene, responsible, driven, hard, but fair—give a true-to-life portrait of an attending ER doctor? What does it take to fill that role at a major urban hospital's emergency room? You must be curious about the actual job responsibilities—not only what he does but who he is "attending" and where he falls in the overall hospital hierarchy.

And what about Doug Ross? He is clearly a good pediatrician, but unquestionably a "cowboy" and a "loose cannon." In real life, do such difficult doctors invariably get fired—unless, like Doug, they wind up on TV after heroically rescuing a child? Or would they be kept on, problems and all, because they are such good doctors? Further, what is the deal with Ross's department? He answers to the head of pediatrics and his fellowship is through that department, but he works, almost exclusively, in the ER. By the way, how many of you with children have ever found a pediatrician on staff in your local ER? How common is that, and are any other specialists kept on staff at a typical ER?

What about doctors such as the gruff yet gifted Peter Benton, a surgeon who takes his personal problems out on his students, is increasingly absent from the ER as he spends more and more time in surgery, and has a medical student (in the first two seasons, that was John Carter) to supervise and teach?

And then there's Carol Hathaway. Is it realistic to believe that immediately upon her recovery from a suicide attempt, she would be allowed to resume the difficult responsibilities of an ER nurse?

How well, in general, do these portrayals reflect the lives and work of the people who staff the emergency rooms of the real world? What role does each fulfill? Are there roles you should expect to find in a real-life ER that do not have counterparts in the television drama? Answers to such questions may not just satisfy your curiosity but save your life. With nearly 100,000,000 emergency room visits a year, you have almost a 1 in 3 chance of ending up in the ER in the next year.

Emergency Medical Services (EMS)

You're as sick as a dog. You are vomiting your guts out, you have a fever, and your belly hurts like hell. You call your HMO, and a doctor you've never heard of tells you to go to the ER. You stumble out of bed. You are too sick to drive, and you are alone. You dial 911, and in a flash the EMS is at your doorstep. Who are these heroes who come to the rescue, often in the middle of the night? How critical are they to determining whether patients get to the hospital in good enough shape for the ER staff to fix up? In real life, the answer may depend on exactly where you live and what kind of training the rescuer has had.

On the show, the majority of the rescue teams are members of the Chicago fire and police departments, and all are part of the emergency medical system for the city of Chicago. Twenty-five or so years ago, however, just around the time Michael Crichton wrote the pilot for the show (that's right—he held on to the pilot of *ER* for more than 20 years!), that system really didn't exist. There were virtually no 911 activation systems, no sophisticated EMS transport, no radio communication among rescuers, hospital, and emergency department. Emergency transports to the hospital were provided by local mortuaries. A patient who didn't make it just wound up giving business to the transport team! (One can only wonder just how fast these hearse-ambulances really tried to get to the hospital!)

Fortunately, in 1973, in response to an earlier report that pointed out the lack of available emergency care for the more than 50,000 Americans who died yearly in traffic accidents, the system you see every week on *ER* was established. It set standards for emergency medical services across the nation, although individual states and communities are free to meet these standards or not.

But even when the standards are followed, all EMS workers and systems are not created equal. The EMS worker who responds to your call may be an EMT (emergency medical technician) or a paramedic. In some communities there are two levels of EMTs. If the rescuer has received only "basic" emergency medical training, frankly, he or she can do very little aside from providing oxygen and general first aid—certainly no intubation, no IVs, no drugs on the fly. Those with advanced EMT training are able to provide some lifesaving procedures, such as intubation and IVs, and some drugs.

If you are in critical condition, pray that your community was smart or wealthy enough to train all its EMS workers as paramedics. They are the most expensive level of EMS worker, the gold standard of emergency care. Only paramedics can give an array of critical medications and perform advanced medical procedures, many that go well beyond the basic three principles of life support (airway, breathing, and circulation). For instance, they can administer Valium or other medications to stop seizures before they cause brain damage, and the diuretic lasix to avert a respiratory arrest for patients with pulmonary edema (fluid in the lungs). They can treat a tension pneumothorax (a collapsed lung that is pressing on your heart and aorta); with no paramedic in your ambulance, if the pressure squeezing your heart and crushing your major vessels isn't relieved and the hospital is more than 10 minutes away, you might be dead. If you're lucky to have a paramedic by your side, he or she can save your life with a needle thoracotomy—basically, a needle inserted into your chest to allow the air to escape. Your odds for survival should be dramatically increased if you are rescued by a paramedic, the Sheps and Reillys of emergency care.

You may be surprised to learn that if you live in an urban area, you are more likely than someone in a rural area to be treated by a paramedic. Now consider this. The 911 system is by no means universal, primarily because it is not affordable everywhere. This lifesaving link is available in only one out of two communities around the country. And even when the 911 system is in place, it may not have the capability to find you if you are at an unknown location. In many places, if you are in a car accident, especially at night when pedestrian traffic may be nil, you may find yourself on your car phone with a 911 dispatcher who can't pinpoint your location. So if you don't know where you are, the dispatcher will have to tell you to go find a stationary phone and call back.

Nearly all communities provide guidelines for which hospital the EMS worker is to take you to, but more often than not, the rule of thumb is the closer the better. Are you surprised to learn that some hospitals provide incentives to EMS workers to bring patients to them? In private community hospitals, for example, paramedics and police find nothing short of a luau—free food left out for them by the administration. (Raiding the fridge is condoned, even encouraged.) Even in county hospitals, administrators may grouse about having to treat violent patients, uninsured patients, patients who have OD'd, but there's a special place in their financial calculations—if not their hearts—for the ER, because a certain number of the patients who come through its doors will inevitably be admitted, fill empty beds upstairs, and have their bills paid by local and state agencies.

When an EMS worker, or for that matter a cop or a firefighter, is himself injured, the ER staff treats it as an assault on one of its own. You may recall the episode when paramedic Raul Melendez was severely burned and lay dying, lucid until the end. Everyone on the staff stood ready to attend to him and suffered with him, as if he were a family member. Indeed, if you have to go into an ER with a serious problem, pray that no cop or firefighter will be injured that night, because if one is, you can be sure that the focus of much of the staff will be on that patient until he or she is stabilized. Firefighters, police, and EMS are part of the ER family, and families take care of their own.

Also, despite the laudable role of Doris, often seen whipping blood-soaked gurneys into the ER, women are the exception among all types of EMS workers. The physical rigors of the job require enormous body strength. Imagine carrying an unconscious 300-pound man down five flights of stairs in a dark, smoldering tenement and you'll understand why women don't tend to volunteer for the work.

In the first season of the show, many paramedics who were viewers felt that their contribution was being underplayed. They wrote in to the producers expressing their disappointment. It was only in the latter part of the second season that the show started to develop stories examining the role of the paramedic outside the ER, when charge nurse Carol Hathaway, to qualify for her recertification in MICN (Mobile Intensive Care Nurse), joined Ray Shepherd ("Shep") and his partner Reilly on ambulance runs.

In the second season Shep became a main character, but his portrayal would certainly not please most real-life EMS workers. First he is shown as a walking time bomb while mourning the loss of his partner Raul. Then there is the highly emotional scene in which a family member of a gunshot victim keeps crowding Shep while he tries to do his job, and in order to get more space Shep gives the guy a violent-looking shove. The man strikes his head against a stone table and is knocked unconscious. Despite Carol's defense of Shep's behavior to the IAD (Investigative and Audit Division) investigator, we come to learn that she is in sympathy with the charge against him. This story line does a disservice to paramedics, who calmly, carefully, thoughtfully, and bravely bust their butts and risk their lives assisting others in need, under great emotional stress, and at times at great risk to their own lives.

En route to the hospital in an emergency, you are in no better hands than those of a paramedic. The person who answers your call will likely be a model of grace under pressure, the ambulance as close as you can get to an ER on wheels. An EMS response by a paramedic will give you your very best shot at staving off the Grim Reaper.

THE CLERK

You've arrived at the hospital. You are not critically ill, but you're still suffering with terrible abdominal pain. The first ER person you are likely to have an extended conversation with is the clerk or secretary. On the show, the character who performs most of the clerical or secretarial work is Jerry Markovic, with less frequent appearances by Timmy, Rolando, and Randy (a kookily, sexily dressed woman with a criminal record). Jerry seems to be the chief cook and bottle washer for the secretarial pool, answering phones, trotting up and down from X Ray, calling physicians, and otherwise doing the business of the ER, always with a cherubic smile and a wisecrack. His reputation as in-house baby-sitter is unparalleled. Jerry delights his charges with medical book illustrations of diseased organs.

In real life, an ER will have a number of support staff performing Jerry's duties. They are often the people you speak with first, and that conversation will reflect the primary, though not exclusive, concern of the hospital with regard to your health care: *money!* Yes, all the doctors, nurses, secretaries, and techs want you to get well, but the hospital wants to get paid. It may be hard to see it this way, but a hospital is a business, and any hospital that doesn't take this hard attitude may quickly slip into the red, losing millions each year.

But the clerks and secretaries have more difficult responsibilities than being toll collectors. They are the scribes of the admitting board (though it is the chief or senior resident who assigns patients to doctors). Clerks facilitate and channel much of the pertinent information between the doctors and nurses and the hospital that implements your ER care. They make the phone calls to the consultants and other physicians, they fill out the slips for the lab work, they schedule X rays.

For the most part, unfortunately, these staff members go unnoticed. When they are singled out, it is usually over an error rather than a job well done. Their names are not included in the thank-you note from a grateful family member or patient, but they are the fall guys if a test is lost or ordered incorrectly.

Even though these support staffers are rarely highlighted on the show and are taken for granted in the real world, one need only watch what happens in the real ER when a nurse, a physician's assistant, or any warm body is recruited to fill in for a clerk who is out sick: tests don't get done or are lost, important phone calls aren't made—the wheels of the ER engine don't get greased. In some cases, the engine grinds to a halt.

THE PHYSICIAN'S ASSISTANT (PA)

You are lying on the gurney waiting for test results. The physician's assistant comes to your bedside and asks you questions about your abdominal pain. On *ER*, that's Jeanie Boulet, once the physical therapist (PT) who cared for Peter Benton's mother. Working full-time as a PT, she attended night school and is now working as a physician's assistant (PA) in County General's emergency department. Jeanie has learned that the husband she is separated from has AIDS, and she has told her former love interest, surgeon Peter Benton, that he is at risk for becoming HIV-positive. So far Jeanie, unlike her counterparts in the real world, does not have an area cut out for her. In fact, she seems to have done nothing of significance so far. When Carol Hathaway has to evaluate her performance, she gives Jeanie low marks for not being assertive in the ER. Eventually Jeanie wins over the ER staff, including Hathaway, Benton, and even Morgenstern, the attending physician, with her fund of knowledge. With each new episode her role more accurately reflects the impact that PAs have on the day-to-day workings of hospitals that employ physician's assistants.

In the real world, candidates for PA spend their last two years of college studying and working in clinical medicine. The degree they earn is a Bachelor of Science. Once in a hospital setting, a PA works under the auspices of the residents and attending physicians, allowing the doctors to spend more time with the most critical and difficult medical problems. According to Janice Tramel, associate director of the University of Southern California's Primary Care Physician Assistant Program, PAs who work in the ER are capable of performing much of the same duties as ER residents: they evaluate patients, suture lacerations, order appropriate tests to determine what is wrong with a patient, and can even put in chest tubes.

Physician's assistants have been around since the late 1960s, partly in response to the population of medics returning from Vietnam. These men needed formal certification that would allow them to continue working and using the experience they had gathered during the war. With a PA degree, they were able to function at a high level in the medical community, though always under the supervision of a licensed physician. In many cases, PAs initially worked as paramedics and other health care professionals before going back to school for additional training. PAs should not be confused with nurses. In most instances the PA has a greater range of duties that can be performed than the RN. For instance, the PA has the authority, under carefully circumscribed conditions, to order tests, to do procedures, and to give medications, all of which must be cosigned by a physician. Oddly, the reverse becomes true when we compare PAs to **nurse practitioners**, who hold a special Master's degree: although they have a similar scope of practice to PAs, nurse practitioners, under certain circumstances, can work independently of physicians, something PAs are not permitted to do.

PAs have had difficulty establishing acceptance in the medical community. In the clinical hierarchy, according to Janice Tramel, they stand above the RNs (registered nurses). Their specialized clinical training allows them more responsibility. More directly bearing on the way they are treated, they frequently make more money than nurses, even when they are younger and less experienced than the nurses they're working alongside. The potential for jealousy and hostility was dramatized in the episode "Dead of Winter" when Carol Hathaway showed an immediate resentment toward Jeanie Boulet. From that point on, anything Carol asked Jeanie to do was met with, "That's a nurse's job," and anything Jeanie asked of Carol with, "That's a PA's job," fueling a petty feud. This tension is a reflection of what we'd expect to find in real-life medicine. A seasoned group of nurses in the ER may not be happy about having a newcomer with a Bachelor's degree, just out of school, come into their territory and make more money and have more discretionary power than they do.

Other ER staff members may be reluctant to accept it, but the growing presence of PAs and nurse practitioners will be critical to the shaping and delivery of emergency care for the next century. With skyrocketing patient volume and continued emphasis on cost containment, physician's assistants and nurse practitioners are a low-cost alternative to more physicians. Since they are capable of doing much that a physician does, they free up ER physicians to perform more critical procedures. Many county and community hospitals are using PAs and nurse practitioners to manage the large number of patients, and TV's County General has joined the trend.

THE NURSES

After the clerk checks you in, the first medical person you will probably deal with after you get to the ER (the paramedics have already seen you out in the field) is a member of the nursing staff, usually a triage nurse. (**Triage** comes from the French for "to sort.") She is the one who will decide whether your injury is life-threatening and needs to be seen to at once, or whether you can wait it out until there is room or a doctor to spare. Remember the episode in which the ER is busting at the seams and triage becomes the name of the game? Mark pleads with Morgenstern to close the ER to any more patients, but Morgenstern is concerned that the county will cut funds if it sees that the hospital is unable to serve the community's needs. So the doors stay open and the people pour in, bleeding, coughing, puking, and dying. Mark doesn't have time to eat. By the time he has a short break, the cafeteria is closed for the day. In the pelting rain, he jaunts across to Doc Magoo's diner, only to be thwarted once again by a fiery car collision.

Hours later, after treating the critical patients, Greene, Carter, and a handful of nurses turn to the less serious cases. In rapid succession, they assess and treat the 40-odd patients remaining in the waiting room, from the woman whom they give placebo eyedrops to "cure" her psychogenic blindness to the child on whom they use a metal detector to locate the batteries he swallowed. This altruistic approach makes Mark and the staff look like heroes—this is the kind of thing people go into emergency medicine to do—but, as we'll see later, liability and billing headaches would crop up if doctors behaved like this in the real world and they would give administrators nightmares.

Under normal circumstances, nurses are the staff members you will see the most during your voyage through the ER. They are the ones who will give you medication (shots or pills), draw your blood, and clean you up after you vomit, and it is to them that you can complain about how long you wait between the stages of your treatment. Under certain circumstances, a pre-established protocol allows nurses to start a "breathing treatment" if you come in wheezing from an asthma attack, or, if you have chest pain, to get an IV going, take an EKG (electrocardiogram, which records the changes in electrical potential during a heartbeat and can diagnose abnormalities), and often give you some nitroglycerin, even before the doctor sees you. As described by Dr. Horace Liang, director of the ER residency training program at Johns Hopkins Medical Center, a major trauma center for the city of Baltimore, nurses are "the key to a great ER. They have to quickly assess a situation and run independently with the info. You live and die with your nursing staff."

Orchestrating the work of the nurses of *ER* is Carol Hathaway, the nurse most prominently featured on the show. Carol is a charge nurse, which means that she is the leader of the nursing staff working the shift and will handle administrative questions, such as scheduling problems and patient complaints, along with her usual clinical duties. She holds an RN (registered nurse) degree and would have either an AA (Associate of Arts) or BS (Bachelor of Science) degree from a nursing college. And she may have taken additional courses and received additional degrees. (Carol has a Master's.) In order to be a charge nurse, she will have had years of ER experience to prepare her to help run a large urban emergency department. There are about 70,000 nurses across the country who consider emergency nursing their area of expertise, and the ENA (Emergency Nurses Association) has certified over 20,000 nurses in emergency care.

County General has an older nursing staff of seasoned, mature nurses—Lydia Wright, Haleh Adams, Lily Jarvik, and Malik McGrath, among others. Typically, most ER nurses have worked the floors and intensive care units long before they come to work in the ER. This is so for two general reasons. The first is that ER practice requires recognizing the symptoms of a wide, wide variety of possible ailments, as well as drug therapies and possible reactions. Second is the immediacy factor, what makes emergency room practice what it is. By the time a patient is moved onto another floor of the hospital, the illness has already been diagnosed and the person has been stabilized, so monitoring the effectiveness of the regimen is more relaxed. Again, according to Dr. Liang of Johns Hopkins, "Nurses just getting out of school haven't seen enough or experienced enough." It's not that ER nurses can do anything clinically different from other nurses, but they often must act with utmost speed and under extraordinary pressure. And it is not until the pressure develops that you see how important the nursing staff is to a well-run ER.

It's after midnight. An adolescent girl named Liz is brought into the ER complaining of shortness of breath. She has a history of asthma, but her usual medications have not been helping her. The evening triage nurse can see that Liz is in respiratory distress: her fingers and lips are blue (**cyanotic**); she is not getting enough oxygen into her lungs. Carbon dioxide is building up in her blood and is making her drowsy and disoriented. The nurse puts Liz in a wheelchair and rolls her into the main area of the ER. Even at this late hour, the place is jumping. If this were County General, you might see Mark Greene zapping a heart attack patient, Malik cleaning vomit off his sneakers, and Peter Benton in Trauma Room 1 stopping a "pumper" (arterial blood spurting out with each heartbeat) from a knife wound to the neck. As the nurse wheels the wheezing girl into a treatment room, she calls out for nursing assistance. Whoever is available comes to her aid and helps hoist Liz onto a gurney. The triage nurse returns to the front. Moments later, Liz's labored breathing stops altogether, but her heart is still beating. A nurse calls out "Code!" signifying a respiratory arrest.

The shouted word reverberates down the hall. It's showtime! Any nurse who is not engaged in some critical procedure drops what she is doing and races to the treatment room. Generally, the magic number of nurses needed is two, unless a patient has to be restrained—then it's the more the merrier. The charge nurse tells the clerk to get a pediatrician and page Respiratory Therapy. As other nurses arrive, and see the quota has been filled, they return to what they were doing. All nurses know they are there to assist in the ABCs (again, airway, breathing, circulation) of life support. The charge nurse grabs a small plastic device called an oral airway from the crash cart (so called because it's used when patients "crash," or suddenly develop major problems like cardiac arrest) to help keep Liz's mouth open. She inserts it, places a face mask over the teenager's mouth and nose, and is ready to **bag** her—to simulate respiration using an ambu-bag.

Like a chamber music duet, two of the nurses play their parts in perfect harmony with each other. One nurse puts in an IV in anticipation that Liz will also need intravenous medication to breathe. No sooner is the IV in than the other nurse attaches cardiac electrodes to the patient's chest to monitor her heartbeat. The pediatrician arrives and knows the first order of business is to **tube** the patient. (How often have we seen Doug Ross, the *ER* pediatrician, do this procedure?) He asks for a size 7 endotracheal tube (ET). (The size measures in millimeters the diameter of the tube and is chosen based on the size of the patient's trachea.) Before he can blink, a nurse has it in his hand. She knows what his next move will be—intubation—and responds by lifting the mask off the patient's face. The doc inserts the tube into Liz's mouth and down into the trachea. The respiratory therapist arrives, attaches the ambu-bag to the ET tube, and begins to squeeze oxygen directly into the patient's lungs. The doc listens for air movement into both the left and right sides of the chest.

Satisfied that the ET tube is in the right place, the doc asks for a chest X ray to check the lungs and tube placement, in addition to three blood tests: a CBC, coag panel, and Chem-7. The coag panel tests the body's ability to clot, and the Chem-7 is a chemistry panel that tests seven elements, the most essential blood chemistries. The nurse knows the protocol without missing a beat. First she asks the clerk to call radiology for the X ray and then grabs a syringe to draw blood for the requested tests. The other nurse is busy checking vital signs. Liz's blood pressure is 160/95 and her pulse is 140. Both high. That's partly due to stress, but the teen is also **hypoxic**, which means the oxygen in her blood is low. The heart tries to compensate by pumping faster and harder, hence higher BP and pulse. The doc orders .5 milligrams **epi** (adrenaline—makes the heart beat faster and raises blood pressure), **IV push** (injecting medication rapidly into a vein to hit the blood system all at once), followed by 125 **solumedrol** (a powerful steroid). An instant later, a nurse is delivering the **meds** (medications) right into the IV. The doc asks the respiratory therapist to give .5 milligrams of **albuterol** as an inhalation treatment through the ET tube. All these medications help open up the blocked air passages. The patient, monitored, intubated, and medicated, shows dramatic improvement. Another crisis averted by teamwork. There is only one job left: once a bed in the ICU (intensive care unit) has been arranged, one of the nurses will escort the patient upstairs to be admitted.

However well schooled, nurses have some special skills not found in any book, skills that come only with working the ER day in and day out. ER physicians work independently of one another, each with his or her own patients. One may be truly unaware of the clinical judgment and competency of a fellow ER physician. But the nurses know! Ever notice that Carol Hathaway is at every attending staff meeting? When a physician may not measure up to his or her peers, it is often the nurses who identify the problem. Doctors are well aware of this unique perspective, and when an ER group is deciding whether to accept a new doctor, the opinion of nurses who have worked with that doctor often weighs heavily in the decision.

Most ER physicians will confirm that the nurses who work in the ER are the best of the bunch. They have to be. In a life-or-death emergency, with no background information on a patient's medical history, it is often the nurse's judgment that makes the difference. If a nurse advises a doctor that a patient must be seen right away, you can be sure the response will be immediate.

There is a unique relationship between ER nurses and physicians that does not exist anywhere else in the hospital. Certainly there is a camaraderie between doctors and nurses in the operating rooms and the intensive care units, but nowhere else in the hospital do physicians spend almost their entire professional lives interacting with the same group of nurses. That personal connection is unmistakable on *ER*, not only in the shared silences when tragedy strikes but in the less frequent revelry and high jinks as well. The belly dancers who were hired for Peter Benton; Lydia, Doug, Carter, and Carol's blitzkrieg on Cardiology to steal back their new crash carts; the DOA turkey that spawned a Thanksgiving feast; the reception at Carol's aborted wedding; and any excuse for a surprise party—all aptly celebrate the warmth and respect among ER staffers.

Despite the respect now accorded nurses for the work they do in the real ER, the show has not always portrayed things this way. In early episodes the nurses were often seen just standing around, waiting for their next orders. According to Marilyn Rice, past president of the Emergency Nurses Association, those first shows were reminiscent of what it was like to work in an ER twenty years ago (when, remember, Michael Crichton first put together a script), not in today's emergency department. Rice thinks the role nurses play in an active county hospital is more accurately reflected on the show now.

She was unhappy, however, as were many ER nurses, that Carol Hathaway was brought into the emergency room as a drug OD, apparently having tried to kill herself over a relationship with Doug Ross. The picture of the charge nurse, stripped naked with a large tube shoved down her throat to suck out her stomach contents, was not the image the nursing profession wanted aired throughout America. But do such things happen in real life? Absolutely. When a group of Los Angeles nurses was asked this question, a similar circumstance was described by one of them. And it is not unique to nurses.

A few years ago in Los Angeles, an ER physician jumped off the top floor of a hotel and killed himself. Others around the country have had problems with drugs, alcohol, and psychiatric disorders. In the first season, the show's attending psychiatrist, Div Cvetic, admitted to his love interest, Dr. Susan Lewis, that he had been clinically depressed from treating the "animals" on his service, but assured her he was coming out of it. Safe to say, this guy has work-related burnout. While Susan awaited his arrival for a holiday dinner, Div was shown standing in the middle of a busy thoroughfare in the pouring rain, pleading to be run over by a car. He survived the suicide attempt, but quit work and moved away (without bothering to let Susan know).

Unlike Div, some staffers have ended up in their own ERs for emergency treatment. People get depressed, whether they are nurses, physicians, salesmen, or cooks, and the ER is there to treat them if they try to hurt themselves. In Carol's case on the show, her ER happened to be the closest one. And her co-workers saved her life. In the final episode of the first season, "Everything Old Is New Again," Carol says it best after County General's Dr. "Tag" Taglieri (an orthopedist also called a "bone crusher") calls off their wedding moments before the ceremony is to take place. The remaining guests, all colleagues, gather around her under the tent where the reception was to have been held. She feels no shame, for the canceled wedding or for being admitted to her own ER. Carol is asked to make a speech and, choked with emotion, she says, "I am glad to be alive." As she looks at Carter, Haleh, Lydia, Mark, Doug, Lily, and Jerry, she adds, "And I have such good friends who care." Carol takes to the dance floor, the party begins, and the first season comes to a close.

"I'm Not a Doctor, But I Play One on TV"

Medical students call the ER "the pit." They see it as a place where diagnoses must be made under great pressure and often without sufficient information, where failure is put up on the board for anyone and everyone to see, where medicine is practiced at that precipice beyond which lies only eternal peace for the patient and eternal guilt for the physician. As fearsome as it can be, the ER remains a favorite training ground for would-be doctors who truly love medicine, because only there can they get exposure to the entire breadth of possible medical problems.

Back to your night in the emergency room. You are sitting on a gurney, your hands on your painful stomach. You're still growling, sick as a dog. Once again you tell your story, this time to the people who will finally be treating you: the doctors. For the third time you describe in detail what brought you to the ER, and it won't be the last, especially if you happen to be in the ER of a teaching hospital (that is, a hospital associated with a medical school), such as County General, loosely modeled on Chicago's famous Cook County General. Then you will be seen by what may seem like countless young men and women in white coats, all laying claim to the title "doctor," many of whom will turn out to be medical students. This is both the curse of the teaching hospital and its blessing, because at a teaching hospital you are more likely to get state-of-the-art treatment.

Now to the white coats. The hierarchy from least experienced to most experienced goes like this:

> Subinterns (third- and fourth-year medical students)
> Interns
> Residents
> Chief resident
> Attendings
> Chief

THE MEDICAL STUDENTS

Not all doctors are doctors. The youngest and least experienced are medical students. Though some institutions differentiate student and doctor by giving the former a short white coat to wear and the latter a long one, there is no standard. Students, however, do wear name tags that usually identify their school—and conspicuously lack the letters *MD*. But should you have any concern that the person ordering brain surgery for your stomachache is a student, fear not. It won't happen. Only an MD can order surgery!

Most medical schools require four years of education for the MD degree. The highest hurdle to get over may not be the work but the expense; at a private medical school such as Harvard, tuition alone is over $24,000 per year. Students have to anticipate that total expenses (including books, food, and a place to live) for a four-year education at Harvard Medical School will come to over $160,000. On the show, we learn that John Carter comes from a wealthy family when Jerry brings a magazine to the ER that lists Carter's father, Roland, as having a net worth of $178 million. Money is no big deal for John, but you can be sure that most of his classmates in the ER are loaned out to the max. In one episode, the doctors have a reverse bragging session in which they each disclose the amount they had to borrow to get through medical school. Mark Greene wins with just over $100,000. For some students that is cheap. Adding up undergraduate and medical school loans, many students graduate medical school in debt to the tune of a quarter of a million dollars.

During years *one* and *two* of medical school, students spend most of their time in three places: the classroom, the laboratory (studying gross anatomy and dissecting cadavers), and the library. Some courses introduce students to clinical medicine (they practice the art of injection on nectarines), but it is not until the third year of school that they spend any significant time in a teaching hospital on what is called **clinical rotation**.

A *third*-year student would be expected to "rotate," or spend time in the service of several basic medical specialties, including general medicine, general surgery, pediatrics, obstetrics and gynecology, and psychiatry. The rotations last anywhere from four to eight weeks. In a large teaching hospital, young medical students can be observed roaming the wards on nearly every floor. Third-year students usually spend a large amount of time studying and reading about the specialty, and often have a written examination at the end of their stint in that area.

During the *fourth* year, there is a fair amount of "elective" time when a student can choose specific specialties to work in, such as ophthalmology, dermatology, and emergency medicine. Again, students are expected to study and learn about the specialty during their rotation (don't forget they are students, paying for the privilege of learning). Part of the fourth year is taken up by "subinternships," where the student acts as an intern on the rotation. The subinternships last between six and eight weeks, and often help students decide what specialty they ultimately want to pursue—a decision they must make by the middle of the fourth year.

Once that choice has been made, these students must endure a process called The Match. It works like this. Fourth-year students rank in order of preference the hospital and specialty in which they want to train during their internship, while the hospitals rank the students in order of their own preferences. Then a computer matches student to hospital. So on a sunny day in March (known as Match Day), students find out what they will be doing the following year and where they will be doing it. The day John Carter finds out, he spends his lunch hour in a bubble bath with third-year medical student Harper Tracy and a bottle of champagne. When he goes back to work, late and inebriated, Dr. Hicks tries to recruit him for a procedure. Carter, being the responsible fellow he is, levels with Dr. Hicks and almost gets himself thrown out of the program before it even begins.

Deb Chen, a third-year student, rotated through the ER during the show's first season. She is eager to try any procedure to outdo her classmates. Most memorable perhaps are her first and last. Carter, showing Chen the ropes, gives her an early shot at a rectal examination. Never the one to say no, she salivates at the chance to "glove up and dig in." Behind a closed curtain we hear Chen ask the patient to turn on his side. A moment later, the patient howls in pain. Concerned, Carter asks if all is well. Chen admits that her finger is stuck in the patient's rectum, leading Carter to ask her whether she used lubrication. Oops!

From that inauspicious beginning to her demise, Chen is unrelenting in her drive to be number one, determined to crush Carter or any other student on her path to becoming a surgical resident. But her "procedure ambition" gets the better of her when she attempts to insert a central line (an IV that accesses the largest veins in the body that go directly to the heart) without supervision and nearly kills the patient in the process.

Chen is replaced by another med student, smart and sassy

Harper Tracy. She arrives during the first week of July, what is known throughout the medical world as transition week. For a patient, transition week is a very undesirable time to be in the ER. It's when the house staff gets replaced—all at once, with totally inexperienced interns—so you could be taking your life in your hands.

As good as Harper Tracy appears to be, no third-year student will ever approach the talents of John Carter, who works in the shadows of Dr. Peter Benton, the surgical resident. As gifted as Carter is, though, he is not infallible. In the "Hit and Run" episode, Benton forces John to ID the body of a teenager, a "nerd," much like himself, whose death he has just witnessed. He looks through the patient's class yearbook to match his face to a name. When the parents arrive, Benton somberly breaks the terrible news and leads them in to see the body. As soon as the sheet is turned down, they explain in shock that it is not their son! Well, at least Carter learned from Benton how to inform family of a loved one's death. Carter rectifies his error and gives the same speech himself to the right family. At the end of his shift, a downtrodden Carter shares his misgivings with Jerry just outside the ER. He is even contemplating leaving medicine when, suddenly, he is confronted by death's counterpart. After delivering a baby in the backseat of a station wagon, Carter is reaffirmed in his mission.

At the conclusion of the show's first year, Carter has completed the longest rotation in a surgical elective in the history of medical school—an entire television season! And at no time during that rotation does Carter attend the formal teaching conferences that he would be required to attend in real life; nor is he ever shown studying in the hospital library, preparing for the exams he will have to take at the end of his rotation. Indeed, if a library exists at County General, no one seems to have found it.

During his third-year rotation in surgery, Carter also would be expected to watch his instructors (the residents, in this case, Peter Benton) and to have opportunities to perform minor medical procedures. In fact, the majority of the work he does is suturing to repair lacerations (cuts) and running errands for Peter Benton.

During the second season, we see Mr. Carter again in the ER for another full television season, breaking his own world record—an accomplishment that would keep him from graduating from any medical school in the United States.

Carter does occasionally have the chance to prove himself, and invariably demonstrates remarkable skill for one so new to the profession. He is also allowed to assume an enormous amount of responsibility for a student in his fourth year of medical school. But John Carter is a unique subintern, or Sub-I. When challenged with questions by the residents in the ER, he shyly, but always accurately, stammers out the right answer. He never seems to be at a loss when it comes to medical questions.

What rings truer and is more reminiscent of many medical students is his compassion for patients and his sometimes sophomoric antics in and out of the hospital. Peter Benton remarked in his evaluation of Carter, "He is one of the truly outstanding students I have ever worked with." The feeling Benton has for his student and the student's feeling for his profession can be no better captured than in the episode called "John Carter, MD," in which Carter misses his own medical school graduation to play cards with and comfort a frightened young girl awaiting a liver transplant. Benton, true to character, is uncomplimentary even when he learns of the sacrifice Carter has made. But when Carter is about to exit the ER, he is handed a package that Benton has left at the front desk for him. Inside is a white lab coat, and embroidered over the front pocket is "John Carter, MD." Carter puts on the coat, and with the confident gait of a physician, walks off into the next season as an intern.

THE INTERNS

Another group of people normally walking around the ER dressed in white coats are the interns, although none has shown up in the first two years of the show. The literal definition of **intern** is "confined, impounded," and this is a perfect description of the year young Carter is about to undertake. A real county teaching hospital is practically home to interns, who work incredibly long hours with very little sleep, truly "confined" during this first year of training out of medical school. Talk to any intern and he or she will tell you it is a living hell. Only after many years does the nightmarish quality of the experience seem to fade. Policy changes over the past decade have tried to limit the allowable working hours of interns.

THE RESIDENTS

You are still in pain. You have discussed your symptoms with the paramedics, the PAs, the nurses, and the intern. It's going to be a long night. Once again it's story time for the next member of the white-coat brigade, the resident. The literal meaning of **resident** is to "reside," and though not as demanding as an internship, a residency in a specialty can make a physician feel as if he or she is residing in the hospital. The length of a residency varies from specialty to specialty, and can even vary from hospital to hospital. For emergency medicine, the residency consists of one year as an intern and either two or three years as a resident. Surgical residencies are even longer (five years, including the internship). Of the three residents that frequently appear in *ER*'s County General, only one, Dr. Lewis, is from the specialty of emergency medicine.

Susan Lewis

Susan has spent the first two seasons of her ER training at County General. In the second season Dr. Kerry Weaver was added to the cast to play the role of the chief resident, but other than Weaver, Susan is apparently the only resident in training in the ER program. We hear about other residents in other hospitals, but we never see them. Where are they? As previously mentioned, the hospital on which the show *ER* is based is Cook County, the largest county hospital in Chicago. At Cook, the ER residency has 18 residents per year for each of the three years of training, so the program actually has over 50 residents rotating at various times through the ER. Such a cast would have been impossible for the viewing audience to keep track of, and so another compromise with reality was made. Here the gap between television's ER and a real emergency room is very wide.

In order to gain broad experience in critical care, Susan and the other ER residents are supposed to rotate through a number of different areas throughout the hospital, including the pediatric, cardiac, and trauma intensive care units that will give them broad exposure to emergency and critical care medicine. Not only does Susan never leave the ER, but the rest of the residents in Susan's program are nowhere to be found.

There are other departures from reality in the show. At real hospitals, ER residents generally attend two conferences each week that last about three hours apiece. These conferences reexamine particularly difficult cases or situations to review what went wrong or to establish procedures for how to handle future cases. One episode of *ER* did feature a morbidity and mortality conference that put Mark Greene in the hot seat for performing a cesarean on an eclamptic patient. Perhaps this conference was the show's attempt to suggest that educational meetings occur on a regular basis at County General. But most training programs have regular Journal Club meetings where residents discuss the latest journal articles, take monthly exams on ER topics, and are expected to read and study the major emergency textbooks. Many residents attend a cadaver lab to study human anatomy. None of these sides of ER medicine seems to have made it onto the show.

Susan Lewis would also have reason to make sure she had some free time away from the ER to spend studying the field. At the end of her training, she knows there will be the difficult and feared Board Exam. The American Board of Emergency Medicine administers this full-day exam, which consists of multiple-choice questions; about 30 to 35 percent of students flunk it. Those who pass must take an oral exam about a year later, which another 10 to 15 percent fail. Those who pass both exams get to call themselves "board certified," and many hospitals are making this a requirement to be on staff.

Still, Susan has yet to make it to the library or sit down to read a journal. Granted, watching a resident read medical journals doesn't make for the most riveting television fare—not much action and a limited number of camera angles to choose from (do you shoot the pages of the article over her shoulder; do you focus on her jiggling foot?). But with the miracle of TV medical practice, despite the lack of evidence of her ever reading anything other than a patient chart, Susan's fund of knowledge is at times astounding. Like Benton, she is capable of coming up with truly amazing diagnoses, often to the bewilderment of her colleagues. In one instance, she diagnosed a pregnant woman with a rare tumor (pheochromocytoma), when no one around her had a clue that that was the problem. Watching the episode in a room full of experienced ER docs, I polled each; not one was brash enough to suggest that he or she might have come close to making the correct diagnosis. With clinical instincts like that, it was agreed, Susan should just skip the rest of her training and be made chief of a department somewhere.

Though women now constitute approximately 40 percent of medical school classes in the U.S., they still make up no more than 25 percent of the applicants to ER residencies. Times may be changing, though. Nearly 50 percent of the ER residents (300 applicants for 6 positions) at the University of California at San Diego's program are women, while at Johns Hopkins (700 applicants for 12 positions) about 40 percent of the 1995 entering ER residents were women.

In the past the overnight work and the frequent weekend and holiday schedules cast a dark cloud on this specialty. But now the benefits are starting to make themselves felt. An ER doc's duty hours are well defined: a shift lasts eight to twelve hours. ER physicians know when they are going to work and when they are going to be off. They don't have to be tied to a beeper. This is a luxury for a working mom (or a working dad, for that matter). As Susan Lewis put it, "We treat 'em and street 'em or turf them upstairs."

When Susan's residency is over, she will be well compensated for her ER training. In Illinois, she can expect to start making as much as $170,000 a year, and possibly substantially more a few years down the line. She will have a lot of free time and a fair amount of money at her disposal. Then all she'll need is for the writers of the show to give her a better social life.

Peter Benton

Peter Benton is a surgical resident who is spending his entire residency in the emergency department of County General— something that would never happen in the real world. A surgical resident in the middle of his training, Benton should be rotating throughout various parts of the hospital, on different surgical services. And he would not be the only surgical resident practicing in the ER. Furthermore, in real life, a surgical resident who is doing a rotation in emergency medicine does not leave the ER to go to the operating room.

In many teaching programs throughout the country, surgical residents do rotate into the ER, perform minor surgical procedures in the department, and assist in the evaluation and treatment of trauma cases. In some cases, especially in large hospitals with training programs, this leads to what is known in the profession as "turf battles" (referring to which department is responsible for the patient's treatment). ER residents like to do major surgical procedures, because it is what they will be doing in practice. Surgical residents look forward to performing these major procedures as well, and may compete with the ER residents for certain types of patients brought in through the ER.

Cook County Hospital, for example, has no full-time surgical resident in the ER. One might be called to the ER for major trauma, but a surgical resident is not going to hang around to suture minor wounds or routinely evaluate abdominal pain. In real life, poor Dr. Benton would be stuck in the ER as a full-timer stitching up patients, while his surgical colleagues upstairs in the OR would be taking out gallbladders, removing inflamed appendices, and repairing gunshot wounds. A situation Peter Benton would surely scorn.

Moreover, in a real hospital as large as County General,

patients brought into the ER involved in a major trauma are likely to be seen by a trauma team, which usually consists of surgical residents, ER residents, and nurses. On the show, it seems that whoever happens to be standing there when a stretcher goes by gets to take care of the patient. But don't forget, we TV viewers get attached to our characters and want to see them acting heroically again and again. No horning in by strangers, please.

Even if the residency program portrayed in the show defies logic, Peter Benton himself typifies the ER perception of the surgeon. These swashbucklers are often seen as brash, brusque, even rude. But Benton has been known to make mistakes. Early in the first season, Susan treats an elderly patient she suspects might have appendicitis. Benton contradicts her and sends the patient home with a stomachache after a cursory examination. When the woman returns with a **perfed appy** (when an infected appendix bursts open and spills into the gut), which requires emergency surgery, Benton takes full responsibility for the error of judgment. He may be the man staffers love to hate, but he is also one doctor they know they can't do without. Which is how real-life ER physicians often feel about the surgeons they do work with.

Most doctors will tell you they need to keep personal distance to be professional, but that doesn't mean they're lacking in humanity. As a patient entering the ER, you are listed on the board, which keeps track of patient flow, according to your ailment, and the doctors will often refer to you as such. You don't have a name. You have a complaint and a bed number: the abdominal pain in bed 15, the broken leg in 9. Benton takes this to the extreme. But near the end of the first season, in the episode called "Motherhood," Peter learns a heartbreaking lesson. His mother, having suffered a stroke, is no longer living at home. She hasn't been in the nursing home long when Peter receives an urgent call from the staff. When he arrives, he is greeted by a staff physician who rattles off a brief canned statement about how his mother's heart was very weak and how the staff used all its capabilities but lost her nonetheless. Shortly thereafter, Peter confides to PA Jeanie Boulet that he has given the same "we-used-all-of-our-capabilities" speech over and over to friends or family of a deceased loved one, but that until that day he had never really heard the words.

As for Peter Benton's social life, it does seem realistic. He has little free time; he is obsessed with the next "great surgical case." For many unmarried surgical residents, the rigors of the residency give them a special attitude toward those rare moments free of crushing responsibility. Fifteen-hour workdays and a lot of nights on call put stresses on residents, and these stresses are not only physical but emotional as well. It's a war mentality. And, being in a large teaching hospital surrounded by lots of other overstressed single young people—medical students and residents, nurses, physical therapists, young administrators—it is not surprising that their romantic partners are likely to be found among their colleagues. Where else are all these people whose jobs are their primary love going to find eligible people crazy enough to go out with them?

Doug Ross

If there is one character whose role on the show has the least in common with the real world of emergency medicine, it is surely that of Dr. Douglas Ross, played by television heartthrob George Clooney. Ross, a fellow in pediatric medicine—which suggests that he has already completed three years of a pediatric residency—appears to be on loan from the pediatrics department, doing a fellowship in the emergency department. This is a most unusual arrangement. According to Dr. M. Douglas Baker, senior staff member in the ER at Children's Hospital of Philadelphia (former fiefdom of C. Everett Koop and the pediatric hospital for the University of Pennsylvania in Philadelphia), pediatric ER fellowships are few in number to begin with (only about 80 positions are available in the U.S. each year), and none are like Doug Ross's. Furthermore, were such a fellowship to be created, it would require that the recipient use at least part of the time to develop advanced training skills and to do research. As far as aca-

demics go, Doug is never seen reading a medical journal, studying a textbook, or engaging in any activity remotely studious.
The only research Dr. Ross is ever seen planning is on the female
staff members of the hospital, research that has been remarkably
successful.

Doug's array of fascinating cases is also fantasy. Even though
Children's Hospital is one of the foremost pediatric hospitals in
the country, drawing over 60,000 children per year, many from
distant states, the majority of the problems seen there are fairly
routine: ear infections, upper respiratory infections, tummyaches,
and the like. On *ER*, according to Dr. Baker, "Doug sees a lifetime of pediatric emergencies in just a few shows!"

Third, in real life, fellows of pediatric emergency medicine
most often work out of a separate pediatric emergency room.
And, with few exceptions, pediatricians take care of *children,* not
adults! On *ER*, Doug Ross, a fellow like no other, saves anybody
who needs his help.

For his social life, as well as his good looks, Doug is the envy
of many a pediatric emergency attending physician. As for his
personal behavior in the ER, Doug is known for his compassion
and for flouting the rules if his sense of humanity tells him doing
so would serve his patient. In one episode, Doug buys asthma
medication and brings it to the home of an indigent woman so
that her child can be treated. In another, a child who has fallen off
a second-story balcony is brought into the ER by her father.
When Doug is shown a footprint on the child's back that matches
the father's boot, he is so enraged that he punches out the man in
the middle of the ER. (Almost every ER physician I consulted
agreed that it would be much more likely for the doctor to be the
recipient rather than the giver of a punch!) Doug's benevolent
gestures, on the other hand, are not out of the range of believ-
ability for a pediatrician in the ER. Pediatric residents at Children's Hospital of Philadelphia seek out the homeless and provide free pediatric care. Similar programs exist from Boston to
San Francisco.

The Chief Resident: Mark Greene

As you lie on a gurney in the emergency department, you may very well see a resident but you are less likely to see the chief resident, who can probably be found teaching, in the library preparing for the next lecture, or handling some administrative problem. On the show, however, the chief resident seems to do little else than take care of patients.

Dr. Mark Greene began the first season of *ER* as the chief resident of County General's emergency medicine training program. After Mark's graduation and promotion to attending in the emergency department in the second season, Dr. Kerry Weaver assumed the role of chief resident.

If Greene or Weaver were the chief residents of Cook County Hospital, they would be part of one of the largest ER training programs in the country. To become chief resident there, they would have completed medical school and an internship and would be in their third and last year of formal ER training.

At Cook County, the two most outstanding third-year residents from a class of 18 are selected to be the chief residents. They are responsible for coordinating the activities of all the other residents, while taking an active role in the academic education of the medical students and residents (the latter, as previously mentioned, are conspicuously absent from the show).

Mark and Kerry were, however, each able to see a lot of patients as chief resident, performing many coveted and bloody procedures such as thoracotomies (cracking the chest to repair major chest trauma) and cricothyrotomies (putting a hole in the neck for an airway). But a recent chief resident of the very real Cook County ER had done only two unassisted thoracotomies and no unassisted cricothyrotomies during her entire residency. While ER residents are exposed to these procedures, they can typically count on one hand the number of times they have performed them without the assistance of the trauma team. Obviously we see these procedures so frequently on the show because of their potential dramatic impact, rather than their verisimilitude. John Carter, still a student, considered doing a cricothyrotomy by himself on one episode, while Doug Ross performed one on a young near-drowning victim in the middle of a rainstorm! The problem, of course, is that an evening of treating ear infections and sprained ankles makes for pretty dull television.

Much of what Mark Greene does in his role as chief resident is medically sound, though he has this habit of performing some medical procedures that are outside the scope of normal ER practice. For example, he performed an upper endoscopy on a person with a bleeding ulcer, a procedure that GI (gastrointestinal) specialists spend years perfecting and covet as their own. It is simply not done by ER physicians.

While ER doctors applaud the altruistic actions of Dr. Greene in the episode "A Shift in the Night," as he goes out into the waiting area one busy evening when the wait for emergency care becomes excessive, the hospital administration would have been up in arms at such behavior. Bandages and prescription pad in hand, Dr. Greene and staff go from patient to patient diagnosing and treating, barely ordering a test or requiring anything more than a cursory examination to make a diagnosis. Though the doctors looked like heroes to us, real-life hospital administrators would have recognized that such a situation would increase the risk of serious omissions in the medical documentation of each case or, worse, inadequate assessment of the medical problem, leaving the hospital open to enormous potential lawsuits. Put more bluntly, any physician who neglected to write up his charts would be given the boot. But in the world of TV, the episode comes to a close with Carter remarking to Greene that the shift was about helping people, what he thought medicine was all about. Mark looks at the idealistic medical student and confirms what Carter is just learning.

When physicians, rather than administrators, are asked to critique the character of Mark Greene, they all focus on the show in which he agrees to interview for another job. At the insistence of his wife, Jennifer, Mark considers joining a posh, upscale internal medicine group. Real-life ER physicians all know that this would never happen. In the show's first season, the writers incorrectly saw the modern ER physician in old-fashioned terms, as a doc-of-all-trades. Not only would an emergency room chief resident be ill prepared, they note, to practice internal medicine, but why would a person like Dr. Greene throw away everything he had trained for over the past four years?

THE ATTENDINGS

You are still lying on the gurney in County General's ER, but eventually you will be seen by an **attending** physician (literally meaning to "look after" or "take charge of"). These are the doctors who are ultimately responsible for your care and who will decide whether you need to be admitted or discharged from the hospital. Attendings also supervise the interns and residents who float through their department for stays of approximately one or two months. It is the job of an attending to ensure that no zealous medical student removes a patient's appendix when the problem is really too many hot dogs at the ballpark. Attendings are part of the fail-safe system that allows students and doctors to get hands-on experience without jeopardizing the health and care of the patient.

Attending physicians have completed their residencies and are now responsible for overseeing the education and medical care given by the residents in the department. Once again, the education one normally finds in the real world—teaching conferences, discussions of the most recent ER journal articles, and formal bedside instruction with the attending staff—is not depicted on the show.

As for medical care, teams most often comprised of an attending ER physician, a senior ER resident, one additional resident, and potentially one medical student rotate through the real-life ER at teaching hospitals at all times. Nearly every major ER training program has at least one attending physician present in the emergency department 24 hours a day! The job is as important as it is prestigious. Full-time academic teaching appointments are often coveted positions, and represent a high level of achievement in the profession.

Mark Greene spent his second season of ER holding one of those coveted positions. He settled in well as a leader and administrator in the ER. The quality of medicine he practices would make most ER physicians proud. He is compassionate in surroundings that often make it difficult to spend any significant time with patients. Apparently Dr. Kerry Weaver, who appears cold, calculating, and impersonal, is about to join him as an attending in the third season. Viewers and residents beware: rocky times may be ahead for County General's emergency medicine residency as these two clash.

THE CONSULTANTS

Your abdominal pain is worse than ever. The ER attending physician might want to call a surgeon to evaluate your problem. If you are having chest pain, on the other hand, it would likely be a cardiologist who is called in to consult. Consultants are doctors who have specialized training in specific fields. It is impossible to be an expert in every area of medicine, and the working relationship between specialists and physicians on the front lines allows patients to receive the best medical care.

On the show, Dr. Jack Kayson, a hard-nosed, unwavering cardiologist whose opinion is always correct (at least in his opinion) continually fights with the ER residents. So does Dr. Div Cvetic, the brash psychiatrist who is always refusing to admit patients to the psychiatric service at County General. It seems that the only consultant who has gotten along with the ER staff is orthopedist Dr. John Taglieri, and that seems to stem from his relationship with Carol Hathaway. The kind of war that goes on at County General's ER between the specialists and the residents is not truly indicative of present-day medical practice.

THE CHIEF OF THE ER

As a patient in the ER, chances are you won't be seeing the chairman of a large emergency department. You may be so blessed if you have a very interesting disease, or if you sit on the board of directors of the hospital or of a charitable foundation. At County General, you certainly won't be seeing David Morgenstern, because he doesn't even work in the ER!

Dr. David Morgenstern, the big cheese, the big kahuna, the buck-stops-here guy, is a thoracic surgeon who has nothing better to do than walk around the ER—sometimes in tuxedo, sometimes in surgical scrubs—to complain to Mark Greene. Morgenstern probably provides the strongest evidence that Dr. Crichton's portrayal of emergency medicine is based on practices of two decades ago. In many large university teaching hospitals in the 1970s, ERs were run by either the department of surgery or the department of medicine. Morgenstern would have fit beautifully into the scheme of things back then, running out of the ER to sew up an aneurysm (a balloonlike dilation of an artery), then returning to see how the old ER was doing.

No more! In real life, Dr. Morgenstern, in his late forties, would be a board-certified emergency medicine specialist with years of experience in the ER. He would be an author, a teacher, a prominent figure in the field of emergency medicine, *not* thoracic surgery! He would set foot in an operating room only as a patient. If County General is like Cook County Hospital, one would think that being chief of an ER with 200,000 patient visits a year and directing a large attending staff and a very large residency program would be a demanding full-time job. Yet Morgenstern seems to do it all with ease, even having plenty of time for a busy surgical practice and social life!

While it is true that the physicians who were the leaders and developed the practice of emergency medicine in the 1970s were trained in other specialties, they have subsequently dedicated their careers to emergency care. Dr. Gail Anderson Sr. was a successful academic Ob-Gyn at the University of Southern California, yet he gave up his position as chairman of the Ob-Gyn department to create one of the first ER training programs in the country, at USC, and is now viewed as one of the founding fathers of emergency medicine. He is a constant figure in the emergency department at Los Angeles County Hospital, and while he still occasionally teaches Ob-Gyn, his priority in practice has been the ER, not the OR. Dr. Peter Rosen trained as a general surgeon, gave up his full-time surgical practice, and was instrumental in developing ER training programs at the University of Chicago and the University of Colorado, while also writing the leading textbook in the field. These two physicians, along with a number of other pioneers in emergency medicine, have devoted their careers to practicing and teaching the art of emergency medicine.

It is clear that the medical consultants and writers have had difficulty with Morgenstern's character. At the end of season one, Morgenstern leaves County General to take a prestigious job at Harvard's Brigham and Women's Hospital. The new chief, Dr. William "Wild Willy" Swift, seemed more likely to participate in a bike race than to manage the ER. Dr. Swift apparently got a better offer (from another producer, probably, not another hospital) and was quickly written out of the show. Morgenstern then miraculously returned, and we were back at square one, with a thoracic surgeon running the ER service.

We end this chapter with comments from the chairmen of some major ERs on the differences between the TV program and what they see in their own ERs. Bob Simon, the chief of Cook County's ER, makes it a policy never to talk to the press about the show. But he told us that he's seen only 10 minutes of it here and there and considers it a soap opera, "an inaccurate portrayal of what goes on in an ER, both in its extereme positives and its extreme negatives."

Dr. Gerald Whelan, chief of emergency medicine at Los Angeles County/University of Southern California, had this to say:

> The show is like an ER of twenty years ago. My major gripe is with the attending or teaching staff. They are almost always greedy, stupid, or arrogant—that is, if they are ever there. The show has done a lot for the image of the ER physician, even

though it distorts what ER training should be really like. The best show was the one about the burned and dying fireman. The hardest thing to do is to work like crazy on someone you know is going to die soon, someone who is alert and awake like that guy with 90 percent burns on his body. It's tough, especially if it's someone you see every day, like EMS crews and firemen. That was realistic.

And here is a comment from Dr. Marshall Morgan, chief of emergency services, UCLA Medical Center:

I know that Crichton wrote the original twenty years ago, and it shows. There is rarely if ever any supervision by the attending staff. That is just not right at a major teaching center. But the show is more accurate than most, especially considering the dramatic demands of television. Even though all the weird events happen at one time or another in real life, they pack a lifetime of weirdness into three weeks of shows.

High Drama

The Story of "Hell or High Water"

Are the emergency procedures that Mark Greene, Doug Ross, Peter Benton, and Susan Lewis perform the methods that real-life ER doctors would use in similar circumstances? Do the patients they treat on the show react as you would? Indeed, how often can the real-life version of those great life-and-death dramas depicted on the show be expected to play themselves out? Probably the most memorable episode of the second season, "Hell or High Water," can best serve to answer some of these questions.

The wild, lovable Doug Ross is on the ropes, his job at the hospital in jeopardy. It isn't Doug's sexual adventures that have gotten him into trouble (professionally, that is), but a relentless, uncompromising desire to see his patients treated fairly, even if it sometimes puts him in conflict with the policies of the ER and his boss in pediatrics. Despite the emotional and professional toll it takes on his career, Doug must always do right by himself. Facing what seems inevitable, he reluctantly considers giving up the guts and glory of the ER for a cush $90,000-a-year job in private practice.

After his job interview, Doug is to escort one of his ex-paramours, Linda, to a fund-raising costume ball. The idea of wearing tights is too much for him, so he opts to go in his tuxedo. The guy looks a million bucks in black tie. Outside, it's a rainy, cold November night. The rain pounds on Doug's car as it races through the streets of Chicago. It's been a rough day for him already, and suddenly things take a turn for the worse: he blows a tire. There is no way he's going to change the flat in a tuxedo in the middle of a torrential downpour. Tired, disgusted, and depressed, he pulls the car over. Just as Doug is about to light up a joint of marijuana to relax, he is startled by a young boy pounding on his window. It is a pounding stronger than the rain and a prelude to the pounding Doug Ross is about to take.

The young boy is crying hysterically for help. He and his older brother had been playing in a large storm drain. During the downpour, a rush of ice-cold water rose in the drain and trapped his brother under a metal grate. Doug doesn't need to hear more. He bolts out of his car and wades through the pond created by the storm drainage as the young boy leads the way to the huge drainage pipe, nearly big enough for Doug to enter standing upright, inside of which is the boy's trapped 12-year-old brother, Ben.

A jammed metal grate keeps Doug from rescuing the boy. Ben's leg is stuck under the metal bars of the grate. The icy water is rising. Doug attempts to examine Ben's leg, which is hurting. Doug thinks it is probably broken, but he can't concentrate on that now. He sends the younger brother to call 911. All the while Doug is fighting to keep Ben awake, insisting that the boy sing a loud chorus of "Take Me Out to the Ballgame" while he tries to pry him loose. At one point he tells Ben to curl up into a ball as tightly as he can. This will help keep his body warmer. They talk about the Cubs. Doug promises to take the kid to a game at Wrigley Field after this ordeal is over. He tries everything he can think of to engage the boy. Yet in all this excitement, why does Ben start to nod off? The problem is hypothermia.

Hypothermia is defined as a body temperature significantly below normal (usually below a rectal temperature of 95°F). A normal *oral* temperature is 98.6°F (plus or minus one degree). If the temperature is taken rectally, it would be expected to be about one degree higher (99.6°F). This is referred to as the core temperature, and better reflects the temperature of the brain, heart, and other vital organs. There are many reasons a person may suffer from hypothermia, but the most likely one for Ben is exposure to the cold elements of the Windy City. About the fastest way to chill a person is in cool water, for water is an excellent conductor of heat, what thermo engineers call a "heat sink." Think of a bottle of champagne: leave it in the refrigerator, surrounded by cold air, and it will take a couple of hours to cool, but stick it in a bucket full of ice and cold water for a fraction of the time, and—*voilà!*—it's chilled to perfection. Well, Ben's body is that bottle of champagne, having the heat sucked out of it by the cold rainwater of a Midwestern November storm.

At first, as Ben's temperature starts to drop just a little, his heart rate and breathing speed up, and he starts to shiver. These are mechanisms the body uses to help produce heat. In exposure to mild cold, shivering can increase the body's production of heat by as much as five times the normal amount, but this doesn't work well when you are immersed in icy water. There just isn't enough heat produced to match the heat being lost.

As the temperature drops lower still, to about 95°F, Ben's body is working at the max to produce as much heat as possible to keep his core temperature up. At about 93°F, amnesia starts to set in, and his speech starts to slur. Another two degrees, and Ben is becoming apathetic, sleepy. At about 90°F, Ben is stuporous. He can't keep his eyes open.

Doug doesn't have much time left. He tells Ben to keep singing songs to stay awake, and he rushes out of the storm drain to get his jack and crowbar from his car. When Doug returns, he pries open the metal bars that have trapped Ben's leg and continues yelling at

Ben to stay awake. But Ben's hypothermia is getting worse—he's just too sleepy from the cold. He starts to sink under the icy storm water.

Just then the grate bursts open and both Ben and Doug are swept out of the pipe and into the flooded drainage area. Ben is under water, lost beneath the icy runoff from the drain. His temperature continues to drop. When it reaches about 88°F, all the shivering stops and his body is defenseless against the killing cold of the water. At 86°F, cardiac arrhythmias begin to develop, and at about 82°F, the heart may start to **fibrillate** (produce a life-threatening irregular beat). Finally, with severe hypothermia, below about 81°F, there is a loss of voluntary movement of the muscles, the blood flow to the brain drops dramatically (assuming the heart is not fibrillating, in which case the blood flow would already be zero), and the blood pressure falls. Ben's body enters a state of suspended animation; if the temperature drops much more, he will lose all heart activity and be clinically dead.

Doug frantically searches under water for Ben. Finally, on a third try, he grabs the boy from his underwater tomb and rises to the surface, cradling Ben in his arms. High overhead, a searchlight focuses on the scene. A local news helicopter happens to be flying by and has been recording the heroics for public broadcast. What a scoop for the lucky helicopter crew! Doug lays Ben on the ground. The boy appears lifeless, without signs of a pulse or breathing. Doug quickly abandons mouth-to-mouth resuscitation when it's obviously not working, but he knows that the best he can do is breathe for the young boy. He starts CPR, pressing on Ben's chest to provide circulation of blood to the brain. It is time for the ABCs of life support. Ben's airway seems to be obstructed with something. Doug has to find a clear airway into Ben if the kid is to have any chance at all.

Finally joined by a police officer, Doug secures Ben's airway by performing a cricothyrotomy, or "crike," right there next to the drainage pond. He creates a hole in the neck into the trachea (through a soft area in the front part of the neck called the cricothyroid membrane) with a pocket knife. He borrows a pen from the police officer to create a makeshift endotracheal tube, inserting the pen into the hole to provide a breathing passageway for Ben.

The paramedics arrive. Time is of the essence. Not only does Ben need critical emergency care for the cardiac arrest, but he needs specialized equipment to warm his body as quickly as possible. The paramedics want to take Ben to Mercy Community, the nearest hospital, but Doug wants him taken to County General's ER. Mercy isn't a Level 1 Trauma Center, and may not have drugs and the competence in the procedures required to work on a hypothermic heart and body. On the other hand, even by chopper, County General will take longer to get to than Mercy. Take him to the nearest hospital, or risk the extra few minutes that could kill him by trying to get him to a place where he will get more skilled care?

Against the advice of paramedics, Doug gambles on the latter. He assumes responsibility for the continued care of the child. Up until this point, Doug has provided care as a Good Samaritan. So-called Good Samaritan laws have been enacted all over the country to provide legal immunity for anyone, including health care providers, who provides emergency aid in good faith with no expectation of financial compensation.

Doug has the right to assume the care of this young boy in the field (provided his parents weren't there to object), but once he does that, he assumes liability for any problems his decisions may create or contribute to. He makes the decision to bypass the closest hospital with a critical patient, a decision that, should Ben reach DOA (dead on arrival), will be second-guessed by everyone at both hospitals and all those watching their televisions at home, not to mention a team of high-priced lawyers. All this happens in front of a news camera. Details at eleven? Nope—live, right now!

Doug is given some rescue equipment and, with Ben in tow, boards the cramped news chopper (as opposed to the well-equipped paramedic ambulance) and heads off to County General. Doug wraps Ben in a blanket, holding him as they soar.

Once again, Doug has put his ass on the line to help a patient, this time a young boy whose life literally hangs on the reliability of his sole judgment.

En route, Doug tries to kick-start Ben's heart with a **defibrillator** (a machine that produces electrical shock to get the heart to beat normally), but the damn thing hasn't been charged. He calls in the emergency to County General. Mark orders the ER to prepare for the patient's arrival with blankets and saline warmed to 106°F. As the chopper sets down on the roof of the hospital, Ben is hypoxic (he is not getting enough oxygen, especially to his brain) and in V-fib (ventricular fibrillation, a life-threatening irregular heart rhythm). His **pulse ox** is 80 (a measurement of how well Ben is breathing—normal is 95 or better, 90 is bad, 80 is ominous). Treatment of his irregular heartbeat is started right on the roof—he is given epi intravenously. On the way down they shock his heart with the now partially charged defibrillator. They take out the paddles and put them on Ben's chest. Mark yells "Clear!" (to warn everyone in the room to stand back—remember the time Deb's paddles landed on Carter?) and they zap the boy with an electrical charge. Still no heartbeat. As they rush Ben on a gurney through the halls, Doug is straddled atop him, still doing CPR.

Once inside the ER, Ben will be saved only if there is still time to treat the hypothermia. Hypothermia and a near drowning can create irregular blood counts and chemical imbalances in the blood, so basic blood lab tests are ordered. A severe jolt to the system like hypothermia and near drowning can be a trigger for **DIC** (disseminated intravascular coagulation) that can cause severe bleeding and death. The ER staff also checks the *coags*, the clotting factors in the blood.

But Ben's core temperature is 80°F, and if he doesn't warm up soon, all the blood tests and medication at County General won't make much of a difference. With a temperature this low, Ben's heart may stay in fibrillation no matter what Doug and Mark try. Ben needs to be rewarmed, and fast!

The choice of method used to get core temperature up depends upon how sick and cold the patient is, as well as what facilities are available to the ER physician. The first option is passive external rewarming, where a patient is wrapped in an insulating material that limits further heat loss from the body. This method relies on the heat generated by the body and conserved by the insulation to bring body temperature back to normal. This is okay for mild hypothermia, but doesn't cut it for a case as severe as Ben's. For his severe hypothermia, Ben needs a heat source in addition to his own body's. This need is met with both external and internal (core) rewarming agents. Ben is given warm blankets to cover his body (external rewarming). But more important, he is given warmed, humidified oxygen to warm his lungs, and warmed IV solutions to start to raise the temperature inside his body.

An additional technique, called **peritoneal lavage** (literally washing the organs inside the abdomen), can also be done. In this procedure, a small incision is made below the umbilicus (belly button), and warmed IV fluids are infused through a catheter into the abdominal cavity. These heated fluids (up to about 110°F) bathe the stomach, liver, spleen, and intestines with warmth, helping to raise the core temperature quickly.

But with Ben running out of time, lavage may take too long to raise his temperature, now up to only 85°F. The good news is that Ben's heart is beating rhythmically again, but he could go back into V-fib if his temperature stays this low. Two additional procedures remain. If Ben's heart is working well, **dialysis** can be done. In this procedure, Ben's blood can be actively warmed as it passes through a dialysis machine (the machine usually used to filter blood for patients with kidney failure). The patient's heart must be working well for dialysis to be used. In Ben's case, his irregular heart rate has made dialysis a risky option. The crew in the ER choose to use extracorporeal rewarming, similar to the cardiopulmonary bypass used for heart patients.

Peter Benton is pulled away from Trauma Room 1, where he had been working on a young girl who had been struck by a car in a hit-and-run. Just a few hours before, this young girl was awake and stable following the accident. Now, she lies dying of internal bleeding just yards away from Ben, who less than an hour ago had seemed doomed to certain death.

Benton places large catheters (tubes) into Ben's circulatory system. They will remove the blood from Ben's veins, and send it off to the bypass machine. The blood will be rapidly warmed and supplied with oxygen, and then returned back into Ben's circulation. Benton secures the lines for the bypass, and Ben is placed on the cardiac bypass machine. His blood is warmed, and as his temperature rises quickly and approaches normal, Ben starts to wake up. Doug smiles at the 12-year-old and lets him know he is a man of his word—he'll be taking Ben to a Cubs game at Wrigley Field, just as he promised when the two were back in the storm drain.

Doug saved the boy's life and, while nobody could suggest that he acted not in the boy's interest but in his own, it is clear that the incident has saved Doug's job at County General.

Is this episode true to life? If so, where do they get this kind of material?

Unfortunately, most people who suffer hypothermia and drowning don't have a guardian angel like Doug Ross sitting conveniently nearby in a disabled car. Drowning claims the lives of 8,000 people each year in the United States, and is the second leading cause of accidental death for people under the age of 45 (motor vehicles are number one). Oddly, cold water and hypothermia can dramatically increase the chances of surviving a drowning, and the writers of *ER* were no doubt aware of a case that happened in June 1986. In many ways, the story of Michelle is even more dramatic than Doug's rescue of Ben!

On a late afternoon in a quiet suburb of Salt Lake City, a mother enjoys a picnic with her three children. The eldest is a son, age four; the middle child, Michelle, is two and a half; the youngest is a baby girl. The mother needs to run inside the house for just a few minutes when Michelle soils her dress, but upon her return, she can find Michelle nowhere. The four-year-old son tells his mother that he and his sister had just been playing across the street, and that Michelle had fallen into the creek. A horrid realization comes to the mother as she looks across the street from her home. The usually quiet, bubbling brook had been recently transformed into a raging creek following a harsh winter of record-setting storms in the nearby mountains. If Michelle were in that stream, there would be no time to lose. The raging brook is icy cold, and anyone in the water would surely succumb to the numbing effects of hypothermia.

Keeping her wits about her, Michelle's mom calls 911 and then gets a neighbor to watch her two other children. She rushes across the street, frantically looking for Michelle along the banks of the creek. Soon she is joined by a search-and-rescue team well experienced in water searches.

Doug Ross could have used such help in his rescue of Ben. These experienced rescue workers use special climbing harnesses and equipment to keep from being dragged downstream, but even their equipment can't completely insulate them from the numbing cold of the water rushing down from the mountain snow. Using their training and experience, they block off one of the reservoir gates upstream to lower the water level in the area of the accident. They probe the bottom of the creek with a long pole, and suddenly one of the rescuers spots an object the size of a small child wedged below a rock. One more probe with the long pole and a tiny hand floats up from the depths of the nearly frozen water. The team scoops up young Michelle and begins CPR.

Unlike Ben, Michelle had been completely submerged for an hour. Her core temperature was 66°F, far lower than Ben's 80°F, so low, in fact, that her **EEG** (electroencephalogram, which measures brain-wave activity) would have been flat if checked. Michelle had no pulse and no respiration. Her pupils were **fixed and dilated** (the center of the iris of the eyes being open and not changing in size in response to light), and the rescue team was sure she was dead. But the team had already made arrangements for Michelle to be transported by helicopter to Salt Lake City's Children's Primary Medical Center. This hospital, just like

County General, was prepared with special equipment to handle this type of emergency. So, instead of a news copter, Michelle was whisked off in a specially prepared rescue helicopter that immediately started warming efforts. Similar to Ben's treatment, Michelle received warmed humidified oxygen and warmed IV solutions, but this treatment began in the helicopter.

Once she arrived at Children's Primary Medical Center, Dr. Robert Bolté, co-director of emergency services, needed to make a critical decision. The extracorporeal warming that had been used for Ben had never been tried before (remember, this was 1986), and no person had ever survived this long under water. How long is too long under water? Until that day in Salt Lake City, every physician would have guessed that an hour was far too long. The odds against survival, even with brain damage, were immense. Winning the lottery seems easy by comparison, but a facility like Children's Primary Medical Center has to believe that its skills, equipment, and training can increase the odds dramatically. Clinically, Michelle was dead, or at least in a state of suspended animation. At this low temperature, the heart and brain can't function. But the other side of the coin is that at this temperature, tissue deterioration is retarded. And so most ER physicians adhere to the rule that a person cannot be pronounced dead until rewarmed to at least 86°F, a temperature at which the heart and brain have at least a fighting chance to work.

Dr. Bolté and Michelle's parents made an agonizing decision. With little hope of survival, they chose to rapidly rewarm Michelle using extracorporeal rewarming, utilizing the expertise of the cardiac bypass team at Children's. This was the first time the procedure had ever been performed; it had to be done because Michelle's heart was too cold to pump the blood through her body. The ER staff continued CPR as Michelle was placed on the bypass machine. Very slowly she began to show some signs of life, much to the amazement of Dr. Bolté and his colleagues. At 77°F, Michelle's eyes opened briefly. As her temperature climbed higher, her heart started beating once again. Within an hour, her temperature was back to normal! Michelle stayed in a coma for nearly a week, but gradually returned to normal. Two months after the near drowning and hypothermia, she walked out of the hospital, and remains a healthy girl today.

For every drowning death, five more (mostly children), like Michelle and *ER*'s Ben, are hospitalized for near-drowning. Nearly one-quarter of these patients will have moderate to severe impairment after treatment. Warm water, as in a swimming pool or bathtub, does not allow for the metabolic changes that helped Michelle in real life and Ben on television survive their extended submergsions. In warm water, as the brain and heart become starved for oxygen, the heart rate and blood pressure increase until death is close at hand. The suspended animation that takes place with severe cold is not available to preserve brain and heart function.

Yes, there are real-life heroes like Doug Ross who can seemingly perform miracles, and, yes, there are stories of real-life ERs that are every bit as dramatic as the show. For Doug, the painful and risky decision to transport Ben by way of the news copter to a more distant but better-equipped center probably saved the young boy's life. For Dr. Bolté, the decision to try a new procedure, even when all seemed lost, saved the young girl's life.

PART

I I

Medical Manual

ER at War

A Look Back at Emergency Medicine

Mark Greene and Doug Ross did not invent the practice of emergency medicine. Its beginnings probably go back many thousands of years, to prehistoric times. Cave paintings confirm that humans recognized injury as a special state to be memorialized. Back then, there were some fearsome adversaries: a falling rock, a hungry predator, a club-wielding stranger. Fortunately, evolution programmed into us certain survival mechanisms that might get us through even in the absence of medical care. For instance, blood pouring from an open wound induces "platelet aggregation," nature's clotting mechanism; infection sets off a counterattack by one's own white blood cells, often successful in fighting off the invaders; the infection-cleansed wound closes with the help of nature's bandage, a scab. Each body is equipped with its own mysterious ability to provide itself some basic emergency care, so the body can go on to the next necessary stage: the rebuilding of injured tissue.

But we expect that soon after early man recognized the danger of injury, some wise elder of the clan became the guy to go to after a collision between flesh and flesh, or tooth and flesh, or stone and flesh. And so was born the subspecialty of ER medicine, even before Hippocrates started swearing his oaths. Though ER practice would have to wait until the late twentieth century to be recognized as a certifiable medical specialty, the desire to deal with the hurt expediently, in its early primitive stages, was the genesis of all medical practice. For centuries to come, the wound would remain the single most powerful force bringing patient and healer together.

Even after the onset of recorded history, the medical picture remains sketchy at best. The Sumerian civilization, which flourished along the Tigris and Euphrates Rivers, has left us texts that mention the treatment of wounds: wash, cover with plasters (a combination of plants and animal extracts), and bandage. Bas-relief art depicts injured people who can't walk or are vomiting blood. But the causal connection between wound and subsequent symptoms—fever and chills from infection, weakness from loss of blood—appears to have escaped the Sumerians, and this stayed true throughout most of ancient history.

In ancient Egypt, just a thousand years before the reign of Tutankhamen, writings describe Egyptians as having been "beaten to papyrus," the semantic equivalent to (and maybe the source of) today's expression "beaten to a pulp." The art and writing of the times also describe certain advances in the treatment of these wounds and, more important, mention the physician.

These early doctors treated injuries with ointments, some made from pine or fir resin. Such ointments may have had some antiseptic value, though the Egyptians were as yet unaware of the existence of bacteria. Often the ointments would be mixed with honey and even animal oils. Honey, which is not receptive to bacterial growth, acts as a sort of firebreak for incipient infections.

There is some suggestion that doctors may have tried, as we know embalmers did, to close wounds by immediate suturing. The materials they employed ranged from adhesives—some kind of cloth covered with sticky resin—to clamping devices made from a thorn or insect mandible and thread (or sometimes a woman's hair). The Egyptians also left physical evidence that they used splints made of bark to treat broken limbs.

ER DOCTORS IN ANCIENT GREECE

The next big leap in the treatment of wounds, at least as is documented, comes from the golden age of Greece. Imagine doctors such as Susan Lewis, Douglas Ross, and Mark Greene transported back in time to around 400 B.C. The Parthenon has just been completed. The Peloponnesian War is raging and the Spartans are kicking the crap out of the Athenians. Hippocrates, the father of medicine, declares that all physicians "who desire to practice surgery, must go to war." To this day, the Hippocratic oath, culled from the still relevant parts of his 60 to 70 books on the healing arts, is recited at medical school graduations every year by thousands of new doctors.

During the siege, many Greeks are wounded. A woman such as Susan Lewis won't be a physician. Despite all her special talents, she would be relegated to the chores associated with the home and child rearing. Close to the warring factions, the doctors, forerunners of Doug Ross and Mark Greene, wait in nearby barracks or tents to attend trampled Greeks. Instead of white coats and latex gloves, they would be clothed in perfumed white togas and sandals—it was way too early for them to understand about sterile procedures.

A middle-aged warrior, about 17 years old, is brought into the makeshift ER. The concept of a hospital had to wait until well into Roman times, still centuries in the future. When a member of the Roman legion was wounded in battle, he would initially be transported to and treated in the home of a wealthy citizen. Medical care improved when the homes of the wealthy were replaced by infirmaries built along the frontiers that offered drugs (hundreds of kinds of plants), surgical instruments, and supplies for those wounded in war.

The idea of a place separate from the battlefield to treat soldiers, however, had a precedent with the Greeks as early as the battle for Helen of Troy. According to Homer, fallen combatants were taken from battle and brought to ships or barracks to be treated, though the treatment they received was hardly lifesaving. Physician's assistants (women of extraordinary beauty) would sprinkle the wounds with wine, grated goat cheese, and barley meal. Usually, the patient promptly expired.

But this being nearly 400 years after *The Iliad* and the age of Hippocrates, these ΣR docs practice a more advanced, state-of-the-art emergency medicine. One examines a patient who has a laceration on his leg and a spear tip embedded in his forearm. The other lays the injured warrior on a cot and makes sure the leg with the laceration is raised. The first doctor applies a towel dipped in water around the patient's foot. He is sure not to put it on the wound, but in an area where blood flows near the wound.

Another cold compress is wrapped around the patient's forehead to draw blood up and away from the laceration. A salve of mercury, arsenic, and lead is loaded into the wound and closed with clips, possibly fashioned from insect mandibles. In the end, this care may have done little harm and some good.

Now to the spear. The doctor pulls out the barb point, and blood spurts out of the forearm as if from a burst water pipe. Add panic to the patient's physical agony. A slave prepares an opium and wine spritzer to reduce the soldier's pain. Applying the first line of defense against severe hemorrhaging, the ΣR doc stuffs the wound with fig-leaf sap. Since sap can curdle milk, it should curdle blood and stop bleeding.

The physicians move on to the second line of defense against bleeding, a tourniquet. This temporarily stops the bleeding, but they don't know that you must tie off the vessel inside the wound, nor how to suture it, so the trade-off will be a likely case of gangrene. (It wasn't until the mid-1500s that Ambroise Paré figured out how to use a tourniquet successfully.) The gaping hole in the forearm is bandaged.

Next, one of the ΣR docs listens for sounds in the patient's chest, trying to hear the state of his patient's humors. *Humors,* not humor. This is certainly no laughing matter! Having been trained at the Athens U. medical school, he knows that the body is made up of four humors: blood, phlegm, yellow bile, and black bile. (The adjectives *phlegmatic, bilious,* and *sanguine* find their roots in the moods Greeks associated with the humors.) Pain, which the Greeks did not understand to be a symptom, was caused by a disharmony of the humors. The key to good, if not successful, treatment is to make sure there isn't too much or too little of any one humor. To be healthy, the humors must be kept in balance, much like the yin and the yang of Chinese philosophy.

To that end, our medical time travelers prescribe a severe regimen of bleeding, purging, and starving. The bleeding is to get rid of bad humors. As if this patient hasn't been through enough, after they have stopped the bleeding at the original wound they cut another part of his body and let it bleed. The other bad humors will be driven out through the mouth and rectum, and this calls for purging. They feed the patient hellebores, a plant in the buttercup family that is not only a violent gastrointestinal poison but is, in high doses, lethal. Fortunately evolution put into humans certain protections from their early physicians, as well as from their other natural enemies, and as soon as the patient bravely swallows the floral offering, nausea and diarrhea take over. The only way the patient will survive the purge is to vomit quickly enough to remove the deadly hellebores from his system. Finally, starvation will prevent new humors from forming.

Even before this ordeal begins, these ΣR doctors are quick to tell the patient what his chances of survival are. They are better trained to give a prognosis than a diagnosis. They are basically weathermen, giving a bright or gloomy forecast, but powerless to do anything about it.

It isn't that they have chosen to go into fortune telling rather than medicine. Good diagnostics all but escape them because Greek knowledge of anatomy is almost nil. These ΣR doctors, the Greenes and Rosses of yesteryear, don't even know that blood is pumped through the body by the heart. The idea of a pump won't be discovered until Alexander the Great's time. They don't even have a word for such a device, so the simple concept of blood circulation is out of their purview.

Not so humorously, they inform the 17-year-old that the mortality rate from laceration and spearing is high. They neglect to add that the follow-up treatment of bleeding, purging, and starvation has an even better chance of killing him.

What was beneficial in the care was that these ancient Greek doctors were at least vaguely aware of sepsis (infection), though they did not know of the existence of bacteria. They used drugs and bandages in an attempt to heal fractures, infection, and hemorrhage—steps, even when alongside missteps, in the right direction for treating trauma. Changes in this groundwork would not come quickly.

THE FIRST TOURNIQUET AND AMBULANCE

Over the next thousand years, emergency medicine would remain in the shadow of religious fervor. In the Middle Ages, the use of the sling bandage for arm injuries and weight-and-pulley traction in the treatment of leg fractures were among the few advances made (the sling is still used for shoulder fractures and the weight and pulley for hip fractures). During the Crusades, there is evidence that wounded soldiers were removed from the battlefield at the end of the day for treatment elsewhere. In Renaissance times, superstition still dominated medical practice, though Ambroise Paré, the barber's apprentice who became a surgeon, not only advanced the use of the tourniquet but accidentally improved the protocol for treating wounds.

The normal practice was to pour oil into a wound to stop the putrid smell and promote the formation of pus. On one occasion, Paré ran out of oil when he came to the last soldier of the day, and had to dress the wound with just a clean cloth. He went to bed that night feeling guilty. The next day, much to his surprise, the soldier he had treated with cloth did not have a fever and was in minimal pain, in sharp contrast to those he had treated with oil.

He told his colleagues, "I dressed him. God healed him." There-after, Paré abandoned the notion of filling wounds with oils in favor of allowing nature to take its own course.

In the 1600s, Harvey's description of the human blood system, supported by the discovery of carbon dioxide and oxygen in the following century, shed light on the roles played by circulation, blood pressure, and respiration in trauma recovery. In the 1800s Virchow introduced anesthesia—ah, relief from pain! The fight against infection was improved by the work of Louis Pasteur and Joseph Lister, though for a long while many doctors continued to reject the notion that infection could be caused by something unseen. This new knowledge gradually forced a rewriting of the procedures for the emergency care of the wounded.

Even before the role of bacteria in spreading infection was known, however, the Napoleonic Wars spurred new attempts to treat the wounded in a timely if not always efficacious manner. In a change from the old practice in which the wounded were left unattended until the end of the battle, Bonaparte's surgeon-in-chief introduced the use of rudimentary carts (think of rick-shaws) to evacuate and transport the wounded soldiers from the battlefield to nearby aid stations, even while the battle raged on. In fact, in 1792 he employed the first air evacuation, by hot air balloon. But oddly, the use of a network of ground "ambulances" to transport injured or ill civilians to treatment centers did not catch on elsewhere until late in the next century. In the interim, anyone injured in the streets of Paris, London, New York, or Boston depended upon the kindness of strangers or a nearby place of business for a place to rest until a doctor could be sum-moned and persuaded to travel to the patient.

The American Civil War was a sad chapter in history and in medical practice. The loss of life was staggering, very much because battlefield medical treatment was a disaster, having fallen far behind the new advances in ways to tear up and otherwise destroy human bodies. The medical corps was disorganized, there were no ambulances, and generals on both sides found medical supply wagons disconcerting to the carrying out of battle plans. Worst of all, everything that was being learned about infection and the treatment of wounds was all but ignored. Surgeons rarely washed their hands, and they reused instruments and sponges without cleaning them between patients. In the end, the Confederate and Union armies lost over 200,000 men from battle wounds. Many of these deaths were a result of infections that could have been treated within the then-current state of the art but which were allowed to fester long after the battle was over.

By the end of the Civil War, the new health dangers posed by a tightly packed urban society demanded more efficient transport of the critically injured. The first ambulance appeared in the city of Cincinnati in 1865. But the first true city ambulance system was developed in association with Bellevue Hospital in New York City a year later. Within three years, Bellevue Hospital received nearly 1,500 requests for transport, and by 1883 the ambulance service to Bellevue and the surrounding hospitals serviced over 10,000 patients. Keep in mind, there were no cars, the phone had just been invented, but was not yet in wide use, and the 911 system was over a hundred years in the future. What the urban populations of the time had, and were thankful to have, were horse-drawn ambulances that carried the driver and a surgeon. This primitive EMS system worked something like this.

> A call bell is by the doctor's bed. This awakens him, while at the same time a weight falls and lights the gas. The doctor hastily dons his boots and trousers, and catching his coat from the rack on the way, rushes for the ambulance. While this is going on, a bell strikes in the stable, a weight falls, opening the doors and unhitching the horse; the animal being trained runs under the harness, which is dropped and clasped in an instant.*

*"The Beginnings of Ambulance Service in the United States and England," *Journal of Emergency Medicine* 8 (1990).

Imagine someone like Peter Benton, surgeon extraordinaire, dressed in heavy flannel and leather to fight off the cold of winter, rushing down to a horse-drawn cart in the middle of the night. He is about to explore the streets of urban America looking for the wounded and sick. Since very little medicine is delivered by these makeshift ambulances, he is on board, for the most part, to pronounce a patient's death at the scene or upon arrival to the hospital. And of course, as in ancient times, to make a prediction about the patient's chances of recovery, a skill still capable of making or breaking his professional reputation.

Like his present-day counterparts, this first EMS doctor was extremely careful about documenting all that transpired. He kept meticulous notes of the ride, noting the time of the call, transport and arrival times, and any other details that "a coroner's jury might possibly require."* Even back then, the legal profession was influencing how doctors treated their patients and kept their medical records.

THE TWENTIETH CENTURY: WAR ADVANCES EMERGENCY SERVICES

As the twentieth century arrived, the combustion engine and gasoline-driven transportation came into its own. In this new world of mechanization, gone were the horse-drawn carriages with their doctors riding shotgun. In their place came an undertaker in a motor-driven ambulance. As previously mentioned, the first emergency transport to hospitals was provided by local mortuaries.

While people in the U.S. were being carried to hospitals in hearses, war abroad was forcing new advances in the emergency treatment of trauma. In World War I, doctors realized that soldiers who were bleeding profusely went into shock, in part because of a loss of blood volume. A doctor from Cleveland introduced the idea of replacing lost blood intravenously with sea

*Ibid.

water (our distant ancestors were, after all, sea creatures, and our blood remains saline), and for the first time shock was treated by fluid therapy. In principle, it is the same treatment seen on an *ER* show. A severely injured patient is hooked up to IV lines running all types of compatible liquids into the veins.

The second great conflict of the century, World War II, saw the creation of field hospitals, called Auxiliary Units, which permitted patients to be cared for closer to the battle zone. Technological advances allowed surgeons to monitor a soldier's vital signs, such as blood pressure and respiration, during emergency procedures. Blood drives in the United States provided massive quantities of whole blood, which were refrigerated and shipped overseas for treatment of the injured. This opened up the widespread use of blood transfusions, the very same as those seen on *ER*. (In addition, penicillin had been discovered between the wars, and it and other antibiotic agents were available for soldiers by the time of World War II.)

The Korean battleground became the theater for helicopters to quickly transport the wounded to the new Mobile Army Surgical Hospitals of 60 beds. Inside these MASH units, greater use and variety of antibiotics decreased infection from battle wounds. The ability to treat **shock** (hypotension, or low blood pressure, and tachycardia, accelerated heart rate due to blood loss in trauma) was dramatically improved with IV electrolyte (salt) solutions. Fluid therapy now meant that a severe traumatic injury did not have to be a death sentence. The problem of kidney failure was finally tackled by dialysis.

The MASH units, run by surgeons, practiced the art of triage (the sorting and classification of patients according to severity) and brought new expertise to early treatment of wounds that otherwise would have caused severe disfigurement or death. Surgically, the single difference that distinguished emergency medical care in Korea from that in World War II was the decrease in limb amputations. In that earlier war, the only option in the case of damage to a major artery was to tie off the artery and hope gangrene did not set in. Amputation was the usual result. New techniques in the repair and tying of arteries meant that arms and legs could be salvaged.

Even though much had been learned on the battlefields of Europe and Asia, little was making its way back to the emergency system offered in the U.S. Where Korea had introduced evacuation of the wounded by helicopter to mobile field hospitals, at home trauma patients were still being transported by mortuary vehicles. Consultants returning from Korea publicly asserted that "a seriously wounded victim's chances of survival would be better in the zone of combat than on the average street in America."* Accidents were the leading cause of death for people between the ages of 1 and 37, while traffic accidents were the most common cause of accidental death in all ages under 75. If a patient was hit by a car, essentially no medical treatment would be given in the ambulance. And in the emergency room, medical practice wasn't up to the standards set on the battlefield. It wasn't just accident victims who were in jeopardy. For patients suffering heart attacks, for instance, there were no Coronary Care Units, no special clot-busting drugs, and very little expertise on the part of the ER doctor. Patients took their lives into their own hands if they sought treatment at a hospital emergency room.

As the 1960s approached, the time of the general practitioner was fading, and insurance coverage favored hospital care over office evaluations. Suddenly, ERs were more accessible and (for the patient) less expensive than a primary care/family doctor's office. The public was demanding immediate access to increasingly sophisticated medical technology, and the ER was believed to be the place to find it. While the volume of patients in urban ERs was increasing at 5 to 10 percent a year in the sixties, little was done to put the emergency rooms on par with the rest of the hospital, particularly with regard to staff training and standards. While American hospitals continued to grow more medically sophisticated as well as specialized, the ERs did not. Many were

---

*"Accidental Death and Disability: The Neglected Disease of Modern Society," *National Academy of Sciences*, September 1966.

staffed by whatever young general practitioner decided to pick up a few dollars (and maybe a few new patients) by applying for part-time work in the ER. Another source of doctors was foreign-trained physicians whose lack of fluency in spoken English held them back from establishing practices.

Emergency rooms in university medical centers (teaching hospitals) were not properly organized. There were no Mark Greenes to supervise inexperienced students and residents, and there were no emergency medicine training programs to prepare physicians for the range of medical problems they would encounter in emergency rooms. The ERs in community hospitals (usually smaller hospitals without major affiliations to medical schools) were no better, and often either had no physician available or had a poorly trained and often inexperienced doctor asleep in some back room, available to be called out if the nurses found something they couldn't or didn't want to handle. Something needed to be done.

EMERGENCY MEDICINE COMES INTO ITS OWN

The year is 1962. Kennedy and Khrushchev stare down the barrel of the nuclear gun over Cuba. In Israel, Adolf Eichmann hangs for his war crimes. *The Music Man* opens in movie theaters. Marilyn Monroe dies of an overdose in Hollywood. And the Justice Department orders the halt of racial segregation in hospitals built with federal funds. In Alexandria, Virginia, a family practitioner named James Mills, completing his year as president of the medical staff of Alexandria Hospital, recognizes the poor quality of ER staffing in his own hospital. "One solution was to on-call the medical staff to serve rotations in the ER. That was met with less than great enthusiasm by doctors who already put in more than 60 hours a week in their own private practice."* Dr. Mills and

*A. Lyons, and R.J. Petrucelli, *Medicine: An Illustrated History* (Abradale Press, 1987).

three of his colleagues, all respected doctors and leaders in the hospital, decided to give up their own successful private practices and become full-time ER physicians.

Dr. Mills had been a naval physician for three years in the early 1950s and wanted to bring the quality of care he had helped dispense in the war zone back to the streets of America. Apparently he succeeded. In 1963, the American Medical Association highlighted what was to become known as the Alexandria Plan. Across the country, others followed the lead of Mills and his colleagues in providing an improved system of emergency care, though no formal training yet existed for teaching emergency medicine to physicians as a medical specialty.

Training in a specialty is not a given in medicine. At one time every doctor was a generalist, each doing everything for his own patients, from treating the sniffles to delivering babies to performing surgery. Specialties grew from the practical experiences of practicing physicians. As an example, some GPs (general practitioners) developed an interest in diseases of the eye and developed medical practices that offered specialized treatment for ophthalmologic problems. After a time, special training was developed. Credentialing examinations (board examinations) were devised to recognize those with this special expertise. Thus the specialty of ophthalmology was created and became the model for medical specialization.

More recently, in 1968, a group of eight Michigan physicians created the American College of Emergency Physicians (ACEP) to "educate and train doctors in emergency medicine, and to provide quality emergency care in the nation's hospitals." They had tapped into a nationwide need. Within one year of the group's formation, 1,000 members had joined. Modern emergency medicine had begun.

Two years later, the first ER training program was started at the University of Cincinnati. A year later, the University of Southern California in Los Angeles set up its own program. Finally, residents were able to receive formal training in emergency medicine. Still, however, there was no true emergency care provided en route to the hospital. There was the concept of the mobile coronary care unit developed in Belfast, Ireland, and in New York City, but the procedures of these roving units were soon incorporated into emergency cardiac care within the hospital setting. What needed to be addressed were those critical first minutes following a heart attack or a major trauma, when the extent of the injury or disability was assessed and necessary first aid commenced. For the most part, these first moments in the golden hour were wasted as the patient, most likely strapped to a stretcher and unattended, was bounced along in the back of an ambulance as it raced toward the place where the first stages of treatment would begin, inside the ER doors.

In 1973, the federal government recognized the need for improvement of emergency care and passed the Emergency Medical Services Systems Act. This piece of legislation made large blocks of money available to develop a comprehensive emergency medical system, which finally included (1) the development of paramedics and ambulance systems, (2) sophisticated communications between hospitals and prehospital emergency transport, and (3) a coordinated effort tied to emergency rooms around the country. According to Dr. Harris Graves, past president of the American College of Emergency Physicians, this is when 911 was conceived. Finally professional ambulance services with trained personnel were about to hit the road. Shep and Reilly's precursors were on their way.

Despite the creation of the EMS, emergency medicine had yet to become a recognized specialty. A specialty requires recognition by the American Board of Medical Specialties. Apparently, the ABMS, made up of representatives of the other medical specialties, was not eager to grant membership to emergency medicine. The feeling was that internists were already trained to deal with the broad array of illnesses, and the surgeons were standing by if invasive steps were called for. Only after an agreement that representatives from the other specialties would sit on the governing board of emergency medicine did the ABMS agree to accept emergency medicine as a new specialty.

Finally, in 1980, ER doctors were given the chance to take a board-certifying examination that recognized their unique knowledge of the specialty. This exam and the recognition by the ABMS gave professional credibility to emergency medicine. But in the minds of other practicing physicians, ER doctors were still second-class physicians. The memories of incompetent physicians staffing ERs, and the feeling that emergency medicine is for physicians who can't make it in private practice, died slowly.

Judging things by attitudes up in the Mecca of medicine, Boston, and at the *New England Journal of Medicine* (a publication of the Massachusetts Medical Society), the debate still raged as to whether emergency medicine was really a specialty as late as 1981. "Anyone who has rotated through a busy, varied intern service should be comfortable with all of the procedures performed in the ER. It is true that one must know a little of everything, but the requisite knowledge need be no more than shallow. It is in essence the knowledge required for the first few moments of general practice."

The academic teaching hospitals in Boston, as late as the early 1980s, did not have professional ER physicians in their emergency departments. Very few graduating students went into emergency medicine training, and there were no ER residencies to be found in the city. If a medical student voiced a desire to enter an ER residency, chances were good that a senior faculty adviser would actively discourage the application. Final recognition of primary medical board status for emergency medicine finally came in 1989.

But back in 1974, when Michael Crichton wrote the first episode of *ER,* the notion of an emergency room physician was yet to take hold. To his credit, and to the credit of his writing staff, the show is attempting to abolish the old stereotypes that plagued this specialty. And it is working. For graduating medical students, it has become one of the most popular and competitive residencies to acquire!

WHERE ARE THE DOCTORS?

Despite the newfound glory of ER medicine, there is and will continue to be a shortage of doctors in the specialty. While the current need nationally is for over 26,000 ER doctors, fewer than 11,000 have passed the board examination. The numbers may actually be decreasing, as more people either retire or switch specialties in greater numbers than are produced by the ER residency training programs.

According to the American Medical Association, the average physician at age 35 today can expect to practice for an additional 33 to 36 years and retire around age 70. In a recent survey of ER physicians (the average doctor surveyed was 41 years old), the majority indicated that they hoped to be doing something other than the practice of emergency medicine within 10 years. This would suggest that the average ER physician will not practice emergency medicine beyond his or her early fifties. It's called burnout. Working through the night and on holidays and weekends, ducking punches as well as bullets, can wear thin as ER physicians grow older.

Yet emergency medicine is so exciting and fun to practice that it remains one of the most popular specialties for medical students to train in. And there will always be patients who need help with a fractured wrist, a finger in the dike for a hole in the heart, and a breath of fresh air (or oxygen) for their shortness of breath. Emergency rooms and people like Mark Greene and Susan Lewis will be there to help, 24 hours a day, every day of the year. The very first form of healing is here to stay.

Lifeline

The Heart of the Matter

The body has an amazing ability to overcome infections, survive trauma, and heal wounds. Break a bone, and in a month or two it will be stronger than ever. Cut your skin, and before you know it, the wound is healed. But the heart doesn't do as well. Just a few minutes with its oxygen cut off or even sharply diminished, and that vital muscle could be compromised for the rest of your life. That is, assuming you survive the experience.

In trauma care, there is the golden hour, where the earliest minutes are critical for the patient's survival. In cardiac care, it's seconds that count. Every second that passes during a heart attack increases the amount of irreversible damage that the heart suffers, and increases the chances that the now out-of-balance heart will develop potentially lethal irregularities in its beat. When a patient comes to the ER with chest pain, there is no time to lose. The patient's chances for almost full recovery depend on fast action!

THE TROUBLE WITH HARRY

It is in the wee hours on a Monday morning, and Harry, a 60-year-old man complaining of chest pain, is brought into the ER by his family. Statistically, heart attacks occur more often in early morning hours than at any other time of the day. Harry has a history of high blood pressure, high cholesterol, diabetes, and a previous heart attack. He is on seven different medications for his heart and blood pressure. He has had **diaphoresis** (sweaty skin) and severe chest discomfort, a pressurelike sensation, for two hours, with the pain radiating from his chest down his left arm and up into his jaw—classic signs of a heart attack. He has had similar pains before, but not this bad. Still, he tries to wish away his worst fears and convince himself that the problem was indigestion. But when the pain does not go away with antacids, Harry has to face that in his heart he knows he is in trouble. And the trouble is in his heart!

The triage nurse rushes Harry in a wheelchair into the ER, leaving his family behind in the waiting area. On the show, families often stand around in the ER treatment areas, witnessing and reacting to major medical problems, but in the real world this rarely happens. Allowing family members in during a critical treatment period not only hinders medical care but will also scare the hell out of them. All too many family members have become patients themselves after fainting in the ER and hitting their heads on sinks, gurneys, floors, or whatever else happens to break their fall. And the patient has enough to worry about without having to be concerned about how the family is taking the bad news. There will be plenty of time for the family to peek in and offer moral support after the patient has been stabilized.

VITAL SIGNS

Once inside the ER treatment room and away from the family, a nurse, such as *ER*'s Carol Hathaway, hurriedly checks Harry's vital signs: blood pressure, pulse, respiration, temperature, and weight. Almost all patients, cardiac or not, entering the ER have their vital signs taken. Vital signs—"life signs," in the vernacular—help the staff differentiate the mildly sick from the seriously sick, as well as the seriously sick from the dying.

Blood Pressure

Blood pressure is a critical vital sign for a nurse to check. What is she actually doing or listening for when she takes a patient's BP? What does it mean when she shouts BP 120 over 80? In real life, she would be more likely to write it discreetly on the patient's pillowcase, for other staff to read as the patient is treated, but this method lacks something in the dramatic-effect department.

Whether written or called out, the numbers represent the pressure of the blood being pumped through the arteries at two critical moments in the heart-rhythm cycle. The upper number represents the pressure when the heart contracts, and the lower number when the heart is relaxed between beats.

Blood pressure responds to the body's mood and situation. Stress can cause the BP to rise, and coming to the ER is a very stressful experience, especially if the patient is in pain or is frightened about what the pain might possibly mean. It is not uncommon to see ER patients with slightly elevated blood pressures. Hypertension is usually said to exist when the peak pressure during contraction of the heart (systolic pressure) is regularly greater than 140, and the diastolic, when the heart is relaxed, is greater than 90. To be sure that the readings are typical of those the patient walks around with all day, they should be taken while the patient is relaxed, unstressed, and not acutely ill; clearly the ER is not a good place to make a diagnosis of hypertension. Very high blood pressure, though (especially when the lower number creeps up close to 130 or even above), can be symptomatic of several very serious medical problems, including an acute heart attack.

On the other hand, low blood pressure, or hypotension, usually refers to a systolic pressure of less than 90. Low blood pressure is normal for some people, but a systolic BP less than 90 must be looked at in cases of an acute heart attack as a symptom that the heart may be failing. The blood pressure starts to drop, and the amount of blood getting to the brain and heart can become dangerously low. Harry's blood pressure is 130 over 90—normal under the circumstances—and the nurse quickly checks his other vital signs.

Pulse

Pulse, unlike any other vital sign, has gained a place for itself as the telltale sign of life in the movies. A child falls off a swing, an unidentified body is found motionless in an alley, and the first person on the scene grabs the victim's wrist and feels for a pulse. A refinement at one stage of movie development was to have the examiner press his fingers into the victim's neck; the medically informed were presumed to know that it was the carotid artery that was being checked.

When the doctor asks for Harry's pulse, she wants a number. A pulse is not a heartbeat but a pulsating artery that gives evidence that the heart is beating. An abnormally fast or slow pulse can be an important marker for disease, especially heart disease.

Normally, the heart beats about 70 times per minute. If a pulse is over 100 beats per minute, the heart is beating fast, a condition called tachycardia. Children's pulses are faster than those of adults, and an infant at two months of age can have a normal resting heart rate of about 130. As with blood pressure, pulse can rise for many reasons, especially exercise, pain, fever, and anxiety. But if your pulse gets up really high (around 140 to 150), especially in heart patients, and you have not just run the marathon, it can be a marker for a serious acute cardiac problem.

Bradycardia is just the reverse—a slow pulse, usually less than 60 beats per minute. Again, conditions must be taken into account. In people who exercise regularly, a low resting pulse may be completely normal. Marathon runners have been known to have resting pulses in the 30s! Bradycardia can also be secondary to routinely prescribed heart and blood pressure medication, but a very slow heart rate in a patient with cardiac disease may be a signal that the electrical circuitry in the heart is damaged and that some beats may be having trouble getting started (this is called heart block).

Aside from too fast or too slow, the pulse may be regular or irregular. As the nurse counts the number of heartbeats, she will also note whether the beats come in a regular cadence. Like the rhythmic marching of soldiers in parade—hup, two, three, four . . . hup, two, three, four—the heart rhythm should follow a regular beat. When the cadence of the heart is disturbed, there could be a serious problem with the normal electrical circuitry that stimulates the heart to beat. The nurse feels for Harry's pulse, and counts 70 beats a minute with a regular rhythm. So far so good.

Respiration

Breathing is automatic. It is controlled by the brain stem as a basic function of life. The average person breathes 13 million cubic feet of air in the average lifetime. That's a lot of breathing, the equivalent of inflating and then deflating one-third of the Empire State Building. Luckily we don't have to think consciously to breathe, but sometimes we have to make an effort to control our breathing when there is a problem. If a patient is not breathing properly, the lungs may not be introducing enough oxygen into the body. No oxygen, no life. How many times have you heard someone on *ER* say "Breathe!" to a patient who is upset, cold, in pain, frightened, or just plain stupefied? This is done to help bring the patient's breathing back into balance. Of course, breathing is not only a helpful first aid tool but its alternative bodes poorly for longevity.

As with the question "Pulse?" the question "Respiration?" requires more than a yes or no answer. The normal breathing rate is about 14 breaths per minute. Much faster or much slower and the patient may be having a problem. For someone having a heart attack, the respiratory rate may be increased by pain or anxiety. The rate of breathing may also increase if there is a problem with too little oxygen in the blood. The decision to breathe faster is not conscious, but actually a result of reflexes in the body that cause the respiratory rate to increase in order to deliver more oxygen to the brain and vital organs. But breathing takes a certain amount of energy, and the faster a patient breathes, the more oxygen he will use up in his attempt to bring oxygen levels up. Giving supplemental oxygen to patients with chest pain helps increase the oxygen in the blood and slows down the respiratory rate, so the patient does not have to work so hard.

The nurse checks Harry's respiratory rate, and he is breathing at 24 breaths a minute. This is a little fast, and she will provide him with supplemental oxygen as the first treatment for his chest pain.

Temperature

Temperature is the vital sign that gives the ER doc a valuable clue to the general state of health of the patient. If the temperature is up above 99.6°F (rectally), the patient probably has a fever and may have an infection. A fever will cause the heart rate to rise, and increase the metabolic state (meaning the use of oxygen and food). This can complicate the treatment of a patient with a heart attack, so the doctor will want to know if Harry's temperature is normal. It is.

Weight

Weight, even though it won't be changing during the evaluation in the ER, is a vital statistic to know for all patients in the ER, especially cardiac patients. While obesity (especially along the stomach) is a risk factor for heart disease, the doctor will want to know the weight of the patient in order to calculate doses of medications. You hear it all the time on the show. Mark Greene calls out 40 milligrams of lasix (a diuretic); Doug asks for 150 milligrams of Tylenol for a child with a fever; Susan asks for a dopamine drip (a cardiac medication) at 5 mics per minute.

The calculations of these doses are based on patient weight, so staff members are not trying to embarrass you when they repeatedly ask for your weight. Very small amounts of medication are involved—a milligram is one-thousandth of a gram, and "**mics**" represent micrograms, each one-millionth of a gram—so the ER staff has to be very careful in deciding how much of a drug is right for you. Never lie about your weight to someone in the ER!

THE ELECTROCARDIOGRAM (SQUIGGLY LINES)

Once Harry's vital signs are recorded and oxygen is being delivered (through the nasal cannula, or small tube, that you see all the time on the show), any nurse worth her salt knows that an EKG (electrocardiogram) is mandatory for a patient with a suspected MI. Yes, even heart attacks carry their own coded names. **MI** stands for myocardial infarction, the death or dying (*infarct*) of heart muscle (*myocardium*—"myo" for muscle and "cardium" for heart). As if arranging the numbers on a clock face, the nurse or technician attaches sticky electrodes to each of the arms and legs, and then across the patient's chest. The wires from each electrode are connected to a machine that prints out squiggly lines on graph paper.

It is termed a 12-lead EKG because doctors look at the heart's electrical activity from 12 different views. It's like piecing together a 3-D picture of a house using a series of regular photographs. You can take a picture of the back of the house, and another from the front of the house, one from the side of the house, and even get an aerial photo from above the house. Piece them all together and you have a good idea of what the house looks like!

Even if the EKG is normal, there could still be a cardiac problem that has not yet shown up as a deficit in electrical activity at any one or more locations, so the patient will be connected to a cardiac monitor while in the ER. This monitor can be viewed not only at bedside but usually also at the nursing station and keeps the staff aware of any irregular heartbeats.

To understand what these squiggly lines tell doctors, it is important to understand just how the heart works. The heart is able to beat in a normal, coordinated manner because of a series of complex electrical impulses that are transmitted from various locations in the heart muscle. The electrical wave normally originates in the upper part of the heart, in an area called the **atrium** (the two smaller chambers of the heart; the two larger chambers are called the **ventricles**). The electrical activity spreads out from the atrium down into the ventricles, stimulating the heart muscle to contract in a coordinated manner.

The monitor conveys the electrical activity of each individual heartbeat, and these can vary in recognizable patterns if the heart is damaged or starving for oxygen (**ischemia**). The monitor can also show if the rhythm of the heartbeat is normal. Because the normal rhythm of the heart originates in a small area of the right atrium called the "sinus node," a normal heart rhythm is called a **sinus rhythm**. When the beat of the heart is no longer originating from the sinus node, the rhythm is abnormal and is called an **arrhythmia**. Arrhythmias can be very serious, even life-threatening. If you have ever danced with someone who doesn't have a sense of the beat, someone who is not moving in time with the music, you know the dance is more chaos than pleasure. Well, so it is for the heart, which beats to its own time signature, a steady beat that, when scrambled, can put the life of a patient in jeopardy.

Just as Susan Lewis did in the episode "Going Home," when she looked at Mr. Flanagan's EKG and treated him for a heart attack, so Harry's doctor arrives and looks at his EKG. She instantly recognizes that the horizontal lines at regular intervals on the graph paper show the unmistakable pattern of an acute MI.

THE HEART ATTACK (MI)

The term **heart attack** evokes fear of imminent death, perhaps because it involves the muscle most associated with life. But a heart attack, while serious, is not a death sentence. Denying or disregarding severe chest pain, on the other hand, drastically raises your chances of dying from a heart attack or suffering a permanent alteration in the way you live. Enduring crushing chest pain for two hours before heading out to the ER was not a good idea for Harry. Tragically, all too many people do the same thing.

According to the American Heart Association, of the 1.5 million people who will have a heart attack this year, about a third will die. But fully half of those (250,000) die within the first hour of the attack, often never reaching the hospital and denying medical personnel the opportunity to save their lives.

When a person does not survive an acute heart attack, it is often because of a syndrome called "sudden death." The world was shocked when the Olympic skater Sergei Grinkov fell dead on the ice at age 28. Can a lethal heart attack really strike an athlete in top condition? Yes. Most likely, Grinkov did die of a classic MI, probably complicated by a lethal abnormal heartbeat.

Today such abnormal heartbeats can be treated with medication, but only if the patient puts himself in the hands of skilled practitioners on time. They then have a chance not only to save his life and enable him to recover fully but to help him before any serious damage is done to the heart. If not, a patient can become a cardiac cripple, unable to walk across a room without severe fatigue and shortness of breath. Harry lost two precious hours at home, but at least he chose to come to the ER. He is still alive, and his vital signs so far are good.

What exactly has happened to his heart? What differentiates a mild heart attack from a severe one? We know that the heart, usually weighing less than a pound, is a strong, specialized muscle that functions as a pump, forcing blood with each contraction to circulate throughout the patient's body. Like all muscle tissue, the heart needs a lot of oxygen, and it gets the oxygen from blood that circulates through the coronary arteries. These arteries feed heart muscle with a rich supply of blood, but if one of the coronary arteries gets clogged, chest pain usually develops. This pain is called **angina**, while the term *ischemia* is used to describe the condition in which there is insufficient blood flow to the heart.

An MI occurs when one of the coronary arteries that supply blood rich in oxygen is clogged for a long enough period of time to deprive an area of the heart muscle of oxygen to the point of injury. If the heart tissue in the area of the clogged artery dies (that's the infarction), the muscle scars and never returns to normal. The longer the tissue is allowed to go without blood, the greater the likelihood of permanent damage. The amount of tissue that is left dead determines whether your doctor will describe the attack as severe or mild. The greater the loss of heart muscle, the weaker will be the heart, even if the patient survives the attack. If the attack is so severe that the pump can't deliver enough blood throughout the body, vital organs start to fail and the patient will die.

Harry happens to have an EKG that is consistent with a heart attack, but many patients with chest pain and heart damage do not. A small heart attack may not give characteristic changes on the EKG in its earliest stages, so the doctor routinely orders other tests that alert ER physicians for heart damage. The most common one of these, as seen often on the show, is the check of cardiac enzymes in the blood. The enzyme most commonly mentioned is **CPK**, which stands for creatine phosphokinase. This enzyme starts to elevate within a few hours following a heart attack, and can be used not only as confirmation of an MI but as a rough marker to gauge how bad the heart attack was.

One additional test you may see someone like Susan Lewis order in the ER is a cardiac echo. Using a special microphone that sweeps across the chest (think of the sonar used in the old submarine movies), the echocardiogram can look at the chambers and valves of the heart. If there are problems with the way the heart is beating, the echocardiogram will help to isolate the abnormality and provide clues to how much damage has occurred from the heart attack.

Now that we and the doctor have a clear idea of what is happening to Harry, what next? Once Susan had a clear idea of what was happening to Mr. Flanagan, she took immediate action. Anyone having a myocardial infarction in the ER is under attack by tiny clots that block the blood flow through the coronary arteries to the heart muscle. The faster these clots are removed, the better chance the patient has to survive with minimum damage to the muscle. The troops in the ER are mobilized, and the response is tantamount to a declaration of war. Harry's doctor comes back with everything she's got to launch the counteroffensive along three major lines: (1) relieve her patient's chest pain, (2) limit the extent of the damage to his heart (remember, once a heart muscle is damaged, it never returns to normal), and (3) watch for and control abnormal heartbeats.

Chest pain that is true cardiac pain is caused when the heart does not get enough oxygen. Paradoxically, chest pain is also anxiety-provoking, and the pain can then cause the blood pressure and heart rate to increase. The higher the BP and heart rate, the harder the heart has to work, and this just makes the heart attack worse. Course of action: relieve the pain, ease the anxiety, and thereby control the blood pressure and heart rate.

Relieve the Pain: Nitro and Morphine

Harry is in a lot of pain. He is clutching his chest, asking for help. To relieve his chest pain, the doctor starts with nitroglycerin. This medication comes in many different forms. You can take it under the tongue (**sublingual**) as a pill, swallow it whole in pill form, have it sprayed as a liquid into your mouth, have it placed as a paste on your skin, or be given it intravenously. Nitroglycerin (they have the same name, but it's not the explosive stuff!) dilates (expands) the arteries around the heart and increases blood flow to oxygen-starved heart muscle. If the drug can increase blood flow and oxygen to an area of the heart with a clogged artery, the patient will feel less chest pain, suffer diminished anxiety, leading, it is hoped, to a lower blood pressure and heart rate. The opening up of the coronary arteries can also limit further damage to heart muscle. Morphine is also sometimes used because, like nitro, it dilates the blood vessels, increasing blood flow through the diseased arteries around the heart. But it has the added benefit (unlike nitroglycerin) of being a powerful narcotic, a painkiller all its own.

The doctor knows she needs to be very careful in the use of these drugs. When we see Susan Lewis concentrate on the type and dosage of medication she wants to give Mr. Flanagan, it is for a good reason. Nitroglycerin and morphine, often used together to treat angina, dilate blood vessels everywhere, not just around the heart, so they can lower blood pressure too much. If the blood pressure drops drastically, less blood will flow to the brain and to the heart, and this can trigger a bigger heart attack or even add a stroke to the patient's miseries! The blood vessels in the head dilate as well, giving some patients severe headaches that mimic migraines because they have the same cause: blood vessels dilate as they fill with blood, pressing on the nerves surrounding the brain.

Harry's doctor gives him a combination of nitroglycerin by mouth (under the tongue) and morphine intravenously. The patient's pain dramatically subsides, and the doctor then instructs the nurse to start a nitro drip (a slow IV). This will help to keep the vessels dilated and treat any recurring angina.

Limiting the Damage with Drugs

The next objective is to unclog the blockage in the artery that is causing Harry's heart attack. There are two major approaches employed by physicians in the ER: thinning the blood and dissolving the obstruction. Thinning the blood with drugs such as heparin makes the blood less likely to form clots. Another thinner that you've heard prescribed on the show, coumadin, isn't used acutely in the real ER because it takes three to four days to work, while heparin works immediately. Plain old aspirin will help limit the formation of new blood clots, too. It helps make platelets (crucial in the formation of blood clots) less "sticky." This is why many people considered at risk for heart disease are advised to take an aspirin once a day.

Unless there is something in a patient's history to cause concern about excessive bleeding, those with severe chest pain and an apparent heart attack are given aspirin and heparin automatically. These medications can help prevent more clots, but neither will unclog the clot or clots already present in the vessel and causing the heart attack.

To clear the obstruction, two powerful medications, TPA (tissue plasminogen activating factor) and streptokinase, are administered. They will not only dissolve clots that form in blood vessels but can also reopen a clogged artery that is causing a heart attack. There are, however, major side effects. These drugs dissolve clots in other parts of the body as well, and the formation of clots is how your body normally controls bleeding. If Harry has a bleeding ulcer, has had a recent bad bump to the head, or has recently had surgery, the doctor will probably avoid these drugs. Even healthy people without heart problems given these drugs sometimes bleed too much, and a small percentage of patients given these medications will develop severe complications (uncontrollable bleeding, irregular heartbeats, even death). But consider the alternatives. To do nothing may mean more and more oxygen-starved heart muscle will die. The doctor understands the trade-offs. Like all ER doctors, she is very careful about how and when these medications are administered. The oldest of medical admonitions plays in her mind: *FIRST, DO NO HARM!*

Limiting the Damage with Angioplasty

Though medication to thin the blood or clear the obstruction is the method to treat a heart attack or MI in the ER, coronary artery bypass surgery in the operating room or an angioplasty performed by a cardiologist in the Catheterization Lab are alternatives. Angioplasty works on the order of a pipe cleaner. A very thin catheter is inserted into the groin and snaked up the aorta (the major artery in the body) all the way to the coronary (heart) arteries. The cardiologist injects some dye and an X ray (fluoroscopy) and looks directly at the patient's beating heart and the arteries around the heart.

If there is a blockage in one of the arteries, the cardiologist will locate it, and may be able to thread the catheter into the obstruction. The cardiologist then blows up a tiny balloon attached to the catheter and crushes the stuff (cholesterol plaques and clots) against the wall of the artery, thereby opening the artery up to greater blood flow. Once the occlusion is relieved, the balloon is deflated. To keep the debris from reclogging the artery, cardiologists are employing a new technique in which they insert an expandable wire mesh called a "stent," designed to keep the artery open. Of course, there are complications associated with angioplasty, such as bleeding and irregular heartbeats, and sometimes the obstruction is so bad that the patient needs to go for emergency coronary artery bypass surgery to survive.

Giving medications versus angioplasty as the method of choice to unclog arteries is one of the most hotly contested points in ERs around the country. This controversy is dramatized through several episodes of *ER,* when Susan Lewis has a heart attack patient whom she treats with medication (TPA) rather than angioplasty to clear the obstruction. She battles it out with County General's Chief of Cardiology, Dr. Jack Kayson, who opts for angioplasty. Kayson brings her decision up for review. After he has his day in hospital court, it seems to be a draw. As fate would have it, Susan is soon faced with another MI victim—Kayson himself. Another cardiologist wants Kayson to go for emergency angioplasty, but Kayson puts his trust in Susan. She gives him medication and he survives. Kayson, who once seemed bent on destroying Susan Lewis, has had a literal and figurative change of heart and winds up with a new respect for Susan. He even develops a short-lived crush on her!

In the real world, there is a tremendous mutual dependence between ER physicians and cardiologists. The decision to treat with TPA, streptokinase, angioplasty, or surgery is ultimately a joint one between patient, ER doctor, and cardiologist. In truth, the cardiologist usually should and does have the most knowledge and expertise to make the final decision, and these are the physicians who must eventually care for the patient through any complications that should arise from the treatment.

Whatever the decision, there may be mitigating circumstances, however. When chest compressions are done during CPR, ribs often crack and chest wall trauma occurs, which could change minor tissue tears into major bleeding events. There is no right course of action to follow in all heart attacks and there are no absolute guidelines, but whatever method is chosen, it must be decided on sound bases and undertaken quickly. The longer the heart endures the attack, the greater the damage.

Knowing the risks and benefits of the treatment, and the type of heart attack Harry is having, the doctor chooses medication over angioplasty. She instructs the nurse to prepare the TPA, and begins the intravenous infusion of the medication. The clots in the coronary arteries should quickly begin to dissolve. But with the treatment comes a potential complication, and the third line of attack: the doctor must watch for any bleeding or abnormal heartbeats (arrhythmias). And whether it is a trauma patient or someone suffering an illness, on any given episode of *ER*, arrhythmias seem to pop up, especially when there is a lull in the story or a need to boost dramatic tension.

V-Fib and V-Tach

Just when everyone thinks Harry is out of the woods, the nurse yells out, "He's arrested! V-fib!" Patients with cardiac problems, despite appearing stable, can change from moment to moment. Bam!—an alarm on the heart monitor goes off. This sets in motion a dizzying cascade of events that are all designed to bring the patient's heart rhythm back to normal. If not, the patient dies.

One of these arrhythmias, **V-tach**, is short for ventricular tachycardia. *Ventricular* because the origin of the electrical activity controlling the heart's rhythm comes from the lower part of the heart, the ventricles. *Tachycardia* (from the Greek *tachys*, meaning "swift," and *kardia* for "heart") is a fast heart rhythm (about 100 to 200 beats a minute). Though the patient may briefly have stable vital signs (blood pressure and pulse), V-tach often does not allow the heart to pump blood effectively to the brain and the rest of the body, and blood pressure soon falls. This rhythm often changes spontaneously to **ventricular fibrillation (V-fib)**. With V-fib, the heart is in total chaotic activity, without any coordinated pumping action. You may remember a scene of Carter massaging a heart when it went into V-fib; later he described it as feeling like a "bag of worms."

As the doctor rushes back to the patient's bedside, she finds nurses beginning to perform CPR (cardiopulmonary resuscitation). CPR provides the patient with artificial breathing (air or oxygen given by a compressible bag) and artificial circulation, also called external compressions (by pressing on the chest over the heart and simulating contractions). The doctor looks up at the cardiac monitor and sees the unmistakable random activity of the EKG consistent with V-fib. As opposed to the normal electrical rhythm and contractions of the heart that produce a steady stream of blood flowing throughout the body, ventricular fibrillation is random electrical stimulation of the muscle that produces no blood flow from the heart, and consequently no blood flow to the brain. In a few minutes without a dramatic change, her patient will die. The staff can provide temporary blood flow and oxygen to the brain with CPR, but for the patient to survive, they will have to get his heart beating normally again. The best way to do this is with a combination of medications and electrical shocks.

The first thing the doctor does is whack Harry in the chest with her fist. It's a frequent occurrence on *ER* to see Susan Lewis do this, which is actually called a "precordial thump." Believe it or not, it provokes a small electrical current across the chest to the heart and may convert the patient's heart rhythm back to normal. It is not a great way to make friends, but the patient is usually unconscious when this technique is attempted.

The thump to the chest doesn't do the trick, so next the doctor electrically shocks the patient with a special machine called a defibrillator. This machine produces electrical energy measured in **joules** (pronounced "jewels"): watts × seconds = joules.

Almost no one remembers this formula—they just remember the amount of joules needed to treat the V-fib. The principle here is to electrically reset the heart's electrical thermostat by jolting it out of its lethal arrhythmia (irregular heartbeat).

The way you see it done on the show is just the way it is actually done in the real emergency room. The machine is set at 200 joules. Whoever has the paddles rubs them together with electrical conducting gel (affectionately called "goop" in the ER). The gel needs to completely cover the surface of the paddles, or the patient's skin will be burned. Performing CPR after a patient has gotten fried by one of the paddles is no fun—it can smell like a hot dog roast in the treatment room. The paddles are placed on the patient's chest and a staff member yells "Clear!," warning everyone to stand back. Anyone who happens to be in contact with the patient during the discharge of the machine will get these 200 joules too. Nearly everyone who works in an ER knows a story of someone who did not get away from the patient. Should that happen, not only will that person get a strong kick but the electrical charge might cause him or her to go into cardiac arrest by resetting a normally functioning heart rhythm. So when the staff hears the word *clear,* they know to jump back pronto.

After the first shock, Harry's heart rhythm has not returned to normal. The shock can be immediately repeated twice more, once at 300 joules and then at 360, the most energy used in resuscitation. The rhythm remains V-fib, so the doctor needs to make sure Harry, who is unconscious and not breathing, is getting adequate oxygen.

In order to do this, she will need to breathe for him. Up until this point, Harry has received oxygen through the mouth via an ambu-bag. This does not work well for long, because a lot of the oxygen will end up in the stomach or escape out of the sides of the mouth. The best way to ensure good ventilation (breathing) is by intubation, and after this is done, the doctor checks both sides of Harry's chest for breath sounds with her stethoscope, and is satisfied that the tube is in the right place. She will need a chest X ray to be absolutely sure, but that will have to wait. Now it's drug time.

Medications are given only as needed. There is no magic here either, because there is a list of actions to perform dependent on what heart rhythm is present. The guidelines are all spelled out in a book from the American Heart Association, and every medical student, nurse, and resident learns these guidelines in a course called Advanced Cardiac Life Support (ACLS). The first round of drugs for V-fib is to help make the heart more receptive to jolts of electricity. If that fails, drugs to suppress abnormal heart rhythms are given. If this fails, there are a few more tricks that can be tried, but by this stage it's probably time for the doctor to start thinking about what to say to the family. If a good heart rhythm can be reestablished, then comes the job of stabilizing the heart rate and blood pressure.

CPR continues, but Harry is still in V-fib. The doctor orders one of the nurses to push a syringe full of epi (epinephrine, or adrenaline) through the IV. The idea of IV push is to rapidly inject the drug into a vein so the medication hits the bloodstream all at once. When it reaches the heart, it will have a very high concentration and maximum clinical effect.

After the epi is given, Harry is shocked again at 360. No change. Still V-fib. It's time to use a drug that suppresses the abnormal rhythms. The doctor tells the nurse to add a syringe full of lidocaine into Harry's IV. After the medication has gone in, Harry is shocked again at 360. They are into a routine now: drug ... shock ... drug ... shock ... drug. ... Every time a medication is given, a couple of minutes later the doctor tries to shock the patient out of the lethal arrhythmia. Epinephrine is given every five minutes, and repeat doses of lidocaine are given as well. All the while, CPR is in process to help circulate the medication around the body and to the heart. But the V-fib continues. The doctor orders an IV bolus of 500 milligrams of beryllium to be given, a drug used as an anti-arrhythmic when most others have failed. (A **bolus** is a small amount of liquid placed into an IV for immediate response; IV push is the act, and bolus is the substance.) They shock Harry again with 360 joules, and suddenly the monitor shows some regular blips of electrical activity. This time, success. Harry's heart has returned to a normal rhythm, but at a very slow rate.

A nurse feels Harry's neck for a carotid pulse, searching for evidence that his beating heart is forcing enough blood through this large artery up into the brain. She can feel a pulse, but it's very weak and very slow. In order to speed up the heart and try to raise the blood pressure as well, the doctor tells the nurse to push a syringe full of atropine into Harry's IV. **Atropine** is a drug that makes the heart go faster. His heart rate speeds up, then slows down again to a dangerously low level.

It's time for a pacemaker. In the ER, the doctor can use a machine that provides regular electrical stimulation to the heart through large electrodes attached to her patient's chest. This is called an external pacemaker, as opposed to the permanent pacemakers that cardiologists attach directly into the heart. This is what Susan Lewis ultimately orders for her patient, Mr. Flanagan. The nurse places the paddles in the correct position, the doctor turns the dial on the machine, and before you can say *zap!* Harry's heart rhythm has picked up the beat of the machine. It's up to 70 beats a minute, and he is on another step toward recovery.

Harry's blood pressure, however, is still low: only 70 over 40. The doctor needs to get Harry's BP up higher to improve blood flow to the brain and the heart. No time to lose. She tells the nurse to start an IV dopamine drip to get the blood pressure higher. Dopamine can raise the blood pressure in patients whose hearts may be weak from a heart attack. The dose (calculated by weight) has to be just right and carefully monitored, for too much can raise the blood pressure too high, and too little may not get the blood pressure up high enough (usually a systolic of at least 90). The nurse advises that 15 mics (pronounced "mikes") of dopamine have been started. This represents 15 micrograms per kilogram body weight per minute in an IV infusion. Though a fairly low dose of dopamine, it has brought Harry's BP up to 100/60. Normal!

Harry is stable. Moments later, though, V-fib occurs again, and the cycle of shock and medication is repeated. A normal sinus rhythm returns. Five more minutes go by, and everyone watches the cardiac monitor in anticipation. The rhythm stays steady. Harry starts to blink his eyes and move his head, but he is unable to talk because of the tube in his windpipe. Success, for now at least. This guy has bought some time instead of the farm.

There is a bed available in the ICU, and he will now be transferred to the Coronary Care Unit. The cardiologist is on his way in to evaluate the patient, but of course he has missed all the action!

It can and often does go the other way. One of the most dramatic scenes on *ER* involved Mark Greene as he took care of a 32-year-old male with a heart problem. His patient had been in great health, but suddenly developed irregular heartbeats that became life-threatening.

The doctors gave him all the right medications: epi, dopamine, atropine. They zapped his heart with joules of electricity, but still the patient "crumped" (went downhill and died), and the cardiac monitor showed only a flat line (asystole), no electrical activity. Greene pulled out all the stops, but this just wasn't a night for one of those miracles. The code was called: all attempts at resuscitation were called off.

FACT OR FICTION?: FOR THE FAINT OF HEART

An article published by the *New England Journal of Medicine* was critical of the way CPR is portrayed on television, including on *ER*. On these shows, only a minority of patients receiving CPR are the elderly, said the article, while in reality a clear majority of code patients are elderly. On television, 75 percent of the cardiac arrests do not involve patients with long-standing heart disease. In the real world, there is underlying heart disease in 75 to 90 percent of arrests. On the tube, two-thirds of the CPR patients survive their codes, when the real figure is closer to 7 to 15 percent. And these figures are for patients whose hearts stop in the hospital. The percentage who survive is even lower for accident victims who arrive in the ER in cardiac arrest.

Not all heart problems are as life-threatening as an acute heart attack or as dramatic as a cardiac arrest. There are many other conditions that can affect the heart, and one seen frequently at County General and in real ERs is congestive heart failure. At times the heart has been damaged so much that it just can't beat hard enough to get blood back out into the circulation, and the blood backs up into the lungs and in the legs. The pressure in the blood vessels builds up so high that the serum starts to leak into the lung tissue. This is congestive heart failure (CHF), and County General has had its (realistic) fair share of these patients. Red Buttons played Mr. Rubadoux ("Ruby"), the concerned husband of a patient suffering with CHF. The most common complaint is shortness of breath. Breathing is usually very rapid (much faster than 14 breaths a minute), and the lungs can fill up with so much fluid (pulmonary edema) that patients feel as though they are drowning. In a sense they are. Pulmonary edema is the extreme, and patients have so much fluid in their chests that they are in danger of expiring if something is not done quickly. The only way to keep the patient from dying is to expunge and eliminate these fluids.

The most common medications to rid the body of fluids are called **diuretics**. This class of medications causes the kidneys to excrete a lot of fluid, essentially drawing all the excess fluid out of the body and especially out of the lungs. The diuretic used most often is **lasix**. Not only is it powerful but it can be given both orally and intravenously.

In addition to diuretics such as lasix, morphine can help to treat severe CHF and pulmonary edema (remember, pulmonary edema is just very severe CHF). ER doctors refer to morphine as MS (for morphine sulfate), and it helps relax severe anxiety caused by the shortness of breath, while lowering the pressure in the veins and reducing the work the heart has to do to pump the blood through the body. Nitroglycerin can also be used, for it helps to lower the pressure, improve the blood flow to the coronary arteries, while also allowing the heart to pump more easily. And don't forget the oxygen. In medical terms, oxygen is a drug, just like any other in the ER: too much can be toxic, and too little can kill you. A patient in severe CHF will need a lot of oxygen, and need it fast. The change with emergency treatment can be dramatic. In little over a half hour in the ER, a patient unable to speak and barely able to breathe can once again be talking and breathing comfortably.

Not all heart disease is limited to the middle-aged and elderly. A number of heart problems in young patients have been seen on the show, and they represent real problems for patients of all ages. This is not coronary disease in the manner that most people think of heart problems. In most of these cases, the coronary arteries are clean of any disease. One problem ERs see is called **pericarditis**, where patients present with a sharp pain that increases with deep breathing. The abnormality here is in the sac that covers the heart, called the pericardium. If this sac becomes inflamed or infected, there can be tremendous pain in the chest. The pain can usually be relieved with Motrin or another NSAID (nonsteroidal anti-inflammatory drug), and the problem is usually more painful than it is life-threatening.

Another form of heart disease not caused by a clogging of the coronary arteries is called **myocarditis**. Heart muscle can be affected by viral infections, and because the heart does not heal well, a severe viral infection (often referred to as viral myocarditis) can leave a young patient with end-stage heart disease and in search of a heart transplant. Certain hereditary forms of heart disease can cause an enlargement of the heart muscle, resulting in a blockage to the flow of blood out of the heart. This "hypertrophic cardiomyopathy" has been associated with the death of a number of young athletes, and is sure to turn up as a problem at County General one of these Thursday nights.

Trauma

Damage Control

The word *trauma* is used loosely in everyday language, but in strict medical terms, a trauma is any injury, accidental or intentional, caused by a harsh object or instrument. In major trauma, that harsh object might be an auto windshield that your head strikes after your car hits a highway divider at 50 miles an hour. Or the trauma might be a GSW (gunshot wound), the harsh object a bullet that comes in contact with one of your vital organs. No matter the mechanism of injury, major trauma is a big deal in any ER, and it seems that almost every week at County General's ER at least one major trauma case is presented. They've got to get the television viewers' blood pressures and pulses soaring as the staff pulls out all the stops in an attempt to cheat death! In real life as much as in a television drama, major trauma will get an ER staff rocking, and the procedures you see employed every week are for the most part the kind of lifesaving maneuvers used in emergency rooms around the country.

Unless a patient is injured right at the door of the ER, County General's trauma cases usually begin out in the field, with the activation of the EMS (emergency medical system).

Suppose you are motoring along at 50 miles an hour, listening to your favorite CD on your four-speaker stereo system, when you hit a slick spot on the road and lose control. Your last view of the world before blackness swallows you up is a telephone pole center stage, rushing at you. Your seatbelt snaps when your car hits the pole, and you are propelled through the windshield onto the hood. Incredibly, to make matters worse, you had just bought your 16-year-old son a new hunting knife at a local sports store and were holding it up and admiring it when you skidded. As you flew through the windshield, your chest was impaled onto the knife.

The paramedics who are called to the scene find a bloody mess. Your face has been ripped open by shards of glass, and blood is oozing from the knife wound to your chest. You are unconscious, and your blood pressure is 50/30. The only thing that may help save your life is the fact that you happened to have your encounter with death two blocks away from an ER such as County General.

THE GLASGOW COMA SCALE (GCS)

It's scoop-and-run time. The paramedics secure your spinal column with a hard cervical collar because, for all they know, you might have suffered a broken neck in the accident. To help protect the rest of your spine, they strap you onto a backboard before they load you into the ambulance and set out for the ER. During your brief ride, the paramedics assist your breathing with an ambu-bag, which forces oxygen into your lungs. They determine that you still have a pulse, and to gauge how alert you are the paramedics will run some quick checks so that they can report an assessment to the ER.

You may recall scenes on the show in which paramedics rush through the doors of the ER, calling out that the patient's "GCS is 3–4–4." They are referring to the Glasgow Coma Scale, an assessment of how the major trauma has affected your level of consciousness. The parameters are simple: (1) A numerical score from 1 to 4 (with 4 being the best response) is given for your ability to open and close your eyes on command. (2) A score of 1 to 5 (with 5 the best response) is given for how well you respond verbally to questions. (3) A score of 1 to 6 (6 is the best) is given for how well you are able to move your body in response to stimuli, including verbal and painful stimuli. These numbers are reported as three individual scores that can then be added to come up with an overall score for the GCS.

The lower the number scored on the scale, the greater the likelihood that your brain is not functioning optimally. The highest you can score is 15. A score of 8 or lower indicates that you have had serious injuries and may be in deep trouble.

The doors to the ER crash open and a doctor, someone like Mark Greene or Peter Benton, falls in alongside the gurney on its way to Trauma Room 1. The paramedics report that your GCS is 2–2–5 (totaling 9), meaning that you have suffered major injuries and are poorly responsive verbally, but that you are still responding physically to stimuli. You are placed onto a bed in the trauma room. An instant later, the trauma team swings into carefully orchestrated action that looks to an outsider like organized chaos. It's show time!

It may not be apparent at County General's ER, but in every major trauma center there is a team of doctors, nurses, and respiratory therapists who work in a coordinated fashion, everyone with a job to do, to help save your life. Though the wounds to your face and chest are obvious, flying out of a windshield at 50 miles an hour can certainly produce severe trauma to other areas of your body. It will be the job of the trauma team to identify all the major life-threatening injuries you have, and you won't be going anywhere, not even to the OR, until they have a handle on what has happened to you.

First things first. For any critically wounded patient with multiple problems, the initial evaluation is a "primary survey" to stabilize any immediate life-threatening injuries. Knowing what to look for in a primary survey is one of Benton's favorite pop quizzes, and Carter always seems to have the right answer. The primary survey's major objective is to check and ensure the ABCs (airway, breathing, and circulation) of life support.

One by one, A, then B, then C, are executed in a series of often aggressive and invasive procedures that in less than five or ten minutes will determine whether you will see the light of day again.

Everyone on the trauma team has his or her own job to do, but they all have one goal: to keep your brain alive. The first priority on the primary survey is A for airway.

You are not breathing well. The paramedics had been forcing air into your mouth through the ambu-bag, but you will need a more effective way to get oxygen. Without an airway, you're dead. The ER physician, your doc, has two choices here. He can intubate or perform a cricothyrotomy.

"CRIKE!"

Your severe facial injuries make it impossible for your doc to see clearly inside your mouth to be confident that he can get the tube down your throat and into your trachea. Which apertures are the ones you were born with, and which have been created by the accident? In emergency situations like this, where intubation is impossible, his only other choice is to cut into your neck and place a breathing tube directly into your trachea. This procedure is called a cricothyrotomy, and is often referred to on the show as a **crico** or **crike** (pronounced "kriko" or "krike"). Peter, Mark, and Susan seem to perform cricothyrotomy routinely on the show, but in real life such procedures are rarely attempted by ER doctors. Most patients, even those who are critically ill or injured, can be intubated.

Touch the center of the front part of your neck. Most of what you feel is the hard tubelike structure that is the outer cartilage of your trachea. There is a small soft area in the middle of all this hard tubing (in men, this is just below the Adam's apple) called the cricothyroid membrane. Doctors don't want to cut through the hard cartilage stuff, just the membrane.

During a crico, a vertical incision is made in the skin over the cricothyroid membrane, followed by a horizontal cut into the membrane. A breathing tube is then inserted into the hole, and a bag or ventilator is attached in the same way as for intubation. Quite a bit can go wrong, though, with this fairly simple procedure: the tube might be put in the wrong place, or one of the vital structures in the neck (big arteries and veins, important nerves, and the esophagus, to name but a few) could be cut with the scalpel. If you think there were problems before the crico, cut a major artery in the neck and see what happens!

"PNEUMO!"

The next part of the ABCs is breathing. A lot can go wrong in your chest in a major trauma. The force that expelled you out of the car could have caused significant damage to your lungs. Your doc listens to your chest on both sides, and can't hear breath sounds on the right side. It won't help to force air into the endotracheal tube if the lung has a pneumothorax (has collapsed), so he will have to re-inflate the collapsed lung. Your doc looks up at your neck. Your trachea is shifting over to the left and the nurse tells your doc that your blood pressure is dropping again, down to 60/40! Air is seeping into your chest on the right side with every breath, but not out, creating a large bubble of air that is compressing the collapsed lung on that side. It is also compressing and pushing your trachea and other vital structures over to the opposite side. Your aorta, along with the other great vessels, including your heart, is being squished by the ballooning mass of air in your chest. This is a tension pneumothorax, and without treatment, your heart and great blood vessels will be compressed so much that no pumping action will be possible, and thus no blood will reach your brain.

Your doc quickly stabs a needle into your upper chest, allowing the tension of air to be released. Immediately your blood pressure begins to rise, and the trachea shifts back to the middle of your neck. But the needle that has allowed the air to escape will need to be replaced by a much larger tube that will help to reexpand your lung.

You need a chest tube to re-inflate the lung and evacuate any blood from the chest. Your doc makes a small incision in the skin, dissects down and into the lining around the lung (called the pleura), and pokes a large tube through the pleura into the chest cavity. The tube will suck out the blood and air, and re-inflate the lung. Your doc listens to your chest through a stethoscope, and now hears good breath sounds on both sides of the lungs.

"Saline, D5W!"

Finally, the last of the ABCs: circulation. Goal: make sure your heart is beating effectively and in a regular rhythm. If there is a problem, the doctors will rectify it with electrical shock (paddles and defibrillator), a pacemaker, or medications (epi, lidocaine). While your doc has been working on your airway and breathing, the nurses have been frequently checking your pulse and blood pressure. They have tried to start intravenous lines that will provide fluid to help temporarily replace the blood you are losing from your injuries. These fluids will help to support your blood pressure until bleeding and blood loss can be controlled.

An IV is like throwing a lifeline inside your body. It allows direct access for medication or fluids (for dehydration or excessive bleeding) into the body via the veins. On the show you will often hear orders for IVs shouted out, such as D5W, Ringer's lactate, or normal saline, denoting which solutions will be introduced. All of these IV solutions used in the ER are basically water, each differing in the amounts of sodium, chloride, and dextrose (sugar) added to the solution. D5W (not to be confused with WD4, which you may use to dissolve rust!) stands for a solution that is 5 percent dextrose in plain sterile water, without sodium or chloride.

Ringer's lactate, along with normal saline (referred to as NS), have no sugar, but do have moderate amounts of sodium and chloride. These two solutions are used most often in trauma to help replace the fluid volume and salts in the plasma lost to bleeding (replacing plasma itself cannot be done nearly as quickly). Remember, the IV replaces some of the salt and water lost from the blood, to try to restore the original salinity of your blood, but if severe bleeding has occurred you are going to need red blood cells as well!

Your veins are in such a state of collapse that the nurse has been unable to get an IV started into your peripheral circulation (the small veins throughout your body that bring blood to the major vessels that lead to the heart). Without fluid to get your blood pressure up, you will likely die. The only way to keep you alive is a central line.

A **central line**, referring to the central location in the circulation of the vein used, is inserted into one of the great veins such as the internal jugular and subclavian veins in the neck, or the femoral veins in the groin. The upside to using these veins is the greater amount of fluid that can be delivered through them. The downside includes complications associated with putting a very large needle into the neck—for example, a doctor can hit a major artery and create a bleeding problem that will be extremely difficult to correct. Putting the needle in the wrong place in the lower part of the neck can puncture your lung. Principle No. 1 of medicine: FIRST, DO NO HARM! No one wants to put a patient in more danger in the process of trying to save a life. But it can and does happen. Deb Chen tried this delicate procedure without supervision on one episode, with dire results.

Your doc quickly puts an internal jugular central line into your neck, and the Ringer's lactate is sent ripping into your blood system. Your circulation is happy to have the extra fluid, and your blood pressure starts to rise.

"CRACK THE CHEST!"

The nurse suddenly tells your doc she can no longer find a pulse. You have another major problem, this time with your circulation.

Your doc takes a stab—*guess* might be a better word in this scenario—that the knife wound may have come close to or hit your heart. Pumping all the fluids in the hospital into your vessels won't help if there is a major injury to the heart and blood can't be circulated effectively. There is no time to spare. The choice is between a pericardiocentesis or a thoracotomy. Pericardiocentesis is done frequently on the show. Peter Benton performed his first one duing the episode "Confidential." It is usually reserved for patients who have bleeding into the pericardial sac (the pericardium is the membrane covering around the heart). If fluid collects around the heart, filling the pericardial sac, it can compress the heart, suppress heart activity, and cause hypotension and death. A needle can be inserted through the chest wall into the sac to aspirate (remove) the blood and relieve the pressure. But a pericardiocentesis will probably not work well when the leakage of blood is from a large hole in the heart, such as from a knife wound. You are going to need a thoracotomy ("crack the chest").

Your doctor grabs a scalpel and makes a 10-inch incision across your chest. Using metal rib spreaders, he reaches into the chest cavity and places a clamp on the lower (descending) portion of the aorta. As the aorta leaves the heart, it divides into two vessels, the ascending (upper) and descending (lower) aorta. By "crossclamping" the lower aorta, your doc has prevented blood flow to the lower portion of the body. The rest of the blood pumped out of the heart has nowhere left to go but into the ascending aorta and out to the heart and brain. Your doc then places his hands around your heart, and gently swings it out into the left side of the chest. He can see a bleeding hole in the lower part of the ventricle, as blood gushes out with every beat of the still contracting heart. He places his finger in the wound to stop the bleeding, and then with the nurse's help, sews three large sutures into the wound. These wounds will need to be inspected again in the OR, but for now, the heart is no longer leaking blood, and your doc slowly releases the clamp from the descending aorta. The nurse rechecks your BP: 85/60. Not great, but certainly better than no blood pressure at all.

Bloody Deeds: Tests on Your Blood

You are still alive, but only barely. As part of the primary survey, your doc will want to have transfusions of blood available, and will need to order blood tests that will eventually check your blood counts and blood chemistries. Finally, he will need to check your urine and stool. All these tests will help him find where all your major injuries are and how bad they are. Your doc calls out for tests that will further locate, confirm, or reveal the extent of your injuries. "CBC, lytes, coag panel, six units of O-negative blood, UA for dipped blood!" There isn't an episode or a night in a real ER trauma center when this mantra won't be heard.

Let's take a look at each of these tests, explore why and how they are done, and what they are likely to tell the staff about the state of the human body before them, your body. Blood may make you queasy to look at, especially when it's oozing out of your own body, but it is a good barometer of your health. And if your supply needs to be replenished, that's not simply a matter of reaching into the blood pantry and plucking out the first pint that comes to hand.

Blood can be drawn out of a vein (**venipuncture**) from any part of your body, but your arm is the most convenient. Blood is collected into separate color-coded vials and will be sent off to the lab for analysis. The color coding on the vials is important, for some have special chemicals in them that facilitate the specific lab tests that will be done (for example, the tube with the lavender top contains medication that prevents clotting, so individual cell counts can better be identified).

Your blood is made up of two basic parts, the liquid part, called plasma (the serum), and the blood cells. When you remove the plasma from the rest of the blood, which is what is done in the laboratory, you are left with just blood cells. Together, the liquid and the blood cells are referred to as **whole blood**. Plasma's function is to carry the chemicals (sugars and minerals) necessary for life via your veins. Your body is the most complex (some would say divinely complex) system on earth, and these chemicals provide the energy that power movement, speech function, even thinking, including remembering and recalling memory. Equally important is your blood, of which there are three major components: (1) red cells, which carry oxygen throughout your body; (2) white cells, which fight infections; and (3) platelets, which help your blood clot when you are bleeding. If you lose too much whole blood—plasma and cells together— there won't be enough life-sustaining chemicals and oxygen circulating through your body to do what has to be done to keep you functioning. That is why one of the first things that needs to be tested is your blood.

CBC, RBC, Crit, Hemoglobin

The most common blood test ordered in all of medicine is the CBC, or complete blood count. The CBC measures the number of the red and white cells, and the number of platelets in your blood. Each reveals something very specific about your health, one of those things being how much blood you have lost. Do you need a transfusion? Questions are racing through your doctor's mind, and he can find some of the answers to his questions through the blood. In severe trauma, your doc will have an eye out for the amount of red blood cells, specifically, the hematocrit and hemoglobin, in order to determine how much blood you have lost (these two collectively tell how many red blood cells are carrying oxygen to your brain and throughout your body).

An integral part of the CBC in severe trauma is the measure of the red blood cells, which should make up approximately 40 percent of whole blood. The term bandied about on the show and in the real world for this percentage is called the **hematocrit**, or **crit**. A normal hematocrit would be about 40, meaning 40 percent red cells in whole blood (no one uses "percentage," just the number). Women have slightly lower hematocrits, while men's are usually a little higher, and the values vary slightly by age.

Chronically low hematocrit, a drop of more than about 10 percent below normal values for your age and sex, is called **anemia**. The body adjusts to the condition when it comes on gradually, but when it is caused by dramatic and sudden blood loss (called *hemorrhage*) following severe trauma, your body may be unable to adapt to the loss quickly enough. The human body does not keep a large reserve of red blood cells, and it takes a long time to replenish those that are lost to bleeding. Because the usual life span of an individual red blood cell is about 120 days (the body ordinarily replaces this population of cells from the bone marrow at the rate of only 1 percent per day), a sudden loss of large amounts of blood can spell trouble.

Because the blood loss in acute bleeding is whole blood, with plasma and blood cells lost together, the hematocrit will initially stay the same. With minor bleeding, the body replenishes the "liquid" (plasma) fairly quickly, drawing on the fluids in other body tissues and driving down the hematocrit percentage. In the acute setting of trauma, the drop is sharp; as IV fluids run wide open into the veins (as fast as they can), the remaining red blood cells in the body are quickly diluted.

In a major trauma, the trauma team cannot wait for the lab results. The blood loss must be gauged by clinical observations, such as how low the blood pressure drops or how fast your heart rate increases. If you are bleeding to death, no ER doctor is going to wait for a hematocrit to return before giving you more red blood cells. But the hematocrit test can be done even as extra blood and fluids are given to you. If the hematocrit drops below 20 (meaning the red cells make up only 20 percent of your whole blood), you are in danger of not having enough blood left to supply adequate oxygen to your brain. At this point, your doc should already have transfusions of O-negative blood running in.

Besides hematocrit, there is another marker that indicates to the doctor that you may have lost too much blood: the test for hemoglobin. Remember, the job of red blood cells is to carry oxygen throughout your body. Hemoglobin is the material inside the red blood cells that actually carries oxygen. The measure of the hemoglobin in your blood tells doctors how well your red blood cells can carry oxygen throughout your body; the figure for normal is about 15. If you are bleeding acutely, from either internal or external wounds, and IV fluids are given, the hemoglobin will drop. When your nurse yells out that the hemoglobin is 10, your doc is worried. As it drops lower, the O-neg is running in fast.

"Cross-Match, 6 Units O-Negative!"

There are two critical considerations in deciding suitability for a transfusion: (1) matching for the four major blood groups, and (2) checking for the RH factor. Almost everyone falls within one of only four basic red blood cell types: A, B, AB, and O. There is also an additional factor in blood called "RH." Here you can go only two ways, RH-positive or RH-negative. When the laboratory reports your blood type back to the ER, both pieces of information need to be included, so they will say, for example, AB-negative or O-positive.

After the lab technicians "type" your blood to identify which of the blood groups and what RH type you belong to, they **cross-match**, which means they mix your blood with a sample from the blood the hospital is planning to transfuse into your veins. This is done to make sure that the two different bloods are compatible.

The matching of blood has been in practice only since 1900. Before then you could have received incompatible blood, suffered a reaction, and perhaps died. Needless to say, quite a few people did die from transfusions before the turn of the century, as well as from not getting a needed transfusion because of the risk. Today, a lab can type and cross-match your blood with amazing accuracy in about thirty minutes. But in an emergency, even that may be too long to wait.

In the event you are profusely bleeding and the ER doctor doesn't have that kind of time, there is a back-up plan. The "universal donor," type O-negative blood, is compatible with every blood type. But only 7 percent of the population is O-negative, compared with 39 percent who are O-positive, so doctors use it sparingly.

WBC

The cells in the blood that have the specialized job of fighting infection are the white blood cells. The CBC includes a **WBC**, or white blood cell count, because it is important to know how many white cells there are for the body to defend itself against bacteria. If you have been seriously injured, the chance of infection will be great, and you will need to call on your white blood cells to help fight off the germs that entered your body on your son's new but nonsterile knife and that dirty piece of car metal that made its way across your face. Whatever their source, infections are common in trauma victims. Many multiple-trauma victims survive initially, only to succumb later to an infected wound or to other complications such as pneumonia, another kind of foreign invasion. It is the role of white blood cells to fight off these infections.

Platelets, PT, PTT, and Coag Panel

Your doctor will want to know your platelet count, another component of the CBC that has been ordered, so that he can determine whether you will be able to stop bleeding. Once nature designed this vast, interconnected hydraulic system able to carry life-sustaining ingredients to every corner of your body, it had to devise a fail-safe plan to prevent the loss of these essential fluids through a breach in the system. What nature uses for this purpose are platelets, small disklike components in the blood that help form clots to plug leaks from bleeding arteries and veins throughout the body. A normal platelet count is about 200,000. If your doc finds that you have a low number of platelets, he may call for a transfusion of platelets to help your body control the bleeding.

On the TV show you are likely to hear Peter rattle off some additional tests that check the body's ability to clot that are not included in the CBC: these tests are called the PT and PTT. This may sound like just so much more alphabet soup, but the next time you view *ER,* watch how often these short bursts of letters pop up.

The chemical tested by the PT and PTT works with your platelets to form clots that halt the bleeding in your body. The test to measure these chemicals is called the PT (**prothrombin time**) and PTT (**partial thromboplastin time**). If the results of the PT and PTT tests are abnormal, your body will not be able to clot effectively and you may bleed to death. Some patients have chronic problems with clotting. Hemophiliacs are perhaps the best-known example, but the vast majority of patients with clotting problems have abnormal clotting tests because of medication (coumadin) prescribed to prevent blood clots, which can cause strokes and heart attacks. To correct the problem, the doctor will order plasma rich in these special clotting chemicals, to be delivered in yet another kind of transfusion, this one called FFP, for fresh frozen plasma.

Chem-7 and Lytes

What else is there in plasma that can give lifesaving information in an emergency? Plenty. The chemicals in your plasma (fluids) each have a similarly specific role in maintaining proper bodily function.

One of the most common tests ordered on the show and in real life to check for chemical imbalance is called **lytes**, an abbreviation for electrolytes, which tests the basic chemicals in the body: sodium, potassium, chloride, and bicarbonate. More commonly in the ER, doctors are interested in a Chem-7 (a test of 7 chemistries); this is a test that includes the basic electrolytes (lytes), but additionally tests three other chemicals in the body: glucose, BUN, and creatinine.

In the ER, this test directs your doctor in how to manage intravenous fluids, particularly in cases of trauma or severe illness.

The four basic chemicals in your body—again, sodium, potassium, chloride, and bicarbonate (the "lytes")—are dissolved in your plasma. They come from the food you eat and the fluids you drink. They are an integral part of the routine blood chemistries ordered by all physicians. Severe abnormalities of these chemicals can kill you. The most common seen in the ER include severely low sodium, which causes seizures, and very high or low potassium, which causes irregular heartbeats and weakness.

Two other components of the Chem-7, the BUN (blood urea nitrogen) and creatinine, are compounds in the body that are dissolved in the plasma. Collectively, they give an accurate reflection of how well your kidneys are functioning. High values of these chemicals are an indication that the kidneys may not be working well or that you may be very dehydrated. If the values are very high, your kidneys may not be working at all—called *renal failure*—and you may need dialysis. (This is when a kidney machine is used to filter the impurities out of your blood, taking over the function of your kidneys.) The values of the BUN and creatinine, along with the lytes, will help the ER doctor manage the fluids given intravenously in the emergency room.

Glucose

Glucose is the sugar that provides you with the energy to be alive, and it is dissolved in your plasma. The food you eat is digested and converted into fat, protein, and sugar (glucose). Very high values of glucose (**hyperglycemia**) mean you probably have diabetes. Patients with diabetes take medication (insulin or pills) that lowers blood sugar. Sometimes the values can be too low (**hypoglycemia**), and a patient can become confused or even go into a coma. The patient's sugar is checked to make sure it is not too high or too low.

Your doctor may decide to order a Chem-23 for you as well. This lab test includes the Chem-7, plus 16 other chemicals found in the blood (such as calcium and bilirubin). The most critical chemicals, though, are usually in the Chem-7, and will provide your doc with a great deal of necessary information to help guide your therapy in the ER.

Blood Gases

Your lungs and heart are working, but are you getting enough oxygen through the ET (endotracheal) tube? If you aren't, you could be on the verge of being brain-dead! There is a test for just about everything, including the risk of **hypoxia** (low oxygen) to the brain. Unlike the other blood tests that have been ordered, which analyze blood from **veins** (vessels that carry blood from your body back to your heart), there is one test that requires blood from your **arteries**, the vessels carrying blood from the heart to the lungs and other organs. (The word *artery* has an interesting etymology, deriving from the Greek for "air pipe." When upon autopsy the ancient Greeks found arteries empty, they apparently thought these vessels were for the transport of *air* throughout the body.)

Here's a brief course in how it works. Let's start in the continuous cycle at the point where blood is pumped from the heart through the pulmonary arteries to the lungs. There the blood picks up oxygen and is then drawn back to the heart, where the oxygenated blood is sent out through the arteries to deliver oxygen to all the tissues and organs of the body. Next, the oxygen-depleted blood (it looks blue through the skin) returns to the heart through the body's system of veins. From there it is sent back to the lungs to be re-oxygenated, continuing the cycle. In order to figure out exactly how much oxygen is being carried to the tissues (most important, to the brain), a sample of blood must be drawn from an artery. On *ER,* you will see a doctor hold a patient's hand firmly against the bed and poke the wrist in search of a pulsating artery. Soon, bingo! Blood flows into the syringe, and this final blood specimen, known as an arterial blood gas, is rushed off to the lab.

Normal oxygen in the blood runs about 80 to 100 (measured as oxygen pressure in millimeters of mercury). With severe chest trauma and the need for intubation, the oxygen content in the blood can go way down. Supplemental oxygen is given through the ET tube to make sure the oxygen content in your blood is high enough to prevent heart and brain damage. For patients who are not so critically ill but still need added oxygen to treat their hypoxia, physicians can supplement their oxygen supply through those tubes we see on the show that are hooked around patients' ears and up to their nose. The two nipples at the front end of the device are plugged, almost like a miniature electric plug, into the patient's nostrils. Called "nasal cannula," these tubes help a patient breathe by maintaining oxygen at a safe level without the patient's having to breathe hard for it.

The Secondary Survey

Once the IVs have been established, O-negative blood and fluids are running in, and the ABCs of life support have been accomplished, it is time for the secondary survey. The secondary survey is a head-to-toe, front-to-back examination of your body, looking for clues that might suggest additional injuries. Some of the injuries found in the past at County General and in real ERs are obvious, like a meat hook in an arm, an antenna in the gut, and an arrow in the head (though the arrow in the head would probably have been part of the primary survey!). Other wounds are not so obvious. You are covered with contusions (bruises) and abrasions (scratches), but there is nothing obviously wrong with you other than the facial lacerations (cuts) and the knife wound to your chest. Your doc will need to do a complete secondary survey to look for injuries he may have missed in his primary survey.

UA and Guiac

While flying through the windshield, you may have damaged your abdomen or kidneys. These injuries may not be apparent immediately in the ER, but you could eventually die if they remain undiagnosed.

In evaluating these injuries, is there anything your doc can learn from what you would usually flush down the toilet? To establish verisimilitude, episodes of *ER* have shown a staff member checking a patient's urine or stool, surely bold new steps for prime-time TV. In the treatment of trauma, these checks are a crucial part of the diagnosis and treatment.

First comes the stool. Early in the development of diagnostic techniques, doctors relied too heavily on the size, smell, and quantity of stool as indicators of a patient's general health. But it remains an article of good clinical practice that the color and shape of a patient's stool can reveal important information. Your doc will most probably defer this critical exam to a medical student, someone like Carter. In trauma, the sphincter tone of the rectum and the position of the prostate can also yield clues to pelvic and spinal trouble. But in the ER what is of greatest interest is whether or not the stool remaining on the withdrawn gloved finger will test positive for blood. This test, known as **guiac**, is used by your primary care physician in his or her office as a screening tool for certain disturbances of the colon, including benign polyps and even cancer. But for you, after a serious accident, if the stool guiac test is positive (the paper turns a shade of blue after some developing solution is dropped on the card), the ER doctor must consider the possibility of your having suffered damage to your bowels. The med student performs the exam quickly, and tests your stool. The solution turns the guiac card bright blue, indicating blood. You may have suffered severe bowel trauma.

The next test is to check your urine. Nearly unconscious, you are not about to jump off the gurney to provide a urine specimen. That's why you see a nurse like Carol Hathaway stand over a patient, cleaning his or her genitals with iodine and holding a long flexible tube called a foley catheter. The tube is placed (using sterile techniques) into the urethra, the opening from which you urinate, and then is pushed all the way up into the bladder. Catheterization allows the doctors to get a sterile urine specimen for a UA (urine analysis), while being able to drain the bladder of all the urine present. Catheterization is not pleasant when awake, but nothing to worry about if you are unconscious.

You may think of urine as nothing but waste, a fluid your body throws out; but to the ER physician, it is liquid gold. After you have suffered major trauma, a test strip dipped in your urine can detect the presence of blood, which suggests there may be severe damage to your kidneys or bladder. In addition, analysis of your urine can tell the ER people if you are dehydrated, diabetic, undernourished, or have a bladder or kidney infection.

Lavage

Because you are unable to tell your doc where you hurt, he must assume, especially with the blood on the guiac card, that you have suffered an injury to your bowels. Abdominal injuries from blunt trauma (meaning there is no evidence of a penetration to the skin, and the injury was caused by a blunt force against the body) can be extremely difficult to diagnose. Your liver and spleen are at risk, and a fast way for your doc to check for injury is to perform a diagnostic peritoneal lavage (DPL). If a major injury has occurred, such as trauma to the bowels, liver, or spleen, there will usually be bleeding into the abdominal cavity. Even in the absence of any external signs of injury, you may be bleeding to death. That's why you often hear someone like Peter Benton order lavage for his patients.

In a DPL, a small catheter is placed into the abdominal cavity through a small incision made into the lower abdomen. A small amount of saline solution is run into the abdomen, washing (lavaging) the abdominal cavity, and then is removed and analyzed. If there is blood in the fluid, it is evidence of a serious bleeding wound and a probable major intra-abdominal injury. It is possible that the bowels were ripped, or that the liver or spleen was fractured. (You can fracture or break a vital organ in the same way you can break a bone. And if you fracture the liver or spleen, you can bleed to death.)

Your doc performs the DPL, and there are signs of blood in the fluid, suggesting that in addition to severe facial and chest injuries, you probably have a major injury inside the abdomen.

X Rays

As part of the routine secondary survey, your doc will order three crucial X rays. He will want to check your neck with a cross-table C-spine; he will want to check your chest with a chest X ray; and he will want to evaluate your pelvis with a pelvic film.

The X ray of the pelvis will help to rule out any major pelvic fractures, while the chest X ray will help reveal the proper placement of the ET tube, along with helping to assess how much lung damage may be present. But if you plan ever to walk again, the cross-table C-spine X ray may be the most important one for you in the initial stages of your secondary survey in the ER.

When the paramedics first came on the scene, they tied you

down and immobilized you on a hard board with a rigid collar around your neck just in case there might be a fracture or dislocation of your neck or back. And where a cervical spine fracture is suspected, the neck remains immobilized in a rigid collar until the doctor can get a portable X ray of the cervical spine to rule it out. The ordered test is a "cross-table C-spine" or "cross-table lateral," which means the X ray is shot across the table or gurney that the patient is lying on, in order to view a side angle of the upper (cervical) spine. Your doc may decide to get a couple of additional views, but the cross-table C-spine will help rule out an obvious cervical injury so you can be unwrapped from the paramedic's cocoon.

The regular X rays done by conventional machinery are limited in their ability to actually look "inside" the human body. If there is an injury to your head or abdomen, regular X rays will probably be insufficient to assess the extent of the damage accurately. A more advanced X-ray technique, the CAT scan (computerized axial tomograpy), is done in a large machine, where the pictures are taken and processed by a sophisticated computer program. CAT scans are painless, and they allow doctors a glimpse inside the body without cutting it open. CTs (common vernacular for CAT scans) can be used to evaluate head trauma (looking for intracranial bleeding) and abdominal trauma (damage to liver, spleen, and bowels), and have become an essential tool for managing the patient with multiple trauma. For any patient who has come into the ER with a low GCS (remember: the Glasgow Coma Scale), your doc will want to get a head CT to rule out a subdural or intracerebral bleed. (Both of these are bleeding inside the head, but **subdural** is outside the brain and under the skull, while **intracerebral** is inside the brain. The latter is far more worrisome.)

Whether to order a CT scan to help evaluate abdominal trauma or perform a DPL is an individual decision ultimately left to the ER doctor or trauma surgeon. For you at the ER, your doc seems to prefer the DPL, and certainly Mark Greene, Doug Ross, Susan Lewis, and Peter Benton have had a great deal of experience performing this procedure on the show.

Another set of useful X rays are the arteriograms. These special X-ray studies are used to assess whether there is a blockage in an artery, or whether an artery has been damaged in trauma. If your doc should find diminished pulses as he examines you, he might guess that you have an injury to an artery that requires an arteriogram to assess the damage. A special dye is injected into the artery and X rays are taken to see the flow of blood (visible from the dye) through the vessel. You have strong pulses in your arms and legs, and your doc will not need an arteriogram for your evaluation.

Your doctor has completed his primary and secondary surveys and reviewed the results of the blood tests and the X rays. You have received O-negative blood, along with IV fluids, and your blood pressure has stabilized at 95/60. You have survived a cricothyrotomy, severe facial trauma, a thoracotomy, a tension pneumothorax, and a chest tube, while you still have evidence via the DPL of an intra-abdominal injury. In real life, as on the show, it's time for surgery. Your doc has provided the surgeon with a road map to all your injuries, and you have been stabilized for surgery. You have survived (so far!) with the help of the trauma team and its dizzying array of tests and gadgets. Now the surgical team must do its job so you can live to see another day.

Sleuthing for Illness

Diagnoses

If you think Lieutenant Columbo had his work cut out for him in those ingeniously intricate TV crime thrillers, be assured that he'd face far greater challenges in medicine. A patient who comes into the ER complaining of aches, a fever, or weakness could be suffering from any one of a hundred problems, many trivial, some life-threatening.

The ER doctor requires all the skills of a master detective to put the puzzle pieces together and come up with an almost instant answer to what is causing the patient's symptoms—a trick he or she has to perform about 5,000 times a year. Unlike the family physician, the ER team doesn't have the luxury of knowing a patient's history, much less knowing the patient personally. The same question and answer—for instance, "How badly does it hurt?" with the response of "Quite a bit"—may mean very different things from different patients. One patient may be about to pass out, while another may be only uncomfortable. Yet the ER people get just one quick shot to gather a large volume of information and to try to answer "What's wrong with the patient?" before the question turns into "What did the patient die of?"

Lab tests on the *fluids, gases,* and *solids* found in the body are integral to the investigative process. The fluids someone coughs, circulates, eliminates, or otherwise gives up provide early clues to what ails him. A fruity smell on the breath may alert the doctor to DKA (diabetic ketoacidosis, where the patient is critically ill with a very high blood sugar and severe chemical imbalances in the blood), a product of severely uncontrolled diabetes. Excessive flatulence (gas), diarrhea, or abdominal noises may point to a colon infection. Even the lack of bowel noise may be important, for it may signal a severe obstruction. Using whatever clues the body will provide them (X rays help, too), the members of the ER team try to figure out what's gone wrong, a necessary prerequisite to planning a repair job.

Usually the most important piece of information comes from the patient very early in the evaluation, what is called the "chief complaint," or main problem that brought the patient to the ER.

Before the new diagnostic tests were developed, doctors had little to go by other than the general appearance of the patient, his or her sensitivity to probing various parts of the body, and, most important of all, the patient's description of what hurt and for how long. In the old days, great professors of medicine would tell their students: "The patient is trying to tell you what's wrong with him. You have to be quiet and listen." This is the same advice given Peter Benton in the episode "Into That Good Night," when he misses a diagnosis by not carefully heeding the patient's own words and sends him home with a "perfed" (for perforated, or ruptured) appendix.

The list of major complaints that bring patients to the hospital are endless. Just take a look at "the board" behind the clerk's station at County General's ER. This is a running tally of patients, all listed with room assignments and chief complaint. Some are weak and dizzy, some have nausea and vomiting, but most come in because of one or more of four common complaints: *pain,* of course, leads to all others; then in no particular order come *weak-*

ness, *shortness of breath*, and *fever*. When Mark picks up a chart, these are the complaints he expects to find, complaints that he must turn into diagnoses. Like Columbo but without the well-chomped cigar and dirty trenchcoat, he has to be alert to any clues that might help him solve his case.

"A Pain in the . . . "

Sometimes the cause of pain is obvious, and the treatment is fast. A young man trips and hears a crack as his arm hits the hard ground. His forearm in excruciating pain and bent at an angle that nature did not intend, he finds himself being examined by a pediatrician, someone like County General's Dr. Doug Ross.

The doctor feels for the pulse in his patient's wrist, and then (probably calling him "buddy") asks him to move all his fingers. This tells the doctor that the tendons which supply function for the hand are okay. He then brushes the skin on his patient's hand, and asks if he feels everything normally. He does. In those 30 seconds, the doctor has determined that the blood vessels are still intact beyond the fracture area, that the nerves are still functioning, and that the patient has normal use of the muscles and bones of his hand. In medical vernacular, he is *neurovascularly intact* with *good range of motion*. The doctor confines the trouble to a fracture of one or two of the bones (the radius and the ulna) in the forearm. His patient will need an X ray, Tylenol (the ER drug of choice) or a narcotic for the pain, and a splint to stabilize the fracture until it knits together.

Unlike the pain of a broken bone, pain symptoms like a severe headache that persists for hours, excruciating abdominal pain that persists for days, or crushing substernal (under the breastbone) chest pain for 18 hours do not have causes that are easy to determine.

"My Head Is Killing Me"

First of all, the ER doctor must learn to separate the severity of the symptom from the severity of the underlying cause. How much pain you feel is not an absolute guide to how severe its cause is; a bad headache can be brought on by a very tense day on the job or be a symptom of a life-threatening ruptured aneurysm in the brain. What goes through the mind of a physician who has a patient with severe head pain? As alarmist as it sounds, ER physicians must think of the worst-case scenario first. It has to be ruled out before they can move to a less serious possibility, even though in most cases something less serious will turn out to be the culprit.

The ER doctor takes a history from a 60-year-old man who complains of a severe headache on the left side—the worst headache he has ever had, he reports. The patient has no weakness in his arms or legs, no history of head trauma or of migraines, no signs of a fever or stiff neck or congestion. Next, the neurological exam, something we see Mark Greene often do on *ER*.

It's the same in real life. The doctor shines a light in the patient's eyes to see whether the pupils are "perrl," which means *p*upils that are *e*qually *r*ound and *r*eact to the *l*ight. They are, which tells the doctor that the area of the brain responsible for vision is functioning normally. The doctor looks through an oph-thalmoscope into the back of the eye for signs of increased intracranial pressure (caused by bleeding or swelling), which if present could indicate bleeding or a tumor inside the head. Again, no problem. Nonetheless the doctor checks the patient's cranial nerves, which allow us to feel and move the muscles of the eyes, mouth, and face.

Some of the ways an ER doctor can ascertain a cranial-nerve problem are by noting whether the patient's face is drooping and whether he can look up and down, as well as to the left and right. The doctor will also look into the patient's ears, and palpate around the left side of the face and head, looking for tenderness or other signs of infection. The doctor does not think there is an infection present, for the patient does not have a fever or stiff neck (a sign of meningitis, a condition in which the fluid that bathes the brain becomes infected). Sinus infections can frequently cause severe headache, but without a recent cold or congestion, this is not likely. And what would a neurological exam be without checking the **DTRs** (deep tendon reflexes)? (It's a common sight to view Susan, Doug, or Mark checking a patient's reflexes on the show.) The doctor taps his patient's knees and ankles with a rubber hammer. Bleeding in the head can cause changes in the reflexes.

Though the patient's neurological exam proves normal, since he has such severe pain and no history of headaches, the doctor will err on the side of safety and order a CAT scan (an X ray that can detect blood in or around the brain). He will also order a CBC and an erythrocyte sedimentation rate (*sed rate,* or ESR), a nonspecific test that can be a marker for severe inflammation. Two hours later (in real-life time), the doctor gathers his patient's information. The CAT scan, neurological exam, and CBC are all normal—only the sed rate is off-kilter. Putting the clues together—a high sed rate of 100 (20 is normal) with headache and tenderness over one side of the head—the doctor can make a diagnosis. His patient probably has "temporal arteritis," inflammation of the large head arteries, which, if left untreated, can cause blindness.

Faced with a clear CAT scan and no signs of neurological problems, the doctor knew not to dismiss the patient's headache as tension-related or as a migraine. His sleuthing looked for *all* the possible culprits, not just the most likely. Using the clues before him, he quickly narrowed it down to one suspect and saved this man from going blind.

"I'm Having a Heart Attack"

Almost all patients who come to the ER with chest pain worry that they are having a heart attack. In many cases, however, the chest pain is a symptom of something else. A 12-year-old boy with chest pain along the sternum (the breastbone) thought he was having a heart attack. Why not? He had stayed up late with his parents the night before and saw an old man with the same symptom on *ER* go through an MI (myocardial infarction). If such a case were to be dramatized on the show, the first order of business would be to reassure both patient and parents that a heart attack is extremely unlikely in a patient so young. An ER doc would press on the boy's chest. If this clearly produced the pain, and the pain was sharp and increased with movement, he would have good clues that the pain was in the chest wall, probably just musculoskeletal pain, not heart-related.

Of course, chest pain in a child can be serious, though this is rare. Let's say another 12-year-old boy comes into the ER, this one with a chief complaint of upper chest pain for three days and a "ripping" sensation into his back. He has been otherwise healthy and appears to be normal, except that he is as tall as the ER doc. He also notices that the boy has long, slender fingers that might one day might make him a great basketball player or concert pianist. The ER doc listens to the boy's chest with his stethoscope and hears a strange whooshing sound, a murmur, similar to the sound of a leaky heart valve that he occasionally hears in older patients. The ER doc has an EKG done, but it is normal. He then orders a chest X ray, and it shows a dilatation (enlargement) of the aorta as it originates from the left side of the heart. This is an aortic aneurysm, and it is dissecting (spreading) through and into the aortic valve of the heart. This same type of dissection recently killed the author of the Tony Award–winning musical *Rent*, though from a different underlying disease. What the young boy has is a disease called Marfan's syndrome, a so-called connective tissue disease that results in very tall stature, long fingers, and aortic dissections. Historians believe Abraham Lincoln may have suffered from this disease. Lucky for the patient, the ER doc did not dismiss the complaint of chest pain in a young child, and instead followed the clues that led him to the culprit before it could strike its deadly blow.

Sometimes age isn't so obvious a factor in ruling out a heart attack. Suppose the ER doc is taking a history from a 40-year-old man who has had crushing substernal chest pain for three hours. The patient has had this pain in the past and is worried it might be his heart. His father died at age 45 from a "heart problem," and now he is sure he is about to die from a heart attack. He tells the ER doc that it feels like an elephant is sitting on his chest, a classic complaint for heart pain. The man wonders if this is the same elephant that sat on his father's chest and killed him. The pain, he says, is especially bad late at night, but is better when he sits up.

The ER doc orders an EKG, which turns out to be totally normal. He is quite sure that the elephant resides in this patient's stomach, not his heart. His pain comes from stomach acid entering the lower portion of the esophagus, an organ not designed to withstand the caustic action of digestive juices. This can feel like a heart attack, but there are symptoms that immediately helped the ER doc pinpoint the correct cause. His pain was worse when he lay flat (allowing the acid to slosh out of the stomach and into the esophagus) and better when he sat up (when the acid goes back down, thanks to gravity). They are classic signs of heartburn, or gastroesophageal reflux (meaning acid **refluxes**, or moves backward into the esophagus), rather than a heart problem.

The patient, however, isn't convinced of the diagnosis and still feels he is about to die. It is only when the ER doc gives him a "GI cocktail" from the ER bar and lounge—a mix of Maalox (an antacid), Donnatal (an antispasmodic), and Novocaine (a local anesthetic) that his pain disappears and he comes to accept that he will indeed live to see another day.

Fire in the Belly

While treating chest pain may require some extraordinary sleuthing skills, the greatest challenge for many ER physicians is abdominal pain. The possibilities seem endless, and often it is nearly impossible to come up with a diagnosis. Here is how an ER physician, such as Mark Greene, might approach the problem.

A female patient enters the ER at 3:00 A.M. in a cold sweat, running a high fever, and in terrible pain. The waiting room is jammed, and she faces a long wait. But moments after arriving, she vomits all over the triage desk—that gets her a bed pronto.

The bellyache is so common a complaint that the expression "quit your bellyaching" has become synonymous with a whining and complaining personality. But as common as abdominal pain may be, its cause can range from something as innocuous as a sausage pizza to a ruptured appendix, so it is important that the patient go ahead and bellyache, holding back nothing from the people who will be taking her history. They will want to know when the pain started, what she was doing when it started, when it seems to get worse or better.

The main problem the ER doctor has in making a diagnosis is that he can't just look into the belly and confirm or rule out what he suspects is going on under that tough packaging we call the skin. So as a next step in pinpointing the problem and perhaps its severity, he will **palpate** (from the Latin "to touch," but doctors do more than touch—they press and even knead) different areas of the abdomen, all the while looking for reactions that indicate inappropriate sensitivity. On *ER* it's not unusual to see Susan Lewis, Peter Benton, or Mark Greene doing this. If the patient should try to push his hand away while he goes about his pressing, the patient is "guarding," and it will help the doctor localize the area of pain.

He presses deeper into that area, and then quickly lifts up. The act of quickly lifting up jiggles the **peritoneum** (the tough covering that surrounds the abdominal contents), and the severe pain it elicits in this patient may be her ticket to the operating room. It is called "rebound tenderness." On the show you may hear this referred to as "rebound," and it represents a nonspecific sign of a major abdominal disorder, such as acute appendicitis. The term **nonspecific** indicates that a cause is suggested, but far from proven. By knowing the internal architecture of the abdomen, the doctor can make an educated guess about where the pain is coming from and start to eliminate unlikely causes. Doctors learn to think of the abdominal area as being divided into four quadrants, to help them isolate the source of the pain.

The Organs That Live Uptown

If the patient complains of pain in the upper-right quadrant, the ER doctor will test the organs he knows are in that area, particularly the liver and the gallbladder. The liver, a large organ that resides just below the lower ribs on the right side, produces many chemicals necessary for normal digestion, including the bile that helps digest fat. There is a group of tests collectively called liver function tests, or **LFTs**, that will reveal whether that organ is functioning normally. The liver can be damaged by many things, including viruses (such as in hepatitis), trauma (a motor-vehicle accident with abdominal trauma), alcohol, and gallstones. The doctor orders the LFTs and continues his search for the diagnosis.

If the patient complains of pain anywhere in the upper abdomen, it could potentially be from too much acid and stomach irritation (gastritis), or even an ulcer. But stomach pain would most often be in the middle or upper-left quadrant, so this diagnosis is less likely. On the show, a large number of patients have had bleeding from their upper GI tracts because of ulcers, and also varices—dilated veins that most people think of only in connection with the legs but which can occur almost anywhere in the body. In one episode, Mark Greene performs an upper endoscopy on a woman bleeding from her upper GI tract. He places the **endoscope** (a long flexible tube with its own special lighting) into the patient's mouth and down into the GI tract and finds varices as the cause of her bleeding. This is a great way to make a diagnosis—but, unfortunately, ER physicians are not trained to do this procedure! It is usually left to gastroenterologists, many of whom would be extremely unhappy if ER doctors started encroaching on their turf.

Bleeding from an ulcer or from varices is usually associated with some visual clues that alert the staff to the problem. If there is a lot of bleeding, bright red blood may be present in the vomit. If there is slow bleeding, the blood will have had a chance to mix with the stomach acid and come out looking much darker and grainier; a typical complaint of a patient bleeding from the stomach is "coffee ground emesis": vomit that looks just like coffee grounds.

In addition, the doctor will check the stool for blood, using the chemical guiac test. If his patient is bleeding from an ulcer, her stool may look black and tarry, for digested blood mixed with normal waste looks like black tar, a condition called **melena**. This is why doctors ask that most charming of bedside questions, "What do your bowel movements look like?"

Another organ in the upper abdomen is the pancreas, a very complex structure that produces enzymes that help to break down the food you eat. It also manufactures important chemicals, such as insulin, that regulate how much sugar is absorbed from your blood. The pancreas can become inflamed (**pancreatitis**), most often from too much alcohol or from gallstones. When the damage is from gallstones, it is usually because one of the stones has traveled into a duct that the pancreas uses to send the digestive juices into the bowel. Pancreatitis is usually associated with nausea, vomiting, and excruciating abdominal pain. When the pancreas is damaged, one of the enzymes it produces shows up as a marker in the blood. The test for it is named after the enzyme itself: amylase.

In the upper-left quadrant lies the **spleen**. The spleen is part of the lymphatic system, and helps to filter the blood of bacteria and impurities. It contains lots of blood vessels, so injury to the spleen can cause massive bleeding. When a patient complains of pain here, the doctor is likely to think of diseases such as mononucleosis (a viral infection), a blood disorder, cancer (Hodgkin's disease), or trauma. The best way to see if there is an acute problem of the spleen would be to do a CAT scan of the abdomen.

The Organs That Live Downtown

If the patient complains of severe pain and is "guarding" and even has "rebound" in the lower-right quadrant, the doctor will focus his inquiry on the "appy"—the appendix. This is sort of a little extra tag of tissue in the small bowel, and it can become inflamed and infected. Everyone knows that an attack of appen-

dicitis is excruciatingly painful—and if the appendix has ruptured from an infection, the pain can be so severe that it can
spread to the upper-right quadrant and, in fact, to the whole
abdominal area. But, surprisingly, out of the many people who
come to the ER clutching their stomachs in agony, few wind up
in the OR to have an appendix removed.

If the doctor narrows his patient's pain to the lower-left quadrant, the problem is probably with the colon. The most likely
cause for people over 50 would be an inflammation of the colon
called **diverticulitis**. But this being a younger woman, the doctor
would more likely suspect a problem in the pelvis, such as pelvic
inflammatory disease (**PID**), caused by an **STD** (sexually transmitted disease). If pain is prevalent on either the left or the right
lower quadrants, it might be a sign that the ovaries are involved.
An ovarian cyst frequently causes pain. In either case, the doctor
would do a pelvic exam to help detect an infection or mass
(growth) around the ovaries or uterus.

If the doctor wants to isolate the bladder as the cause of his
patient's pain, he will order a **UA** (urine analysis) to check for the
presence of blood, bacteria, or pus in the urine. And if the patient
is of childbearing age, she, like every woman in that category
with abdominal pain, will get a pregnancy test. Loads of ER
physicians have seen women who have indignantly proclaimed
that there was no way they could possibly be pregnant—insisting
they had not had sex in months, or even years—but somehow
were miraculously pregnant nonetheless. In the episode called
"Dead of Winter," a 300-pound woman suffering severe abdominal pain is being evaluated for surgery by Peter Benton; what
seems like a case of appendicitis turns out to be labor—with
twins!

The pregnancy test can be done on either blood (serum) or
urine, and either way the test checks for the presence of a hor-
mone called HCG (human chorionic gonadotropin) that rises
dramatically early in pregnancy. A pregnancy where the fetus is
not in the normal position, or outside the womb or uterus, called
an **ectopic** pregnancy, can present as abdominal pain. And this lit-

tle fetus can be anywhere, even hiding in the liver or under the bowels. If the fetus grows into a blood vessel or ruptures it, massive internal bleeding can occur.

There was a case of ectopic pregnancy in the pilot for the series. A 13-year-old girl whom Carter questions denies she could be pregnant. When Carter tells Benton, Benton tells him she needs to be firmly questioned, suggesting that she has a lot of symptoms consistent with ectopic pregnancy. After firm questioning by Bention, she breaks down and admits she is sexually active. Benton then explains that she has an ectopic pregnancy and what it is.

Will an ER doctor like a Mark Greene really request a CBC, a UA, blood cultures, LFTs, and a pregnancy test—all for a patient's bellyache? Yes. And all the while he probably will try not to give the patient anything for the pain. It's not that he is sadistic. But if she will need to go to the OR, and the decision is dependent upon a surgical evaluation, the doctor will probably hold off treating the pain until the surgical consultation is finished. Unlike the patient having a heart attack, in whom pain can make the heart attack worse, the concern here is that painkillers might mask the major symptom. Pain, its location and severity, is always a valuable clue, at times the only clue, in making a diagnosis. About the earliest his patient might get something for pain (in real time) would be about the time the late evening news is winding down, or possibly as late as the middle of *Late Night with Conan O'Brien*.

Besides having to wait for pain medication, the patient may not even get a glass of water. In medical terms, until it has been decided for sure that she won't be needing surgery, she is NPO, from the Latin *nil per oram*: "nothing by mouth." On the show, Carter learns this lesson the hard way when he mistakenly honors a patient's request for a glass of water, forcing an angry Peter Benton to cancel the patient's scheduled surgery. Many drugs used to put you to sleep can cause vomiting, and the last thing the anesthesiologist wants is a patient throwing up into the anesthesia mask, with material from the stomach ending up aspirated into the lungs.

"You Take My Breath Away!"

If Columbo tried to draw in a deep breath, he might well end up coughing and gasping. He may just need a better brand of cigars or to stop smoking altogether. At the ER, a patient's difficulty in breathing is usually a major clue in evaluating the medical case.

A 28-year-old man, who has been coughing and increasingly short of breath (called **dyspnea**) for the past five days is brought into the ER. He has no fever, no chest pain, and no history of lung problems. He did have an allergy to cats as a child, though, and his girlfriend is currently taking care of a friend's cat.

The ER doc checks the patient's vital signs, and sees that his breathing (respiratory rate) is very fast, about 40, and his pulse is 130 beats per minute. Moreover, the patient's whole chest is heaving with each breath. Normal breathing is a nonlabored, coordinated action of muscles in the upper chest. But a person with a severe breathing problem may call on lots of other muscles in the chest and abdomen to help. This is referred to as using accessory muscles of respiration, and it is a sign that the patient is working too hard to breathe.

For the patient, using all those extra muscles in the chest and abdomen to breathe requires a lot of energy, and that can be very tiring. For the ER doc, it's a clear sign of an acute medical problem. Often seen on the show are people with chronic breathing problems, usually older patients with a long history of smoking who have a condition called chronic obstructive pulmonary disease (**COPD**). And to boot, we sometimes see them sneak off for a cigarette when no one is looking! This patient, however, is another matter. His problem is **acute**, not chronic. That means it's a sudden, intense flare-up, not an ongoing problem.

Suspecting asthma, the ER doc listens to the patient's chest and hears wheezing throughout both lungs. What exactly causes wheezing? Think of air going in and out of your lungs as water flowing down a quiet stream. As the stream narrows, the water becomes turbulent and starts to make noise. Your lungs are something like that quiet stream; when something narrows the stream bed, as in asthma, it becomes turbulent and noisy.

The ER doc checks the pulse ox on this 28-year-old patient. **Pulse ox** (short for *oxymetry*) is a simple procedure that checks how much oxygen is being carried in the blood. Doctors like this test because it is fast, painless, and easy. A small plastic clip is slipped on the patient's finger. The clip has an electrode that is attached by a wire to a machine that reads the oxygen content in the blood right through the skin. The oxygen is read out as a percentage from 1 to 100. Normal is about 95; anything below 85 to 90 suggests a serious problem with the lungs. The patient has a pulse ox of 90. With the wheezing and the history of allergies to cats, the ER doc is sure the patient is having an asthma attack and orders medications to alleviate the wheezing and bring down the swelling in the air passages.

WEAKNESS

A 20-year-old male comes to the ER by ambulance with a complaint of weakness. He tells the doctor he had a cold about a week ago, probably just a little virus, but in general he has been remarkably healthy. Over the past three days he has felt weak in his legs. Initially it was only slight, but now he is having difficulty walking. When the problem spread to his arms, he got terrified. He is not in pain and feels no change in sensation (the response to touch and temperature), but he can no longer walk on his own. When the doctor asks him why he waited so long to come to the ER, the patient replies that things just started getting really bad in the last few hours. What is going through the doctor's mind as they talk is that unless the patient is having a psychosomatic manifestation and the symptoms are not real, this guy is in deep trouble. These are very unusual complaints for a young man, and he will need to look for as many clues as possible to solve the mystery.

First, the doctor performs a complete neurological examination. All is well except for the strength and the reflexes in the man's arms and legs. The DTRs (deep tendon reflexes) are diminished, nearly absent. There is severe weakness in the legs, and moderate weakness in his arms. In the ER, cerebrovascular accidents, better known as strokes, are probably the most common reason for people to have "focal weakness." This means that if a person comes to the ER because of weakness in the right arm and leg and has a "facial droop" on the right too, he or she probably has had a clot or bleed into the opposing side of the brain. The doctor would perform a CAT scan for this type of problem, and most of these patients will then require admission into the hospital.

Generalized weakness is a whole other proposition. Where the findings are "nonfocal"—no specific area of weakness, just "all over" weak—the reasons may be extremely varied. Blood chemistry changes can do it, and a low potassium level can even cause paralysis. Severe anemia, low blood sugar, thyroid disease, heart failure, and depression are just a few of the many reasons that a patient can feel overall weakness. The medical evaluation in the ER is intended to "put the fire out": if there is a serious medical disease, the doctor will diagnose and treat it. But often with this type of complaint, the ER evaluation is just the beginning, and if the patient is well enough for discharge, a primary care physician will need to follow up.

The symptoms of the young man at the ER don't fit into any of the usual patterns for stroke or the medical problems of general weakness. The doctor is perplexed, and checks a Chem-7 just to make sure his patient's potassium and the other blood chemistries are okay, and they are. During the course of the examination, the patient becomes weaker. Within an hour, he starts to have problems breathing. The doctor calls for a neurologist. By the time he arrives, the patient is about to be intubated in order to assist his breathing.

The neurologist examines the young man, and finds that the extreme weakness in the arms and legs has extended to the very muscles that allow the patient to breathe. What could this strange problem be? It could be botulism, a paralyzing disease caused by a toxin from a bacteria in contaminated food. But botulism usually affects the eyes, causing double vision, and does not start in the legs and work its way up the body. There are some other unusual diseases that the neurologist considers, but the diagnosis he makes is Guillain-Barré syndrome. This is a paralyzing disease that works its way up the body, usually wiping out the DTRs. The disease can progress very quickly, but the essential clue in this case was the patient's recent viral illness. Guillain-Barré is thought to be an unusual reaction to a viral infection, and though the paralysis can leave a patient on a ventilator because of respiratory failure, most patients eventually do recover completely from this mysterious illness. For the ER doctor, this unusual case was solved by the characteristic findings in the history and physical exam, not to mention the help of a specialist's consultation.

FEVER

One of the most important clues to help establish a diagnosis in the ER is the presence of fever. A patient's temperature is a great marker for an infection. The normal body temperature is between 96.5°F and 99°F. If more heat is created than lost, body temperature can briefly rise—this is what occurs during vigorous exercise. Sweat cools off and lowers the temperature during and after vigorous exercise. The body temperature of a marathon runner on a warm day can get up over 104°F! These are only brief elevations in temperature, though. When it rises for a sustained time in association with an illness, this is a **fever**.

On the show, as in real life, an electronic probe is inserted into the ear canal to get a body temp because it can be more accurate than the mouth. Too many patients like to drink cold soda or hot coffee in the waiting room, which can temporarily affect the results of a temperature taken orally, and those with breathing problems may have trouble keeping their mouths closed long enough for an accurate reading to be obtained. It is certainly preferable to having a rectal temperature taken!

Though a fever could represent a number of medical problems, it most often reflects the presence of an infection somewhere in the body. But the ER doctor needs to know exactly *where* and *how bad* it is. One important test to help determine this, the CBC, provides a great deal of critical information, but when it comes to infection it is the white blood cell count (WBC) that tells the story. A normal WBC is about 7,000 (that's how many cells are in 1 cubic millimeter of blood), and though many different conditions can affect it, a very high "white count" (greater than 20,000) is usually indicative of a serious infection.

To see if the infection is in the blood itself, doctors do a blood culture, putting a small sample of blood in a special bottle and incubating it at body temperature. If bacteria grow in the blood, this is a sign of a very severe infection (**sepsis**) that may require prolonged treatment with antibiotics. Unfortunately, the cultures of the blood take one or two days to grow. Though they may help guide therapy down the road, they will not help the ER doctor make a diagnosis.

A faster test, the UA (a urine analysis), can detect the presence of bacteria and white blood cells in the urine. The presence of white blood cells might suggest the infection may be in the bladder or kidney. Most patients with urinary tract infections do complain of burning on urination or back pain (the kidneys are anatomically situated along the back, and filter metabolic waste from the blood and create urine).

Patients who come into the ER with high fevers and a stiff neck and who seem confused and disoriented may cause the physician to suspect meningitis. (Very young children with this disease may just seem lethargic and have a fever.) The brain and spinal cord are completely surrounded and protected by a tough skin, called the *meninges*, which manufactures a clear liquid known as cerebrospinal fluid that cushions the brain and spinal cord from minor trauma (such as a bump to the head). Sometimes the fluid can get infected, causing meningitis. The only way to diagnose meningitis is with a procedure that has sent chills up the spine of viewers—a lumbar puncture, otherwise known as a spinal tap. Remember the sad scenes of Harper Tracy holding down a young boy who had to have two lumbar punctures performed by Doug Ross?

Press your thumb in the middle of your back and then slowly move the thumb down along the bony prominences. You should notice the undulations of the spinal column as you approach the buttocks. Each undulation represents a single vertebra, and it is possible to place a long skinny needle between the bulging bony vertebrae, piercing the tough meninges that covers the spinal cord to extract some spinal fluid for analysis. Don't worry—sticking a needle into your spinal cord won't paralyze you! Your spinal cord only goes down as far as the lower portion of the middle of your back. Doctors pick an area far below that to extract the fluid. By looking at the fluid under the microscope, they can look for bacteria or white blood cells.

Horses, Not Zebras

Mark and the staff at County General know how to evaluate pain, what to do about shortness of breath, and how to proceed with a patient who has a fever. Unfortunately, medicine does not draw lines in the sand separating these clues, and it is the astute ER doctor who can take all the clues and make a quick diagnosis.

There is an old saying in medicine that when you hear hoofbeats, think horses, not zebras. In fact, bizarre and unusual cases are referred to as "zebras," and any doctor who is always looking for zebras is going to spend a lot of money on unnecessary tests and miss the most common and obvious diagnoses. (This is the very advice Div Cvetic gives neophyte John Carter in one of the show's earliest episodes.)

There are those times, though, when the hoofbeats do mean zebras. In the episode "Full Moon, Saturday Night," Susan Lewis treats a young man, Mr. Flaco, a groom-to-be with a case of uncontrolled hiccups. It seems innocuous enough. But, after observing abnormalities on the patient's chest X ray, Susan zeroes in on AIDS as a possible suspect, stunning both patient and viewer.

It may seem mystifying how quickly Susan and other doctors on *ER* solve the puzzle of illness. Just like Columbo knows just the moment to uncover the culprit (usually right before a commercial break or at the end of the show), so it is with the physician who arrives at a diagnosis. But if there is something magical in emergency room medicine, it isn't sorcery but extensive medical training and experience—and, perhaps a dash of luck.

CHAPTER EIGHT

Things Not Normally Found in Your Body

In the episode "The Birthday Party," an incoherent Renee Franks is rushed to County General on the brink of death from an OD. Susan Lewis, joined by Mark Greene, orders "CBC, lytes, toxic screen, and a BA." As they go about trying to save her life, they intermittently shout out, "Lavage!" "Ewald!" "Charcoal!" This is not unlike what you find in a real ER.

It's Friday. 2:00 A.M. Late December. Full moon. Some people believe this time of the year, and this time of the month, portend hectic nights at the ER. The year-end holidays, happy times for most of us, further sadden those who are already depressed about their social and family situations. And when there is a full moon, well, it just seems to make matters worse.

The paramedics bring in a sobbing 18-year-old who admits

she ingested a lot of tranquilizers following a fight with her boyfriend. Doctors who face these patients need to have answers to three basic questions before they can decide on a proper course of action. *What* drug or drugs were taken? *When* were they taken? And *how much* was taken?

What was taken. To properly treat an OD before major toxic side effects occur, the ER doctor must identify *all* the substances ingested. Though this patient says she took Valium, the ER doctor, smelling alcohol on the patient's breath and hearing her words slurred, asks if she's also been drinking. The patient admits to having a few beers, but denies having taken any other drugs.

When taken. If the ingestion was recent (within an hour or so), much of the drug will still be in the stomach. Much longer than a couple of hours, and many of the pills will be on their way through the intestines. The doctor asks her when she took the pills and, through the tears, she says it's been four hours.

How much taken. Even if the patient says she took only a handful of pills and had only a "few drinks," doctors must assume a worst-case scenario. The paramedics have brought her empty pill bottle. When new, the bottle contained 50 two-milligram tablets of Valium, with instructions on the label to take one pill three times a day. Normally the ER physician would have to count the remaining pills to see how many could have been taken. In this case, it's easy.

If the ER physicians do not carefully ascertain what was taken, how much, and when, they may treat for the wrong ingestion, or miss treating for toxic medications other than the ones the patient has admitted taking.

To avoid such a catastrophe, the ER doctor, just as Susan Lewis and Mark Greene did for Renee Franks, asks the nurse to draw blood for a BA (blood alcohol level), a toxic screen, CBC, and lytes. In addition, he will want to check an EKG and a chest X ray.

The **BA, or blood alcohol level**, quantifies the amount of alcohol the patient has ingested. Too much alcohol, of course, can be toxic but it can also affect the patient's "level of consciousness" to the point that her speech is so slurred and she is so disoriented that nothing she says can be relied upon. Moreover, alcohol can compound the effect of certain drugs, such as Valium, and the two working together can severely depress the patient's ability to breathe.

The **toxic screen** identifies whether other drugs may have been taken, such as cocaine, marijuana, amphetamines (uppers), barbiturates (downers), and opiates (narcotics such as heroin).

The CBC and lytes ensure that the patient's blood count and blood chemistry are okay. Results that are not normal provide clues to what else the patient might have ingested that did not show up on the toxic screen.

The **EKG (electrocardiogram)** checks the rhythm of the heart. Some medications, such as the tricyclic antidepressants (such as Elavil, or amitriptyline) can have disastrous effects on the normal rhythmic beating of the heart.

The **chest X ray** will show whether there are any abnormalities in the lungs. Severely drowsy or comatose patients can inadvertently breathe food or vomit into their lungs, causing pneumonia or burning of lung tissue. Some drugs, such as heroin, can cause fluid to build up in the lungs (pulmonary edema), making respiration difficult or nearly impossible.

Long before the results of these tests are known, the most important action the ER doctors take is to prevent the digestion and absorption of as much of the drug from the stomach or intestines as possible. To accomplish this task, they have two choices. One is to give ipecac, a liquid medication that causes vomiting. But since the young woman now in the ER took the pills four hours ago, the majority of the Valium is probably out of the stomach and already in the intestines, so vomiting out the stomach contents won't help much.

Another factor to consider is that our patient is in an altered mental status. If forced to vomit, she may inhale it. Inhalation of stomach contents into the lungs, including the acid in the digestive juices and other articles that don't belong in the lungs, can do these vital organs no earthly good.

THIS STOMACH PUMPING DOESN'T BUILD GOOD ABS

To avoid aspiration, we use the second alternative to get the remaining pills out of the stomach: sucking out the stomach contents with a large tube, called an Ewald. In common vernacular, this is better known as "pumping out your stomach." In ER slang, it is called "down your nose with a garden hose." A tube large enough to suck out pill fragments is placed through the patient's nose or mouth, forced down through the esophagus and into the patient's stomach. The outside end of the tube is connected to suction, and any pill fragments are sucked up into a container.

The stomach is flushed out with clear water and then a slush of charcoal and a cathartic (fluid that passes through the bowels quickly) is passed down the tube. The charcoal will absorb any remaining medications in the gut. To say the least, this is most unpleasant, and usually leaves a lasting memory for patients who have had to undergo it. Viewers of this procedure will not be likely to forget it, either. Many a viewer may have cringed during the episode in which Carol and Mark physically restrain a young woman who is brought into the ER after what appears to be a suicide attempt (prompted, we later learn, by discovering she is pregnant with her brother's child).

As the nurse inserts the tube down the young woman's nose, assuring her that this must be done and it will make her better, the ER doctor readies the charcoal to pour through the tube. As a general rule, ER physicians perform this procedure on most of their adult overdose patients to make sure that they get all undigested pills and that they limit absorption of toxic medications.

WHY A 72-HOUR HOLD?

Once the lab tests are back, the ER doctor learns that Valium and alcohol are indeed present, but the rest of the toxic screen is negative: the patient has not taken any other medications. The patient remains uncooperative and, until the Valium and alcohol have left her system, still runs the risk of a respiratory arrest. In such situations, the ER can request a **72-hour hold**.

This allows physicians to admit the patient for observation and treatment, even against the patient's will. She will first go into the ICU to make sure she doesn't slip into respiratory or cardiac arrest, and then be transferred to the psychiatric ward once the staff is sure the alcohol and Valium have been cleared from her system. A psychiatrist will use the 72 hours to determine the mental stability of the patient—a critical determinant of whether or not patients pose a threat to themselves or to others or are gravely disabled. In this case, if she is not a threat, the law in most states requires that she be released, even if she is clearly not completely competent to manage her life.

WHAT KIND OF FUEL AM I?

Overdoses are often the most challenging of all ER cases. Not all paramedics remember to search out the pill bottle and bring it along, and family members bringing in a loved one are even less likely to do so. Often the ER staff doesn't have a clue about what the patient may have ingested. On the episode "A Shift in the Night," Mark Greene treated Omar, a patient who appeared to be a case of alcohol intoxication. But not everyone who seems drunk has actually had too much alcohol to drink. The level of ethanol (the alcohol in wine, beer, and cocktails) in Omar's blood was zero, so Mark had to look elsewhere for the cause of the intoxication.

The remainder of the toxic screen was negative, so he knew that ingestion of drugs was not the problem. Through astute laboratory work, Mark was able to deduce that the patient had ingested methanol (known as sterno, now used as antifreeze but ingested as contraband liquor during Prohibition). Oddly, the treatment was the administration of intravenous ethanol! It may seem strange to treat an apparently intoxicated patient with alcohol, but *ethanol* prevents the formation of toxic chemicals in the body during a *methanol* OD. Greene quipped that here's a case where a shot of bourbon (a good source of ethanol) would prevent brain death and renal failure, rather than contribute to it.

ONE DRINK TOO MANY

Alcohol is one of the most common ODs seen in any ER, real or dramatized. The legal limit for driving an automobile is a BA of .08—you might hear people on the show refer to this as a level of "80." If you are driving a car and are found to have a blood level in excess of .08, you will be arrested for drunk driving.

The ER often sees patients with blood alcohol levels substantially higher than this standard. County General staff members have been known to bet on the blood alcohol level of a local drunk before the blood test comes back. Lydia Wright uncannily makes the winning guess from just a whiff of the patient's breath. A BA of around 150 (.15), and you may start to slur your speech. Over 200 (.20), and you will probably start to wobble all over the place. On one episode a college student had been at a party drinking shots of beer mixed with Tequila and was brought into the ER in a coma. His BA was an extraordinary 832 (.832)—higher than most ER doctors will ever see in real life, but not beyond the realm of possibility.

One of the ironies of ER medicine is that about the only people who would not have suffered a respiratory arrest and died from a BA this high are chronic alcoholics, whose bodies become acclimated to high levels of alcohol. At this incredibly high level, alcohol suppresses the body's normal breathing activity, and in real life the young man portrayed on the show would not have been likely to survive his foolish macho challenge to death.

WHO AM I ANYWAY? (SWEETS FOR THE SWEETS)

One especially unusual case of poisoning on the show involved a group of cheerleaders who had been brought to the ER because they were acting disoriented and confused, though happy. Each cheerleader had an **altered mental status (AMS)** or **altered level** of consciousness (ALOC). If a patient is confused and disoriented and does not know what is happening, the doctor can determine whether he or she has ALOC by giving a basic mental status exam. The questions include:

- Do you know what day it is?
- Do you know your name?
- Do you know where you are?
- Do you know what is happening to you?

You will often hear the doctors on *ER* asking their patients these questions. If responses to these four questions are correct, the patient is "alert and oriented times four" (on the show you may hear, "A and O times four"), but patients who are unable to answer some or all of questions have an ALOC. ALOC comes in many shapes and sizes: the patient who is extremely sleepy and difficult to arouse, incapable of answering the simplest of questions; the patient running through the streets of Chicago wearing nothing but a Chicago Bulls hat; the combative patient who is trying to strike anyone around him or her; the cheerleaders who "just weren't acting right."

The cheerleaders present a diagnostic dilemma for the doctors of County General's ER. Checking a CBC and a Chem-7 won't help. Getting X rays won't help, nor will talking with them. But checking a toxic screen does the trick! Valentine chocolates they had ingested turned out to have been spiked with LSD, and it is this drug that is causing their ALOC.

READ THE LABEL

Remember the *ER* episode when Susan Lewis has a patient she suspects is suicidal? Mr. Delanova is an elderly man whose chief complaints are blurred vision, nausea, and trouble breathing. In a private moment, Susan asks the patient's daughter whether her father is on any medications. The daughter hands over a plastic bag filled with medicines. Susan suspects Mr. Delanova might be depressed, but the daughter immediately assures her that her father is not suicidal. Susan's interest is piqued by the bottle of digoxin in the bag. She reads the label and the date the drug was prescribed. She counts the pills, and too many are gone. Mr. Delanova is "dig toxic," which means the digoxin level is too high in the blood, causing the severe side effects.

Susan comes to realize this was not an intentional overdose, but a case of a man who accidentally took too many pills because he was too proud to let anyone know he couldn't read the proper dose on the bottle. Here Susan doctored a heart in more ways than one.

There are cases where an OD or poisoning is not the cause for an ALOC. Low blood sugars in patients with diabetes can cause an ALOC, and these otherwise normal people can become very violent and confused if the blood sugar drops too low. A severe abnormality in the electrolytes in the blood can sometimes cause an altered mental status, and these so-called metabolic derangements may cause patients to be very sleepy and confused and to act bizarrely. A bad bump on the head can make a patient confused and disoriented, while a stroke can leave a patient with an ALOC. And of course, a patient with a psychiatric problem will act the same way. Who can forget veteran singer Rosemary Clooney's (George Clooney's real-life aunt) touching portrayal of a patient with ALOC? She plays a wayward singer lost somewhere back in 1948, where Harry Truman is president and the hit song of the day is a vintage Cole Porter number.

While adult poisonings (ODs and accidental ingestions) are commonly seen in most ERs, the vast majority of patients who accidentally put toxic substances into their bodies are children. We have to remember that for the first few years of their lives, the sense that most frequently provides children with useful information is that of taste. While adults respond to anything that has engaged their curiosity by examining it visually, and then by touching it, children will try to identify something new to them by tasting it. This is why tykes have a tendency to swallow Grandma's little red cardiac pill or drink a little bit of the pink liquid under the kitchen sink. Over 40 percent of accidental poisonings occur in the kitchen, and about 20 percent in the bathroom. In terms of sheer numbers, over-the-counter analgesics are the most common accidental poisoning, with household cleaning substances, cosmetics, and plant ingestions following closely behind.

A two-year-old boy is found by his mother playing in the backyard with a mouthful of chewed leaves. She recognizes them as oleander, and she calls the poison control center. They suggest that she immediately give him ipecac to make him vomit and then go to the nearest ER for treatment.

Oleander is a common plant whose toxicity is similar to the heart medication called digoxin, which also comes from a plant (foxglove). It doesn't take much to affect a little child's heart. It can cause cardiac arrhythmias and, in high doses, death. By giving the boy ipecac soon after he ingested the leaf, the mother hopes to prevent most of it from being digested.

Even though ipecac is a medication that all homes with small children cannot do without, there are certain types of ingestions that it should not be used to treat. These include caustic ingestions, and one of the most common and deadly is lye. Contained in many common products like Drāno and Liquid-Plumr, lye can cause severe burns to the esophagus and stomach. Vomiting will make the burn more severe, while a glass of milk can be a lifesaver.

FOREIGN BODIES IN OR ON THE BODY

Patients have come into the emergency room with nearly every type of foreign body imaginable in or on them. A "foreign body" is any substance placed into the body that would not normally be there. A piece of glass under the skin is a foreign body; a knife in the chest is a foreign body; a swallowed toothpick stuck in the esophagus is a foreign body; and a flashlight flickering in the colon is a foreign body. In the episode "Fire in the Belly," John

Carter, eager to assist in what would be his first appendectomy, is disappointed and unnerved during surgery to discover that the patient's appendix is perfectly healthy. A defensive Carter assures Dr. Hicks that the patient had all the symptoms of appendicitis. The expert Dr. Hicks discovers the source of the patient's pain: a toothpick in the terminal ileum (part of the intestine). So that things will not be a total loss for the overenthusiastic med student, Hicks congratulates Carter on his first "toothpickectomy."

The foreign bodies adults knowingly attach to or put into their bodies—spoons, razors, lightbulbs, soda bottles—defy imagination. A real ER reported the case of a man who was admitted with a vacuum cleaner hose around his neck. In the treatment room, the man removed his fur coat and stood before the nurse and resident stark naked. The vacuum hose spiraled down from his neck to his penis. There the nozzle was firmly affixed. Apparently, the man had been engaged in a novel form of oral sex play with his Hoover. The blood vessels inside his penis burst, and his enlarged member had become so swollen that it got stuck in the hose.

Despite the initial intent of the patient, these objects of art or desire, whether attached, swallowed, or inserted through rectum or vagina, can obstruct, perforate, and otherwise cause severe damage. You may think that an ER professional has seen it all, but many a doctor has been stunned by the size, shape, and variety of objects patients have placed on the body or in one of its cavities. The following are two true accounts.

Ho-hum

A third-year medical student at a County Hospital presses firmly on the abdomen of an 18-year-old female. The patient is uncomfortable and seems embarrassed. Her complaint is abdominal pain, and the med student is in the midst of a thorough examination. The senior ER resident comes to assist the student, and presses his hands on the young patient's abdomen. He feels the unmistakable hum of a vibrating mechanical device. Turning to the student, he asks her if she had felt anything unusual in the patient's abdomen. When the student says no, he has the patient turn on her side for a rectal exam.

The student places a gloved finger into the patient's rectum, and jumps back as her finger hits the hard edge of a vibrator. Using a speculum, the resident and student easily remove it from the girl's rectum. The patient had been too embarrassed to provide a complete history, but now confesses that she and her boyfriend had inserted the vibrator into her rectum, but were unable to retrieve it. The vibrations were a crucial clue that the student had missed.

Animal Lovers

A 26-year-old male arrives at the ER complaining of rectal bleeding. He too is too embarrassed to provide an accurate history but provides the examining doctor a clue: "There might be something stuck in my rear end." Examination reveals a non-tender abdomen, but a rectal exam shows blood coming from his anus. A speculum exam reveals bloody stool and a dead gerbil. Apparently, through the cardboard tubing from a paper towel roll, the rodent had been forced into his rectum. Once the animal was in, the tube was pulled out.

The idea is that as the gerbil suffocates, it scratches and claws at the lining of the rectum, providing an intense sensation to the patient. The rodent should then have been defecated, but the swelling and bleeding had caused the retention of the animal. The patient required pain medication and antibiotics after the animal was removed, but was then allowed to go home.

EATING HABITS OF CHILDREN

Children are one of the ER's most regular visitors for foreign body retrieval. They place beads, peas, pennies, toy parts, almost anything shiny, into their noses and ears. Sometimes such objects are removed with a suction device, but more often an invasive procedure is called for: the cavity has to be irrigated with a jet of water to loosen things up. The exception is if the object in question is composed of vegetable matter. Such objects can absorb fluid and swell, making the problem far worse. Animate objects, such as live insects, which have an uncanny ability to find their way into human ears, first have to be killed, with mineral oil, alcohol, or Novocaine. Then they are washed out with warm water.

The orifice that offers the best opportunity for ingesting objects—the mouth—also presents the greatest danger. Children seem to consider coins, batteries, and pins delicacies to be savored and then swallowed. Coins usually pass through the digestive system without difficulty, and are by and large harmless if they do not obstruct breathing as they pass through the esophagus, which lies alongside the trachea. To retrieve a swallowed coin requires a stool watch. It usually makes a bottom-line appearance within a day or two.

Batteries, a favorite appetizer among one- and two-year-olds, are a different story. Small alkaline batteries used in hearing aids, watches, and cameras can cause severe damage to the esophagus if they get stuck on their way down to the stomach. Corrosive material can leach out of the battery, causing disastrous consequences for body tissues. If the battery makes it to the stomach most of the problems are over, but the physician will still need to make sure there are no toxic reactions from the chemicals that may be absorbed from the battery (most pass through without harm).

Sharp-edged objects such as an open safety pin or a sewing needle can get stuck in the esophagus or bowel. These objects are usually removed by a gastroenterologist under direct visualization with an endoscope (a long flexible fiberoptic tube that allows doctors to visualize internal structures) before problems begin. If the object does not move in a 24-hour period, or if abdominal pain should occur and the object causes an obstruction or a perforation, surgery may be required for repair and removal.

But for children, the greatest danger occurs when the foreign body doesn't go down the gullet but is inhaled. If the airway is blocked, the child can die. This causes about 2,000 deaths in children each year in the United States. Major culprits are small hard foods, and this is the reason whole hard nuts should not be given to children under the age of three.

Though there may be regional and cultural variations (for example, Budweiser versus Corona beer bottles) in the type of things people put inside them, the phenomenon runs across all populations. Objects have been found and removed from the body cavities of both rich and poor, famous and obscure, gay and straight. We're sure to get letters now from ER personnel across the country topping each other's crazy stories of strange things inserted into body orifices and cavities for which nature did not intend them.

A Little Too Greene

The Story of "Love's Labor Lost"

Who can forget the Emmy award–winning episode in the show's first season where Mark Greene delivers a baby by cesarean section? The episode poses challenging medical questions leading to judgments and then actions that are dramatic, even heroic, yet ultimately turn out to be tragic. But the question for us to consider here is this: Should and could such a sequence of events ever be allowed to unfold in a real-world ER?

It is 1:00 P.M. County General's ER is unusually calm, not much different from the sunny winter's day outside. But this is Chicago. Without warning, winds can whip up with such vehemence that they will startle even old-time residents of the area. Mark Greene interrupts Sean O'Brien, snuggling his very expectant wife, Jody, whose "CC" (the chief complaint that brought her to the ER) consists of a stomachache, and frequency and burning on urination.

Jody reports that other than having to hit the bathroom every 30 seconds lately, it's been an uneventful pregnancy so far, and this trip is merely a precaution. She and her husband are clearly happy, vibrant, in love. This is the time when the excitement of a pregnancy crescendos for such loving couples, for Jody is due in two weeks. That means she's been carrying a new life inside her for 38 weeks (normal pregnancy lasts about 40 weeks).

Mark conjectures the obvious, "It sounds like a bladder infection." But being the conscientious chief resident he is, he needs to find out whether there are any signs of complications in the pregnancy or impending labor. Any vaginal bleeding? he asks. Cramping? Vaginal bleeding at this late stage in pregnancy could be an ominous sign. But she's not bleeding.

It sounds like Mom is in pretty good shape, but until she is discharged, Mark has two patients to consider, both her and her unborn child. If the baby is not moving normally, it could be having a problem. "Still feel the baby moving?" Mark asks. Jody chuckles. The baby is kicking up a storm. Mark measures the size of the baby using a paper tape marked in centimeters. One end of the tape is placed on a bony area in the pelvis called the pubic symphysis (it's in the middle of the pelvis, the first bony area that can be felt as you press south of the belly button), and the other end is placed on the upper end of the uterus (called the fundus). The distance in centimeters gives a rough approximation of how far along the pregnancy is. Mark deduces that the baby is small for 38 weeks, and approximates the baby's weight at 5 or 6 pounds.

Two problems here. This method of measurement isn't very accurate late in pregnancy and is not a reliable way to approximate either the weight or the age of the baby. But there is a reliable way to check out exactly how the baby's heart is doing. Mark takes a Doppler, a sensitive hand-held machine that can detect the faint sounds of the baby's heartbeat, and puts it on Jody's belly. A heartbeat between 120 and 160 is normal. A slow rate (less than 120) could be a sign that the baby is having a problem, such as not enough blood and oxygen. A faster than normal heart rate may be a sign of anxiety in the mother, or of the presence of fever or dehydration. Not to worry: the heartbeat of Jody's baby is normal—a new life floating peacefully in amniotic bliss.

Mark is not too worried about Jody's frequent urination. It is normal for a woman at the end of a pregnancy. The baby takes up an enormous amount of room in the mother's pelvis and abdomen, squeezing the bladder so that there is hardly any room for it to expand as it fills with urine. This provides an almost constant feeling of a full bladder. But urinary frequency is also a common complaint of a patient with a bladder infection (commonly called a UTI, for urinary tract infection), so Mark orders a urine analysis (UA) to rule out a diagnosis of UTI. Later, med students Carter and Chen accompany Mark, urine test results in hand, to see Jody. Her sample showed bacteria and large quantities of white blood cells, telltale signs of infection. Surprisingly, she also has 2-plus protein, signifying a lot of protein in her urine. Mark could have expected a trace amount with a simple UTI, but a 2-plus level, while not alarmingly high, is unusual.

Protein is often a marker for a problem in the kidney, the organ that filters toxins from the blood so that they can be excreted as urine. Is Mark missing something here? Jody also had an initial blood pressure of 130/90. In pregnancy, that is on the border of being high (usually defined as above 140/90). The combination of the borderline elevated blood pressure and the protein in the urine should have alerted Mark to a potentially much more serious problem. Unfortunately, it didn't.

Any alarm Jody and her husband felt dissipates when they learn that she has cystitis—a good old-fashioned bladder infection—and that the abdominal pain and frequent urination are both accommodated within this diagnosis. Deb Chen suggests bactrim (a sulfa-containing antibiotic) as a treatment for the infection, but Mark wisely corrects her: sulfa is metabolized poorly by a baby's liver, and the drug has been associated with newborn jaundice. He suggests Macrodantin, a nonsulfa antibiotic that will not hurt the unborn baby. Mark discharges Jody, advising her to get plenty of rest and drink plenty of fluids and to call her own doctor in the morning.

Was Mark wrong to send her home at this point? Did he misdiagnose the problem? Should he have looked further into what might have caused the protein in the urine and borderline blood pressure in a pregnant woman?

Hypertension in pregnancy can be a serious problem. It occurs in nearly 10 percent of all woman. A number of women have high blood pressure before they get pregnant, and these women face some increased risks (such as stillbirth). More worrisome are women who have normal blood pressure and develop high blood pressure only after they become pregnant. This is called PIH (pregnancy-induced hypertension) and is responsible for 70 percent of hypertension in pregnancy. In these cases, when the woman is beyond the 20th week of pregnancy and her pressure breaks the 30/15 rule (that means the systolic pressure rises more than 30 or the diastolic rises at least 15 from the woman's normal baseline), or the BP is over 140/90, PIH is probably present.

The problem is not very common, occurring in less than 3 percent of all pregnancies, but the consequences can be dramatic. The blood supply to the major organs can be reduced. This is caused by a vasospasm, where the arteries spontaneously constrict and cause a decrease in the flow of blood to the vital organs. The kidneys can suffer, releasing protein into the urine as they are damaged. The liver can be damaged as well, and the brain is particularly susceptible to harm. Intracerebral bleeding (strokes) is a sometimes lethal complication of PIH.

In the early stages of PIH, when the blood pressure starts to rise and protein is in the urine, and the woman starts to retain fluid and becomes swollen (edema), the term used is **preeclampsia** (also known as toxemia of pregnancy). More than likely this is what Jody had when she entered the ER. Of course, she still had it when she was sent home.

Mark never asked Jody if her blood pressure was usually low before her pregnancy, for if her BP a year ago (before she was pregnant) was 90/60, then the reading of 130/90 would have been a clear marker for PIH. Add to this the presence of 2-plus protein in the urine, and a diagnosis of preeclampsia could have been made. For sure, it should have been considered.

Was he wrong to send her home? Experts don't always agree about how best to manage preeclampsia. Some obstetricians, having made the diagnosis, might still have sent Jody home, recommending bed rest and careful observation by her obstetrician, considering the changes were mild and the patient was likely in an early stage of the condition. Jody's blood pressure normalized in the ER to 120/80 (but this still could have been a disturbing finding if it violated the 30/15 rule). Others might suggest that Mark should have called Jody's obstetrician or, at the very least, ordered more blood studies to rule out a liver or bleeding problem associated with preeclampsia. He didn't. And that is the basis on which doctors are judged—what they did, not what they might have done if they had been aware of this or that factor, or what they thought of doing but decided not to do in the end.

7:15 P.M., approximately six hours after Dr. Greene's initial examination and diagnosis. Jody is outside the ER, unconscious in the car. Carter, Chen, and Hathaway race down the hall with a gurney. As Jody is rushed into the ER, her blood pressure is 160/110. High. Very high. Mark knows damn well he has a problem on his hands, well beyond a bladder infection. It's obvious with skyrocketing blood pressure that Jody has PIH. With the benefit of hindsight, he now knows she had preeclampsia.

Mark figures that Jody had a seizure and is now *postictal*, a temporary state of confusion that ususally follows a seizure. Preeclampsia is just the warm-up (preeclampsia plus a seizure) is the main event.

Mark now orders a series of tests including a Chem-23 to help tell him whether there has been any damage to Jody's liver and kidney. Clotting problems can be another complication of eclampsia, and so Mark also orders a coag (coagulation) panel, which will test Jody's ability to clot her own blood. He orders nurse Haleh to start an IV on Jody so he can give her meds as necessary.

Jody starts to seize, her body uncontrollably convulsing. Mark orders an IV push of magnesium sulfate (injecting the med directly into the established IV). This drug helps control the seizures in eclampsia. But the seizure is so violent that Mark decides to put the medication directly into the jugular vein in her neck. In seconds, Jody's seizures subside. But her high blood pressure still has to be dealt with. She is given the drug of choice, hydralazine, and her blood pressure begins to normalize. She is stable.

Mark wants to check the baby. The heart tones are 140—normal. Could Jody be closer to delivery than anyone had thought? Mark isn't going to hedge his bets. He performs a vaginal exam. Whoa! This lady is getting ready to go into labor: 2 centimeters dilated and 80 percent effaced. This means that the cervix, the exit route out of the uterus for the baby, has started to open and to thin out in preparation for the final stages of labor and delivery. It's baby time when you are 100 percent effaced and 10 centimeters dilated.

There is no telling, though, just how long labor will last. If this is her first baby, she could remain in active labor for many hours.

Mark assures Jody's husband that her life is not in danger but that his baby will be on its way sooner than planned. Mark asks the nurses to call upstairs to find out who is on call for OB (obstetrics). This should be the end of the story for the patient in the ER. In most if not all hospitals with an active OB service, patients like Jody O'Brien would now be sent to an ICU or to a labor and delivery suite. In fact, at Cook County Hospital, any woman having problems related to labor and delivery after 20 weeks of pregnancy would be sent directly to labor and delivery. Many hospitals use the 20-week mark as a milestone for viability of the fetus (meaning that, with medical care, the fetus can live outside the womb), and any problems after 20 weeks need a place where delivery and any complications can be best handled. And this place is *not* the ER! If the patient were unstable, the immediate problem would be stabilized, which Mark has already done. But either the OB resident would be sent for to escort the patient up, or the patient would be taken directly to L&D (labor and delivery). Only rarely does a patient in the very end stages of labor deliver in the ER, and then it is almost always because there is no time to get her upstairs.

Jody O'Brien was kept in the ER because L&D was too busy, an inappropriate and unacceptable reason, one that would not be tolerated in a large academic hospital. There would have been more than one OB resident available in the hospital, and even if all the residents had been tied up, someone would have been called in from home. Jody had an uncommon, life-threatening obstetrical problem, and she needed to be on the OB service. It is surprising how seldom the show can be caught sacrificing verisimilitude for drama, but here is a clear case.

7:48 P.M. Mark performs an ultrasound to assess the baby's position. It's a boy! He checks the "biophysical profile" using a scoring system to rate the baby's movements, tone, breathing, heart rate, and amniotic fluid. There's probably not an ER doctor in the country who could have attempted this test, unless that doctor had previously done a residency in Ob-Gyn or radiology. Even among those few ER physicians comfortable performing their own ultrasounds, those most often done in the ER are to look for gallstones in the gallbladder, an ectopic (outside the uterus) pregnancy in the pelvis, or an enlargement (aneurysm) of some part of the aorta, the largest vessel in the body. Ultrasounds are not done in the ER to perform complicated assessments of near-term pregnancies!

Mark then instructs John Carter on how to get an "amniotic fluid index" using the ultrasound. This test assesses the amount of amniotic fluid in the uterus, and for Jody the test is normal. If any experienced ER doctors are reading this book, they will now learn what these tests are, because it is highly unlikely they would have any idea what Mark could have been attempting during this *ER* episode!

9:00 P.M. Why is Jody still in the ER? So that we can follow the story, apparently, without the producers having to introduce a whole new cast of characters: the staff at Labor and Delivery. Susan Lewis is willing to take over for Mark, but he is feeling guilty about missing Jody's preeclampsia and so insists on seeing the patient through until she is in the hands of an obstetrician. He contacts Dr. Coburn, an Ob-Gyn who is tied up with a repeat C-section at another hospital but says she will be there in about an hour. Whenever there is a complication at the end of pregnancy, the rule is to get labor going and get the baby out ASAP. Dr. Coburn asks Mark if he is comfortable starting an induction with pitocin, a medication that causes more forceful and frequent contractions of the uterus. If labor can't be started soon, then the Ob-Gyn may want to consider a C-section. The last thing anyone wants is another seizure!

Even though Jody is believed to be in her 38th week, neither the Ob-Gyn nor Mark would expect complications associated with a premature birth (such as respiratory problems, which usually occur only in deliveries earlier than 38 weeks). It is not clear whether Dr. Coburn knows about Jody's eclampsia and the unstable nature of her pregnancy. If she is supposed to have been told, she should have expressed shock that the patient was still in the ER, and should have ordered the patient to be sent immediately up to L&D. Instead, the Ob-Gyn resident on call makes a brief visit to Jody. He doesn't see any problem now that Jody is stable and returns to his department, which is "jammed" with patients. Jody wants to try to deliver through natural childbirth, and Mark has no reason to object. He orders the "pit" to induce labor per Coburn's suggestion. The wheels are set in motion to bring Baby Boy O'Brien into the world.

10:12 P.M. Jody is 5 centimeters dilated (halfway) and 90 percent effaced. She is having contractions every ten minutes. It could still be hours until delivery. Where is Dr. Coburn? Why is Jody still in the ER three hours after it is known that she is in a complicated labor? No one expresses concern other than over what the baby's name will be. With Mark's help, the parents decide on Jared.

11:47 P.M. Sean O'Brien, having kept a watchful eye on the fetal heart monitor, comes running out to find Mark to tell him about the decreasing heart rate of his unborn child. Well, at least someone is minding the store. The fetal heart monitor's digital readout is an unmistakable "90." Too low. Mark is convinced it's just because the baby is napping. He zaps the fetus awake and the heart rate returns to normal.

Mark, his voice less confident, asks the staff to get an ETA (estimated time of arrival) for Coburn, who remains unavailable. He has reason to be concerned. These drops in the baby's heart rate are called decelerations and can be indicative of any one of several serious threats to the baby's health; this type of deceleration or lower heart rate may mean that the baby is not getting enough oxygen. When the heart rate drops for any prolonged period of time, a baby must be delivered as soon as possible to avoid irreversible brain damage or even death.

Jody's contractions are now three minutes apart. It's getting close to crunch time, and she is definitely in need of an obstetrician. Instead, as the pain of labor intensifies, Jody cries out, "I believe I'll have an epidural!" and is given one. This is an anesthetic injected into the lower area of the spine to ease the pain. Jody probably needs a crash C-section, and if Mark can't find an obstetrician, he should start calling for a surgeon to help. Benton is elsewhere in the hospital watching his mother's hip repair, so he is unavailable. Of course, Benton (the doctor, not the actor) would be amazed if he came to the ER and saw what was happening!

2:30 A.M. Jody is 8 centimeters dilated and 100 percent effaced. Susan checks the fetal monitor. The baby has late "decels" (decelerations), and it's not because he is sleeping. Clear signs of fetal distress. Minutes are precious now, and if these decelerations persist much longer, a cesarean section will need to be done. Mark puts an intrauterine catheter through Jody's vagina to measure the quality of the contractions. He also attaches electrodes onto the baby's scalp to monitor little Jared's pulse more accurately.

Like the ultrasound he performed earlier, this procedure is not part of the training that emergency medicine specialists would receive. Not only is it outside an ER doctor's normal scope of experience but it would likely be held to be malpractice for any physician to perform these procedures before having demonstrated proficiency with them under supervision. Considering the fact that, in large institutions like County General, patients would always be sent up to L&D for such procedures, Mark would have had little opportunity to develop experience with these procedures prior to this crisis.

Any physician watching this episode would know that by any measure of reality, things have gotten absurd by this point. Jody O'Brien has languished in the ER for 7½ hours, and should anything go wrong, the hospital and every person in it who has touched her so far will get sued for malpractice. Even if everything should turn out fine, this entire set of events would bring down the severest censure on the entire ER staff.

3:15 A.M. Things go from troubling to out of hand. Mark wants to send Jody up to Ob-Gyn but, for reasons only the show's director fully understands, can't. Jody is fully dilated. Mother and baby are on the launch pad. Where is the OB resident or Dr. Coburn? By this time, medical people watching the show are squirming and screaming out, "Just find some OB somewhere, anywhere, to get his or her butt in there!" With all the time they have taken, they could have flown in a specialist from Mass General in Boston or even UCLA! Jody does her best to push the baby out, but the labor isn't going well. Little Jared develops worsening decelerations. His heart rate is dangerously low. Mark sends for the Ob-Gyn resident and does a pudendal block to give Jody additional anesthesia, because the epidural is wearing off—yet another procedure for which ER personnel are not trained.

4:13 A.M. Jody is apparently fine, but her baby is in trouble. Little Jared's decelerations are lasting longer. Mark says the fetal monitor can be read only one way: deliver now or the baby won't make it. Under normal circumstances an obstetrician would have already performed a C-section, especially in view of the late decelerations, the seizures, and the eclampsia. By this time, the baby would be close to brain-dead. Still, Mark, stumbling along, attempts a vaginal delivery. Jody's blood pressure is starting to rise again, to 150/100. The baby's heart rate drops even lower. Medical malpractice attorneys in the audience start perking up, imagining how they would be the first to reach the surviving husband/father. They haven't seen a case this good since an orthopedic surgeon amputated the wrong leg of a one-legged man!

To make matters worse (or ludicrous, if you happen to be an OB watching the show), the child has a shoulder dystocia, which means the baby's shoulder is getting stuck as he makes his way down the birth canal. This occurs in only about 1.5 in 1,000 deliveries, but we have long since suspended disbelief. The shoulder dystocia means that the baby is too large to deliver through the mother's pelvis. Mark has apparently miscalculated the baby's size; he thought it was only 5 or 6 pounds. That's a problem with using a method that is inaccurate at Jody's stage of pregnancy, or with misreading the ultrasound.

To get this big baby to pass through the birth canal, Mark tries some special maneuvers (the main one is the McRobert's maneuver, which involves raising the mother's legs higher to make a better angle for the baby to be delivered). No dice. Mark attempts to grab the child with forceps to bring him out. Again, no luck. As a last resort, an obstetrician would then have tried to break the baby's shoulder or clavicle and ease him out. But no. Mark does something that seems logical only if you are making a roast and the company's late. You push it back in the oven to keep it warm. Well, it's not such a good idea with babies. I reviewed the episode with Ob-Gyns who have years of experience, doctors who have delivered thousands of babies, and not a single one had ever tried pushing a baby back into the uterus. But that's exactly what Mark tries.

Mark tells the father that he needs his consent to perform a C-section in order to save the baby. They rush Jody into Trauma

Room 1. In preparation, Mark orders a "flash and crash." That's where betadine is poured over the abdomen where he will make the incision. It's time to pull out the OB textbook, because if Mark pulls out an ER textbook, he won't find anything in there about doing a C-section on a live patient. Remember, the show is supposed to take place in Chicago, not Bangladesh. About the only indication for an ER physician to perform a cesarean section in an emergency room is to salvage a living baby from a mother who has just died.

No Ob-Gyn has been available for over 9 hours in one of the busiest hospitals in the country. Mark finally asks the nurses to find Peter Benton. But he is nowhere to be found. Apparently he is the only surgeon who can be called in this large urban hospital!

Now both Mom and child are in trouble. Jody seizes. More mag sulfate. She stabilizes and is prepared for surgery. Not in the OR but in the ER. Carol doesn't know the names of the surgical instruments (she does not know which are the Metzenbaum scissors, common surgical scissors for the OR). Carter nearly passes out as he watches the procedure, groaning "oh, man" with his eyes rolled back. As Mark starts the C-section, Susan Lewis warns, "Isn't there something about a bladder flap?" No one seems to know what exactly they are supposed to do. Susan makes it clear she doesn't have a clue about what Mark is doing.

This won't save Susan's malpractice carrier, for Susan can now expect to be named in the malpractice suit as well. Finally, and not unexpectedly, Jody "crashes." She is going down fast. And she is taking her baby with her. There is an abruption of the placenta. What does that mean exactly and why is it so serious? The baby is inside the uterus. Attached to the uterus is the placenta. A large network of vessels between the uterus and the placenta feeds blood filled with oxygen and food from mother to baby. In an abruption, the placenta tears away from the wall of the uterus, the network of blood vessels is ripped open, and massive bleeding ensues. Bells start ringing in the background, evidently signifying unstable vital signs.

4:42 A.M. Jared O'Brien makes it out of his mother's womb. He is not breathing. His blood sugar is dangerously low, and he needs an IV line and intubation. Where the hell is the neonatal (newborn) ICU team? There should be a neonatologist, or at the very least a pediatric intensive care specialist, on hand to receive and take care of the baby. The only one doing procedures today, though, is Mark Greene. He starts an IV using the vein of the umbilical cord, and intubates the newborn boy. The baby's Apgar scores are taken. This is the equivalent of a newborn report card that grades a child new to this earth on a scale of 0 to 2 on each of 5 qualities (heart rate, respirations, muscle tone, irritability, and color). The sum of the five scores is the total grade, a score of 7 to 10 being normal. At first Baby Boy O'Brien's scores are very low, but after five minutes Susan Lewis reports that they have markedly improved, and the total is reported to be 8. It's been a struggle, but one of Mark Greene's patients is finally out of the woods and into the world. Now Mark must deal with his other patient.

Dr. Coburn finally makes an appearance, sees the incredible bloody mess, and tells Mark it looks as if he has cut the patient open with a chain saw. Carter is holding down the aorta in Jody's abdomen to limit the bleeding from the placenta. (The aorta runs quite a way from the heart.)

5:30 A.M. The neonatal intensive care unit (NICU) team finally arrives to take the child up to the NICU. Dr. Coburn criticizes Mark for underestimating the size of the child and for misreading the placental abruption on the ultrasound. In fact, it is not difficult to miss an abruption on ultrasound, and an OB whose tardiness was instrumental in helping create a disaster would have a motive in taking a resident to task. Dr. Coburn must surely be thankful she has paid her malpractice premiums on time.

Suddenly, Jody's blood pressure plummets and she develops another problem. She starts to bleed internally everywhere. It's the most serious complication of an abruption, called disseminated intravascular coagulation, or DIC. While DIC can happen in association with many medical disasters (such as severe infections or hypothermia), for an Ob-Gyn it is usually a complication of an abruption. In DIC, the body's ability to clot goes haywire. It's a chain reaction. Too many of the blood platelets and the clotting mechanisms that stop bleeding are used up, and uncontrolled massive bleeding ensues. That is Jody's problem. Her blood can't clot well, if at all, and she starts to bleed from everywhere. The only solution is to give her FFP (fresh frozen plasma) rich in platelets, along with blood-clotting factors to help stop the bleeding from the abrupted placenta. If Mark can control Jody's bleeding and then raise her dropping pressure, she has a chance.

5:42 A.M. Jody "codes": suffers a cardiac arrest. Her heart and body are giving out. She is in V-fib and has a life-threatening irregular heartbeat. A small stream of blood oozes from her nose, and there may well be oozing and bleeding throughout her body. Mark goes to work. Here at least, he and his team are finally back in their element and doing what they do best: trying to bring people in cardiac arrest back from the brink of death. Mark and the ER staff swing into high lifesaving gear. They pull out all the stops. They start CPR to keep air going through Jody's lungs. They defibrillate her to try to shock her heart into a normal rhythm. Jody is loaded up with lidocaine, pronestyl, and beryllium in rapid succession to treat her lethal arrhythmias. Also IV dopamine to raise her blood pressure. Epinephrine to kick-start the heartbeats. Transfusions to replace the blood lost from the bleeding.

Alas, it is all to no avail. Mark continues to pump Jody's chest furiously, well past the point when it is obvious to all around him that the battle is over. It is one of those great *ER* moments when a doctor is still working away on a deceased patient, and his colleagues stand back in silence, respecting his reluctance to acknowledge that he has lost this one.

Finally, Coburn "calls" (stops) the code. It is 6:46 A.M.

A despondent Mark goes to find the father and deliver the devastating news. The baby was brought into the neonatal ICU barely an hour ago and would more than likely stay there for another day. But we're playing fast and loose with reality, so by some miracle the baby is in the nursery being rocked by his father. Twenty-four hours in the life of Mark Greene have passed in the episode. Of his two patients in a life and death struggle, one has been lost. We see but don't hear him inform the father, and the grueling episode comes to its sad conclusion.

This episode scared the dickens out of many a pregnant woman across the country. Yet the sequence of events it depicts must be described as unlikely at the very least in a major city hospital in the 1990s. Yes, there are cases of preeclampsia, but it is easily treated and there are very few reasons for a woman to die from it. It is conceivable that a woman with preeclampsia could languish in an ER without the benefit of OB care if the hospital were located in some distant suburb of Timbuktu, where an OB makes only monthly rounds. But it is hard to imagine anywhere in the United States. where this could actually happen, much less in downtown Chicago. Much of what went wrong could have been averted had Jody gone to Labor and Delivery. The real Mark Greenes would never have performed the exotic tests and procedures that the fictional one jumped in to do. The directors of some of the largest ER training programs in the U.S. consider a C-section as performed on the show by an ER doctor to be malpractice, no matter what the outcome.

For sheer drama, however, the episode "Love's Labor Lost" can't be beat. It may well be the favorite of many of the show's faithful followers. While the actions of the ER staff would in real life have enriched an army of medical malpractice attorneys, the writing staff of the show was rewarded with an Emmy. That's show biz.

PART

III

Laughter and Tears

Lightning Can Strike Twice

Unusual Occurrences

Day in and day out, people sprain ankles, crash cars, catch the flu, eat spoiled food—and then find themselves in the ER. Some of the problems are serious; others don't even deserve mentioning. But every once in a while a patient comes in whose story suggests that some of us, sometimes, can defy the laws of fate. These are the patients who have been hit by lightning, submerged under an icy pond, or bitten by a venomous viper or deadly arachnid—traumas most of us would not survive. Yet, miraculously, they have lived to tell their story. Surely some of them owe their good fortune to chance, but others survived because of some ER physician's quick thinking and the recent advances in the treatment of traumas.

SHOCKING BUT TRUE

In the episode "Men Plan, God Laughs," a cyanotic (not enough oxygen in the blood) patient with signs of "feathering" on the skin is rushed into the ER. One of the doctors suggests that Carter carefully observe the patient because "this isn't something you see every day." Indeed. The patient has been struck by lightning—a very rare occurrence, but it does happen.

In real life it happened recently, on what seemed like a perfect spring day. Lightning struck a middle-aged man out for a walk. Let's go back to that day and see what happened.

Despite billowing cumulus clouds in a bright blue sky and warm afternoon temperatures, this day is about to turn nasty. A cold high-pressure front is heading in, and when it arrives it will turn the skies ominously dark. In the upper atmosphere, winds in the clouds cause air particles to move rapidly, and the friction (like feet rubbing on a new carpet) creates some very powerful electrical forces.

Far below the turbulence, on the dry flats of the valley, our walker sees the oncoming thunderheads rolling his way. He stays calm. Everyone knows that the chance of being hit by lightning is remote. But most people would be surprised to learn that in the United States, lightning actually tops the list of natural events responsible for human deaths—exceeding blizzards, earthquakes, tornadoes, and even floods. As the wind picks up and the lightning cascades across the black clouds, the walker reconsiders his nonchalance and runs for cover.

Nature's onslaught, moving faster than any human can run, strikes the man with a single bolt. A force nearly 1,000 times more powerful than that carried by a high-voltage power line (100 million volts) surges around his body and knocks him to the ground. His heart has been electrically shocked, just as a person in cardiac arrest might be shocked in the emergency room by the use of a defibrillator. But no defibrillator ever gave a jolt comparable to what this man just received.

Even mild electric shocks to healthy hearts can be quite destabilizing. Remember, every time Mark or Susan goes for the defibrillator to try to restart a patient's heart, he or she always reminds everyone else near the patient to stand back. The last thing a normal heart needs is a surge of electricity running through the body; the unaccounted-for electricity may induce abnormal heartbeats or even cardiac arrest. When a lightning bolt, with its enormous electrical power, strikes a healthy beating heart, it gives it such a wallop that it most often stops the normal beating completely. It *causes* cardiac arrest.

Interestingly, it does so not by damaging heart muscle, but by shutting down the natural cardiac "pacemaker" that regulates your heart rate. Your breathing then stops. In most cases, after a brief pause, this internal pacemaker starts itself up again, and your heartbeat as well as your breathing return. But if your heart does not restart, or if you fail to breathe on your own shortly after being struck, you die.

Every year in the U.S., about 1,000 people are hit by lightning, 250 of them fatally. Though you might think that this much voltage would toast you, the lightning strike is so fast that very little energy actually penetrates into the skin. The resulting burns are usually superficial.

For the man lying motionless after being struck by lightning, fate smiles. His heart and breathing activity return quickly, on their own, but he lies unconscious, unaware of what is happening. Fortunately a witness calls 911, summoning paramedics who quickly assess their new patient in the field, intubate him to protect his airway, and transport him to a nearby trauma center for emergency care.

The ER doctor on duty, however, has never seen a person hit by lightning. She knows from the literature that a bolt of lightning can lift a victim off his feet and throw him quite a distance, sometimes slamming the person against a wall or a tree. Anticipating that her patient may have sustained just such injuries, she assembles a trauma team in preparation for his arrival.

As the paramedics come through the doors, the ER doctor makes her primary survey. The patient's heart is beating, the airway is stable after intubation, and there are good strong pulses throughout the body. Even though this patient is unconscious, there are no obvious signs of major trauma. As the ER staff removes the patient's clothes, they notice typical physical changes that occur after a lightning strike. In this case, the lightning flashed over the outside of the victim's body, causing only minor superficial burns to the skin. But as with any victim who had fluid or sweat on his body when the lightning struck, the liquids superheat and then rapidly cool, causing clothes to tear away.

Sure enough, the seams of the patient's pant leg have torn wide open, and the patient's beeper has exploded; only parts of it remain attached to his clothing. Moreover, the staff notices a "feathering" or fern pattern on the victim's back, not a true burn but a reaction caused by a showering of electrons over his body. Some small amount of electricity has penetrated the body through the mouth and ears, because the patient has evidence of a spasm of the arteries in the right leg. This spasm has reduced the blood supply to the right foot, giving the lower right leg a white appearance. Slowly, the spasm relaxes, and normal blood flow returns to the patient's foot.

The patient also has one other typical finding. The tympanic membrane (eardrum) in the left ear has been ruptured, a finding made in nearly 50 percent of all victims of a lightning strike. Most likely secondary shock waves—we're talking thunderclap beyond your wildest imagination—did the damage. Nonetheless, within days, the patient is up and about, able to give numerous interviews to the local press.

On *ER*, a patient who has been struck by lighting arrives at the emergency room with a cataract in one eye, the result of secondary shock waves. Most of the medical problems that occur following a lightning strike are transient in nature, and most patients make an excellent recovery.

But those who attend the annual Lightning Strike and Electric Shock Victims International Convention in Gettysburg, Pennsylvania, see their plight differently. Many say they continue to suffer stuttering, memory loss, blurred vision, even impotence. One conventioneer observed that he has never been cold since the day in 1969 when a lightning bolt blasted him out of his boots and threw him 50 feet. In winter he walks around outside in shorts facing temperatures as low as 44° below zero! In summer, he luxuriates in a bathtub of cold water filled with eight bags of ice. Some doctors dispute claims of such long-lasting effects.

Survivors are looked upon with a certain reverence. There has always been something mysterious about lightning strikes, and many superstitions and "old wives' tales" have contributed to the mystique of the bolt of lightning from the sky. Dr. Mary Ann Cooper, in a discussion of lightning strikes in a 1992 issue of *Emergency Medicine,* tried to set the record straight. Contrary to popular belief, she wrote, lightning does not turn its victims into "crispy critters" or piles of dust, and people struck by lightning do not remain "electrified." The belief at one time that victims of a lightning strike still have the capacity to cause electrical injury from "stored-up electricity" caused terrible delays in their medical treatment. Rescuers were afraid of getting shocked themselves!

Another wives' tale is that lightning is unlikely to strike twice in the same place—don't ever repeat this notion to the people who work in the Sears Tower in Chicago, hometown of *ER*'s County General. From personal experience, they know better.

Lightning generally strikes the tallest object in the area. If, for example, a group of people in a park find themselves standing underneath a tree when lightning strikes and that tree happens to be the tallest object in the area, it is not only likely that the lightning would strike that tree (and the people standing under it) but it would not be unthinkable that it would strike that tree twice.

Even more startling, lightning can hit more than one victim with each strike. The electricity can spread through the ground and "zap" others in the surrounding area. Fully a third of all lightning deaths occur in multiples, affecting two or more people at one site.

Most electrical shock injuries do not occur as a result of having been struck by lightning. Accidents in the home are much more frequent. The problem is that the electricity that comes into our homes is alternating current (AC) rather than direct current (DC). AC is about three times more dangerous than DC, and at 60 Hz (the most common electrical frequency in the United

States), contact with an electrical source can cause muscle spasm. This means that if you touch an AC electrical source with your hand, your fingers will involuntarily contract or spasm. As the energy is transferred from your hand to your body, you hold tight, unable to let go.

The more serious problem with alternating current is that unlike lightning, it does tend to flow into the body, resulting in the death of tissue. In the episode "The Gift," a man receives a power surge of 86,239 volts from his enormous Christmas-light display—and lives. Most stories about individuals who accidentally sustain high-voltage electrical injuries from AC current do not end happily. Given the choice, it is better to be struck by a bolt from the heavens than to be plugged in on earth.

"FIRE!"

While high-voltage AC injuries cook you from the inside, fire and flame will roast you from the outside. Approximately 20,000 people die each year from burn complications, many following the downward course *ER* depicted so well in the case of Raul Melendez. This character was a paramedic who suffered massive third-degree burns over his body in the line of duty, and slowly died in front of his colleagues. Many ER physicians point to this show as the best of the season.

Of course, not all burns end in death. With a first-degree burn, your skin turns red and may be a little painful, and you may peel within a week or so. Basically, a sunburn is a first-degree burn, and Tylenol or aspirin will do just fine. Second-degree burns are deeper into the skin, characterized by blistering and extreme pain. It takes about three weeks for decent healing to take place.

But come in with extensive second-degree burns, and you are admitted into the hospital. If this type of burn gets infected, it can turn into a third-degree burn. Third-degree burns are the real "roastings." The skin has been burned completely through, and the area is insensitive to the touch. It doesn't hurt, because the nerves have been completely destroyed by the heat. The skin is dead, and only a skin graft or scarring will eventually cover the area.

In many cases, though, the burn is not the major problem. Nearly 60 percent of deaths from fires are caused by the gases that are produced and inhaled during the burning, especially carbon monoxide.

BITE ME

Americans have become fascinated with collecting exotic pets. From rare dogs and cats, to pigs, exotic birds, tarantulas, and venomous snakes, pet owners have fallen in love with the unusual and sometimes bizarre. Unfortunately, most people are not familiar with how to handle unusual animals, and oftentimes it is the emergency room physician who is called in to deal with the consequences.

Even for an uncommon pet, a bite wound to its human owner is quite common. It is estimated that over a million animal bites occur each year. Dog bites are the most common (80 percent), followed by cats (10 percent) and rodents (2 percent). (Human bites account for 3 percent!) These wounds run a high risk of infection because of the number and type of bacteria found in saliva, and because all wounds need to be cleaned and sometimes treated with oral antibiotics. Cat bites are especially bad, for a cat's long slender teeth act like hypodermic needles, injecting contaminated saliva into wounds.

Of the wide variety of animals found in the U.S., the most dreaded animal-bite complication is rabies. Around 1950, in the U.S., approximately 20 new cases of this potentially lethal disease occurred a year. Because of animal control and national vaccination laws, currently there are usually fewer than 5 cases per year. Nearly 90 percent of rabies in the U.S. have come most recently from wildlife—specifically, skunks, bats, raccoons, and foxes. Rodents, including rats and mice, even though they may scare you and cause an elephant stampede, are not usually carriers of rabies.

The risk of rabies, though small, is real, and over 18,000 people are annually given treatment for the possibility. So if you are bitten by a skunk or raccoon, expect to be given rabies treatment from your local ER or health department. Years ago, this meant multiple painful shots in the abdomen. But now it's a simple series of injections in the arm or leg.

While snakes are becoming more and more popular as pets, many local laws make domestic ownership of a venomous snake illegal. Should one of these animals escape, as snakes are wont to do, it poses a real danger of illness and death to the community.

Though many ER physicians have never seen or treated a venomous snake bite, nearly 50,000 snake bites occur each year in the U.S. One of those incidents was captured humorously in the *ER* episode in which Harold, a young boy who had been bitten by his pet yellow pit viper, brings the snake to the ER in a paper bag. Of course, the animal escapes, and the hospital is on viper alert until Carter finds it at the end of the episode. As it turns out, Harold does fine.

Not everyone is so lucky. About 7,000 venomous bites cause an average of 15 deaths per year. Almost all (98 percent) of the venomous snake bites in the United States come from the category of pit vipers, including the rattlesnake, copperhead, and water moccasin. (Coral snakes, which are not pit vipers, are venomous as well, but have not proven to be a serious problem for fatalities in the U.S.) Pit vipers are native to nearly every state in the country, with the exception of Maine, Alaska, and Hawaii. They don't usually seek trouble or people, but can appear in the most civilized and unexpected of places. And a bite by one of these creatures can cause harrowing consequences.

"Teed Off" (A True Story)

On a hot day in early August, a golfer reaches into the brush to grab a ball he's sliced on the final hole. Instantly, he feels a sharp burning pain in his lower leg. He yells to his three golfing partners that he has been bitten by a rattler. As they rush to his aid, he races out of the brush. One of the fellow golfers knows first aid, and tries to calm down his hysterical friend. Anything that increases heart rate or movement of the extremity could make the venom circulate into and around the body faster. The group lifts their fallen comrade into the golf cart, and immobilizes his leg with a couple of golf clubs (they use the driver woods, for these are the longest and stiffest clubs). They all had seen old Westerns where an "X" is carved over each one of the fang marks, and then the blood is sucked from the wound. This method can actually help to remove some of the poison if done during the first 15 minutes after the bite, before the venom has a chance to seep out of the local area and into the bloodstream.

In this era of heightened awareness of HIV and hepatitis, however, the group quickly decides, no way! Better to rush him to the nearest hospital without sucking out the wound. One of the men ties a piece of clothing around the leg just up from the bite marks, restricting the blood and retarding the flow of venom out of the leg (but not so tight that it stops the pulse to the foot). They speed off toward the local ER.

The group carries the stricken man, his leg strapped to his clubs, into the ER and onto a gurney. The toxic effects of the venom are already taking hold. The leg beyond the tightly tied clothing has started to swell, and an area of red dots has started to appear, indicating bleeding under the skin.

Some of the common systemic side effects of the venom are also beginning to kick in. Victims develop nausea, fever, and vomiting as early symptoms, and often complain of a metallic taste in the mouth. The smaller the person, the worse the consequences. Children are especially at risk. Pit-viper venom often interferes with the nervous system as well, causing bizarre behavior, breathing problems, convulsions, and seizures. The venom also affects the circulatory system. It can disrupt the normal clotting mechanism in the blood, resulting in massive internal bleeding. The inner lining of the smallest blood vessels, called *capillaries*, is also affected, and fluid can soon start to leak out of these blood vessels into the tissues and lungs. This, in combination with massive bleeding, can kill the victim.

Though unusual for many ER doctors, the one at this hospital has seen a number of rattler bites, mostly golfers who have gone off into the dry brush to look for lost golf balls. The first thing the ER doctor does is to assess the bite to determine the necessary treatment. Its severity is graded on a scale of 0 to 4—our poor golfer is rated a 4.

Fast treatment is of the essence, and luckily for the stricken golfer, the antivenom is available in this particular hospital. But this antidote is made from horse serum (blood plasma that has antibodies to the venom), and many patients have severe allergic reactions to it. This patient does not show any sensitivity to the horse serum after a small test dose; if he had, special measures would have been taken involving steroids, antihistamines, and the like. Up to 20 vials of antidote serum may be necessary— often more than a hospital carries in stock.

As frantic phone calls are being made to other hospital ER's to find additional antivenom for a Grade 4 bite, the stock on hand is administered, first in the ER and continuing in the intensive care unit. The patient is lucky. Without the antivenom, he could have lost his leg or even died.

Snakes are not the only venomous animal bites that ER physicians treat. Far and away, the most likely cause of death from animal venom is from a bee or wasp sting (yes, bees and wasps are animals), usually due to a severe allergic reaction called *anaphylaxis*. With anaphylaxis, the air passages can swell up, making breathing difficult or impossible. There can be cardiovascular collapse, with severe hypotension and death. The treatment is adrenaline and antihistamines.

THE REAL CASE OF CHARLOTTE'S WEB

Arachnophobia is the name of a movie and of a real fear of spiders. There is good reason to fear some of these creepy little creatures. They bite. Nasty poisonous ones. These are unusual cases for an ER doctor to treat, but victims of poisonous spiders are admitted who are seriously ill or even at death's door.

In the United States, the two most common venomous spider bites are from the black widow and the brown recluse. The black widow is found throughout the U.S., is about 1½ inches long, and can usually be identified by a red hourglass marking on its abdomen (not that you would want to pick it up to look!). The bite can cause a dramatic systemic reaction—meaning that the bite itself is not nearly as severe as the illness the toxin causes to the body. There is a commercially available antitoxin for the bite. But not for that of the brown recluse, whose bite can cause a much more severe local reaction. Following is another true and harrowing story of a bite.

A 14-year-old girl is working in her backyard, sipping a soda as she moves some old wood away from a group of newly planted rosebushes. As she lifts up the last piece of wood, she feels a sharp sting on the thumb of her right finger, and instinctively looks down at the ground. There she sees a large spider, probably now well fed from the piece it has just taken out of her finger. As she looks at her finger, she can see two small fang marks on the side of her thumb. Through them, the spider has left her a little present: some black widow spider venom.

The teenager pours out the remaining soda from her paper cup, places the cup over the spider, and scoops it up. She looks inside the cup and sees the spider struggling upside-down in the remaining drops of fluid, revealing its telltale hourglass sign. She has been bitten before, and she knows exactly what she must do. She places the plastic top on the cup, and runs inside to get her parents. She is going to bring the spider with her to the hospital, because the last time the physician didn't believe the spider was actually a black widow. This time she has proof, and she is going to show it to the ER staff.

As her mother drives the car, the girl begins to feel a dull crampy pain in the bitten hand. By the time they get to the hospital, her entire body is hurting, particularly her chest. Soon after that, her stomach starts cramping. She becomes nauseated, and vomits numerous times as she is helped into the busy ER. These are all signs of a severe reaction to the venom.

The ER physician is confronted with a dilemma. He has never seen a reaction so severe, and while most patients may think they have been bitten by a black widow, in reality most are bitten by a nonvenomous spider. The physician needs to decide whether or not to use antivenom (also made of horse serum) and risk causing a severe allergic reaction, perhaps even more deadly than the spider bite.

While he examines the teenager, she picks up the cup and lifts the lid to show him the proof. In that instant, overwhelming nausea hits her again, and as she wretches, the cup shakes out of her hand and the spider comes flying out onto the floor. The doctor looks down just long enough to see the upside-down spider, hourglass and all, turn itself upright and scamper beneath the gurney, just escaping being squashed by one of the ER nurses. With no doubt that it's the real thing, the physician orders antivenom to treat the reaction to the toxic bite.

The three other patients who were in the treatment area when the attacker escaped, along with the original victim, are all evacuated to other areas of the ER pending the apprehension of the spider. The patient feels dramatic relief within an hour following the treatment, but the spider remains at large, finding a new home somewhere in the ER.

Triage

The "Blizzard" Episode and
Real-Life Disasters

As the *ER* episode "Blizzard" opens, there are 17 shopping days left before Christmas. The snow gently falls in big soft flakes, blanketing the Windy City. Jerry Markovic fumbles happily through the powder on his way to work, singing a refrain of "Jingle Bells." Inside the ER at County General, the mood is no less festive. Wendy Goldman rollerblades through the halls, Malik raps over the intercom, Susan and Mark wrap a leg cast on a sleeping Carter as a prank, staff members scoot about on the chairs playing ball. It's not only slow and eerily calm in the ER; there isn't a single patient.

Meanwhile, in contrast, a blizzard outside is dumping nearly two feet of fresh snow on the city, creating hazardous conditions for anyone out in it. The peace in the ER can't last much longer. Soon a dispatcher's radio message to Carol Hathaway sounds the first alarm. It's a mass-casualty alert. Not a drill, but the real thing. A disaster. The staff turns on the news and watches in rapt attention the vivid images that will bring them the first of the patients. More than 30 cars and trucks have crashed on the Kennedy Expressway, after a single car spun out of control in the blinding, slippery snow. There are at least 18 major and 29 minor casualties. Mercy Hospital is without power, so County General is the only game in town. The staff responds calmly, silently, but Mark knows that the oncoming wave of blood and carnage will change the atmosphere of the ER in an instant, testing it to its very limit. Disasters always do, and the victims just keep coming.

The Joint Commission on Accreditation of Health Organizations requires every hospital to have a disaster plan. In such an event, every department and every employee has a prearranged job to do, and twice a year every hospital must test that plan to remain prepared.

County General's plan will be put to the test in a few short moments. Mark knows that however well they prepare before the injured arrive, dozens of patients arriving at the same time will nearly overwhelm the ER's ability to provide optimal health care. He utters, "Here we go," and the staff at County General springs into action. The entire hospital is alerted. Nurses in the ER begin to restock IV fluids, blankets, and all the supplies that will be needed. A media room is created to allow the press access to information, and though the television viewer could not see it in this episode, the ORs would be preparing for any patients needing immediate surgery. As preparations finish, the staff of the ER, plastic goggles over their eyes, latex gloves covering their hands, stands and waits in quiet anticipation, knowing all hell is about to break loose. The sound of approaching sirens grows louder.

BLACK

Out in the raging storm, the Chicago Fire Department has already handled the difficult initial evaluations and sorting of patients. Search-and-rescue teams composed of fire and rescue personnel arrive on the scene. Vehicle lights create an eerie carnival atmosphere. The cold is biting. Pandemonium erupts as the rescue personnel attempt to gauge the extent of the disaster. Next is triage, stabilization, and transport. Victims are grouped by severity of injuries, and early treatment takes place out on the highway, in the freezing snowstorm. The treatment is limited to the ABCs (airway, breathing, circulation), along with stabilization of the spine. The severely injured patients are put in rigid cervical collars, strapped to a backboard, and given oxygen. Pressure bandages are placed on wounds to control severe bleeding. Ambulances transport some of the severely injured to County General's ER. The most critical are facing imminent death, perhaps having arrested at the scene. These patients are "black-tagged" for transport later, for they are expected to die and won't be transported until those patients who stand a chance are sent to County General. In all, over 70 patients will arrive, including one man whose leg has been sheared off at the knee; rescuers at the scene continue to search for his leg.

The wave of carnage hits the ER's shores. Doug is stationed in the front hallway to triage patients a second time as they roll in the door. Triage in a disaster is meant to be a dynamic process, for a patient's condition can change and needs to be reviewed from time to time. Mark runs around the department, a walkie-talkie in his hand, attempting to keep the lines of communication open with his staff. The phones are jammed, probably unusable, as they nearly always are in any disaster. Too many people are calling for information about loved ones. Morgenstern arrives. He asks how it's going, and a fireman replies, "We're a step ahead of the reaper." That's what ER medicine, especially in a disaster, is all about.

RED

The patients who are severely injured but who have a reasonable chance of survival with emergency treatment, but who could die or have severe permanent disabilities without it, are "red-tagged." This group gets the highest priority for initial transport and treatment. In the frenzy at the scene it seems that nearly all the patients merited a red tag, but now Doug trims the number down to just 18. Of these, some suffer extensive second- and third-degree burns, one has an amputated thumb to be reattached, while many others have suffered severe blunt trauma to the chest, abdomen, and spine. Doug, usually known for his hot temper, is cool as a cucumber throughout the crisis. In the throes of sorting patients, a new member of the cast arrives on the scene and introduces herself to Doug as Angela Hicks. Doug hands her a stack of receptacles for bedpan detail. Angela smiles and clarifies that she is *Dr.* Hicks, the new surgical attending in the ER.

Dr. Hicks and Dr. Benton make each other's acquaintance over the man who lost his leg. Fear not—the leg arrives later and is reunited with the patient courtesy of Benton and Hicks. What makes this unusual is not the sewing skills of the surgeons but the site of the procedure: in the ER. Ten of the red-tagged patients have already gone directly up to the OR for emergency surgery, inundating the six operational ORs at County General. Hicks is ready to "fly this puppy" right then and there.

YELLOW

Nineteen patients are tagged yellow. They arrive at the ER just after the red-tagged patients. These are the moderately injured patients, those with large lacerations, fractured bones, concussions. They will survive, and a short delay in treatment of their wounds won't lead to serious problems.

GREEN

Finally come the green-tagged patients: the walking wounded, patients with minor lacerations, back and neck sprains, or uncomplicated bumps and bruises. One man has a lighter stuck to his chest. Doug triages 33 patients as green tags, by far the largest category. That's lucky for the crew at County General, since any more critical patients would overload the system.

In any disaster, mistakes are made and problems seem to pop up out of nowhere. One of the patients that Doug Ross green-tags, Mr. Ramos, though elderly, does not seem ill. His illness becomes apparent all too late, however, when he suffers a cardiac arrest in the midst of the disaster. Doug admonishes himself for triaging incorrectly. But triage conditions can shift, and there is always the chance that patients will take a turn for the worse.

An integral part of any disaster team are the non-health-care workers who help to make the treatment run smoothly. Social workers and clergy help families and the dying cope with the emotional suffering. Often they help parents reunite with their lost children. The nun who prays over Mr. Ramos clearly has an impact on Doug and the entire staff. These clinicians and clergy help us reflect on the sanctity and fragility of life.

Bob

Probably the most uplifting and serendipitous event in this episode came as a surprise to both the ER staff and viewers. During the disaster code, everyone is pitching in to help. As the day wears on at County General, additional physicians and staff come to relieve those who have been working nonstop for hours.

Susan Lewis goes to look for a surgeon for a patient who has an AAA (aortic aneurysm in the abdomen) that is about to blow. Bob—Bogdanalivetsky Romansky, the shy housekeeper—interrupts her cleaning as the patient languishes, about to die in a corner of the ER. Reluctantly Bob grabs a scalpel and slices open the belly of the patient. Much to the amazement of Malik, Wendy, and Lydia, Bob cross-clamps the patient's aorta just in time to save his life!

When Susan returns and asks what has happened, Lydia tells her it was Bob. Unknown to the staff, Bob had been a vascular surgeon in her native Poland. She confesses to Carter in broken English that she had been hoping to take the board exam to become a physician in the U.S., but now is sure that performing this medical procedure will destroy her chances. Carter offers to help Bob with her English for the boards, and the staff applauds her actions.

The day is coming to a close, and every patient has been attended to. As Dr. Hicks compliments the staff on a job well done, there is a sudden blackout. When the lights come back up, Christmas lights are glowing along the walls, "The Christmas Song" is resonating over the intercom, and the halls are filled with the warmth and cheer of holiday spirit. The staff shares pizza and the afterglow of their heroics. Their performance was as smooth as the voice of Nat King Cole.

As well as the disaster plan was executed, how does the response of County General's staff stack up against real ERs that have recently faced mass casualties?

THE HEARTLAND BLEEDS

It is April 19, 1995. At St. Anthony's Hospital, just blocks from downtown Oklahoma City, Sylvia Buckner Amundson has just begun her shift as the day charge nurse in the ER. So far the morning has been uneventful. She has one young man in the major trauma room with a stab wound to the chest. It isn't serious, though, and he will eventually be treated and released. At University Hospital, Dr. Gary Quick, chief of the emergency department, is beginning his day as he greets the ER residents at the start of their shift. Over at Children's Hospital, Dr. Tom Lera is teaching some of his pediatric residents the art of taking care of young children with ear infections and pneumonia. All three hospitals and their staffs have routinely practiced disaster drills in the past, but the thought of a true disaster is the farthest thing from anyone's mind. This morning at 9:02 A.M. all that will change.

A deafening explosion rocks St. Anthony's ER. The walls seem to move. Supplies fall out of carts. The staff is sure a terrible accident has occurred in the hospital. They are wrong. Dead wrong. The Alfred P. Murrah Federal Building six blocks away has been the target of a terrorist bombing attack. The first information anyone has comes from the TV in the waiting room of the ER. Reporters interrupt the local news for a special bulletin and give early reports of an explosion downtown.

Like at County General, disaster drills are put into effect in the hospitals around the city (in Oklahoma City, they refer to this as Condition Black). At St. Anthony's on this day, patients already in the ER are discharged as quickly as possible, operating rooms are cleared, and the alert goes out for available nurses and physicians to report to the ER. Supplies are quickly restocked, and the staff braces themselves for the wave of blood and carnage that is about to hit. One piece of good news: at least all the local hospitals are undamaged, and St. Anthony's, though the closest to the bombing, does not stand alone, as County General had in the face of the blizzard disaster.

At the bombed Federal Building, emergency medical response teams are arriving, beginning the task of triage, stabilization, and transport, but many people, even those with serious wounds, manage to transport themselves to the closest ER: St. Anthony's. Sylvia Amundson looks up the ER driveway just minutes after the blast to see a sight she will never forget: dozens of limping, bleeding people, many disoriented and unaware of what has happened. It is a scene right out of *Night of the Living Dead*.

The scene is so unimaginable that anything Doug Ross witnessed on *ER* the day of the blizzard pales in comparison. Scores of patients with abrasions, lacerations, broken bones, and busted eardrums are triaged through the ER. One man has been pierced over 100 times by flying glass and metal. It's as if someone had loaded a shotgun with shrapnel and aimed it straight at this whole group of people stumbling into the ER. If there is anything to be thankful for about the explosion, it is that it at least occurred in the spring, allowing the triage area to be set up outside the ER. Whenever possible, this is the way disasters are usually run, freeing up necessary space for patient care in the ER.

The driveway outside St. Anthony's becomes the major triage area, where patients receive an initial assessment. The minor injuries, the "green tags," are sent to a treatment area that only minutes before had been the hospital's dental clinic. The major injuries, the yellow and red tags, are triaged (whether or not they are literally tagged) directly into the ER, stabilized quickly with IVs and splints or whatever else is needed, and then, if necessary, sent up to the floors for continued emergency care.

One of the problems during this crisis inadvertently comes about out of the goodness of the human spirit. Doctors (particularly ophthalmologists, who know there will be eye injuries from shattered glass), nurses, EMTs, and just plain folk, hearing about the bombing, come from far and wide to volunteer their services. In fact, too many people show up, and the lack of communication doesn't allow the hospital to utilize the extra personnel effectively. So many physicians respond to the disaster call that patients wheeled up to a hospital bed often have their own personal doctor pushing them along. Luckily, every room in the hospital is made available, and patients usually spend less than 20 minutes in the ER during their initial evaluation.

With so many patients, identification becomes a major problem. Many patients are unconscious because of major head trauma, or in shock from the blast. Unable to give their names, these patients are toe-tagged as either Jane or John Doe, all with different middle initials. Supplies are used up quickly. Local companies rush extra medical equipment to the hospital. All told, 75 patients come through St. Anthony's ER—as many as they see over the course of a typical 24-hour day. And not one died while in their care.

The medical director from St. Anthony's sends a team of doctors to the disaster site to help with triage. These doctors are joined at the scene by an army of rescue workers, but the vast majority of those who are destined to survive got to an ER within the first two hours. The national disaster plans designed by the Federal Emergency Management Agency are called into action, and the Federal Building soon becomes a beehive of both medical and military action. FBI counterterrorist specialists share coffee with local physicians as the horrible reality of the bombing becomes explicitly clear.

But in the ER there is an inexplicable lull as workers wait for the second wave of victims to arrive from the blast. They never do. Slowly it dawns on the staff of all four ERs that the second wave of victims lay buried under tons of rubble. There will be very few survivors. One of them, Dana Bradley, a 20-year-old mother of two, is trapped under tons of concrete and metal, her leg wedged under massive fallen girders. With her blood pressure dropping, and with the fear that the remaining parts of the building might soon collapse, the three doctors at the scene are forced to amputate her leg. Dana is unaware at the time that her two children and mother have perished in the blast.

The last patient found alive in the rubble is 15-year-old Brandy Liggons, who is trapped for nearly 12 hours beneath the tottering remains of the Federal Building. She is transported to Children's Hospital, where Dr. Lera and his staff in the ER have already treated nearly 20 children from the blast. Children's Hospital sees its share of glass and metal injuries that day. There are children with open skull injuries, many broken bones, and a number of abdominal injuries from blunt trauma (heavy objects hitting the abdomen and causing injury to internal organs)— nearly all seen in the first 90 minutes after the blast.

As do all ERs in Oklahoma City, Dr. Lera's has practiced disaster drills twice a year every year in preparation for a catastrophe they hoped would never come. In retrospect, Dr. Lera feels his hospital could have handled many more patients than it did after the blast. But communication often turns out to be a stumbling block. The cellular phone system gets overloaded, and people are confused about who is doing what to whom and where. St. Anthony's received a huge volume of patients in a very limited time, as did County General's ER, but the surrounding hospitals in Oklahoma City did see patients, just many fewer than St. Anthony's.

Another problem in a real-life catastrophe is how to coordinate ambulance traffic and medical care. Because of poor communication, the parents of some of the children injured in the blast think all the injured and missing children were sent to Children's Hospital, and they swarm to the hospital looking for their sons and daughters. But they aren't necessarily there. Social service workers and chaplains become an integral part of the disaster team, as they did on the show, but in this case they are matching parents with children found alive, while informing many other parents that their children have not been seen in the ER or are dead.

The next day, as the hospitals, families, and survivors try to make sense of what has happened, Dr. Lera is challenged with yet another disaster. Four calls warning of bombs in the hospital come in rapid succession. The callers threaten to finish off the children they had missed in the bombing. Specially trained dogs are brought in to search for explosives, and they go wild as soon as they smell the residue of the blast on the children in the ICU. Dr. Lera has to make the painful decision whether or not to evacuate the hospital. He decides to stay put, and no explosives are found.

Volunteers by the thousands open their hearts and pocketbooks to give their time and money to serve the community in this time of crisis. All told, 442 people were treated in area hospitals, with 83 requiring admission; 168 people died as a result of the blast, 80 percent between the ages of 20 and 59.

There are a great many similarities in the type of response given to a medical disaster between *ER*'s "Blizzard" episode and the Oklahoma City bombing. In fact, we were surprised to realize that the disaster in Oklahoma took place *after* this episode aired; the show's writers and medical consultants did such a good job investigating disaster responses for ERs and hospitals that it was easy to think they had based the show on the Federal Building bombing. And the real emergency response in Oklahoma City was handled superbly.

In both cases, the hospitals had time to prepare (even if only minutes) and were not themselves affected by the disaster. What happens when a catastrophic event involves and nearly destroys the hospital?

The Day the Earth Opened Up

Dr. Ed Lowder has worked as an ER physician in a community hospital in Los Angeles County for nearly a decade. The hospital's ER is designated as a Level 1 Trauma Center: it is equipped for all major trauma and has an experienced surgical crew available 24 hours a day.

It is 3:30 A.M. on January 17, 1994. Lowder has just finished his portion of the night shift and gets into bed in the on-call room outside the ER. Sixty minutes later he is knocked out of bed. At first he thinks he is dreaming, but then he hears all the car alarms that are going off and feels the first aftershock shaking the hospital. He jumps up and races down to the ER to find the staff running around trying to upright supplies, carts, and even a patient or two who had fallen to the floor. The emergency power is working (hospital generators kick in if the city's main power lines go down), so the lights are still on. The phone system is down, however, and communication inside the hospital is nearly impossible. Dr. Lowder has experienced minor tumblers before, but never in his 10 years at Northridge Hospital has he felt one like this. He doesn't know it yet, but he is near the epicenter of one of the deadliest earthquakes in American history.

Dr. Lowder and his colleagues are in the thick of a major disaster, without so much as a few minutes' warning to restock their shelves or prepare the staff. The hospital sustains structural damage, and the nursing administrators quickly try to assess the problem. The infants in the neonatal care unit need to be evacuated to one of the trauma rooms; they are on the fifth floor, where the power is out and major structural damage has occurred. Two of the babies are on respirators, and rescuers carry them by hand downstairs to the ER with nurses at their sides supplying life-sustaining oxygen via ambu-bags. The hospital goes into disaster mode in readiness for patients, who will be arriving quickly, too quickly for anything to be done about the damage to the ER itself. The triage area is set up outside the entrance to the ER, where patients are to be assessed and tagged, and then treated in the emergency department as needed. The staff braces themselves not only for the aftershocks but for the hoards of walking wounded they know will be arriving soon.

The Northridge Hospital's ER reports through a countywide interhospital radio system that it is "closed to internal disaster," which should effectively stop incoming ambulance traffic and with it any major trauma from the quake. But this does not stop people from walking or driving themselves into the damaged ER. On a normal day, Northridge Hospital's emergency room treats a little over 100 patients, but on the day of the earthquake they see over 500. The regular ER staff is helped by other staff physicians, nurses, and volunteers who risk their own safety to come in and treat the wounded. Dr. Lowder attends many patients with broken arms and legs, sustained as televisions and furniture fell onto them as they slept. Lacerations are probably the most common injury, as people jumped up from bed and out of their homes as the earthquake hit, stepping with their bare feet onto broken glass, which littered nearly every home in Northridge. Then come the MIs (myocardial infarction—heart attacks), the patients with a history of heart disease who are so stressed by the earthquake that their hearts can't take it. Such patients (and there are quite a few) truly tax the emergency system at the Northridge ER, but the doctors and nurses manage to take care of the sickest without missing a beat.

Getting patients up to undamaged areas of the hospital becomes a test of physical endurance, for the elevators are out and many of the stairs do not have adequate lighting. Patients are carried out of the ER and up flights of stairs to their hospital beds, literally on the backs of volunteers. While transferring patients up to medical floors is a challenge, it is nearly impossible to get some of the patients out of the ER and up to other floors. These are the people who have experienced major earthquakes in Mexico and South America, and they do not want to be up on the floors when the next aftershock hits!

Dr. Lowder is astonished by the incredible number of pregnant women who are thrown into labor by the physical and emotional stress of the earthquake. With its neonatal ICU in shambles, the ER is forced to transfer some of these premature newborns to other hospitals in the area. The other injuries that surprise him are all the dog bites. Apparently, most of the fences and walls in the community came crashing down when the earth shook. Many dogs escaped their backyards in panic, and roamed the streets of Northridge. These animals were as shocked, confused, and in many cases injured as their human brethren. A hand extended to a dog that day would likely result in a trip to the overcrowded Northridge ER.

Thanks to the foresight of the administrators, even though most of the area is without running water, Northridge Hospital has a new special backup water supply. Without water, the lab and X-ray facilities cannot function, not to mention the lack of water to drink. With the auxiliary water system in place, the ER and the rest of the hospital can still run lab tests and get most of the X rays done. Most of the equipment in the hospital has been tied or bolted down, and the damage inside the ER has been minimal.

The hardest part for Dr. Lowder is not knowing what has happened to his own family, about half an hour away. With the phone lines down, he has no idea whether his wife and children are safe. This is the greatest fear for anyone caught away from home during a disaster, and it plays on Dr. Lowder's conscience throughout the day as he takes care of hundreds of shaken and injured patients.

Outside the hospital, the bustling community has come to a standstill. People injured in the earthquake continue to come into the ER for days. Those with broken hands and feet stay home until the pain and swelling get so severe that they are forced to seek medical attention. Lacerations that have not been repaired start to get infected, and patients with chronic diseases like diabetes begin running out of medication and become ill. Those with chronic kidney failure, needing dialysis but not sure where to go—other area hospitals have been more severely damaged—start coming to Northridge's ER for help. With no phones, food, or water in the rubble of Northridge, the ER becomes an oasis.

In the end, because of 30 seconds of shaking ground, nearly 60 people are dead, 9 highways are destroyed, 250 gas lines are ruptured, causing fires everywhere, and over 3 million people are without electrical power. The doctors in the ER at Northridge can only shake their heads in amazement. How can they possibly prepare for the next one, which potentially could destroy even more hospitals and freeways, not to mention airports and harbors?

When the "big one" comes, the basic mechanism to deal with disasters that was seen on *ER* will hold true. No matter how much we try to avoid them, disasters will happen. But disaster planning works, as much in real life as on TV. If there was ever a model for a hospital disaster plan in action, the "Blizzard" episode on *ER* is it.

CHAPTER TWELVE

The Madness

Dangers, Bloopers, and Gallows Humor

There is madness and there is madness. In the episode "Hit and Run," Doug Ross examines a young boy named Ozzie for deafness. The concerned mother tells Doug her son no longer hears the ice cream man's truck or his grandmother. Moments later we learn that the grandmother is dead. Apparently Mom is hearing voices. Madness on an individual level is much easier to address than the epidemics of craziness like drugs or disasters. As goes society, so goes the ER.

At one time, accidents, particularly car crashes, dominated the ER. That has changed. Now the streets are a place for not only cars but people to hit each other. Victims of street violence are coming to the country's ERs in growing numbers. In Los Angeles, nearly half of all major trauma is a result of gunshot wounds or stabbings. Nationwide, as many as one-third of female patients who come to the ER have been assaulted or battered. These themes have been dramatized and echoed in one form or another on the show.

ABUSE AND DOMESTIC VIOLENCE

A news story ripped from the headlines turns up in the episode "Dead of Winter." Twenty-two children ranging in age from six months to nine and a half years are found by police shivering together in an apartment without electricity, heat, or parents. Almost all of the children are malnourished, and some have impetigo, welt marks, or cigarette burns on their skin. In real life as on the show, these innocent victims would be treated in the ER and turned over to children's services for placement.

There have been numerous episodes involving families dealing with alcoholism, domestic violence, and abuse. There was the mother who imprinted a star-shaped burn into her daughter's hand for masturbating. A little boy named Noah had to call 911 frequently to rescue his father, drunk and lying in his own vomit. This boy openly acknowledged his father's problem in the ER, as opposed to the teenager named Corky, who refused to talk about his father's alcoholism. It turns out the teen was protecting his mother, who had been repeatedly battered by her husband while under the influence. And there was the catatonic child whom doctors believed had witnessed the shooting death of his mother by an abusive boyfriend. In fact, we find out, in an attempt to stop the abuse, the little boy accidentally killed his mother himself.

DRUGS

Ask any ER professional, and he or she will tell you the drug problem is getting worse. Heroin, cocaine, PCP, and prescription pain killers are all part of the madness that ER staff deal with on a daily basis. (According to a 1990 article in *Time* magazine, 75 percent of trauma victims in the trauma center at Philadelphia's Albert Einstein Hospital tested positive for street or prescription drugs.)

The show has certainly not shied away from the issue. In one episode, a patient on PCP, the gurney still strapped to his back, goes on a wild rampage and nearly destroys the ER. In another, a 5-year-old girl almost loses her life when doctors come close to mistakenly diagnosing heart disease instead of a cocaine overdose. Doug Ross suspects the father, a single parent, but it turns out to be the man's 15-year-old daughter who is the source.

In real life as on the show, there are people who come to the ER as a source for their drug habit. If the patient complains of migraines and back pain, no lab test or X ray can really substantiate the symptoms. Although most patients who come to the ER with these complaints have real medical problems, these are the complaints most often used by people seeking drugs. Unless a patient is a "frequent flyer" (has made many trips to the ER) and has abused the ER many times, pain medication will be given. Complaining of kidney stones is a little different. It usually leaves some evidence of blood in the urine. In the episode "Men Plan, God Laughs," a middle-aged man claiming to be a urologist wants pain medication for his kidney stone. Dr. Lewis insists first on confirming the diagnosis by urine analysis. The lab work comes back and indeed indicates blood—but it isn't human (it's from a chicken!), and the man isn't a doctor. He is another drug addict looking for a fix of Demerol. Those who are seeking narcotics know every trick of the trade. Many have been known to prick their fingers with a needle in the ER bathroom and drip a few drops of blood into the urine in order to fake the presence of a kidney stone.

GERMS

Patients bring not only their personal foibles to the ER, but also their germs. The risk of an infectious blow to the ER worker is as great as any fist or bullet. The three infectious culprits on the ER's Most Not Wanted List are hepatitis, HIV, and tuberculosis. The staff looks at every patient as a potential carrier and takes the proper precautions, like wearing latex gloves to protect themselves against the transmission of body fluids. Fortunately there is a vaccine for hepatitis, but a worker who gets stuck with a needle from an HIV-positive patient, as happened to Carol Hathaway on the show, has a 1 in 250 chance of contracting the virus.

Tuberculosis has become so common, so contagious, and so dangerous that the ER staff often will place special masks on patients who are coughing. They must assume that everyone is contagious, for even an innocent cough in the face of an ER staff member can transmit a deadly case of TB. The mask prevents the spread of bacteria, and is the best—perhaps the only—way to protect the staff from exposure. In the frightening case presented in "House of Cards," Mrs. Salizar probably has TB, but leaves the hospital AMA (against medical advice). Despite Mark Greene's eloquent plea, Mrs. Salizar is apparently more afraid of being exposed as an illegal alien than of exposing others to TB. Mark breathes a sigh of relief when Mrs. Salizar returns later with her children for treatment.

Violence in the ER

On the show we have seen staff members nearly take a nasty blow—from a drugged-out teenager attempting to avenge the girl who cut off her ear and from "Buttonman," who suddenly goes berserk and nearly chokes one of them to death. These incidents in the heat of the moment are nothing foreign to the practice of ER medicine. What is new is that violence has spilled over from the streets and into what was once sacred territory: the emergency room.

No episode better than "Feb. 5, 1995," captures this new trend. A 12-year-old boy, with a GSW to the chest and drenched in blood, is rushed into a trauma room. The ER staff desperately tries to stop the bleeding and bring the boy back from the brink of death. While they are trying to resuscitate him, another child wanders into the ER, seemingly a friend in search of the boy who has been shot. When Bob tries to stop the young boy, he pulls out a handgun big enough for Dirty Harry. He enters the trauma room with his gun trained on the bloody victim, and Benton tells him he's too late—the boy is already dead. Mission accomplished, he exits, gun in hand, keeping everyone at bay. A stunned Carter breaks the deadly silence and says it all with two words, "It's madness."

Today physicians and their staff are, being threatened, punched, kicked, and shot in unprecedented numbers by gangs, disgruntled patients and their families, and psychotics. This may sound like the stuff of future episodes on *ER* (and indeed may be), but the pain inflicted, the blood shed, and the bones shattered in the following stories do not belong to the world of acting, special effects, and clever writing. They belong to a very real and frightening trend unfolding in ERs everywhere.

1:40 A.M. Over 50 gangs rule supreme over the streets around this inner-city hospital. On these streets they are Hispanic, but other areas have black, Asian, or white gangs. Territorial control exists, with strict geographical borders by streets and businesses. All these gangs seem here to stay. Entire families, crossing generational lines—fathers and sons, and now even grandfathers—are members of the same gang. Though the gangs rarely ever bother other gangs outside the local precinct, they are at war with each other. Over the past decade, the firepower they use has escalated from low-caliber handguns to powerful semiautomatic weapons.

Unlike in many other parts of this city, the violence is not random. If you are an *otro*—an outsider—you usually are not bothered. The hospitals and the churches here are *otro*. The ER is a safe haven, a place where gang members can seek medical attention. In fact, this hospital may be one of the only places in this area where gang members can get medical help. It is *their* hospital. Most of the hospital workers come from the neighborhood. The people know the doctors, and the doctors know the community.

At this late hour, a very young gang member lies dying in the ER. He has been shot in the head. His family is in the waiting room, shielded only by a pane of glass, clearly visible to the street outside. Young members of a rival gang, *not* the one that shot the dying patient, drive by and recognize rival gang family members in the waiting area.

This group of gang members, armed with 12-gauge shotguns and other high-caliber weapons, opens fire on the emergency department. Glass flies everywhere as people hit the floor looking for cover. Miraculously, the only wounds are cuts and bruises from the falling glass. The shattered glass and holes in the walls are an immediate reminder to those in the room of just how lucky they are that they are not joining the young man inside dying from a bullet wound.

2:30 A.M. An ER physician is working the emergency department of a hospital located in a middle-class suburb. A 20-year-old female with lower abdominal pain is undergoing an emergency evaluation. The thoughts running through the mind of the physician include the possibility of appendicitis or a bladder infection. More likely, though, because the pain is very low in the abdomen (in the pelvis), it may be an ectopic pregnancy (a pregnancy growing outside the uterus that can cause severe bleeding and death) or a pelvic infection. The physician orders the appropriate lab tests (including a pregnancy test, a urine analysis to look for a bladder infection, and a CBC).

As part of the workup, the woman needs a pelvic examination to help determine whether the problem is in her pelvis or her abdomen. The exam is crucial to differentiate appendicitis from a pelvic infection, with the former needing surgery and the latter needing primarily antibiotics.

The examination is done in the presence of a female nurse chaperone (a requirement in most ER departments). Just as the physician finishes the exam, a critical patient is brought into the department by ambulance after a 911 call. The patient is in severe respiratory distress from congestive heart failure, and the ER physician rushes off to evaluate and stabilize the critically ill man.

While the ER doctor initially stabilizes the new patient, the boyfriend of the young woman comes into the department. He speaks briefly with his girlfriend, then bolts out of her exam room and out to where the ER physician is working feverishly on the other patient. Without warning, the boyfriend rears back and slams his fist into the doctor's jaw, this in apparent retaliation for the "violation" of his girlfriend. The doctor falls back, strikes his head, and lies on the floor unconscious. Security guards subdue the boyfriend, and the police arrest him.

3:00 P.M. In his 20 years at the ER of this county hospital, a doctor has been threatened, cursed, maligned, slandered, and otherwise intimidated by irate patients. Once a female patient tried to stab him from behind with a large knife, but she was unable to pull the knife out from a concealed area in her dress. The woman had been placed on a psychiatric 72-hour hold (involuntarily admitted because she was a danger to herself and others), and three days later the doctor was informed by the psychiatry staff that they were reasonably sure she would not try to kill him again.

A few weeks later the doctor is working with two other physicians in the ambulatory walk-in area of the ER. Unbeknownst to these three, a disturbed male, approximately 35 years old, has been writing in his diary for weeks that he is going to shoot an ER physician at County. He had been seen at the ER before, primarily for a complaint of abdominal pain. His evaluations had been negative, and he was thought to be eccentric, but recommendations for a psychiatric evaluation had been refused by the patient. He was convinced, however, that these medical evaluations had given him AIDS, and that the County Hospital had ruined his life.

This disturbed man now weaves his way through the hallways of the ER looking for victims. One of the physicians thinks he recognizes the deranged man as he walks toward the desk, and volunteers to care for him. As the man approaches, he unbuttons his trench coat and pulls out a .44-magnum pistol, a shotgun, and a .380 automatic. He is open for business. The next diary entry will be written in blood.

He methodically shoots all three doctors and then takes two women hostages. Eventually, the gunman is apprehended by police and the hostages are set free. Of the three physicians who are shot, one has a badly damaged right arm with neurological damage to his hand, and the other has a collapsed lung with internal bleeding (a pneumohemothorax). The third, the one with 20 years' experience, with a peach-size hole in the left side of his brain, somehow survives.

What could the hospital administrators do in the face of such madness but step up security? ER physicians, in addition to acting and thinking fast to save patients' lives, must now do the same to save their own.

To the Gallows and Other Laughing Matters

Not all of the madness in the ER leaves you crying, dumbfounded, or stunned. Sometimes it is a cause of laughter, even release, in the face of enormous stress and death constantly breathing down your neck. Watching *ER,* we have chuckled at the air-conditioning repairman who revived an arresting patient by falling out of a ceiling duct and landing on the patient's chest. One patient arrives with chest pains, and the staff has to frantically release him from the handcuffs that lock him to his dominatrix mistress (his wife's secretary) before his wife arrives. Jerry posts the results of Carter's venereal disease test on the bulletin board for all to see. The staff ribs Peter Benton by comparing his surgical handiwork to that of another surgeon. Prominently displayed is a large jar of bowels from one surgeon next to a small pill bottle containing Peter's effort of the day: a puny kidney stone. Carter rushes to a "Code Brown" that turns out to be a patient who has the runs.

Here is a cornucopia of humor and other maddening oddities from real-life hospital workers that may leave you in stitches (no pun intended) or simply have you scratching your head.

What You Hear Is What You Sometimes Get

Fascinoma	interesting or unusual case
FOS	full of stool

Larry Parker Syndrome	accident victims complaining of whiplash and pain, who just want to bilk the insurance company
Road rash	concrete or asphalt embedded in the skin
PID shuffle	the walk of a patient holding her belly (usually from pelvic inflammatory disease)
Quack	if it quacks like a duck, it is a duck (go for the likely diagnosis)
Code Brown	someone took a nasty dump
CYA	cover your ass (against medical malpractice)
Bite	go deeper into the skin when suturing
Buff and turf	stabilize patient and ship them out
Down your nose with a garden hose	stomach pumping
GOMER	get out of my emergency room
Frequent Flyer	people who repeatedly come to the ER
Crispy Critter	burn victim
Pimped	being harshly quizzed on medical knowledge
Liver rounds	social event in hospital where alcohol is served
Advanced taxi service	people who abuse paramedic service
Donorcycle	motorcycle
Gun and Knife Club	inner-city hospital
Gorked	not with the program; poorly responsive

Timex

A paramedic finds an arm in an accident that still has the victim's wristwatch. He sees the watch is still working and quips, "Takes a licking and keeps on ticking!"

Strange Patient Request

An older gentleman goes to the ER requesting sustained rectal insertion by a doctor's finger to release prostate swelling. Some interns actually fell for the ploy, but as one seasoned ER doctor told the patient, "Not in my lifetime."

You May Not Be a Redneck, But You May Be a Gomer (Get Out of My Emergency Room) If...

- Your entire wardrobe consists of surgical gowns and diapers.
- Your toenails are longer than a legally concealed weapon.
- You think KY is an after-dinner mint.

On the Right Tract

A couple went to a costume party in unusual costumes. He had an army shirt and helmet. She wore army pants and combat boots. They went as upper and lower GIs.

Testing Reality

Here are some sample questions on a spoof exam for life-support exam recertification.

I. During CPR, aspiration of gastric contents:
  A. Is really gross.
  B. May follow placement of a rectal tube.
  C. May cause widespread nausea and vomiting by members of the code team.

II. The initial setting recommended for defibrillation for a 75 kg male is:
  A. Crispy
  B. Extra crispy
  C. 1000 watts.

III. Patients presenting in the ER with radiating chest pain should be:
  A. Referred to surgical services.
  B. Allowed one phone call.
  C. Asked their religious preference.

IV. The usual method for opening the airway of the unconscious adult victim of trauma is:
   A. The jaws of life.
   B. Head jerk with neck snap.
   C. A tablespoon.
V. It is legally and morally acceptable to terminate CPR when:
   A. The patient is an attorney and you have no morals.
   B. No response is obtained with a verbal stimulus.
   C. Pizza ordered during exam arrives.

Music to My Ears and Other Organs

A hospital recently started to play 14 seconds of Brahms' lullaby over the public address system every time a baby was born. Co-workers, feeling the rest of the units shouldn't be left out, came up with a list of songs for various situations found throughout the hospital. A sampling:

Amputation	"Why Not Take All of Me?"
Kidney Stone	"Love Me Like a Rock"
Colonoscopy	"Bad Moon Rising"
Hemorrhoidectomy	"Great Balls of Fire"
Respiratory Distress	"I'm Mr. Blue"
Trying to Keep Your Patient from Coding	"You Say Goodbye and I Say Hello"
Suicide Attempt	"Fifty Ways to Leave Your Lover"

Charting the Course (actually written on patient charts by doctors and nurses):

Second day the knee was better. On the third day it completely disappeared.

Father died in his 90's of female trouble in prostate and kidneys.

Pelvic exam will be done later on the floor.

Large brown stool ambulating in the hall.

Patient has 2 teenage children but no other abnormalities.

Vaginal packing out. Doctor in.

Urine Like Flint

An elderly woman brought a butterfly mounted under glass to her doctor's appointment. Said the receptionist: "It's very pretty, Mrs. Smith, but it's not the specimen we had in mind."

The Sound of Medicine

A singing quartet of doctors calling themselves "The Four Skins" have recorded songs about medicine, including, "It's Beginning to Look a Lot Like Syphilis" and "Red Cells in the Urine."

Doctor's Orders

One physician in the telemetry unit likes to write the following order: "Patient may shower with nurse."

Signs of the Times

Sign outside hospital: IF YOU MUST SMOKE, DON'T EXHALE.

Sign in hospital lab: BE NICE TO BACTERIA. IT'S THE ONLY CULTURE SOME PEOPLE HAVE.

Mad About You

For a doctor or nurse on night shift, sleep is like sex. They're always wondering when it will happen and how long it will last.

BLOOPERS

There are actually very few medical mistakes on *ER*. What is more common is exaggeration—dramatic license to hold an audience in cases where complete faithfulness to reality would be boring if not impossible to watch. Here are ten outstanding "stretches" in the show and the chapter in which they are discussed in more detail. (The last two are mentioned only in this list.)

1. House Staff: the longest rotation in history; absence of interns; contentious relationship between Attendings and House Staff (Chapter 2).

2. ER doctors don't do endoscopy (Chapter 7).

3. Time for tests (Chapter 6).

4. Family allowed in the treatment and trauma rooms (Chapter 5).

5. Representation of CPR (Chapter 5).

6. A lifetime of crikes and thoracotomies in a few shows (Chapter 2).

7. Thoracic Park runs the ER department (Chapter 2).

8. An ER doctor would never perform a cesarean (Chapter 9).

9. Intubating the dog: In the episode "Make of Two Hearts," Al the cop brings a dog hit by a car into the ER. The doctors haul out a veterinary textbook and read how to intubate the dog. According to leading veterinarians, the dog would have long expired by the time it was "tubed." Also, no dog in their experience would have kept as still as this dog did, keeping the young Russian girl with AIDS company.

10. Doug Ross misses bone cancer: In the episode "The Match Game," a young male comes into the ER complaining of a knee problem. Doug reads the X ray and discovers the teen has an osteosarcoma, a cancer of the bone. The young man had seen Doug four months earlier, and somehow Doug had misdiagnosed him then. Anyone can misdiagnose a patient, but this incident is a blooper: all X rays are read within days of an ER visit by radiologists—who certainly would have caught the error.

HOW TO LESSEN THE MADNESS: A SURVIVAL GUIDE TO THE ER

1. Bring any medications you are currently taking with you to the ER.

2. Don't smoke, particularly if you are on or near oxygen. You could go up in flames.

3. Remember your mother's advice when you leave the house: "Wear clean underwear!" Patient gowns don't close well in the back.

4. Bring reading material. The wait to see the doctor can be worth *Gone with the Wind* or six months of *People* magazine.
5. Don't use someone else's insurance card. It may not cost you any money in the ER, but it can cost you your life. One young man was given a drug that killed him because doctors thought he was someone else. (True story!)
6. Remove expensive jewelry and leave valuables at home. Many possessions develop "legs" in the hospital and walk away.
7. Avoid if possible coming to the ER in a teaching hospital during the first week in July. This is the week of new interns, and with the change in staff you will be treated by people with no experience.
8. Don't be afraid to ask questions. Don't say you understand unless you really do.
9. Don't sign anything you don't understand, from after-care instructions to informed-consent forms. With informed consent, feel free to depend on the expertise of doctors to advise you honestly and correctly.
10. Try to be a patient patient. If you antagonize the doctor, you just might have your chart hidden behind the water cooler.
11. Know the last time you had a tetanus shot.
12. Don't stop for burgers, fries, and a malted on your way to the ER if you have an upset stomach.

CHAPTER THIRTEEN

Fast as McDonald's
at Tiffany Prices

Just what are all the state-of-the-art heroics at the ER going to cost you? Although the service in the emergency room, once you see the doctor, can be as fast as McDonald's (that is, of course, if the ER happens to be quiet that day), you can expect the prices to approach Tiffany's! As for that sore throat, what might cost you $70 at your doctor's office (less if you have insurance) can run you anywhere from $125 to $250 at your local ER, and that's just for two minutes of the doctor's time, before any tests or medications! What you routinely see on the show are the most critical and urgent cases, and obviously these are the most expensive cases to treat in the ER. Throughout the country, these cases have an average charge of $600, many significantly higher.

Prices vary in different parts of the country and even within the same city. What you will be charged depends upon many factors, most important of which are special designations available through the American Medical Association, known as "CPT codes." These CPT codes (current procedural terminology) place a dollar value on most everything that is done to you in the hospital. What is actually paid, however, is a whole different story. Prenegotiated rates with insurance carriers (including the federal government for Medicaid and Medicare) will pay out at rates often substantially less than what was actually billed.

What kind of bill (hospital, ER physician, and radiology all send separate bills) would the people on the show rack up for the tests and treatments during a typical hour of *ER*? During the episode "House of Cards," at least 11 patients were treated. There were other patients in the department, but these were the patients given the most attention during the show. This particular episode was unusual, for the writers made special mention of the prohibitive costs of health care. The treatment in a number of cases was influenced by these costs, as it is every day in real life. Realizing that costs and prices vary across the country, here are some of the average prices you could expect to see at your local hospital for the services rendered that day at County General.

PATIENT 1

The show opens with Dr. Mark Greene evaluating Mr. McDowell, a middle-aged male, for crampy abdominal pain. While the diagnosis is most likely acute gastroenteritis (simple stomach flu) or colic (gas), Mark orders a Chem-7, LFTs (liver function tests), a CBC, and an abdominal ultrasound to rule out other causes that could be more serious, such as appendicitis.

Dr. "Wild Willy" Swift arrives, feels Mr. McDowell's abdomen, cancels all the tests Mark ordered, and sends the patient home. He admonishes Mark, stating that he would have wasted $1,000 worth of tests for a man who just has gastroenteritis or the flu. How close to the mark was Wild Willy's estimate?

Hospital ER Physician

Blood draw	$6.00
Emergency evaluation	$155.00
LFTs	$57.70
Chem-7	$35.00
Abdominal ultrasound	$230.00
Radiologist reading (of the ultrasound)	$135.00
CBC	$18.85
Nursing level 3	<u>$125.00</u>
TOTAL CHARGES	$762.55

Charges for Dr. Swift's abbreviated evaluation:

Hospital ER Physician	$100.00
Nursing level 2	<u>$106.00</u>
TOTAL CHARGES	$206.00

Dr. Swift's guesstimate wasn't far off. With luck, neither was his diagnosis, or the $500 Mr. McDowell saved will hardly have been worth it.

PATIENT 2

A male around the age of 30 is brought in by paramedics for evaluation of a 20-foot fall with third-degree burns to his arms after touching a utility line. Mark Greene, Susan Lewis, John Carter, and Peter Benton are all there. Though we don't hear orders for extensive blood work (like CBC, urinalysis, Chem-23), they are more than likely to be done in a case like this, jacking up the price tag by another $200 from what we list here.

Hospital Ambulance Transport	$330.00
	(plus about $11.00/mile)

X ray

Chest X ray	$106.00
Cross-table C-spine	$260.00
Pelvic	$83.00

ER Physician Charges

Medications	
Central line placement	$113.00
Emergency Care Evaluation	$423.00

Radiologist Charges

Read chest, C-spine, and pelvis	$90.00

Other Charges

Tetanus toxoid	$27.00
Blood draw	$6.00
12 lead EKG	$15.00
IV starts	$72.00
IV supplies	$62.00
Central-line supplies	$174.00
Assist central-line placement	$20.00
IV monitoring	$15.00
Burn dressing	$135.00
Cardiac monitoring	$65.00
Dynamap (BP machine)	$75.00
Oxygen mask	$50.00
Spinal immobilization	$135.00
Pulse ox	$75.00
Level 5 nursing charge	$597.00
TOTAL CHARGES	$2,928.00

Add extra blood work and he has gone over the $3,000 mark.

PATIENT 3

A young girl comes in feeling dizzy and nauseated. Doug Ross examines the child and thinks she probably has the flu. Then he detects an abnormal heart rate and suggests running some tests. The mother, who doesn't have insurance, is concerned about the cost.

The people who get screwed by the system are those without insurance. They are left out in the cold, trying to negotiate a bill that may be astronomical. Many insurance companies now pay a greatly reduced negotiated rate, but the individual without insurance is left to the mercy of the billing department of the hospital. Doug Ross assures the mother that social services will help her work it out. The reality is it's not so easy to work out. Social workers often have very limited resources, and at times there is little they can do. Hospitals are businesses: if you pay quickly in cash, you might be able to cut a better deal. Public hospitals, in particular, are known to give patients without insurance a lesser charge.

All of sudden the child develops a lethal arrhythmia and is shocked out of the irregular rhythm. Suddenly the bill seems irrelevant. But here's the breakdown:

Meds (Adenocard)	$100.00
Level 6 charge (1:1) care	$750.00
IV start and supplies	$93.00
IV monitoring	$15.00
Cardiac monitoring	$65.00
Dynamap	$75.00
Oxygen mask	$50.00
Oxygen cannula	$50.00
Pulse ox	$75.00
Defibrillation	$40.00
ER physician charge	$400.00
Additional tests*	$400.00
TOTAL CHARGES	$2,113.00

*Although not specifically ordered, Jeanette would more than likely have had a cross-table C-spine, CBC, Chem-7, and chest X ray and reading.

PATIENT 4

Mark Greene believes Anita Salizar is probably suffering from TB. She refuses definitive testing or treatment and signs out AMA (against medical advice), but later returns with her family. Her first visit included the following:

Sputum AFB and C&S (culture and sensitivity)	$82.00
Chest X ray	$106.00
Radiologist charge	$29.00
Level 4 charge (acute admit)	$250.00
Isolation charge	$93.00
Isolation face mask	$5.00
ER physician charge	$155.00
TOTAL CHARGES	$720.00

PATIENT 5

Two elderly sisters were in a minor traffic accident. One sister was dizzy and had headaches. The other had a small laceration to her nose. Susan Lewis was about to order a CAT scan to the tune of $710 and the reading another $350 for the dizzy sister who apparently also had a vision problem. Before ordering this extra thousand-dollar photo op, Susan realizes the woman is wearing her sister's glasses. The ambulance ride and the laceration for the other sister still totaled over $700.

Level 3 charge (acute-delayed)	$125.00
Suture supplies	$75.00
Paramedics	$258.00
ER physician charge	$245.00
TOTAL CHARGES	$703.00

PATIENT 6

A woman has abdominal cramps. She requests Carter because his magic touch seemed to help a friend of hers get pregnant some weeks before. Some tests would have been ordered in a case like this that may not have been mentioned in the show, including CBC. The pregnancy test and UA could have run an additional $100. The patient's desire for Carter's sorcery cost her nearly a half a grand . . . that's a lot of diapers.

Level 3 charge (acute)	$125.00
Pelvic exam and supplies	$45.00
Pelvic exam assist	$9.00
ER physician charge	$155.00
Additional tests	$100.00
TOTAL CHARGES	$434.00

PATIENT 7

An infant is brought in with a fever. Doug Ross and John Carter along with Carol evaluate the baby. It is Carter's first shot at taking a urine sample from an infant. Doug tells him not to push too hard on the baby's belly for the sample. Carter rightly asks how you know if it's too hard as he presses on the infant. A moment later the baby hoses Carter. For a sepsis work-up on a baby, they would have probably also ordered a CBC, UA, blood culture, chest X ray, and a shot of antibiotics for an additional $400 than what was specifically ordered or done in the scene.

UA and C&S	$66.00
Level 3 charge (acute)	$125.00
Two baby bottles	$2.00
ER physician charge	$155.00
Additional tests	$400.00
TOTAL CHARGES	$748.00

PATIENT 8

A woman in her sixties is acting bizarrely. The patient, pleasantly paranoid, carrying her purse full of weapons, is evaluated by Susan Lewis. Other tests that probably would have been ordered to rule out anything organic are a toxic screen, CBC, and Chem-7, totaling about $140.

Level 4 charge (acute admit)	$250.00
Close observation	$93.00
ER physician charge	$155.00
Additional tests	$140.00
TOTAL CHARGES	$638.00

PATIENT 9

Smiley comes into the ER drunk as a skunk. He's been in a rollover (traffic collision). Greene and Benton have to find out the extent of his injuries—the primary and secondary surveys. They find that the patient has an injury to the femoral artery, and he is sent to the X-ray department for an angiogram (billed separately). Smiley probably won't be so smiley when he sees that one too many drinks costs him over $6,000.

BA	$46.00
CBC	$19.00
Chem-7	$35.00
Type and cross-match for 4 units of blood @ $125/unit)	$600.00
Cross-table C-spine	$260.00
Chest X ray	$106.00
Femur X ray	$117.00
Radiologist charge	$87.00
Level 6 charge (1:1)	$750.00

IV starts x 2	$72.00
Other IV supplies	$112.00
IV monitoring	$15.00
Blood draw	$6.00
Oxygen per nasal cannula	$50.00
Spinal immobilization	$135.00
Dynamap	$75.00
Cardiac monitoring	$65.00
Pulse ox	$75.00
Gastric lavage and supplies	$230.00
N-G (nasogastric) tube	$58.00
Suture and supplies	$83.00
Dressings	$33.00
Paramedic charge	$330.00
ER physician charge	$390.00
Angiogram	$2,750.00
TOTAL CHARGES	$6,499.00

PATIENT 10

A 40-year-old junkie is in the ER for an evaluation. Medical student Deb Chen, who is competing with Carter for the highest number and the greatest variety of procedures, takes it upon herself to put a central line in this patient without supervision. Bad move, Deb. She loses the guidewire, and the subsequent charges mount up, not to mention the threat of malpractice. Peter Benton and Wild Willy Swift save the day. Other tests not mentioned but probably ordered were a CBC, BA, Chem-7, toxic screen, coag panel—for an additional $180, not that the junkie has to worry. The hospital will pick up the tab for Chen's mistake. (It will certainly be a lot less than the court settlement.)

Chest X ray	$106.00
Level 4 charge (acute admit)	$250.00

IV starts (unsuccessful x 2 tries)	$72.00
IV supplies	$62.00
Central line	$113.00
Central-line supplies	$174.00
Additional tests	$180.00
ER physician charge	$248.00
TOTAL CHARGES	$1,205.00

PATIENT 11

Billy is hit while riding a bicycle and arrives in the ER in respiratory arrest. He has the kitchen sink thrown in to help resuscitate him. Not spelled out, but other items that would have been ordered are a type and cross ($120), Chem-7, coag panel, and several units of blood (@ $100/unit) for another $400.

CBC	$19.00
H/H (hematocrit and hemoglobin)	$17.00
Cross-table C-spine	$260.00
Chest X ray	$106.00
Level 8 charge (trauma arrest)	$997.00
IV starts (x 2), supplies, and monitoring	$149.00
Blood draw	$6.00
Cardiac monitoring	$65.00
Dynamap	$75.00
Pulse ox	$75.00
Spinal immobilization	$135.00
Chest tube	$302.00
Chest tube tray and nursing assist insertion	$200.00
Pericardiocentesis	$113.00
Pericardiocentesis tray and nursing assist	$287.00
ETT (Endotracheal tube)	$22.00
Nursing assist repiratory arrest	$93.00
Radiologist charge	$58.00

Paramedic charge	$330.00
Additional items	$400.00
ER physician charge	<u>$390.00</u>
TOTAL CHARGES	$4,099.00

THE COSTLY FUTURE

Probably the greatest change coming for both the patients and practitioners of ER is managed care. This is alphabet soup for most patients and physicians, with HMOs (health maintenance organizations), PPOs (preferred provider organizations), and IPAs (independent practice associations) leading the way. Though the knee-jerk reflex of physicians is to bash managed care, there are some changes that will reflect positively on health care. Medicaid patients are being enrolled under the umbrella of many managed care organizations, and will no longer be treated as second-class citizens when it comes to obtaining a family doctor. This change will create greater access to medical care for underserved patients and families who have used ERs for their primary care when no other physician would make himself or herself available to them. The volume of nonemergent visits should drop, and this will allow ERs to better treat patients with true emergencies.

But there is a downside to managed care from the ER perspective. A major thrust of managed care is to limit access to the ER. The managed care businesses see this as only natural and good business practice, for care in an emergency room, as you have seen, is expensive, and is a financial drain for the medical cost-containment experts. This is probably what the future will hold.

You find yourself at the triage desk of County General late some weekday night. You have a terrible sore throat, have tried the usual over-the-counter stuff, but just can't get to sleep because of the pain. At the triage desk, a phone call is made to a gatekeeper (usually a nurse or doctor employed by the insurance company) for permission to treat. This really means agreement to *pay* for the visit. Often, the gatekeeper is at an 800 number and has never met you. It can take up to an hour and multiple phone calls to get someone to finally evaluate the case by phone and give the authorization. In the meantime, federal law says that the ER staff needs to see you and make sure you are medically stable. The law does not state, however, that your insurance company will pay for the visit.

If the gatekeeper/insurance company feels you can wait until the next day, when you can see your primary care provider, they will refuse to pay for ER treatment. You may then be given the option to leave the ER or assume financial responsibility for the bill. This will probably make you extremely angry, and no wonder! The decision to authorize the visit is usually based on very limited information (basic vital signs and a cursory history).

While such procedures may limit access to some people who abuse the system with minor medical problems, it can potentially hurt patients who really *need* to be seen in the ER. Denial of authorization should oblige the insurance carrier to arrange emergent evaluation somewhere for your medical problem and to assume responsibility for your treatment. Not all plans assume this responsibility.

Some plans reserve the right to retrospectively deny payment of an ER visit, based on a diagnosis that can be interpreted in hindsight as describing a nonemergent problem. So if you come to the ER with severe abdominal pain and feel like you're going to die, and the problem turns out to be constipation and not a ruptured appendix, you might get stuck with an ER bill of over $1,000 that the insurance company states is your responsibility.

In addition, you may not be able to pick what doctor you want and where you will have a problem treated. Let's say that you have a knee problem. Two years ago, during a college ski trip, you tore a ligament in your knee and had surgery at the local hospital. Now during a playground basketball game you hear a loud pop as you crash down on the same knee.

But now your insurance is a new PPO that no longer uses your local hospital. Should you be brought to an ER of a hospital that is not contracted with your insurance carrier, and you need admission into the hospital, expect to be carted off by ambulance to another facility that is on the insurance list (you have to be medically stable, for example, not having a heart attack). It may be 3:00 A.M. and the hospital may be 20 miles away, but off you go. If your doctor is not on the list, even if he or she operated on you for the same problem in the past, you're out of luck. You will be treated by the doctor and hospital they assign to you. If you don't like it, you can pay for the treatment yourself.

At the end of *ER*'s second season, Carol Hathaway didn't like managed care, either. A newborn who had a congenital heart problem was prematurely discharged from County General under financial pressure, only to return the very next day in crisis. A middle-age construction worker who didn't have insurance and couldn't even afford a work-up for lung cancer (radiation and chemo could cost an additional $50,000) left AMA. A child with an unstable fracture was transferred across town at the request of the insurance company. Carol is frustrated and disgusted. A system that allows patients to be mistreated or not treated because of the dollar goes against the grain of everything health care means to her—and she quits. But be assured she'll be back with a renewed sense of mission. It is the discontented hearts of the Carol Hathaways of the world that bring health care back to those it was meant to serve: everyone who needs it.

EPILOGUE

The Viewing Hour

An hour can feel like an eternity when you are anxiously awaiting something. You feel as though you are experiencing all 3,600 seconds. In the hour you sit in front of the TV to watch *ER*, those seconds and minutes rush by. It is an exciting and involving medical drama, and you feel as though you'd like to spend much longer than a mere hour with the characters. During those 60 minutes that you've watched *ER*, from the surging opening theme music to the closing credits, you've stretched your legs, petted the dog, or relieved those three iced teas you had at dinner. Outside the world of County General, real hospitals surge with intense life-and-death dramas all their own.

During that one entertaining hour of television viewing, emergencies have been taking place all over the country. Here's a sampling of what sent—or should have sent—people to a real ER:

150 heart attack victims, of which 50 have died
57 cases of pneumonia
53 acute asthma attacks
1 drowning victim
14 diseased gallbladders
13 sufferers of severe constipation
29 upper-GI bleeds
57 acute strokes
1 baby with Sudden Infant Death Syndrome
12 rape victims
765 poisonings
114 abused and neglected children
20 DOAs (from traffic accidents, GSW, suicides, and so on)
548 psychiatric disorders
114 bites
1 spinal cord injury
104 assault victims
and 548 complaints of abdominal pain, of which 24 are
    acute appendicitis.

Interestingly, the prime-time viewing hour is also prime time at the ER. You were lucky. You watched *ER* on television, while 10,000 people ended up in a real ER.

Now you can click off the TV and turn out the lights. . . . There's always next week.

ACKNOWLEDGMENTS

Many people have given their time and energy in helping us prepare the material for this book. First, great thanks are due to Stacy Bowton Gleason for her tireless efforts as our "humble research assistant."

In researching the material for the book, we spoke to countless emergency medicine physicians, nurses, and paramedics; we would like to make special mention of Dr. Gail Anderson Sr. of Los Angeles County, USC Medical Center, and Dr. Peter Rosen of the University of California at San Diego, who stand as inspirational leaders in emergency care. They gave freely of their time and experiences, and we hope we have captured some of their enthusiasm in the pages of this book. Also of particular help was Dr. Ed Lowder of Northridge Hospital, who provided us with some hair-raising experiences of the Northridge earthquake.

Dr. Bryan Johnston of White Memorial's Emergency Department in Los Angeles, president of the L.A. County Medical Association and president of the medical staff at White Memorial, remains a constant source of both information and leadership, and is an example of the best that emergency medicine has to offer.

Many emergency department chairmen, ER residency directors, ER residents, and nurses gave of their time and experience, and we would like to thank Dr. Gerald Whelan of the University of Southern California, Dr. May of Los Angeles County, USC Medical Center, Dr. Davis Guss of the University of California at San Diego, Drs. Horace Liang and William Mysco of Johns Hopkins Medical Center, Dr. Alan Gelb of the University of California at San Francisco, Drs. Bob Simon and Paula Ward of Cook County Hospital, Dr. Wally Ghurabi of Santa Monica Medical Center, Dr. Rachel Chin of San Francisco General Hospital, Dr. M. Douglas Baker of Children's Hospital of Philadelphia, Dr. Alan Kuban of Janzen, Johnston & Rockwell, and Drs. Pablo Villablanca, David Schriger, Jerome Hoffman, and Marshall Morgan of the UCLA Medical Center. In addition, we would like to thank the house staff and nurses of Harbor General ER in Orange County, California, and their chairman, Dr. Robert Hockberger, who provided us with invaluable information about their county hospital.

We would like to thank Marilyn Rice, past president of the Emergency Nurses Association, and Judy Brown of Los Angeles County, USC Medical Center, and all of the numerous ER nurses who were so helpful in providing us with a perspective on emergency nursing.

In addition, Janice Tramel helped us to understand the role of physician's assistants and nurse practitioners in the emergency department.

Of special note are the physicians and nurses of Oklahoma City's hospitals, specifically Drs. Gary Quick and Tom Lera, and nurse Sylvia Amundson. Their memories of the emergency care after the bombing of the Alfred P. Murrah Federal Building gave us a vivid account of the excellent job done by the medical community in the face of a man-made disaster.

Thanks also to Dr. Kolbe of Salt Lake City, whose account of the revival of a nearly frozen young child made medical history (and a most remarkable story).

The assistance of the American College of Emergency Physicians was invaluable, and they remain a guiding force in emergency medicine for all of us who work in ERs around the country.

Thanks to *The Journal of Nursing Jocularity*, its publisher, Douglas Fletcher, and David Priest, who provided us with a good laugh and some excellent and funny material.

Thanks to Dr. Jim Stone and the staff at Janzen, Johnston & Rockwell, who always seem to come through in the clutch.

Special thanks to colleagues and friends at Glendale Adventist Medical Center—especially Drs. David Friend, Richard Benedon, and Edgar Aleman, who provided much needed moral support; Judy Grimaldi, who provided invaluable information; and Vic Stadnyk, whose work was greatly appreciated.

Thanks to friends who read the manuscript and voiced their opinions, especially Liza Hall. To someone, more than a friend, MK (alias "Mousie Kookie" and "Hoon"), whom we love, adore, and thank for unending support, a way with words, and a way with the heart. For his way around other parts of the body, we want to thank Dr. Alvin Luftman, whose knowledge of Ob-Gyn was a major asset in preparing the chapter on eclampsia.

It is with tremendous respect and thanks that we acknowledge the work and dedication of the staff at Basic Books—in particular, Susan Rabiner, whose name should probably appear on the cover of every book she edits. Without Susan there would not have been a *Medicine of ER*. An acknowledgment would be incomplete without thanking Kermit Hummel, who not only inspired this project but brought all of us together. We would like to thank Tom Selz and Joseph Dapello for their legal guidance and wisdom. Among those at Basic who helped us get this book out in record time are Juliana Nocker, Kim Lewis, Matthew Martin, Elliott Beard, Karen Klein, Rick Pracher, Heather Rogoff, and Trent Duffy. A special note of thanks is due to Linda Carbone at Basic, who was given the monumental job of line-editing our work, a task not easily done with sanity.

INDEX

Page numbers in **bold** indicate the definition of a term.